THE ZINZIN ROAD

by Fletcher Knebel

NIGHT OF CAMP DAVID

THE ZINZIN ROAD

by Fletcher Knebel and Charles W. Bailey II

CONVENTION

SEVEN DAYS IN MAY

NO HIGH GROUND

FLETCHER KNEBEL

THE ZINZIN ROAD

DOUBLEDAY & COMPANY, INC.
GARDEN CITY, NEW YORK

To the Peace Corps Volunteers—

"the children of Kennedy."

THE ZINZIN ROAD

1

He drove with his moist palms gripping the wheel of the jeep wagon. He could feel a trickle of sweat on his cheek and he knew from the vague itching that the perspiration was cutting a rivulet through the grime. His backbone ached from the pounding of the ruts and potholes in the dusty red laterite road which snaked through the fetid bush all the three hundred miles from Ft. Paul to Zinzin.

The sun was setting, casting monster shadows on the road from the dabema trees, those jungle sentinels, so strangely like pillars of dirty concrete. A coucal, with its white-splashed breast and long black tail, flew clumsily away, trailing its gurgling "coo-coo-coo" song behind. The air should be cooler now as the jeep jounced downward into a shaded valley. A swamp on one side of the road held a tangle of rotting brush. On the other side, on burned-off ground, an old, wrinkled tribesman, all but naked, swiped at a blackened stump with his cutlass. But the heat was still intense, cloying with the humidity that pressed against the flesh like a spongeful of tepid water.

Lewis Corleigh could never shake the feeling of oppression that always enveloped him at this hour of heavy twilight. He knew that the rolling hills had a primitive beauty and that, save for

the road and the scattered, burned-off plots, the land lay as verdant
and lush as it had for uncounted centuries in this bush country
of West Africa. But that was a beauty he might appreciate on a
painter's canvas or perhaps on a color film if he were sitting in
an air-conditioned theater back home. Here, amid the clotted
growth that still seemed dank despite the long dry season, he
could think only of the alien perils, of the parasitical schistosomiasis in the swamp water, of the festering leg sores on tribesmen who walked the bush trails, of the heat, the insects, the malaria. He could never elude the thought of mambas and leopards
in this silent, steaming bush, and almost every twilight on his
jeep run he recalled a time when he had hiked alone through
miles of jungle. It was late afternoon, and he was near a rotted
tree trunk when he heard the ominous rustle. There, fixing him
with hypnotic eyes, was a black mamba. It lay beside the trunk
and its long, narrow head formed the top of a looping S figure.
Lewis froze. Snake and man eyed each other, transfixed, for what
seemed like an hour. Actually, it was perhaps only a minute until
the mamba slid away from the trail. But it had been five more
miles to the road and Corleigh's heart fluttered like an old man's
most of the way.

It was at this time of day that Lewis Corleigh, a Peace
Corps volunteer leader, began counting the minutes until he
reached the next Peace Corps house, a refuge of kerosene lamp,
boiled water and an extra cot for which he brought his own sheets.
Tonight it would be Zinzin, the end of the line, a shambling town
of the Mola tribe where seven Peace Corps volunteers lived and
worked.

He glanced at his wrist watch and noted the time, 5:15. He
would reach Zinzin in a few minutes and he began to plot the way
stations of his creature comforts. First, his shower. There was only
one decent place to take a shower, at Arlene Offenbach's house
at the Lutheran mission school. She was a new girl, Group VII,
and he'd have to listen to her twittering recital of numberless
projects which Arlene, in her still pristine fervor, actually believed
she would accomplish some day. Arlene, with her eager eyes and
bright lipstick, scoffed at "Wawa." Corleigh sighed. Oh well, she'd
learn.

Then on to the mud-stick house of Ted Kramer and Arch Lettermore, the city-pale white man and the jelly-fat country Negro. Kramer had nicknamed his roommate "Archie the Rat Fink" because of his skill at slaughtering rodents. One night, in a burst of trapper's zeal, Lettermore killed seventeen rats around their house. Both men were Group VI. (Volunteers arrived in crews of fifty or sixty persons and each group was numbered chronologically.) Ted and Arch had been in Kalya a year now and, in the first guilty pangs of disillusionment, were beginning to wonder why they had preferred the Peace Corps to the draft. He'd have two drinks of Scotch with Arch and Ted, listen while they languidly damned the latest staff follies in Ft. Paul, then move on to the next stop.

That was the turbulent household of Alice Franklin and Dorothea Wyzansky, the best cooks in Kalya. They were plain women, shabby in dress and too neglectful now to bother about make-up, but he found their boisterous cynicism refreshing. They were Group V, with only three months to go on their two-year service, and they had begun marking off the days on a calendar with a red crayon.

And then the best mattress for the night was at Jim Osterlord's. Jim was a loner of Group VI who had "gone bush." He preferred the company of Mola tribesmen to that of the Peace Corps; he had almost mastered the difficult Mola language and sometimes, in a distant, trancelike state, he said he was never going back to America. Jim was taciturn and aloof, but his extra bed was the softest in Zinzin, and Lew didn't want to stay up all night yammering about foreign policy, Peace Corps motivations or any of the standard topics that so engrossed the others.

That left only Cynthia Fuller and he wondered why he hadn't fixed Cynthia on his schedule of animal comforts for the evening. He would surely see her, at one house or another, but if not, he would call at her house, for he had mail, a box of textbooks and a volley ball for her. He smiled as he thought of her, the loose-limbed mulatto girl from Atlanta with her easy disposition, her unhurried pace, her humor flicking racial quips at white volunteers, and her knowing ways with the Africans. Cindy was the most effective one of the lot in Zinzin. She had never known frustration, for she had come to Africa without illusions. She was a skilled, patient teacher. Lewis had listened to her several times in class and realized that, slowly, doggedly, she was forcing a thought or two into the little black heads, those heads that resisted any departure from their customs of rote learning. He had thought increasingly of Cindy ever since the night, during the big bash at Kramer and Lettermore's house, when he kissed her in the kitchen over glasses of warm palm wine. She had responded, affectionately, and when she pulled away, she smiled and said: "So that's how it is with a white man." Yes, he'd see Cindy somewhere tonight.

Suddenly he whipped the wheel to the right and the jeep slid through a bank of pulverized clay. A cloud of dust, as thick as mist, poured through the window. He saw the black Mercedes-Benz rush by. The driver grinned proudly at the near miss and Lew caught a glimpse of a black face with a thin mustache and, in the same flash, a shoulder holster against a white shirt. In the blur of movement, another face beside the driver had a startled expression. The Mercedes, an exotic vehicle for a jungle road three hundred miles from the capital, had come roaring around the wrong side of the blind curve, going at least sixty miles an hour. If Lew had waited a second longer to jerk the wheel, both vehicles would have ended in a twisted heap of metal. Corleigh had seen such accidents twice, and now he felt shaken at the thought that this time it had almost been his turn.

The idiot! The crazy, dumb, heedless bastard! Then, in a quick plunging of memory, he knew the face. It belonged to Colonel Hulbert Booth, the chief of Old Number One's security police. The revolver shoulder holster on the white shirt was his trademark. Of course, Lew thought, Booth recognized him too, probably with as little pleasure. They had not spoken since the day when Booth raced his powerful motorcycle around a corner in the capital city, Ft. Paul, and knocked down a tribal boy who was standing in the gutter. The boy's head thudded against the pavement and he lay unconscious with blood seeping from his mouth. Corleigh had been walking nearby and when Colonel Booth remounted his cycle, apparently to ride away from the scene of the accident, Corleigh instinctively seized his arm. Lew could still recall the exchange.

"Aren't you going to get that boy to the hospital?" Corleigh demanded.

"What business is it of yours?" Booth asked in the studiously proficient English used by The Family.

"The kid's badly hurt," said Corleigh. "You've got a hell of a nerve leaving him. He might die."

Booth ignored the possibility. "You're one of those Peace Corps snoopers, aren't you? Well, take him yourself. And next time keep your nose out of my business. You vex me."

Booth pushed a rough hand against Corleigh, then started his motorcycle and rode off. Lew took the bleeding boy to Ft. Paul's lone hospital in a taxi and gave a report to the doctor in the unscoured emergency ward. The Kalya physician appeared frightened at the mention of Colonel Booth's name, but at Lew's insistence, the doctor laboriously wrote out an account of the accident with Booth's name in it. The boy recovered. Several weeks later, at the Ginger Baby bar, Corleigh heard that Booth was calling him "that Peace Corps liar," contending that Corleigh had falsely accused him of riding down a tribal boy. According to the gossip, Booth was maintaining that he had not even been in Ft. Paul that day and he warned, so went the rumor, that he had ways of dealing with people who told lies about him.

One morning, not long afterward, Corleigh came out of the Peace Corps hostel where he lived to find all four wheels of his jeep missing and the word "liar" crudely chalked on the side of the car. Again, later, one of the motorcycle policemen in Booth's security platoon charged him with reckless driving in front of the Prime Minister's palace. Corleigh knew that he hadn't been moving faster than twenty-five miles an hour, but he had to go to the moldering bureau of motor vehicles and pay a fifteen-dollar fine.

The incidents were still tunneling through Corleigh's mind now when a "money bus" passed him. The rickety money buses were the sole form of public transportation in outcountry Kalya. This one was tightly packed with humans, chickens and ducks, and the driver was speeding foolishly on the loose, dirt road. Had Corleigh and Booth collided, Lew could imagine the bus plowing into the wreckage on the blind curve. The women would have screamed while their fowls pecked about amid torn, broken bodies. Jesus, what a country! Corruption everywhere, even down to the driver's licenses which any numbskull could get with a ten-dollar bribe, whether or not he knew enough to shift gears, work the windshield wipers or slow down on the treacherous outcountry roads.

And the result was the carrion of automobiles, with crunched hoods and crumpled tops, which appeared along the road from Ft. Paul to Zinzin much as bleached buffalo bones marked the wagon trails of America's old West. Lew felt nauseated from shock and he wiped an arm across his sticky forehead. Had the near-collision with Booth been accidental, or had the security chief spotted him first and intentionally tried to force him off the road in the notorious Kalya game of "chicken"? Lew wasn't sure. All he knew was that the chances of surviving a bad smashup here were small. The nearest hospital was about one hundred miles away at Loli and first aid was an unknown art. Three more months to go on this frenzied jungle raceway, he thought, and dozens of maniacs yet to confront on the blind curves. And Lew had thought that Peace Corps life would be safer than his three-year Army stint. He recalled the last letter from his old roommate at Penn State, a man now snug aboard a carrier in the Pacific, eating ice cream every night and making shore leave in Tokyo and Hong Kong.

And what had Lewis Corleigh accomplished, anyway? He had come here to bring enlightenment and succor to the poor tribes of Kalya, and here he was, nothing but a high-class messenger and a low-class truck driver. They called him volunteer leader, but he led no one. He was neither simple volunteer nor staff member and he was a target for the niggling complaints of both. Today had really tied it.

On his first stop that morning at Katherine and Barbara's in the sweltering, stinking mud-hut village of Kpapata, he had found both young women sprawled listlessly in their house, listening to Nat King Cole records on their portable. They were supposed to be in class, setting an example for the shuffling Kalya teachers who sometimes didn't show up for days at a time. But Katherine and Barbara were fed up. Katherine said she was running a fever, and Barbara was weary of quarreling with the principal over the CARE food that he and the town chief were pilfering from school stocks. Lew found it hard to cloak his irritation. Sure, he understood their disenchantment, but, like him, they were Group V with only three months yet to go. Why couldn't they stick it out to the end without surrendering? If he had been a staffer, he could have ordered them back to school. But, leader or no leader, he had only volunteer status, making the same $157 a month subsistence allowance, and he had no authority to order anybody. What's more, he knew he wouldn't betray them to the staff back in Ft. Paul. Lew had his code, and informing on other volunteers wasn't part of it. But the dilemma irked him and ruined his day.

Then there was Bart, the supercilious beanpole with the scraggly, beatnik chin whiskers. Bart had sulked because Lew brought arithmetic texts instead of the spellers Bart had ordered. It was the fault of the Kalya boy in the mailroom, not Lew's, but Bart eyed him frostily as though Lew had erred on purpose.

Then Susan at Loli, whimpering because her kerosene refrigerator hadn't worked for five days. He wrestled the big box upside down, trying to renew its circulation, and promised he'd right it on his return trip. Susan watched him accusingly, shaking her head. Her look seemed to imply that he had failed the United States. Jesus, he was a history major, not a mechanic. And he wasn't the only man in the Peace Corps who couldn't repair appliances. Washington seemed to have recruited every thumb-fingered liberal arts graduate in the country, looking askance at anybody who could tell a gasket from a fly wheel.

More problems at Dnoga, at Chestertown and at Balapi, all up the long, hot road to Zinzin. Oh well, only ninety-one days to go before the jet took off for Europe. Two long weeks in Paris, with hot showers, untainted vegetables, wine, girls, newspapers, breakfast in bed, and then home to Chicago.

The shadows were fading into the gauze of evening as he drove past the first huts of Zinzin. Long, black lines of people filed along the road, returning from the rice paddies and the rubber plantation. A Mola woman, her pendulous breasts bare above her green skirt wrapper, eyed him from beneath her headload of newly washed clothes in a battered tin basin. She walked with a proud sway of her hips, shuffling on her heels to maintain balance for her burden. A tiny, naked boy, his belly button protruding obscenely because of umbilical rupture, waved and yelled, "Peezkor!" A withered old man with eyes yellowed by jaundice carried a bundle of sticks on his head. In the town proper there was the chaotic clamor of an African evening, a jabbering of tongues, tall Mandingos walking erect in swathes of bright cloth, torpid goats and dogs slouching across the road, Lebanese merchants peering from the dim recesses of their open shops and, at a food stall, women squatting by their wares. Their hair was plaited in identical pigtails, laid straight back like ropes on a counter. At an oil drum culvert a boy urinated into the creek while another boy beside him splashed the muddy waters over his own body. The sounds of early night, a distant bark, the murmur of many voices, the crying of a baby, mingled in the air, which was still stifling despite the setting of the sun.

Zinzin, with its endless clutter of movement, always seemed larger to Lew than it actually was. Last year the commissioner had collected the hut tax, Kalya's primitive real estate and income levy, from 943 dwellings. A handful of these were cement-block houses. Thirty or forty were mud-stick houses with cement floors and metal roofs. All the rest were circular, mud-walled huts, built on bare, packed earth and roofed with dried palm fronds which peaked sharply like straw sombreros. Some huts sheltered as many as eight persons. Lew guessed that Zinzin's population might be four thousand, but nobody really knew. The town had two main streets, crossing at right angles, and a dozen lanes which began bravely at the streets and straggled off into bush trails. Zinzin had fourteen Lebanese and Mandingo shops, an open market, one gas station, two churches, one public school and one Lutheran mission school, the district commissioner's building, a dilapidated, one-room courthouse and a large round palaver hut, thatch-roofed and open-sided, where the town elders gathered to ponder the affairs of the Mola tribe.

Lew turned off the road and bumped over the eroded earth, laced with gullies, to the Lutheran mission compound. A month from now, when the rains of late May came, this route would be an impassable stretch of gummy mud. Now the ground was baked hard and each lurch of the jeep jolted his backbone.

Arlene Offenbach's house consisted of three small rooms of mud blocks built about long wooden sticks that were driven into the ground. Under its zinc roof the house was neatly whitewashed. Lew stood at the screen door and, in the Kalya manner, cried, "Bock-bock."

Arlene appeared from the rear. She was smiling, obviously pleased to see him. As they exchanged greetings, he noted approvingly that her full, black hair was newly combed, swept upward to an ivory ornament which adorned the crest. Her lips were bright with carmine lipstick. Lew wondered how many months it would be before this new volunteer began neglecting her appearance. Maybe never. Some, like Cindy, never gave in.

"Did you bring my CARE tools, Lew?" she asked.

He nodded, went to the rear of the jeep wagon and hauled out a long cardboard box. Breaking it open, he handed them to her one by one. She greeted each with a flutter of pleasure, the spade, the rake, the hoe, the trowel. Such implements were not obtainable anywhere outcountry. From nowhere, a ring of small black boys clustered about the jeep, their envious eyes caressing each shining symbol of American largess.

One youngster of about eleven or twelve took the spade and fondled it. He was handsome, with finely chiseled features and a guileless grin. The boys all wore almost identical ragged khaki shorts as their sole items of clothing. The only touch of distinction, Lew noted, was that the boy with the shovel had a matchbox squeezed under one of his belt loops.

"Dis one you keepin' fo' me, teach'?" he asked.

Arlene hesitated. Lew stepped forward and took the spade from the boy. "No way," he said. "Dis one for da school."

The grinning boy voiced no complaint. Arlene frowned as she entered the house, carrying the other tools. Lew, with the spade, followed her. As they stacked the implements in a corner, the boys pressed against the two window screens, watching their every movement.

In the kitchen Arlene poured Lew a cool drink of boiled, filtered water from an old Haig & Haig bottle. She kept it in the kerosene refrigerator, an item which the Peace Corps supplied to all volunteers in Kalya.

"That was Morfu Gilli," she said, "one of my neighbors' children. You should have let him keep the shovel. He just wanted to hold it overnight. He wouldn't steal it."

"Maybe not," said Lew, "but some visiting aunt or cousin would. You'd never see it again."

"You're too hard on them." She bit her lip, not quite sure of

her ground with this veteran volunteer. "Morfu did me a good
turn yesterday."

"I'm not hard," said Lew, "just practical, and so will you be
after a couple of months. It's a Mola custom. Anything the kid
gets from an outsider, he's supposed to share or give to the first
freeloading relative who asks for it."

She brought him a clean, blue towel, nicely fluffed.

Lew grinned. "You're still in the giving stage, Arlene. We all
go through it. How much money have you given away in the
two months you've been here?"

She pursed her lips as she thought. "Well, I paid one girl's
tuition for teacher training. That's seventy-five dollars and I . . .
well . . . loaned maybe another twenty-five or thirty dollars."

He laughed. "Loaned, huh? Don't hold your breath until you
get it back, honey. Well, time for my shower."

The bath shack in the rear of the house was the finest shower
in outcountry Kalya. Built by the male volunteer who had pre-
ceded Arlene at the mission school, it had a whitewashed, baked
mud wall, rafters, a pitched metal roof, a soap rack and a cement
floor sloping to a drain through which water actually ran out.
Four fifty-five-gallon oil drums in series collected rain water from
the house roof and supplied the shower nozzle. Lew took off
his sweaty clothes and hung them on a peg. He laid out fresh
drawers, socks and sports shirt from the suitcase he had fetched
from the jeep.

"Lew!" It was Arlene outside. "I forgot. You'd better look at
the rafters. I saw a mamba up there yesterday morning and Morfu
had to kill it for me. Sometimes there's a mate."

"Now you tell me!" he said. He wrapped a towel around his
waist and stepped quickly back to the door. It was almost dark
now and he took the flashlight from his suitcase and shone it
on each beam. When he found nothing, he stepped under the
water, which was confined to a thin trickle to preserve water during
the long dry season. However small, the stream cutting the dust
and grime of the day should have been refreshing, but the snake
warning ruined any sensation of luxury. He lathered quickly and
stayed under the shower only long enough to wash the soap off.
He kept glancing at the rafters as he dried himself. He began to

perspire at once and when he pulled on his fresh clothes, he was already sticky again.

Arlene, waiting in her little living room with its cheerful chintz curtains and Peace Corps wicker furniture, was still thinking of the neighbor boy.

"Morfu is such a darling," she said. "He tries so hard and he's so proud that he's begun to read. And the Gillis don't have a thing. His father is making twelve cents an hour working on Jim Osterlord's road and that's the first cash they've had in weeks."

Lew groped mentally for a moment, then remembered that Morfu was the small boy, enamored of the spade, with the matchbox in his belt loop.

"By the way," he said, "what's the idea of that matchbox stuck in his pants?"

"That's a piece of iron ore that Cindy used one day in class to show them the valuable minerals they have in Kalya. Morfu loves it. He carries it everywhere."

Lew listened to Arlene a few minutes while she bubbled on over a dozen pending projects in the mission school run by Kalya Lutherans: a school garden, a new kitchen in which to cook the CARE lunches, an effort to install office records, her letter home asking her mother's church auxiliary in Akron to send over an old typewriter. These new women were always going to change the face of Africa tomorrow. Lew was surprised that she hadn't thought about forming a PTA in Zinzin. One girl actually tried it last year at Bopi. She got twenty mothers at the first meeting, three at the second and none at the third.

"Thanks for the shower, Arlene," he said. "Gotta make the rounds."

She handed him a letter to be mailed in Ft. Paul. Outcountry in bushland there was no mail service, no telephones, no running water, no trains, no sewers, no electricity. Lew was tired of enumerating all the things Kalya didn't have.

Arlene waved good-by to him and turned back purposefully to her house. Morfu and another boy, their white eyeballs glistening in the dark, were already at the door, prepared to do their nightly lessons at the kerosene lamp on her living room table. As Lew turned the jeep, the headlights picked up Morfu inside the house. He was stroking the new spade.

Corleigh drove slowly through Zinzin. People and animals threaded the unpaved, unlighted streets and once he almost hit a limp, short-haired dog whose mange-ridden legs and belly were a sickly purple.

Ted Kramer and Arch Lettermore, who taught in the government school with three other Peace Corps volunteers and three Kalya teachers, lived on the other side of town from Arlene. Their house was a duplicate of hers. The walls, however, were adorned with glowering devil masks. On the forehead of one, Arch had pasted a Lincoln University car sticker. On the back of the door was a red-bordered poster which Ted had taken from the bulletin board of a fundamentalist church in Ft. Paul: "Jesus Christ is coming soon. Will you be ready?" Kramer was a mordant atheist who liked to provoke Lettermore, a practicing Methodist, into religious arguments.

Arch and Ted were lounging in wicker chairs with their loafered feet propped up on the coffee table Arch had made out of a packing box. They were drinking Scotch and Arch held out a third glass, the whiskey already poured, for Lew.

"We heard you were in town," he said. "Bring any mail?"

Lew handed over three letters, two of them for Arch, and both men read in silence for a few minutes, oblivious of Corleigh. He sipped the Scotch. It tasted good after the long drive and his right foot, which had tromped all day on the sticky accelerator, began to tingle pleasantly.

"They've indicted the city auditor back home," said Arch at last. He was a chubby man, with a bush of hair and brown eyes, who found life more amusing than dismaying. Arch came from North Carolina and his drawl melted the language. "Boy, Ah'd like to see a grand jury in this place. They'd indict the whole government, from Ol' Number One down to that thieving principal of ours."

"More rhubarbs with Genghis Khan?" asked Lew. Almost every trip brought new scandalous tidbits about the principal of Zinzin's government elementary school. His name was Moses Harter, but the volunteers had nicknamed him Genghis Khan. He was a stout, yellowish man, more Asian than African in appearance, with a scar on his cheek and an inclination to pillage and promiscuity.

"You kidding?" asked Ted. He was a slouching young man who

had played basketball for City College of New York. His face was
chalk-white and pimpled. "He couldn't get in Cindy Fuller's pants,
so now it turns out he's knocked up the Kalya second-grade
teacher. Not only that, but he put the lug on her for a whole
month's salary, claiming there's a new rule out of Ft. Paul that
every teacher has to give a month's salary to the principal. The
poor girl knows it's a lie, but she has to kick in to keep her job."

"What'd you do?" asked Lew.

"Do?" echoed Arch. "What can we do? Last week you brought
up that load of free textbooks from the department and this week
ol' Genghis nicks the kids a dime a book. He says it's a com-
pulsory rental fee, and the kids don't know the difference."

"I could report it to Williams and he could carry a protest
over to Downing," said Lew. Carter Williams was the Peace
Corps representative in Kalya, chief of the Ft. Paul staff. Downing was J. Richardson Downing, the Commissioner of Education.

"Fat lot of good that will do," said Ted Kramer. "Genghis
Khan gets his job straight from Old Number One and Downing
knows it."

Lew knew that Moses Harter, or Genghis Khan, was on the
patronage list of Prime Minister Alexander Vining, known
throughout Kalya as "Old Number One." But more, in some
way Lew did not fully understand, Harter was also the political
power in Zinzin. He was the town's sole lawyer, although he
had no legal training. He was the building contractor and the
school principal. He also had ties with the Mola tribe's town
chief and with the town devil, a personage of reputed mysterious
powers whose identity was never revealed and who danced in
weird, matted costume in times of tribal peril. Harter was of the
country's ruling "Family" and possessed more influence than the
ranking government official, Steven Muo, a Mola tribesman who
held the post of district commissioner.

Downing, the education commissioner, forever boasting that he
was "elevating educational standards" throughout Kalya, turned
a deaf ear to most complaints against his schoolmasters. Still,
perhaps, Williams could bring some pressure on Downing to curb
Harter. Genghis Khan's own schooling had halted at the sixth
grade.

"Well, I'll tell Williams anyway," said Lew. "Maybe we can do some good."

Ted Kramer shook his head. "Wawa," he said, screwing his white, pimply face into a grimace. They all laughed.

Peace Corps volunteers in Zinzin had learned the word "Wawa" from Forrest Stevenson, a weathered district U.S. AID official who lived in the town of Loli, a hundred miles down the road. Stevenson was a gentle cynic who'd spent almost his whole life in Africa, first as a mission child, then as a missionary and now, in the decadence of full surrender, as a man who distributed the bounty of the U.S. government without the faintest hope it would do any good. "Wawa—West Africa wins again," he'd say at every new AID blunder. His pale blue eyes would mist with regret, and he'd wave his delicate hands in a gesture of despair.

The houseboy, bare save for his khaki shorts, came in from the kitchen with more ice for the drinks. Arch passed the bottle.

"You wanna stay for chow, Red?" he asked. "Country chop to-night."

"Well . . ." Lew hesitated.

"Knock it off," said Ted. "The redhead's going to eat with Alice and Dotty. Why mess around with chop when he can have maybe roast lamb and hot biscuits?"

Lew grinned and drained off the refill of Scotch at a gulp. "On my horse. See you guys next time. Leave any mail and I'll pick it up in the morning."

"Adios, Red. Tell the staff we're still alive," said Ted. "If I ever saw one of them babies up here in Zinzin, I'd have heart failure."

It was but a three-minute drive to the house on the hill where Alice Franklin and Dorothea Wyzansky lived in cluttered squalor. Rounding a turn, Lew's headlights picked out the legend scrawled on the bright blue outhouse: "Welcome home, Dotty. Hope you're not blue too." Dorothea Wyzansky had flown to Nigeria during the school's spring vacation. During her absence Alice had painted the mud-brick outhouse a lively blue. Inside, above the crude wooden latrine, she lettered the old cautionary reminder for male visitors: "Men, we aim to please. So please to aim."

Alerted by the rattle of the jeep, both women were at the

door to greet him. Alice, a small, dumpy girl, stood with her hands on her hips. Her uncombed hair fell over one lens of her spectacles. Dorothea, tall and angular, wore her brown hair pulled so tightly into a bun that it seemed to stretch the sallow skin of her face.

"Hi, Red," Alice yelled. "Ninety days, twenty-one hours and seventeen minutes to go. How about the Heineken's? No Heineken's, no dinner."

"Blackmailers," said Lew. But he went back to the jeep and got six green bottles of beer from the cardboard case.

The mud house, larger than the other Peace Corps dwellings, was in its usual state of disarray. Old magazines, a tangle of yarn, a Scrabble board and some albums for the battery-powered record player littered the cement floor, which obviously hadn't been swept in days. In the corner, near the Peace Corps book locker, was a pile of dirty laundry. Joe-Joe, the houseboy who wore a soiled sweatshirt with the legend "Sweet Briar," smelled as if he needed a bath. He grinned with a flash of teeth as he took the beer.

Dotty slumped on the sofa, which exposed the batting in several places where the fabric had worn through. She lit a cigarette and tossed the match on the floor.

"When were you here last?" she asked.

"Wednesday, I think. Yeah, Wednesday. Why?"

"Then it was Thursday," she said, scowling. "Thursday was Endsville. I mean the living, breathing, screamin' end."

"Brother, we've had it," said Alice. She plopped down beside her roommate and fixed Lew with a resentful glare as though it were all his fault. The household of Franklin and Wyzansky, always spiked with crises, obviously had been skewered by another one. Lew was tired. He suppressed a yawn.

"What now, ladies?" He smiled.

"Laugh if you want," said Dotty, "but wait'll you hear. Driver ants, and I mean driver ants. Not a thousand, not a million, but jillions of them. They came marching through that crack beside the door and spread out in three columns. We were eating breakfast and didn't notice until they were at our feet. Cripes, how they bite. You ever felt 'em? They're like hot tongs. Look!"

She thrust out her sandaled feet. Dozens of tiny red dots

speckled her feet, ankles and lower calves. Alice lifted her legs too. They were streaked with calamine lotion.

"Two whole stinkin' days they marched through here," said Alice. "We had to get out and bunk over at Cindy's. There wasn't a crumb left on the floor when they finally left."

"Too bad they didn't take a broom and sweep out the joint," said Lew.

"Wise guy!" Dotty ground out her cigarette butt on the floor with her sandal. "We should try to keep this place clean when all the fauna of Africa come prowling through here? Cripes, I mean this is the living end. If I ever threaten to serve humanity and all that jazz again, I hope they take me to a head-shrinker."

"And last night!" exclaimed Alice. Her laugh was a high-pitched, giddy one. "Tell him about last night."

"Last night we had a visit from two lover boys out of Ft. Paul," said Dotty. "They drove up in the black Mercedes, all three hundred miles to Zinzin, just to touch our fair, white flesh. Us, I mean. Look at us! Hysterical, no? Anyway, one was Hulbert Booth, that colonel who runs Old Number One's security police. You know him?"

"Know him?" echoed Lew. "He almost ran me down on a blind curve a while ago. He must have been doing sixty. Yeah, I know him. I had a run-in with him once in Ft. Paul too. The big guy with the shoulder holster."

"That's our lover boy," said Dotty. "I hear he brags that his minimum requirement is a new dame every month. The other was a fellow named Tommy who plays the saxophone and—if you'll pardon the expression—works in the Agriculture Department. Agriculture! He wouldn't know a tractor from a hand trowel."

"So?"

Alice took over the story. "So, they claimed they were up here to check on Hulbert Booth's outcountry farm. We had a wrestling match all over the living room and the kitchen. I said I'd scream and they said, go ahead, they liked fighting women. They turned on the record player, so we danced with them. But, oh no, they wanted to jump in the hay right now. God, what a night!"

"Well, don't leave me now," said Lew. "What happened?"

"The Peace Corps to the rescue!" Dotty's voice was shrill. "Ted and Archie just happened to come by, thank God. They

got the picture, so they just sat and sat. Finally, the Ft. Paul
Don Juans figured they'd lost out to two other guys, so they
got in the Mercedes and drove over to the farm. For the night,
I guess. And all because I told that Tommy fellow one night in
Ft. Paul that he was pretty hot on the saxophone. You know,
establishing meaningful contacts with the indigenous population,
Peace Corps Goals Numbers Two and Three. Cripes. Meaningful? If I could find that recruiter who came to Mt. Holyoke, I
mean I'd strangle him with my bare hands."

Humidity steeped the room. Dotty wiped her moist forehead
with the back of a hand. Alice's glasses were fogged from the
body heat generated by her excited rendition of woes. A fly buzzed
in loops at the fringe of the yellow glow cast by the pulsing
kerosene lamp. Through the screen door, on the softest stir of a
breeze, came rich odors of the Zinzin night, a blend of rotting
vegetation and animal and human excrement. Alice scratched at
her calamined legs. Sweet Briar and Mt. Holyoke seemed a
world away.

"I don't get it," said Alice. She batted at the droning fly.
"Everything the Peace Corps tries to do is stymied by The
Family. They steal the supplies, they bleed the teachers' pay, they
loot the textbook fund and then they come up here and try to
go to bed with us, like it was their God-given right or something.
And the staff plays their game too. Why doesn't the rep get his
backbone up once in a while?"

"Williams tries," said Lew. It was the old discussion, as pre-
dictable in its course as the parade of Kalya holidays, and Lew
had no stomach for it tonight. He was fatigued by the drive
and he wanted no Peace Corps theorizing. Besides, these conversational rambles all wound up at the same dead end.

Old Number One was a fast friend of the United States, a
moderating voice among the leftist African demagogues. Old
Number One invited the Peace Corps into his country, paid a
fraction of their subsistence allowance. Old Number One built
roads and gaudy, extravagant government buildings, but he let
his ruling hierarchy, a finely meshed patronage web of a dozen
families, loot the people, filch supplies and divert U.S. AID
money into private pockets by a score of adroit devices. The Peace
Corps was here to help the tribes emerge from centuries of igno-

rance and apathy and from a culture still fastened to village devils and bush witchcraft rites. The smallest of Peace Corps efforts in this direction met resistance from Old Number One's arrogant, non-governing government. The Ft. Paul Family wanted no change, and the Peace Corps was its hireling. Round and round went this endless discussion of the volunteers like a record under a stuck needle. No one knew the solution, and so a majority of every Peace Corps contingent ended its two-year contract, as Group V was doing now, in a tangle of disillusion and shriveled dreams.

"They ought to bulldoze the whole country and start over again," said Dotty. Lew Corleigh yawned.

"The hell with it," he said. "What's for dinner, ladies?"

The houseboy dragged in, scratching at his Sweet Briar sweatshirt. "Okay, now," he said. Corleigh and the two girls went to the table in the kitchen. On the red gingham tablecloth, spotted with grease, were three bottles of Heineken beer, steaming barley soup from the girls' stock of cans, fried chicken, hot biscuits and a mound of juicy slices of fresh pineapple. The women sat down and began eating immediately. The hissing of the kerosene lamp and the clink of table utensils were the only sounds for many minutes.

Suddenly Dotty pushed back her chair and ran from the house, the screen door banging behind her. Alice spoke through a mouthful of chicken.

"Our little intestinal friend," she said. "She's had it for two days."

Lew continued to eat without replying. In the first weeks in Kalya, scenes like this upset his stomach and made the taste of food repugnant. Now, so long as his own alimentary tract stayed in reasonable working condition, nothing bothered him. When Dotty returned, she grimaced without speaking, took her beer and went to sit in the living room.

"Terminate me now, dear Lord," she called to them in her high, thin voice. "I mean terminate me right this living, bloody minute."

"That reminds me," said Lew. "On next week's trip, I'll bring up the termination kits. You're going down to Ft. Paul in groups of twenty for the medical, the termination interviews, all that stuff."

"I don't believe it," called Dotty. "You're a mirage, Dr. Livingstone. You're a ghost. You don't exist."

Alice and Lew finished their pineapple and went into the living room. Alice was picking her teeth with a matchstick.

"I'm sorry, Dotty," said Lew. "The dinner was swell. Too bad you couldn't finish it."

"Just autograph my termination kit. I mean that's all I ask." She looked at him dyspeptically through a haze of cigarette smoke.

They gave him the Zinzin gossip. Houhab, the leading Lebanese merchant, had gone to Ft. Paul with a gangrenous hand. He had cut the palm badly, but the "dresser" at the government clinic had run out of antiseptics and bandages and had wrapped the wound in an unsterilized cloth. There were rumors that Genghis Khan had filched the clinic's supplies and sold them over the border. . . . Arlene Offenbach found a black mamba in her shower. Lew nodded. He knew all about that one and still felt unwashed. . . . Arch and Ted were still collecting for Jim Osterlord's road from Zinzin to the border and were doing pretty well now that the townspeople knew that Jim was holding the money instead of Genghis Khan or his friends. . . . Nobody had seen Osterlord for a week. He'd made a bush trip with the district commissioner, Steve Muo, and he'd been due back today to renew working on the road. God knew what else he was up to, he was so uncommunicative. Something about a filing system in the commissioner's office.

"Cripes, a filing system yet," said Dotty, "and nobody in the whole town can read the alphabet. . . . Wawa!"

"Wawa," echoed Alice. They both giggled.

"Bock-bock." It was Cindy Fuller at the door.

"Come in, dear," yelled Alice. "We're having Wednesday night prayer meeting, rendering thanks for all our blessings."

Cynthia Fuller wore blue jeans and a white jersey pullover sweater. Both were newly laundered and spotless. Her black hair was combed to one side in a full bob. Her lipstick was a pale rose, a subtle foil for her coppery skin. She took a wicker chair and stretched out her long legs. Her toenail polish matched the lipstick. Lew grinned appreciatively. The contrast with the frayed appearance of the other women was refreshing.

"Evening, white folks," she said with a small grin. "You talkin' about us-uns?"

"No, dear," said Alice. "Kalya. What else?"

"It could be worse, but I don't know how." Cindy smiled with a flash of china-white teeth. "What you keeping for me, Red?"

"Couple of letters postmarked Atlanta," he said, "the textbooks and a volley ball. Just like you asked. What Cindy wants, Cindy gets."

"So how are things in Dixie?" she asked. "What white bastions is my leader, Dr. King, assaulting today?"

Cindy, unlike the other Negro volunteers, brought up color at once in any gathering, as though to remind her Peace Corps friends that they were living under conditions of a racial truce which would dissolve once they stepped aground at Kennedy International Airport. But her remarks were never barbed, never intended to incite, always gently teasing in tone. Her manner nettled Lew and he never quite knew what she really thought of her white colleagues.

"I don't know," he replied. "I haven't heard a radio. Been driving for two days."

"You look smashing, Cindy," said Alice. She flicked a hand at her own limp hair. "I don't know how you manage in this crummy weather."

"Ditto," said Dotty. "You make me feel like an old rag."

"A sieve, you mean," corrected Alice. She turned to Cindy. "Dotty's got it."

"That's too bad, Dotty," said Cindy. "Have you been eating lettuce from the market again?"

"Small-small," replied Dotty. She wrinkled her nose. "And let's drop it, huh? I mean it's bad enough without talking about it."

Suddenly, like a giant punctuation mark for Dotty's sentence, the room exploded with noise. The zinc roof rattled and rang as though a thousand boulders had struck it at once. It was a hollow, drumming sound, deafening in volume, and it seemed as though the roof would surely collapse under the barrage. They had to shout to hear one another. Water began to splash on the floor in a corner and Alice quickly brought a pail from the kitchen to catch the leak. Conversation became futile and the four volunteers merely sat and looked at one another. The temperature dropped ten degrees within a few minutes. Dotty clasped her arms and shivered. The first of the "little rains," precursor to the summer wet season, had come.

The booming sound, as steady as the throbbing of village drums, continued without a single rise or fall in volume. The pitch was full-throated, violent, yet so unwavering in intensity that it seemed to give a kind of curious comfort to those inside the house. Nothing so incessant, so unchanging, could be perilous. Rather the fierce, steady onslaught of the storm seemed to have the quality of a heavenly jest.

In ten minutes it was over. As quickly and as overwhelmingly as it began, the rain stopped. The sudden quiet seemed unnatural, and the scattered drops on the metal roof from the dabema and banana trees sounded as distinct as gunshots. Lew went to the screen door and looked out.

"The water's up to the rims of the jeep tires," he said. "We must have had three, four inches."

"Ninety days and nineteen hours to go," said Dotty bitterly, "and about sixty sopping days of it will be spent in mud up to our knees."

Cindy stood up and looked at her sandals. "Wet feet tonight," she said.

"No," said Lew. "I'll ride you home. I've got to deliver your stuff anyway. Take it easy, ladies. I'll come by for the mail after breakfast tomorrow."

"Bye, now," said Alice. "If you had any chivalry, Red, you'd carry the lady to the jeep."

Lew had thought of that, but Cindy was already out the door, picking her way gingerly around puddles on her way to the car.

But at Cindy's house, he did carry her from the jeep, his path lighted by the kerosene lamp she'd left burning on the coffee table. She was not a slight girl, but he didn't notice the burden. The warmth of her body felt good in the new night chill after the downpour.

"Nightcap?" she asked when he put her down. "Bourbon's all I've got, I guess."

"Straight bourbon's great," he said.

"All right, Red. The same for me, too."

The small living room was tidy, the floor swept clean and the woodwork newly scrubbed. Two hooked rugs, which she'd brought over via sea freight, hung on opposite walls. They were taken down periodically for cleaning and airing in Cindy's constant battle with mildew. On a desk stood a picture of her parents, her father very black and her mother the same coffee hue as Cynthia. There were bright orange chintz curtains at the windows and a number of carvings of African faces, in rosewood and ebony, decorated the end tables and Peace Corps book locker.

She brought the drinks and sat down beside him on the sofa, patting his arm as she did so.

"You're a nice man, Red," she said. "I like you."

"Thanks," he said. He eyed her over the rim of his glass. "The same to you, woman, only more so."

Her smile was a slow, warm one. "Meaning?"

"Meaning that you're a damn good-looking girl and we're both four thousand miles from home, and well, I feel like a feeling man should, as the cigarette ads say."

"Uh-huh." She studied her drink and idly stirred the ice cubes with her finger. He saw the trim profile of her breasts beneath the white jersey and he wanted to hold her. They sat silently for a few moments.

"What did you think when you kissed me the other night?" she asked, still looking down at her glass.

"I thought, well . . ." He paused. "I thought I'd like to try it again, the sooner the better."

"No," she said, "I mean about the difference. We're not the same color, after all. I mean about that."

"You really want to know?" he asked.

"Yes, I do." She turned to face him. Her look was candid, but there was a subtle air of challenge in it too.

He wondered how to tell her. He had thought about it two nights ago, on the porch of the hostel in Ft. Paul. He was thinking of her and there, under veiled stars in the muggy African night, he tried to understand just what he did feel about her race and his. He had always gone to school with Negroes in Evanston and there were two Negroes in his Army platoon. Later, at Penn State, one of his friends on the track team was black. Intellectually, he knew, he favored the big civil rights crusade and he grew indignant when he read a newspaper story about racial killings. But emotionally he never got drawn into the Negro revolution, never became a freedom rider, never carried a picket sign or helped repair a bombed Negro church in Mississippi. He had taken people as they were, regardless of color, and let it go at that. But he had never visited a Negro home, never really talked about race with Negro schoolmates or Army acquaintances, never made an effort to explore their feelings.

Then he came to Africa two years ago and suddenly found himself a member of a minority race. It was a shock at first and then, when the shock faded, he began to admire the black skin and to feel oddly resentful at times because his own skin was so pale. With his red hair and fair complexion, he couldn't even take much sun without risking a sickening sunburn. Then, he ruminated, there had come a third phase. Working day in and day out with Negro volunteers and staff members of the Peace Corps —eating, sleeping, arguing and relaxing with them—he began to forget completely about the difference in skin pigmentation. It was all so natural and easy that he read news magazine accounts of new racial explosions in the States with a sense of bafflement, as though it were all happening on another planet and Governor George Wallace of Alabama was a strange, incomprehensible creature from another world. He had a fanciful impulse to fly back home and try to tell the sachems of segregation how wrong they were and just what he had learned. He knew now what America could become some day when it emerged from the canyons of racial strife, and he began to feel a pride in the Peace Corps for leading him to his new understanding.

Cindy sat watching him with a patient, quizzical smile. "Well?" she asked.

"I've learned a lot," he said, "but saying it would sound kind of corny. I guess, oh hell, I've learned to take every person for himself. I knew it with my mind all along, but now I feel it in my gut. Maybe in two years out here I haven't helped Kalya or the U.S. much, but I've sure learned a lot about myself and other people, and that's worth the price of admission."

She shook a finger at him. "But you didn't answer my question. How do you feel about us? You know, black girl, white boy."

"Well, for one thing, Cindy, you're not black, you know."

She tensed. "Why, what's wrong with being black?"

The sudden edge to her tone surprised him. "Nothing," he said hurriedly, "but as long as you want to level about feelings, we might as well be factual too."

She gestured toward the picture of her father. "And if I had my father's skin, you wouldn't be here. Is that it?"

"Oh, for God's sake, Cindy." He felt helpless. Had he learned so much after all? "No, that's not it, and you know it. You asked me how I felt. Well, I feel great. I don't think about color any more. The hell with it. You're a woman. I like you. Period."

"No, semi-colon," she said. "Maybe it's because you're an ocean away from home and any female looks good when a man's hard up."

"Negative." Her taunting tone irritated him. "There are dozens of white girls over here. They're hard up too, I guess. I happen to like you, Cindy. You."

She smiled. "I know you do, Red. I guess maybe I could say the same thing in reverse, but there's a difference. Deep inside me there's a lump of bitterness against white people that won't go away. Remember, last year, when we had that argument about the Los Angeles riots?"

Lew nodded. "You blamed it on the police and I blamed it on the young Negro hoodlums. Maybe we were both right."

"I was mad at the cops because they were white," she said. "It's the old feeling. Maybe it isn't reasonable, but there it is—from all the wrongs of centuries."

"But I never did anything," he protested. "Do you resent me too?"

She laughed. "No, Red. Not you and I guess not any of the other volunteers over here. It's just, well, it's just in my bones."

He put down his drink and drew her slowly to him. She nestled against his chest, turned her face upward and closed her eyes. They kissed for a long time. When they parted, she ran a finger along his arm, raising goose bumps as she brushed the hairs.

"Red hair against that lily-white skin looks funny," she said. "Nice funny. I like it."

"Now who's an ocean away from home?" He grinned at her.

"You're taking advantage. I just meant I like you."

"Better than Archie?"

She wrinkled her nose. "Archie! Nothing vibrates when he looks at me. For one thing, he's too fat."

"Cindy," he asked, "did you ever make love with a white man?"

She shook her head, slowly, seriously. "And what about you—the other way?"

Lew shook his head. They grinned self-consciously.

"You suppose it's any different?" he asked.

"I've wondered sometimes." She ran her fingers through his hair.

"Could we?"

She said nothing. They sat for a moment, not speaking. They finished their drinks and then Lew took her hand and pulled her upright. They embraced and over her shoulder he could see the mosquito netting which hung by a strap above her bed in the next room. After their kiss, she held him off and looked into his eyes.

"They're green," she said. "You're green and red, like a Christmas ornament."

"You've got color on the brain," he said, but he dwelled on the deep brown of her eyes.

She continued to search his face as though in quest of something. Then she shrugged, sat down and patted the sofa beside her.

"No, Lew," she said. "We're going to talk. Sit down with me."

"Too different?"

"No, not that. This is woman stuff. Too much, too fast. We really don't know much about each other, do we?"

And so he sat, reluctantly, and they talked. They talked for hours, about the Peace Corps, about Kalya, about her girlhood in Atlanta and her four years at Morgan State College, about his growing up near Chicago, where he traveled in the Army and what he studied at Penn State, about their likes and dislikes. Oc-

casionally they kissed and it was very late when she took a handkerchief and wiped her pale lipstick from his mouth and cheeks.

"You're an okay article, Red," she said. "On your next trip,
how about having dinner with me instead of the crisis girls?"

"It's a deal."

She walked to the door with him, her hand in his, and then
she kissed him softly as he left.

It was after 3 A.M. when Lew got back in the jeep and drove
to Jim Osterlord's house to spend the rest of the night. The stars
were out again, brilliant on the black cover of the sky, and the
freshness from the season's first rain was still in the air. Far away,
a lone dog barked, and from the bush came the oddly descending
coo-coo-coo notes of a coucal. Lew Corleigh was very tired and
almost content.

2

Lew awoke to the rasping, undulating sound of a short-wave radio. He hadn't had enough sleep and the static coughed at his eardrums. Clad in his undershorts, he walked groggily to the front room, almost colliding with Freddie, the houseboy, who was carrying a mug of coffee.

Jim Osterlord was seated before the radio which he manned every morning at 7:30 for conversation with Peace Corps Ft. Paul. The radio at the other end was in the house of Prudence Stauffer, a primly industrious staff member who automatically assumed any duties that her other colleagues considered too onerous. Jim was pressing a key on a microphone when Lew entered.

"This is Peace Corps Zinzin, Peace Corps Zinzin," he said in a toneless voice. "How do you read? Over."

"This is Peace Corps Ft. Paul." Prudence's voice over short-wave had a gruff, growling quality. "I read you fine. Glad you're back from the bush, Jim. Any emergencies up there? Over."

"Nothing, nothing, Prudence. Got in late yesterday. Everything quiet here, I think. Just a minute."

Osterlord squinted inquiringly at Lew as he held his hand over the microphone. His shaggy mop of black hair, uncut for weeks, fell over his eyes. "Anything we ought to tell Prudence?"

Lew shook his head. "Dotty's got diarrhea, but she'll be all right. Everybody else is okay. No problems."

"Nothing's humbugging us, Prudence." Like other volunteers, Jim used the Kalya idioms. "We need another drum of kerosene up here. You might mark that down in case Lew forgets. Over."

"Is Lew still there, and if so, when does he return?" The voice rose and fell, static crackling around it.

"Yes, he's here. He'll make Ft. Paul tomorrow night. Right, Lew?" Corleigh nodded.

"Okay, Prudence. Signing off Peace Corps Zinzin. Over and out."

Jim Osterlord switched off the set with the air of a man glad to be finished with an uninteresting chore. Peace Corps housekeeping details bored him. He swung around to the table which the houseboy had set for breakfast. There were grapefruit slices, corn flakes with tasteless powdered milk, eggs and coffee.

He pointed a fork at the food. "Eat the eggs before they get cold," he ordered. "You can wash later."

Lew sat down, scratching aimlessly at his bare chest. He felt his usual testiness in Kalya's early morning heat. "Someday I'm coming back and air-condition the whole damn country," he said. "Good idea for a Ford Foundation grant."

Jim said nothing as he ate. He was a handsome volunteer with black, wavy hair and a faint olive cast to his skin that gave him an appearance vaguely suggestive of an Arab. He wore an unbuttoned blue polo shirt, khaki pants, sweat socks and moccasins. He was newly shaved after a week in the bush, and his outer cheeks and jaw line appeared lighter in hue than the rest of his face. He said something to the houseboy in Mola, and Freddie answered swiftly with a rippling, musical inflection. Kalya's official language, taught in the schools, was English, but few tribal inhabitants ever used it. Osterlord was the only Peace Corpsman in Zinzin to steep himself in the native Mola tongue.

"Can you really understand him, Freddie?" asked Lew.

"Ya, man." Freddie grinned in appreciation. "He spea' slow, bu' he spea' good."

"What did he say?"

"He say boil plen' wat' dis day. I say okay, boil all dis day."

Lew looked at his host. "You're hot with the lingo, Jim. Shows what Harvard will do for a man."

"Balls," said Jim.

Osterlord, in Zinzin a year, was assigned to what the Peace Corps called "community development." He had a mania for building, anything from latrines to roads, and he literally shoveled town improvement plans at his friend Steve Muo, the district commissioner. He had even convinced Muo that some day they might build a water system for Zinzin. The project was considered preposterously visionary by other volunteers, since any connection between pure water and health seemed as remote to the tribal Kalyan as that between a government job and work.

"How was the trip with Muo?" asked Lew.

"Swell. Didn't see a white man for eight days."

Corleigh noted the relish in Osterlord's tone, as though Jim's own race had become repellent to him. There was silence. Conversation with Osterlord was somewhat like fishing. He was elusive, wary, and he responded only when hooked.

"Genghis Khan pulled another one while you were away," said Lew. "They say he made the kids ante up a dime each for those free textbooks I brought up."

"Oh?"

"I don't dig that guy," said Lew. "How can he get away with so much? I know he's part of The Family, but God, he overdoes it. Maybe he's just a fast-buck operator who needs money."

Osterlord put a finger to his lips and nodded toward the kitchen. Houseboys in Kalya were notorious for relaying everything they overheard. Jim snorted, then spoke in a low key. "Money? He's got the stuff coming out of his ears."

"From what?"

"He owns half the houses in town," said Jim. "Did you know he owns this one and also the one Cindy lives in?"

"I never heard that."

"Steve told me on the trip," said Osterlord. "Genghis rents them to the Peace Corps through another guy. Gets four hundred bucks a year on each, which is more than it cost to build the shacks."

Lew pushed away the corn flakes with a grimace. The powdered milk tasted chalky. Some nights, Lew dreamed of a huge tumbler of fresh milk. There were milk cows in Kalya, but Doc Zerwick banned the drinking of fresh milk by volunteers on the ground that many of the cattle were tubercular. Lew sipped at his coffee, vaguely resenting the new day. The heat was rising as though from a recently opened furnace.

"How does Commissioner Muo get along with Genghis?" asked Lew.

Jim made a thumbs-down motion. "Steve's mind may move kinda slow, but he's honest, and he knows Harter is a crook."

"You'd think since Muo is the commissioner, he'd have the muscle to keep Genghis in line."

Osterlord's grin was a sour, crooked one. "You know better than that, Red. Genghis is like that with Old Number One." He raised two crossed fingers. "Old Number One appointed Muo because he had to make some concessions to the Molas, but Genghis is his real boy up here. It all takes time. Steve's learning."

Last night the thought of rehashing Peace Corps Topic A— the venality of the ruling Family—had bored him, but this morning Lew felt an urge to explore it again. Perhaps it was Jim's reticence. It took more than gossip trivia to lure Osterlord into conversation.

"What I don't get," said Lew, still in a low voice, "is the lack of opposition in this country. Almost every town has its Genghis Khan. The Family runs everything and everybody, getting fat off the tribes, but nobody tries to stop it. You'd think there'd be at least one outfit, or even just one guy, fighting The Family."

Osterlord surveyed him rather patronizingly, then pulled a thin cigar from the pocket of his polo shirt and lit it. The cigar was of a home-made variety supplied him by a Mola tribesman. On the first billow of smoke, a powerful, acrid stench enveloped the table.

Osterlord eyed Corleigh through the smoke. "How do you know there isn't?"

Lew noted the challenge in Osterlord's voice and a quickened interest in his face. Lew had the feeling that Jim, for some reason, was measuring him.

"I ought to know," he replied defensively. "I travel this country seven, eight hundred miles a week, and nowhere have I ever heard a single beef against Old Number One and his crew."

Osterlord studied him a moment through a second puff of smoke. Then he called the houseboy, spoke to him in Mola and handed him some coins. Freddie grunted and went out the front door.

"I sent him down to the market," explained Jim, "and told him to have a Coke. He'll be gone a half hour."

Osterlord piled up the breakfast dishes and carried them to the kitchen, then returned and carefully swept the crumbs off the table onto the floor. He waved the cigar as he sat down again.

"Red," he said, "you're not a bad guy, but you're as dumb as the rest of the Peace Corps crowd."

Lew grinned. Osterlord's disdain for his fellow volunteers was an old story. Jim mixed with them only rarely. Many of his nights, Lew knew, were spent with his "country wife," a pliant young Mola girl who was a cousin of Steve Muo. Now, Lew surmised, Jim was willing to speak seriously of The Family, but not until Osterlord's pet antipathy had been saluted.

"That's a charitable note to start the day on," said Lew.

"Dumb!" announced Jim into a cloud of pungent smoke. "How the hell can any of you know what's going on when you don't know the language? Name one PCV besides myself and Roger, over at the leper colony, who can speak to anybody but The Family."

"I can't," said Lew. "But, let's face it, Jim, there are about twenty languages in this country. And who can learn twenty languages?"

"Balls. That's just a staff excuse for laziness. There are only two main ones, Mola and Fizi. Every volunteer ought to be made to learn one or the other. Otherwise, they might as well all be shipped back home."

"You mean all the teaching we do in the schools is worthless just because it's done in English?"

Osterlord waved the protest away with his cigar. "Oh sure, the teaching sounds great. But what's the sense of training a lot of kids to read and write English when all they can do with it is get a job, maybe, in a lousy, looting government? It's the system that has to be changed. Otherwise, the Peace Corps is just playing patty-cake."

"I'll buy that," said Lew, "but nobody's trying to change it. Not a single native in the whole country."

"You're wrong, sonny boy." Osterlord smoked a few moments. "You're wrong. You don't know the language, so you can't hear what's going on around you."

"I take it you know something to the contrary," said Lew. "Big Mola palaver man hears rumbles of revolt."

"I listen."

"Well?"

"What I hear I don't tell." Jim's face was blank in a haze of cigar smoke. Lew could sense that he was savoring the intrigue.

"Can the secret agent bit, Jim," he said. "If something's going on, I'd like to know about it."

"Why?"

"Curiosity," replied Lew. "If I can't help anybody over here, at least I ought to learn something. The taxpayer ought to get something for his money."

Osterlord merely stared at him. He really does resent other volunteers, thought Lew. To Osterlord, we're all poachers on his private jungle preserve. Osterlord rolled the cigar in his mouth and propped his moccasined feet on the table.

Lew again had the feeling that Osterlord was appraising him, more intently this time. Why that cautious weighing, he wondered. Peace Corps talk of Kalya politics was always loose and voluminous. Yet Osterlord seemed even more guarded than usual. Why was Jim studying him? Did Osterlord really know something, a secret opposition to Old Number One, or was he merely fencing as usual with another volunteer whose knowledge of Kalya and its intricate ways he deemed deplorably lacking in insight?

"You mean well, Red," said Osterlord at last. "I'll give you a lead. You ever hear of a guy in Ft. Paul named Lincoln Beach?"

Lew shook his head. Osterlord brought down his tilted chair with a thud and went to a corner desk. He burrowed into a heap of papers, found a clean sheet and a pencil. He wrote something and handed the slip to Corleigh.

"Link: The bearer of this is Lew Corleigh. He is Peace Corps and a friend of mine. You can trust him. Jim Osterlord."

Lew folded the slip and tucked it in his wallet. "Very enigmatic, 007," he said.

Jim shrugged. "When I give my word I won't talk, I don't. If you really want to know something, you look up Link Beach. He works at the Utility Authority, billing section. . . . Well, time to go. How about following me out to the road and see how we're doing?"

Osterlord kept his motorbike, standard Peace Corps gear for community development workers, propped against the wall of the living room. Any small vehicle left outdoors would vanish in the night. Even inside it was not entirely safe. Jim had been "rogued" twice in a year, the thieves making off with food, beer, kerosene and tableware.

After Lew had washed and dressed, Osterlord wheeled the cycle outside, donned his white crash helmet, started the motor and went slithering precariously down the gutted hillside road, still mucky from last night's downpour.

Lew followed in the jeep wagon. The sun already blazed dully, high in the east, and the great bush steamed in reply. They rode past the round mud huts with their thatched palm frond roofs and the bare ground swept clean of animal droppings. Beside the huts, skirted women with long, shrunken breasts, raised and lowered heavy pieces of wood shaped like teardrops. They were husking swamp rice in thick wooden receptacles and their strokes had the rhythm of pile-drivers. The women all gleamed with sweat and by midday they would be brutally tired. In Zinzin proper, at the one gasoline station at the main crossroads, a crowd had gathered about a battered money bus whose driver tinkered with a smoking engine. A dozen frizzled heads bent under the hood with him while women squatted with their carrying sacks beside the bus and gabbled their irritation to one another. The town was alive with its endless, shambling parade of people who thronged the road on a variety of missions. Jim blew his motorbike horn constantly while waving to friends in the open shops and market stalls. Lew fell behind. A small goat trod stiff-leggedly directly in front of the jeep's bumper and refused to veer aside until nudged in the rear. Then the goat vaulted toward an open Lebanese grocery, tossing an indignant look over its shoulder.

Osterlord turned east out of Zinzin on the first leg of the new road which he proposed to push to the border. It was Jim's prize project. Assisted by Ted Kramer and Arch Lettermore, he had tediously collected Kalyan nickels, dimes and a few dollars to finance the construction of eleven miles of road, designed to open up the Zinzin markets to the tobacco, rice, oranges and pineapple of half a dozen mud-hut villages now linked only by a narrow, winding bush trail. At first Osterlord met sullen resistance, for twice in the last decade Moses Harter had collected town funds for the road and then had "eaten" the money in traditional Kalya style. The Molas viewed Genghis Khan's self-appropriation of the money with cynical apathy. To them, it was just another form of The Family extortion which they had endured for years. Osterlord gradually whittled down the barrier to contributions by continuously exhibiting the money he had collected. He kept it in a cigar box and showed it everywhere in town. Steve Muo helped. He told his fellow Molas that "Peace Corps never eat money" and that Osterlord could be trusted. Now Jim had enough to pay a squad of hand laborers and occasionally to rent the district's lone earth-mover, which was owned by Itambel, the Italian-American-Belgian iron ore consortium that mined an iron mountain seventy-five miles from Zinzin. Two miles of the Zinzin road had been constructed and Jim was pressing to complete several more before the big rains came.

They halted in a gully where about twenty barefoot men in shorts were wielding shovels near a gray, viscous creek. Oil drums, their ends knocked out, were being installed in the roadbed for a culvert. Jim parked his motorbike. It was promptly surrounded by a swarm of small boys who had been watching the men work, a rare sight in Zinzin. Jim hung his helmet on the handle bars and his uncut mop of black hair flopped down over his face. Jim fought a constant, losing battle to keep hair out of his eyes.

He beckoned one of the workmen and introduced him to Lew. "This is Oon Gilli," he said, "Arlene's neighbor."

Gilli, wet with sweat, shook hands with Corleigh and, in the Kalya manner, ended the handshake by clicking his index finger against Lew's. Gilli pointed at Osterlord.

"Jeem big man," he said. "Peez-kor."

Osterlord grinned. "Great for the ego, huh, Lew? At home I'm just another guy out of Harvard. In Zinzin, I'm the Peace Corps man."

He turned his head and spoke rapidly to Lew. "Oon's a good worker. I'm thinking of making him the foreman and raising him to fifteen cents an hour."

Osterlord, abrasive and taciturn with other volunteers, was a man transformed on the job. He bustled about, inspecting, ordering, brimming with Mola chitchat, joking, lending a hand to pack dirt firmly about the oil drums. With his olive skin and bright blue polo shirt, he looked like a young Arab landowner on his feudal estate.

"I've got to head back down the line," said Lew. "The road's going okay. I'll tell the rep."

"If we can stretch it two more miles before the rains," rejoined Osterlord, "we'll have it made next fall. We can open the whole road by Christmas."

"Good luck, fella," said Lew, but Osterlord already had turned back to the culvert work gang. His hair hung over his eyes and his shirt and khaki pants were splotched with mud.

Lew made his mail-collection rounds. The volunteers were all out teaching, five of them in the government school and Arlene in the Lutheran mission school, but Lew found letters to the United States tucked under the door of each house. There was one letter under Cindy's door and also a penciled note: "If you have time, Red, come by my class. I'm trying something new."

The government elementary school was an L-shaped mud-stick building with zinc roof where two hundred and fifty children crammed into five small classrooms. The first six grades shared two grades to a room. Beside the building stood an open cement-block structure where hot CARE lunches were cooked over a wood fire. The CARE kitchen finally had been completed last year under Peace Corps direction. It was not more than twenty feet square, but it had taken three years to finish, even with the cement donated by the U.S. embassy wives in Ft. Paul. Behind the kitchen stretched a sloping soccer field between sagging, termite-ridden goal posts. The field itself was strewn with rocks which bruised hundreds of bare toes. Arch Lettermore last fall had tried futilely for two months to organize a gang to remove the stones. The pupils stubbornly refused, insisting such work was up to the government.

Several cows, which Lew knew were owned by the principal, Moses Harter, grazed drowsily on the soccer field and flies circled the droppings. A drone of voices came through the paneless and screenless windows of the school. Lew walked to the end room, where Cindy Fuller taught her seventh-grade class, and leaned on the window sill. Cindy, in a neat blue linen dress, waved to him from her place by the cracked blackboard. About thirty pupils, some of them actually husky young men, sat on wooden benches. There were no desks. Flies, fresh from forays to the latrines and cattle dung, looped hazily through the classroom.

"Students," said Cindy, "this is Mr. Lewis Corleigh. He's a Peace Corps supervisor, so we must show him how attentive we are."

Thirty heads rolled toward this white man with the strange red hair, then turned back reluctantly to face the blackboard. Cindy had covered it with figures in three columns labeled "Base 2," "Base 10," "Base 12." As she talked, Lew realized she was teaching the new mathematics, adapted for Africa by the Entebbe method. In the winter vacation Prudence Stauffer had instructed a small group of Peace Corps teachers, including Cindy, in methods of teaching the Entebbe math.

Cindy ordered her class to work out problems of addition, using a base of 12 instead of the customary system. They fell to work, leaning over to write on notebooks in their laps. Cindy strolled to the window.

"The day we ever get desks," she said, "I'm really going to celebrate."

"Do they actually understand that stuff?" asked Lew. "I don't. The new math missed me in school by a couple of years."

"It's amazing," she said. "Five or six of them are doing beautifully, which is more than I hoped for. But comparing number systems makes them all think a little." She hunched her shoulders. "The progress is small-small, but that's Kalya. I'm not discouraged."

"I had a good time last night," said Lew. "Is that dinner invite still open next week?"

She smiled the slow smile that wreathed her whole face and crinkled about her eyes. "Of course, Red. Any night." She turned back to the blackboard and Lew gratefully withdrew his head from the window. As hot as it was outside, the air inside the room, stoked by the metal roof, was torrid. He could see a broad, damp streak on the back of Cindy's fresh dress.

It was nine o'clock by the time he turned into the long road to Ft. Paul. The sun, pale as beaten gold in the white haze of the sky, shed a glare already hostile with its promise of midday ferocity. Here the sun was a thing to fear, a brute, implacable force. Lew could remember the rising of the sun over Lake Michigan where the rays dispersed the chill of dawn and seemed to stroke a man in a small boat with friendly fingers, hinting at the pleasant warmth to come. In West Africa the cool dawn vaporized in a blast of heat which swelled through the day and left the land and its people limply defeated at the hour of heavy twilight. Now the sun's intensity already had drawn the moisture from the jungle which walled the road from Zinzin. Only the puddles in ruts of the still-shadowed road attested to the rainburst last night.

The bush stood tall and thick as he drove south on Kalya's only highway, a raw, red cut, just wide enough for two vehicles to pass. Only ten years ago this had been a snaking bush trail over which but few men trekked the whole way from Zinzin to Ft. Paul.

Outcountry Kalya lay a century distant from its capital in those quite recent days. The government in Ft. Paul, a hybrid of the British and American systems, had established its shaky sovereignty years before the anti-colonial winds stormed through Africa. It had decreed English as the official language, largely because of the influence of the early missionaries, who also gave the nation its veneer of Protestantism. Lutherans and Baptists predominated, but Ft. Paul also had several Methodist churches, one of which boasted Old Number One as its leading communicant. The monetary medium was dollars and cents, borrowed from Liberia, whose freed slave founders had brought it from America's Old South along with a wardrobe of customs peculiar to the white plantation aristocracy. The old Ft. Paul, like a tramp steamer with no home port, tossed uncertainly on modern seas. If its boiler was patchwork American and its machinery European, its hull was planked with ancient jungle woods and, belowdecks, the shifting mass of cargo, irretrievably entangled, was pure West African. Underway she wallowed, half in apology, and thus her whistle, a vent for Kalya nationalism, was understandably strident.

Until a decade ago the overland trip from Ft. Paul to Zinzin took a month. The travelers, a few Mandingo traders, government tax collectors and European explorers, required platoons of tribesmen to headload their personal supplies. Sometimes rice could be obtained at the hut villages, but travelers could not count on food along the way, for some jungle towns were destitute. Dozens of creeks and a few wide rivers had to be crossed. Frequently a party would be delayed for hours while swinging vine bridges were repaired.

Then came the road, financed by U.S. foreign aid funds and constructed by gangs of Kalya workmen who followed the giant yellow earth-movers from America. The road ran through fifty villages and towns on the meandering route from Ft. Paul to Zinzin, and overnight the tribes of Kalya found themselves brushed by the strange baggage of Western civilization. Suddenly came tires and trucks, gasoline fumes, watches, whiskey, Coca-Cola, long pants and shirts, shoes, pumps, dishes, cameras. Most of these oddities came in the lumbering trucks of the Lebanese merchants who seemed to arrive only a few hours behind the earth-movers.

The tribes saw this jumble of goods, but few could buy, for theirs was an existence tied to rice and goats, coconuts and chickens, or meat from the occasional kill of a leopard, water deer or bush cow. With the peddlers of goods came the peddlers of education, hitherto confined to several widely separated mission schools. The government in Ft. Paul, once only a distant power which sent ragged soldiers to force infrequent levies of rice on the town chiefs, now dispatched commissioners, tax collectors, principals and teachers. Mud-stick schools were built near the palaver huts, and the children were ordered to attend for the learning of English. All this was a tremendous wrench for the tribes. For centuries they had lived with witchcraft, monstrous town devils and secret societies—Golo for the men and Mata for the women—which instructed youth in bush lore, performed bloody circumcision rites and occasionally resorted to human sacrifice despite the government's ban on the practice. The Family might prey upon the tribes with Old Number One's tacit consent, but the tough patriarch did insist that education and the new ways must prevail. By the time the U.S. Peace Corps arrived, the tribes were torn between the old customs, harsh but of bone-deep familiarity, and the gaudy enticements of the new. They were fascinated by the new, but they clung to the old, seeking the shelter of ancient habits, much as a voyager in far lands yearns for home.

The conflict—the Peace Corps called it the "culture clash"—left the tribesfolk bewildered and often defenseless. They lived with the old and the new in baffling proximity. A mud hut might now have a transistor radio side by side with a vinzinja dog whose historic chore it was to eat the feces of babies from the earthen floor and to lick the naked baby's rump clean after a bowel movement. A youth would go to the Lebanese store and buy a Seven-Up, bottled under hygienic conditions, then come home and drink water hauled from a creek which festered with typhoid germs and schistosomiasis. A mother might open a can of pork and beans one day, then labor the entire next day threshing swamp rice with crude implements which had not changed in a thousand years. A father would work at one of The Family's rubber plantations for eight cents an hour, then spend the earnings to ride the money bus one hundred miles to Loli and palaver for a day over purchase of a goat from the clan chief's brother.

To Lew Corleigh there was something pathetically tawdry about the tribal regions today. He called them "the tin-can jungle" and he often mused about the paradox on his long rides up and down the gutted road. The questions were all familiar, endlessly debated by volunteers, but they kept recurring in his mind like a repetitive dream. Were the tribes better off now than one hundred years ago? Was it right for the Peace Corps to lead the tribes to a life that brought new torments to replace the old? Was that progress? What was progress? Was it a service to slash the high infant mortality rate in a country where the people and the land had been equitably balanced for centuries? What could a boy do better with English in a bush village than he could with his native Mola? Didn't it make more sense for a boy to learn to grow swamp rice, as his father did, than to learn to change a tire on a car he would never own? Knowledge for its own sake was prized in the West, but in the bush of Africa, did that justify English grammar, the new math, the history of Europe? But could the new age be avoided? Jet planes swept over the jungles, far overhead whirled the space satellites—and round and round went the theories and judgments.

It had all seemed so simple back in his senior year at Penn State, when he elected the Peace Corps, but the longer Lew Corleigh stayed in Kalya, the less sure he became about what he was accomplishing, or, more fundamental, what he ought to be trying to accomplish.

That was the unsettling thing about the Peace Corps. He had joined chiefly because, in that last college year, he had sensed that he was drifting and he wanted to find his course. The Peace Corps would give him the time to decide, perhaps even provide the goal and the drive he needed.

The sense of drifting had come upon him only in manhood. As a boy he had always known what he wanted to do when he became a man. His ambitions might change with his years—from pilot to actor to soldier to businessman—but in any particular era, the goal seemed fixed and unalterable.

He had been reared in Evanston, a skinny, red-haired kid who grew fast, made friends easily and fought only rarely. His temper spurted like a geyser, but subsided as quickly. In the sixth grade, he was in love with airplanes and firmly intended to become a Navy carrier pilot. A plane provoked his first fight. Walking home from school with Harry, the fat boy next door, he spotted a Navy fighter winging west. "Look at the Grumman," he said. Harry looked. "That's not a Grumman," he replied, "it's a McDonnell." Lew insisted. "It's a Grumman, stupe," he said. "It's not," said Harry. "You don't know your ass from a hole in the ground." Lew fumed and demanded Harry take back what he said. "I won't take it back," said Harry. Lew struck the first blow and they fought until they were both crying and bloody and too weak to raise their arms. Both boys limped home, sobbing, each to be comforted by his mother. The next morning, Lew apologized timidly for hitting Harry and they walked to school together. But Lew never recanted on the make of the plane. Even now, he could see it vividly. It was a Grumman F9F.

At New Trier High School, where his grades were average, Lew decided he would become a television actor. He reached his full height of six feet in his junior year, he ran the 880 on the track team and he became aware that he was attractive to girls. They let him know in small, flattering ways. His hair was red and curly, his eyes were green, his shoulders were wide and he weighed a trim one hundred seventy pounds. Timmy, who affected lassitude and who bleached an artificial white streak in her brown hair, thought he was "neat" and they dated steadily. He took her to country club dances, where one night he drank too much beer and woozily made love to her in the sand trap beside the ninth green. It was his first time, but, he guessed, not Timmy's. It was a flustered melange of hands, clothes and legs and he really couldn't remember much about it the next day. Timmy had sighed tremulously and whispered, "You're great," but his chief physical reaction was dizziness.

That summer he took her to an afternoon beer party on the beach of Lake Michigan, and the gang played a half-tipsy brand of touch football in the shallow water. The next day he got a call from an advertising agency which produced television commercials for a Chicago beer company. One of the partners had seen the beach romp and wanted it re-enacted with Lew as the star. They shot the scene the following Saturday with Lew and his friends all made up to appear older. The clutter of cameras, reflectors and stage props intrigued Lew. He got five hundred dollars for the day's work, the others one hundred dollars. He decided on the spot that he would become a television actor and promptly wrote a letter of inquiry to the Yale drama school. He made repeated calls at the advertising agency for further roles, and later made the rounds of Chicago television studios, but the prospect of his steady services produced less than electric response.

He drank too much beer that summer and fall, stayed up too late at house parties and began to study less. His grades fell. One night his father called him into the study for what proved to be The Lecture. Henry Corleigh, a successful fuel oil distributor, was less successful as a parental disciplinarian. For one thing, he drank too much himself, and for another, he secretly envied his son's effortless appeal to women. Henry was gaunt, clumsy, and often stuttered under pressure. Their session was more corrosive than illuminating. Father said the boy had to settle down or become a teen-age bum. Lew said he knew it. Henry said otherwise he'd be a failure in life. Lew said he realized that too. "You've got to sh-sh-shape up and f-f-fly right," said the elder Corleigh heatedly. The stammering ruined the effect and the scene deteriorated into the comic. Lew kept his eyes fixed on his hands, which he rubbed restlessly together. He was embarrassed for his father. The trouble with The Lecture was, he knew, that he already had made up his mind what he had to do. The track coach had warned him earlier in the week and he was determined not to be dropped from the team. Lew thought his father was weak and he felt sorry for him.

The next inflexible career decision followed within a few months. He would lead the hard life, toughening his muscles and his psyche. On his eighteenth birthday, a few days after graduation from New Trier, he walked into a Chicago Army recruiting office and volunteered for a three-year hitch. His father was delighted, his mother disturbed, but both wrote him encouraging letters as he trailed through three Stateside infantry posts and then was sent to his permanent station in Mannheim, West Germany. Army life excited him at first, especially when he proved his own stamina in combat maneuvers, but then the routine, as drab as barracks paint, dragged at the days. He learned a smattering of German with frauleins during leave, he won the half-mile at an inter-service track meet, but his promotions stopped at corporal. As a career, the Army had palled. When his hitch was up, he was ready for college.

At Penn State, where he was admitted more for his time in the 880 than for his B-minus high-school grades, Lew again changed his sights. In his freshman year he decided that he would return home after graduation and work in the Corleigh Fuel Supply Company. He intended to apply himself, learn the business, expand his father's outlets and some day make a great deal of money. He fixed on the new plan in the spirit of some self-denial, for what he already knew of the business bored him. Like his prior decisions, this one became immutable. It heartened his father, it steadied his habits—and it lasted until the fall of his senior year.

He was majoring, for lack of anything better, in history. He took one course in contemporary foreign policy and another in Latin American history. That fall the world seemed to unfold about him. He thought of Argentina, he wondered about Mexico, and he hungered to visit Chile. He had never been to Latin America, and the service in Germany had whetted his appetite for travel. Now a lust for far horizons set in. A kind of panic seized him. He could see himself surrounded by tank trucks and fuel hoses in the Chicago suburbs and he could see his red hair fading to a frowsy rust and his belly growing a pot front.

Then came the bright November day when President Kennedy went to Dallas. Lew heard the news while throwing a football behind the fraternity house. He went to his room in a daze and wept. After that, for some reason, the idea of the fuel oil business became unthinkable. He thought of returning to the Army, and even of the Navy and Air Force, but in the end he rejected military life. He knew it too well. Besides, the Vietnam war was slowly building and Lew had no hankering to kill or, more importantly, to be killed. By the time spring brought a green sheen to the land around University Park, Pennsylvania, the itch to be gone—anywhere—had become intolerable. He told himself he wanted to help other people, but knew vaguely that he was rationalizing. What he really wanted to do was to travel in Latin America, and perhaps there he could decide on the future. By that spring, Lewis Corleigh was a soft target for the Peace Corps recruiter, a burly young man of staccato sincerity, who came to the campus. Lew filed his application after listening to the man for an hour. He listed his choice of area as Latin America.

But he had no Spanish, so the Peace Corps assigned him to Kalya and sent him off for eight weeks of training. He was popular with his fellow trainees at the University of California at Los Angeles, and when Group V arrived in Ft. Paul, it elected him one of four volunteer leaders. The honor made Lew wince privately, for the first sight of Kalya and its mass of untrained, unknowing blacks made him acutely conscious of his own poverty of skills. He couldn't teach. He couldn't build anything. He could not survey and all he knew of plumbing and sanitation was the bit he had learned in training. He realized forlornly that he'd used a hammer and saw only a few times in his life.

The training yearbook, "Who's Who in Kalya V," which carried photographs and one-paragraph biographies of the volunteers, revealed his paucity of preparation for the job of remaking Africa.

"Lewis N. Corleigh, Age 25. 400 Winding Way Lane, Evanston, Ill. Lew spent three years in the Army before receiving his B.A. from Pennsylvania State University in 1964 with a major in history. He won his varsity letter in track. Lew worked several summers driving a truck in his father's fuel oil business. His hobbies include swimming, golf, tennis and reading."

The profile did disclose his one solid accomplishment: he could drive a truck.

And so here he was, driving the Zinzin road in a jeep wagon that pounded worse than the Corleigh tank trucks, hammering at his pelvic bones and upsetting his kidneys. He'd made almost a hundred round trips on the skidding road and in one bout of depression he had even counted the bug-a-bug hills between Ft. Paul and Zinzin. Along the road there stood exactly 1027 of these conical clay mounds that looked like great, inverted ice-cream cones nibbled by rats. They were abandoned spawning homes of flying termites which periodically descended on the villages to devour any piece of lumber in a human habitation. Two weeks earlier Alice Franklin and Dotty Wyzansky had awakened one morning to find the entire back doorjamb eaten away by the pests.

Lew sighed and turned his attention to his duties. At the village of Balapi he picked up mail tucked behind the screen door of the house where two volunteers lived. At another house of two teachers in Chestertown, he found a note with the mail: "Lew, please bring up some new paperbacks, mystery stories if possible, and a roll of Scotch tape. Money attached." Two one-dollar bills were pinned to the note. Lew wondered where they'd found the pin.

He approached Dnoga with foreboding. He was scheduled to have lunch with Roger. That meant trading a bottle of Heineken's for a greasy sardine sandwich and some of the chocolate cookies Roger wheedled from a girl volunteer in the next town. It also meant finding another excuse to avoid visiting Roger's leper colony located two miles off the main road. Roger, a bony, whiskered man from Iowa, had adopted the half hundred lepers as his own, and he loved to exhibit their truncated fingers and toes and their gathering sores to visitors. He would touch the rotting flesh and put a finger on a raw, skinless bruise, explaining that the leper had banged his hand because he had no feeling in it. Roger showed off his worst cases with pride, as though some of his own handiwork had gone into the production of such medical monstrosities. He would handle the wounds with elaborate casualness, proving his own lack of fear. "Don't worry," he'd say, "it takes years of body contact to catch the stuff." The afflicted tribesmen would grin sheepishly while Roger berated them for sloth. They had to work, he'd scold, for who else would provide for them.

Roger was a stern taskmaster, a leper psychologist, and no doubt his methods were the correct ones, but two visits to the wretched, dusty village were enough for Lew. The visible pain, the filth, the poverty and the suffocating heat made him recoil in private horror. After each visit, he couldn't wait to reach Loli and the hot shower in the AID trailer where Forrest Stevenson lived, and to scrub himself mercilessly, forcing soap between all his fingers and toes in a feverish effort to wash away the memory of the leper village. Roger was part saint, part dictator, part exhibitionist, but Lew was content to sound his praises without further personal contact with his sanctuary.

Today when Lew peered into Roger's house and called, "Bockbock," the lord of the lepers was ready with two sardine sandwiches and a piece of coconut pie. Roger wore shorts and a V-necked shirt made of country cloth. His blond beard had grown luxuriantly for a year and now was trimmed to a dagger point below his chin, lending him a conquistadorial look. They chatted as he placed cubes of ice in two glasses to cool the beer which Lew brought from the jeep station wagon.

"I've got 'em started on a new rice paddy," said Roger. "I think you ought to take a look, so you can report the progress to Williams."

The genius of Roger as a Peace Corpsman, thought Lew, was that he believed his project to be the only one in all Africa worth staff attention. Roger had started two years ago as a geography teacher in Dnoga, but within two months he left the school to run the leper colony which the Kalya government conveniently ignored. The Peace Corps staff in Ft. Paul accepted the switch without protest, merely changing Roger's designation in the records from "elementary teacher" to "leper specialist."

"I'd like to," Lew lied, "but I've got to make time on the road back. I won't get further than Loli tonight, so that means two hundred miles tomorrow."

Roger nodded without sign of annoyance. The conversation was a familiar one. "All right, you can go in with me on your next trip," he said. That too was part of their routine, and Lew mumbled a vague response from which a wishful listener might extract an affirmative.

"Some smart-ass guy in the Agriculture Department swiped our fingerlings," said Roger. He did not seem upset about it. "More hanky-panky of The Family, I guess."

Roger and the lepers had formed a large pond by damming a stream, and then Roger ordered trout minnows from the Agriculture research station. The lepers rejoiced at the prospect of fresh fish within a few yards of their huts.

"Jesus," said Lew. "You mean The Family has stooped to stealing from lepers?"

Roger nodded. "It figured. Still, you ought to report it to Williams."

"And how, I will. Have you got any idea who it was?"

"No," said Roger, caressing the point of his beard, "but I'll bet Bill Fess will have some nice, juicy trout in his pond next year. His farm's down the road, you know."

William Fess, the commissioner of agriculture, was another favorite Family villain of the Peace Corps. As a matter of course he diverted government-paid laborers on the Kalya agricultural research station to work on his own farm. Last year, thanks to Israeli technicians, the station developed thousands of orange, lemon and grapefruit budwoods to improve the fecundity of Kalya's citrus crop. Jim Osterlord and several other outcountry Peace Corps volunteers came to the station for two weeks' instruction and then planned community citrus farms in their areas. But they waited in vain for the budwoods, for Fess took almost the whole supply for his own farm.

"Now they're down to roguing the lepers," said Lew. "That really frosts it. Talk about robbing the blind!"

"Oh, we'll work out something," said Roger calmly. The greater the obstacles, the better Roger enjoyed his work. "Maybe I can rustle up some minnows from the CARE people. Sure you can't spare an hour to see the new rice paddy?"

"No," said Lew. He could envision the sores and the fingernails growing freakishly out of knuckle stubs. "Some other time. Okay?"

Roger nodded and handed Lew two letters to be mailed in Ft. Paul. Lew got into the jeep, adjusted the seat belt and turned south for the next leg to Loli.

His afternoon chores duplicated those of the morning and the sun was lowering when he drove into Loli, a neat mud-hut hill village which marked the southern boundary of the Mola tribe. The heat was less enervating here, for Loli was in hill country with an altitude almost two thousand feet higher than Ft. Paul. In certain seasons, the breeze was brisk in Loli and sweaters were needed at night. This evening, however, the air was hot and still, less humid than Zinzin, but still uncomfortable.

He drove to Susan's house, found no one home and entered anyway. He struggled for ten minutes, righting the old kerosene refrigerator which he had turned upside down the previous day. He relighted the fuel beneath the icebox and waited. Miraculously, within a few minutes the box began to cool inside. He had no idea why turning a refrigerator on its top should revitalize its mysterious mechanism. All he knew was that sometimes it worked. He stepped back, not without pride, and surveyed the mechanical triumph of a Penn State history major. He felt, suddenly, almost competent and he drove to the home of Forrest Stevenson in the pleased mood of a man who has bent the machine age to his will.

The district official of the U.S. Agency for International Development lived in a spanking modern trailer home which crowned a parkland knoll under a foaming dabema tree. It had all the conveniences: inside plumbing, septic tank, a heavy-duty generator supplying lights, stove and air-conditioning units. Stevenson, long versed in the ways of Africa, lived in easy, unapprehensive camaraderie with the Loli natives, yet his home had all the protection of a fortress. The reason was Mrs. Stevenson.

The year before, Stevenson had taken a new wife, a small, nervous woman from Los Angeles who started at every bush sound and who viewed each new African caller as a marauding savage ready to plunge a spear into her back. She lived in a state of perpetual, frenetic fright and she talked incessantly and nostalgically of the abandoned amenities of southern California, where some of the inhabitants had been known to walk away unharmed from a seven-car wreck on the Harbor Freeway.

In a futile effort to assuage his wife's fears, Stevenson had arranged protection in depth, a four-stage system that had everything but moat and drawbridge. First, he placed double rogue bars at all windows. The fittings were so tight that a man with a crowbar would have to work half an hour to gain entry. Next he brought a German shepherd from Europe and trained the dog to regard everyone save Mr. and Mrs. Stevenson with bristling animosity. The animal bayed at every strange footfall and his fierce challenges could be heard a mile away in the huts of Loli. Third, Stevenson installed a complex wiring system which emitted a shrill alarm should anyone attempt to enter the house after the inmates had retired. Finally, he hired an ancient Mola warrior to patrol the property all night with bow and arrow.

This frail, scarred veteran, who boasted that he had tasted the human flesh of a Fizi in his youth, wore nothing but a loincloth and a soiled yachting cap that somehow had found its way to Loli. The watchman contended that he could split a stake at fifty yards with his metal-tipped arrows, and everyone but Lew believed him. Lew gained his own insight into the warrior's prowess when he returned to Stevensons' home late one night to the booming welcome of the German shepherd. The moon shone brightly and Lew asked the watchman to demonstrate his skill by hitting an acajou sapling about forty feet away. The old man flashed a snaggle-toothed grin, swiftly whipped an arrow from the quiver on his back and fitted it to the bowstring. He let fly on a bulge of biceps muscle—and missed the little tree by five yards. They both snickered.

This evening, as Lew drove up, the watchman had not yet made his appearance, but the dog barked the jeep wagon all the way up the hill. Stevenson stood in the yard, trying to quiet the animal. "Geronimo," he admonished, "you know Lew." Geronimo bounded against Lew's legs, sniffling damply at his trousers and leaving wet marks at the crotch.

Stevenson was a thin man, delicately boned, whose expression was one of monastic resignation. The eyes were pale blue and often, when he was immersed in thought, they seemed to grow misty. His manners were gentle, his voice reflected weary cynicism and Lew had never seen him in a buoyant mood. But he was a wise man who savored conversation with Peace Corps workers and his home offered comforts which Lew found irresistible.

"I hope you can stay for dinner and the night," said Stevenson.

"I accept," said Lew. "Some day, though, when I've got a paying job, I'm going to write to you for my board bill."

"Forget it," said Stevenson. "Feeding the Peace Corps is one of the few worthwhile things I do."

The Stevenson home, like most of the trailer houses supplied by AID to its officials, was opulent by Peace Corps standards. Air-conditioning units, run from a diesel generator, emitted a cool, bracing air that Lew often dreamed about in the close mugginess of the hostel in Ft. Paul. A huge porch, with aluminum screening and louvered windows, was built out from the three-room metal trailer. The furniture, brightly upholstered, was low, spacious and inviting. Against the trailer proper, Stevenson had installed three sets of shelves which were filled with books, most of them dealing with Africa. Fabrics, carpeting and clothes stayed crisp and fresh in the air-conditioned house, and visiting Peace Corps women invariably thought of their own limp garments hanging in plastered mud houses. Even the wealthy members of The Family in Ft. Paul did not live as comfortably as did the out-country officials of U.S. AID.

Mrs. Stevenson, small, plump and skittish, came through the trailer door and greeted Lew. Her smile was an anxious one.

"Lucky you," she said. "Forrest tells me that you're going home this summer. Aren't you thrilled?"

"Yeah, I guess so," he replied. "I only wish I knew what I'm going to do. I've got applications in to three grad schools, but no word yet."

Stevenson flicked a small, sad smile. "Still trying to remain inside the womb, huh?"

"You think so?" asked Lew. "I hadn't looked at it that way. It's just that I'm not sure what I want to do yet. Business doesn't send me. I don't know, maybe government or some kind of service outfit overseas."

Stevenson went to the refrigerator inside the trailer and returned with three tall, frosted glasses. The amber liquids were topped by sprigs of mint which Stevenson grew in a back plot. It amused him in Africa to serve mint juleps, the product of Kentucky, a state he had never visited. The first sip jolted Lew. Very little of the crushed ice had melted into the straight bourbon, which Stevenson, like other AID officials, obtained tax-free at two dollars a fifth from the U.S. embassy liquor dispensary in Ft. Paul.

"Ah, the Peace Corps," said Stevenson, sinking into an armchair and balancing his drink. "How many fine young Americans has it subverted by supplanting their natural instincts for cupidity with the dry blooms of humanitarianism?"

Lew laughed. "A good many, I guess. Is that bad?"

"A little of it goes a long way," said Stevenson. "A good plumbing salesman does more for mankind than a bad missionary."

"Oh, for heaven's sake," protested Mrs. Stevenson, "let's not start down that road again tonight. After several hearings, Forrest, your canned philosophy isn't very funny any more."

"It's not canned and it's not intended to be funny," said Stevenson. He waved a thin, blue-veined hand. "It's just the voice of experience, Grace."

Grace Stevenson snuggled into the back of the chaise longue. Geronimo, who had been pacing fitfully, sank on the floor with his head between his paws, his ears rigid, and his eyes alertly on his mistress.

"I'd rather talk about Lew going home," she said. "We've got thirteen long months here yet and after that fantastic thing today . . ."

She sighed and her husband winked at Lew. "She's dying to tell you the latest," he said. "More culture shock."

"I hate that phrase," said Grace, "but if I live to be a hundred, I swear I'll never understand these people."

Her story, interspersed with acid comments from Stevenson, took almost half an hour. As near as Lew could follow the intricate plot, an old, bare-breasted Mola woman had come to the front door that morning while Stevenson was away. The woman contended the Stevenson houseboy owed her thirty-nine

cents for three nights' lodging some time in the dim past. The
houseboy said he'd paid her. The woman broke into a torrent of
acrimonious Mola while Geronimo accompanied her with frenzied
barking. She went away, making faces at the dog. Several hours
later a large black man appeared. Geronimo barked his alarm.
The man said, in primitive English, that he was from the magistrate's office and he had a summons to serve on Mrs. Stevenson
for alleged non-payment of a three nights' lodging bill. Now the
houseboy switched his story and contended he had never stayed
at the old woman's house. Grace Stevenson told the man she
wasn't responsible for her houseboy's acts and anyway he denied
owing the money. The official insisted she was responsible. She
became afraid of the sheathed cutlass hanging from his belt and
ordered him off the property. He grew angry and said it was
Kalya land. The German shepherd barked hysterically, bounding
against the louvered windows in on effort to get at the intruder.
The big man finally left. Later three women and two men
showed up under the dabema tree. They said they were relatives
of the defrauded woman and would remain on the premises
until Mrs. Stevenson promised to accept the summons. ("First
Loli sit-in," remarked Stevenson.) Mrs. Stevenson finally gave
in while Geronimo rasped an epilogue. The crude summons, at
last delivered, ordered her to appear in court next Monday and
answer charges that she failed to pay thirty-nine cents rightfully
owed. Kalya tribesmen loved litigation.

"Wawa," sighed Stevenson. "So it'll cost us two days in court
and two dollars and thirty-nine cents. The two dollars is for the
court costs."

She flared at her husband. "Well, what would you have done?"

"Very simple, Grace," he said gently. "You just invite the
magistrate's man into the house, pour him some of the houseboy's palm wine and offer to settle the affair. It would have cost
twenty cents, maybe two bits."

"The man with the cutlass?" she shrieked. "Don't you understand? He had a cutlass. He could have slashed me to ribbons."

"Dear," he said wearily, "these are the least combative people
in Africa. Besides, Geronimo would have torn him apart at the
first move." Stevenson turned to Lew. "She lives in mortal
terror when there's nothing to be afraid of."

"That's easy for you to say," she said, "but you're not here alone all day surrounded by . . . by . . . a bunch of savages."

"Wawa," said Stevenson again. His pale blue eyes misted as he studied his mint julep. "It takes many forms, including the spiritual defeat of a woman who won't take the trouble to understand."

"Hmph! You and your bargain-basement theories."

Lew felt ill at ease as a ringside spectator at the family wrangle, but neither Stevenson appeared the least embarrassed. Mrs. Stevenson promptly veered into a discussion of where she wanted to live when they returned to the States. Mr. Stevenson poured a second round of juleps and they chatted of home until the houseboy announced dinner.

The meal constituted Grace Stevenson's further rebuke to Africa for the anxieties the dark continent thrust upon her. The houseboy served a jellied consommé and spaghetti with tomato meat sauce, both from American cans; *petits pois* from France; a sharp cheese from Denmark; beer from Holland. Only the watermelon was Kalyan and that had been grown by Stevenson in his garden.

After dinner Mrs. Stevenson prepared to retire to bed with a copy of Saul Bellow's *Herzog*, a man whose derailment from the tracks of Western civilization at least had the solace of familiarity. Grace admired Herzog for having the good sense to wrestle with his mental miseries in the United States, and she merely sniffed when her husband argued that the fellow would have had no problem in Kalya. For one thing, Forrest said, Herzog could have had his two wives simultaneously over here, thus compressing rather than prolonging a central source of anguish.

Stevenson took the chaise longue vacated by his wife and stretched out his pipelike legs. His face was deeply tanned, even in the grooves the years had cut.

"What's new in Zinzin?" he asked. "How are the crisis girls and Jim Osterlord, the master builder?"

"Not too bad," said Lew, thinking of Dotty's diarrhea. "The volunteers are having their usual troubles though with Genghis Khan."

"Good old Genghis," said Stevenson. "I admire his talent for thievery. He never fails to blaze new trails to plunder. What's he come up with this time?"

Lew described Moses Harter's appropriation of one month's salary from the second-grade teacher he'd impregnated.

"A wonderful form of taxation!" exclaimed Stevenson. "Think what the world would be like if every man could exact a stud fee for his services."

Lew added Harter's latest feat of charging his pupils ten cents each for free government textbooks that had been brought to Zinzin in a Peace Corps vehicle.

"See what I mean?" asked Stevenson. "The fellow's inventive. He has larger ideas too. I happen to know that he'd like to get a fellowship for study in the States. Now for a man who only went through the sixth grade, that shows real aptitude for beating the game. A fellowship! That's not greed. That's a magnificent imagination."

Lew shook his head. "When I think of guys like him, and they're all over the country, I get depressed. Look at that citrus steal last year. Sometimes I wonder whether the Peace Corps is making any headway at all."

"You get depressed?" echoed the older man. "How about me? My outfit is determined to build things—anything—in this country. Most of it is an idiotic waste. Unless the African learns to help himself—and our projects almost never require that—nothing is accomplished. He merely accepts the item as charity to which he's entitled and which the rich United States is foolish enough to provide. You've been here long enough to know that."

"I can't see that the Peace Corps is much different."

"Sure it is," countered Stevenson. "AID just gives things and if left to us, this country would become one vast relief dump. But the Peace Corps at least insists on some self-help. Look at Jim Osterlord's road. That's a good example. A couple of years from now, after learning with Jim, the Molas may—I say 'may'— even be able to build a road for themselves."

Geronimo growled and Stevenson leaned over to calm him. "Oh, I have no illusions about the Peace Corps. God, I was a missionary on this continent for thirty years. But we Americans are a great, restless nation of busybodies. We're all over the world, trading, giving, touring, bombing, fixing, lecturing, fighting and moralizing. All I say is that the Peace Corps is the least obnoxious organization we have abroad. I mean it. I firmly believe the Peace Corps does less harm than any of the rest."

Lew laughed and Stevenson smiled fleetingly at his own irony. If he relished anything, it was these talks with the volunteers. Some nights he would talk until almost dawn.

"It's not us that discourages me," said Lew, "but The Family. They seem to sabotage everything we do. If you can't steal it, knock it, seems to be their motto." Lew was silent a moment as he thought of Genghis Khan . . . and Jim Osterlord. He said casually, "Let me ask you, Forrest, do you know of any Kalyans who want to change the system?"

Stevenson shook his head. "No, I don't. That doesn't mean there may not be some, but I don't know them. If there's any opposition to Old Number One, it's clandestine as hell. This country isn't in the revolutionary phase—yet. I've lived all over Africa and I can smell revolution. Here, I smell nothing. The tribes are still too close to the bush. It'll take them another ten or fifteen years for any kind of real opposition to get going."

Lew was tempted to relate his conversation with Jim Osterlord, but something warned him not to. After all, Stevenson was a U.S. government official, for all his free-wheeling criticism of his government and his agency. They talked for another hour and then Lew began to yawn. Cindy and he had stayed up too late last night.

He slept in luxurious, cool, fresh sheets that night, lulled by the hum of the air-conditioners, and the next morning he was up before breakfast and driving the long, red road to Ft. Paul.

3

Peace Corps headquarters in Ft. Paul, a suite of air-conditioned offices over a garage, hummed with good works when Lew arrived there Friday morning after his long drive from Zinzin and a sound sleep in his upper bunk at the hostel. A few volunteers waited patiently on chairs outside Dr. Samuel Zerwick's office, but elsewhere there was the clatter of early morning activity. Typewriters hammered behind beaverboard partitions, the receptionist looked happily agitated and Prudence Stauffer strode briskly across the lobby without pausing to banter with Corleigh. Lew noted the oversight, for with Prudence it was a matter of principle to speak to every volunteer. The care and feeding of the troops came first with this bustling, somewhat severe field officer, for she had been a volunteer herself only two years before. Today she appeared distracted.

Lew leafed through the tabloid eight-page Ft. Paul *Daily Voice*. The lone newspaper in Kalya was a government-subsidized organ specializing in drab, self-serving handouts from the Prime Minister's palace and local crime dramas written by a staff of two reporters whose zeal for the lurid was surpassed only by the waywardness of their syntax. The lead article this morning concerned the demise of the "Very Rev. Dr. Pulaja Inole, divine primate

of the Temple of Holy Guidance," a fundamentalist sect that
had migrated recently to Kalya from Ghana. The story carried
the byline of Oliver Downing, a pleasantly owlish young member
of The Family who had been educated in England.

The Very Rev. Dr. Pulaja Inole lies inexorably, yes brutally,
slain this morning from a knifing from his rear.

The divine primate was knelt in prayer over his bedside late
yesterday when an enraged parishioner, said to be the alleged
killer, softly treaded up behind him and plunged the eight-
inch knife into the back. The vicious blow at once was
severing the spinal string and went all through his upper
organs to come out from the chest.

At the time of the slaying, Mrs. Sophie Abdollum, the
alleged killer's wife, was in the divine primate's kitchen with
preparations for the evening repast. Mrs. Abdollum said she
was staying with the primate to minister to his physical needs
in return for the spiritual succor she is received from the
primate himself.

Police said the alleged Abdollum, the slayer, recounted
to them that he blamed Dr. Inole since his wife had not
been home in six days and nights altogether missing from his
bed.

The blood was flowing all over the primate's poor body
(see picture) and Mrs. Abdollum screamed when she sighted
the terrible wound and then did beat her own husband with
her fists.

Police are stressing to our readers that no one of those
involved in the bedside murder is or has been Kalyan. All
three, in addition to many of the Temple of Holy Guidance
members, are shortly from Ghana. The alleged knifer is
hold without bail and the fatal weapon is on display for all
at police headquarters. . . .

Lew dropped a dime in the cup on top of the small refrigerator
and took out a Coca-Cola. He walked over to scan the bulletin
board for items posted during his absence. Today's notices were
monopolized by Dr. Zerwick, whose style was as unique as was
that of the *Voice*. He had thumbtacked two announcements to
the board.

TO: All Volunteers
FROM: Dr. Samuel Zerwick, staff physician

1. A female volunteer was evacuated to the U.S. Army Hospital at Frankfurt this week with a severe case of amoebic dysentery. I remind all PCVs that this disease may lurk in tainted water or may be carried from feces to mouth.
2. PCVs, boil and filter your water!
3. PCVs, wash your hands in boiled water!
4. PCVs, clean your latrines!

Below was the second notice:

TO: All Volunteers
FROM: Dr. Samuel Zerwick, staff physician

1. A panel of physicians has unanimously endorsed the findings several years ago by the Surgeon General's committee on the harmful effects of tobacco.
2. The link between the cigarette and lung cancer is now incontrovertible.
3. In view of the findings, any PCV continuing to smoke cigarettes is either stupidly contemptuous of medical science or he has a latent death wish.

Lew grinned as he sucked at his Coke bottle. Sam Zerwick, the heavy-set medic with the myopic eyes behind the great horn-rimmed spectacles, might blaze with the wrath of Jehovah in his official stance, but privately he was a tender man. He carefully guarded the health of the volunteers as though they were his own brothers and sisters, and in the privacy of his medical confessional, he soothed the volunteer psyche and dispensed sage advice on an infinite variety of problems. He secretly counseled the women on birth control devices. He inspected every caller for signs of crumbling morale. He treated sores, cuts and bruises as though they were intricate compound fractures. He advised the men to stay away from the Ft. Paul half-caste bar girls, and when they didn't, he treated the venereal disease cases without lecture or reprimand. At night he often manned the emergency ward at the city's only hospital, for he had a towering contempt for Kalya medicine and its practitioners. He had driven hundreds of miles through the night to set bones of volunteers injured in

money bus accidents. Sam Zerwick's concerns and his rages were
the delight of the Peace Corps.

The young blonde volunteer who served as office receptionist
plucked at Lew's sleeve as he stood before the bulletin board.

"You're wanted in staff meeting."

"Me?" Even as a leader of volunteers, he had never attended a
staff meeting. "You sure?"

"Yes," she said. "They're all in Williams' office now. They're
waiting for you. Special feature attraction today—Miss Sutherland."

Maureen Sutherland, Lew knew, was a staff official from Washington. He vaguely placed her somewhere in the echelon that
dealt with Peace Corps contingents in African countries.

Except for the two field officers absent on outcountry tours,
the staff was assembled around the desk of Carter Williams, the
representative, when Lew entered.

"Hi, Lew." Williams was a portly man with sparse black hair
who gave the impression of a reluctant Atlas precariously balancing
two hostile worlds, one on each shoulder. He had darting, inquisi-
tive eyes that seemed to be searching a person's face for instant
reactions to Carter Williams. He was uniformly polite, if apprehensive, and now he shook Lew's hand heartily. "We want you
here, Lew, as an adviser on the households of outcountry volunteers. This is Miss Maureen Sutherland from Washington. She's
the deputy assistant regional officer for Africa. You know everybody else."

Miss Sutherland, a slim, willowy young woman, stylishly dressed,
arose from her chair and offered a hand. She wore elongated
dark glasses, and a sheaf of black hair fell loosely over one eye. Her
skin, as creamy as enameled china, hinted of regular facials
and a variety of expensive oils and ointments.

"A pleasure," she said. She spoke through tightened lips, as
though not quite willing to release the words, in the manner
fashionable in eastern women's colleges.

Prudence Stauffer sat primly, her corn-colored hair gathered in a
severe bun. Sam Zerwick rolled a toothpick in the corner of his
mouth and managed to look alertly combative. The other staff
member was Rachael Frisson, a tall, stately Negro beauty who
wore her hair in a high, teased pile and who always appeared some-

what aloof and forbidding. In disdain for Zerwick's posted notice, she smoked a cigarette in an ivory holder. She was the staff member who supervised the Peace Corps teachers within the city of Ft. Paul.

"Miss Sutherland is here on her first inspection and get-acquainted tour," said Williams. He spoke with a smile, but he looked as though Miss Sutherland's mission would be a tribulation. "She's been to Nigeria, the Ivory Coast, Liberia and Somalia so far and now she's favoring us with a day or two. How are things in the other countries, Maureen, as far as the Peace Corps goes?"

"Frightful in Somalia," she said, "perfectly wonderful in Nigeria. You all know the problems in Liberia. As for the Ivory Coast, my best insight into our progress there came from Huve de Valon, that charmer who's, you know, something in protocol." She said it as though De Valon, his characteristics and his position were household bywords.

Miss Sutherland lilted on for half an hour, festively dropping names from Lagos to Washington, with even a side excursion into the Turkish foreign office. She apparently knew everyone and everything, and, in her buttoned accent, she gave them a glittering panorama of the world of great affairs, its intrigues, its grand policies and even its illicit loves. Once Sam Zerwick leaned over to Lew and whispered, "She's kind of an overseas Leonard Lyons, isn't she? I'll bet she calls De Gaulle 'Charlie.'"

She concluded on a pitch of finishing-school breathlessness and looked about brightly as though waiting for applause.

"Well," said Williams, overwhelmed by the torrent of inside information, "I know we all appreciate getting this intimate picture of what's going on outside Kalya. I gather that Peace Corps Kalya is a bad apple at the bottom of the barrel."

"Not at all," said Miss Sutherland. "Washington thinks you're doing a t'riffic job, you know, under terrible handicaps . . . Old Number One, Downing, Fess and the rest."

She dropped the names with the aplomb of an old Kalya hand and Lew surmised she had ploughed through a folder of reports on the plane to Kalya. Miss Sutherland, obviously, was not a woman to be outpointed or outployed.

"Maureen has brought out a matter from Washington," said Williams. "Why don't you just explain it to them, Maureen?"

"Right." She adjusted her dark glasses and pursed her lips. "Washington is disturbed about the volunteers' refrigerators here in Kalya. As I was saying to Carter, everybody on the staff knows that outcountry Kalya is a place of hardship and trial for the PCVs. As I said, Peace Corps Washington appreciates the perfectly t'riffic job you're all doing. Still, those refrigerators, you know."

"What about the refrigerators, Miss Sutherland?" Dr. Sam Zerwick was instantly embattled.

"Well, they don't quite fit the hardship image, do they?" she replied.

"Oh, for Christ's sake!" Zerwick exploded.

"Don't think Washington understands," said Prudence Stauffer, quickly troubled for her volunteers. "The PCVs, at least in my area, have plenty of hardships to put up with. There are insects and snakes, and schistosomiasis, the rains and malaria. Sometimes I wonder how they manage."

"I know, dear, I know," said Miss Sutherland through snugly set lips. "We all realize and appreciate that. If it were just, you know, Kalya, Washington wouldn't worry. But stories have gotten back to Congress about the good life in other Peace Corps countries. In the Ivory Coast, for instance, some teachers live in five-room houses with adorable Danish furniture, hot running water and electric lights. Of course, the host government supplies the quarters, so what can we do? Unfortunately, congressmen don't always distinguish between one country and another and we do face the Senate appropriations committee hearings next month."

"Screw the committee," said Zerwick darkly.

Miss Sutherland showed by her smile that she was not shocked. "It can't be done," she said. "Then, of course, you know, there's old Phil Taggard."

The name fell like a heavy branch on a roof. Congressman Philip Y. Taggard of Utah was feared worldwide by Peace Corps staffs for his one-man vendetta against the agency. He accused it of high living, ineptitude and gaudy propaganda, and he frequently staged lone, unannounced investigations in Peace Corps countries to gather ammunition for his charges. Taggard's chief indictment of the Corps was that its efforts often ran counter to the foreign policy aims of the State Department and Central Intelligence Agency and thereby played into Communist hands. The Peace Corps was touchy on the charge, since some staffers and many volunteers looked upon both State and CIA as unfriendly powers, as hostile to the aspirations of the impoverished as a military junta.

"Taggard pokes around for anything that would embarrass us," said Miss Sutherland, "and he'd just love to light on something like refrigerators in the jungle. It's all—you know—a matter of general policy, Dr. Zerwick, and I'm afraid, you know, Kalya may have to suffer a little, as unfair as it may be."

"I'd like to get Taggard out here in malaria country with no chloroquine tablets," said Zerwick.

Carter Williams frowned at the image evoked of a congressman stricken in Williams' own territory. "What is the exact situation in Washington on the refrigerators, Maureen?" he asked. He clicked open a penknife and began paring his nails, a habit in times of common stress.

"They're in the process of being reassessed," she said. "By the time they get here, what with shipping and all, they cost about three hundred dollars a unit and in cold budget figures that might look extravagant to somebody like Taggard. Of course, you know, before any action is taken, Washington wants the full and free advice of you people."

"What do you think, Rachael?" asked Williams.

Rachael Frisson, who lived a studied social life in a new air-cooled apartment in Ft. Paul, straightened in her chair, carefully removed the cigarette from its ivory holder and snubbed it out. She was wearing a snug dress that tracked her topography like a contour map.

"I think Washington should do what it thinks necessary for policy," she said. "Frankly, my attitude is if the volunteers came over here to have it rugged, why deny them?"

"Of course, Rachael," said Prudence, "that's easy enough for us to say here in Ft. Paul. We staffers live pretty well."

"I intend to," said Miss Frisson. "I am not a volunteer. I'm a staff officer." Her tone indicated the wide social gulf between the two.

Williams turned to Corleigh. "You're the real expert on morale,

Lew. You see more outcountry volunteers than the rest of us. What's your opinion?"

"I think it would be a lousy deal to take out the boxes," he said. "A girl up in Loli had one kaput for a few days, and her food was a mess. I was afraid she'd get sick. You've got to realize, Miss Sutherland, that the volunteers have it rough enough as it is."

He described the predicament of Alice Franklin and Dorothea Wyzansky under the invasion of driver ants and told of Arlene finding a black mamba snake in her shower. Arch Lettermore, he said, once killed seventeen rats in one night around his house in Zinzin.

"It's not logical," he added. "Junking the boxes now would waste a lot of money. After all, the volunteers are supplied with a kerosene lamp and a kerosene stove too. It would make just as much sense to take them out."

"Now, Lew," Miss Sutherland chided. "They do have to cook and they do have to read."

"And, by God, they have to stay well too," roared Zerwick. "Last month I had sixty-eight volunteers reporting in sick. Of all the idiot ideas out of Washington, this icebox bit is the worst." His tone became acid. "I would think, Miss Sutherland, that before you make a recommendation on this subject, you ought to live outcountry with the volunteers for a week or so."

"I plan to next time," she said defensively, "but this is just a, you know, flash, get-acquainted trip. I just don't have the, you know, time now."

Zerwick plunged on, his spectacles glittering. "If those desk jockeys in Washington take out the iceboxes, they ought to be sued for criminal negligence. And so help me, Christ, if there was a legal way to do it, I would. You just tell Washington for me that if those refrigerators go, Sam Zerwick will not be responsible for the health of a single PCV in this country."

"Oh, now really, Dr. Zerwick," said Miss Sutherland. "Let's not be overly dramatic, shall we? We're not talking about, you know, a life and death matter, after all."

"Bull." He glowered at her.

Carter Williams saw matters drifting too far from the placid middle way to suit him. The time had come to seize the problem and climb back on the fence with it.

"I think you see the consensus here, Maureen," he said, quickly conciliatory. He darted a glance at Miss Sutherland to gauge her reaction. "The staff takes a dim view of tampering with the health of volunteers here. Now, of course, the question is, are there over-riding concerns of Peace Corps policy that aren't apparent to us here? Well, of course, we can't answer that in Ft. Paul, but I think you know how we all feel."

If it was not apparent to Miss Sutherland how Carter Williams felt, she did not reveal it. Instead she turned her dark glasses in a swoop toward Rachael Frisson.

"It may be a consensus, but it's not unanimous," she said with a touch of triumph for thus isolating Miss Frisson's position. "Any-way, I'll report back what was said."

Miss Frisson waved her cigarette holder toward Maureen Suther-land in a gesture of appreciation. Rachael, Lew felt, was pleased to establish this ideological rapport with another woman of the world.

The meeting slid into other subjects, including an indecisive discussion of whether male volunteers should be made to shave off beards. Then it broke up. As Lew left, Maureen Sutherland was telling Williams about a perfectly ghastly reception she had attended at the Upper Volta embassy in Washington. However, she noted, she did have chats with Bobby, Sarge and Eunice there.

In the hallway Prudence Stauffer reached out and shook Lew's hand. Her grip was firm. She knit her brows and her determined lit-tle chin protruded like the prow of a small boat in choppy seas.

"Glad to see you stand up and be counted for the volunteers, Red," she said.

"Well, I'm one myself, Prudence, so it figures."

She folded her arms and planted her legs apart. "All for protect-ing the Peace Corps image, but can't abide this unrealistic attitude in Washington about what we face out here."

Lew grinned. "Oh, Maureen's just one of those well-meaning broads who doesn't know the score. One trip outcountry with me would straighten her out."

"You're a good PCV, Red." She cocked her head, appraising him, and her intense look made Lew for some reason want to laugh.

"I try—sometimes," he said. "You're not so bad yourself. If it will help your morale, Prudence, the guys and dolls outcountry think you're the most. Best on the staff."

"You making fun of me?" She squinted suspiciously.

"Hell, no. You're the volunteers' favorite. Well, I've got to go. Don't forget to ticket that drum of kerosene for Zinzin."

Miss Missionary, he thought as he turned away. Thirty years ago a Prudence Stauffer would have come to Africa as a Baptist or Lutheran missionary. Now it was the Peace Corps. Something fetching about her, though, the small, plain girl with the serious eyes, the stubborn chin and the stamina and protective juices of a lioness. A man had to admire her. Still, she amused him too.

Then, as he left the building, he thought of the meeting and he became irritated. Here the Peace Corps dilemma was what to do about Kalya's marauding Family, and yet Washington preferred to worry about image and refrigerators in the mud-stick houses of the volunteers. Oh well, only three months to go until blissful termination. He turned his mind to the chores of the day. There would be a weekend rush of outcountry volunteers at the hostel. He'd better get back there and get the place tidied up.

He was wheeling the dusty jeep out to the street when he thought of Jim Osterlord's note. He had some time, so why not look up that Lincoln Beach today? Utility Authority . . . that was right next door to the First Methodist Church.

Downtown Ft. Paul was awash with moist heat. The refuse in the streets stewed in the morning sun. The city choked on its tangle of shuffling pedestrians, bleating taxis and money buses. Weathered frame houses, battered reminders of the old town, stood next to new concrete buildings that, because of the tropic humidity and listless workmanship, seemed already old the week they were completed. Blackening streaks outlined cracks in the cement structures.

Every unimproved lot was jammed with one-room metal shacks, glistening fiercely in the sun, around which naked children played in the dirt. Tribal women, many newly arrived from outcountry, squatted on their haunches as they mixed bowls of country chop under circling patrols of flies. Dignified Mandingos in bright, sheetlike wrappers played chess as they sat on long straw mats in open-air lean-to "hotels." Others slept, using folded garments for a pillow. Customers crowded the market stalls where wrinkled old women sat and bargained, in peevish cackles, over the price of their wares—bananas, mangoes, rice, chocolate, eggs, chickens, festering cuts of lamb and pork, and cigarettes sold singly or in pairs. In a filthy creek, fringed with rusty cans and old auto parts, bare-breasted women scrubbed clothes on the rocks. The sidewalks swarmed with Africans, some wearing tribal gowns of black-and-gold country cloth and others in European dress. They overflowed the curbs and wandered in front of cars whose drivers blew horns constantly. The city was a bedlam of blaring horns, shouts, curses, barking dogs and crying infants.

Lew drove by the glistening "Cathedral of Justice," with its tiled mosaics, its white, fluted columns and its red tile roof. Further on was the modern Treasury Building, a small copy of New York's glass-and-steel office penitentiaries. Both structures were flanked by ramshackle tin and zinc huts, all of which seemed about to collapse on their tribal residents.

Then came an open space with a sweeping green lawn, neatly hedged. A long, curving asphalt driveway was bordered with roses, flowering jasmine and yellow and red tulips imported from Holland. There were two great flagpoles, both circled with flowers. One flew the flag of Kalya, a white star against alternating spangles of yellow and red. From the other floated the banner of the Prime Minister, Old Number One. On a field of blue, it bore his family crest in white, a leopard rampant dangling the scales of justice from its fangs. Behind the flagpoles, after another stretch of weedless, carefully nurtured lawn, stood the Prime Minister's palace, a huge, bizarre pile of marble. Ornate pillars framed the entrance and on top of the building, beneath a gleaming, white tile Bermuda roof, perched the Prime Minister's penthouse. Aside from an annual formal reception, few people were ever invited to this eyrie. The nation's business was conducted on the ten floors below. The whole structure was so incredibly lavish and garish that visitors, at first sight, often stood dumbfounded. Peace Corps workers said it reminded them of something conceived by Conrad Hilton's architect the morning after.

On the edge of the lawn, facing the street, stood three white stone guardhouses, manned by Old Number One's special security police. They wore white shirts, the right sleeves adorned with the Prime Minister's family crest, black motorcycle pants, black puttees and gold-trimmed white crash helmets. In the driveway stood a dozen motorcycles with motors idling.

The large center guardhouse held the office of the chief of security police, Colonel Hulbert Booth. He was standing now outside the building as Lew drove by, and Lew felt a flash of resentment at the sight of the man.

Booth's rugged black face was framed, as usual, by gold-rimmed goggles. His men wore revolvers at the hip, but Booth's rested in the shoulder holster which hugged his white shirt. Booth's epaulets were crested with silver eagles, symbol of his rank. As he stood now, talking to one of his men, he had the stance of authority, a man who knew he was respected and feared throughout the republic. Booth had once been boxing champion of Kalya and he had the reputation for quiet, methodical brutality in enforcement of the many laws governing the protection of Old Number One's person. To be "boothed," in Kalya slang, was to disappear in the middle of the night. There were sinister tales of the aftermath at Kpali, the jungle prison camp, where, it was said, political prisoners had their hands severed at the wrists with two slashes of a cutlass.

Lew granted that the colonel, huge and broad-shouldered, was an imposing figure, and his own brushes with Booth lent credence to the horror tales. Yet Booth was a handsome man whose mouth usually wore a genial smile, as it did now, under his meticulously groomed pencil mustache. Whether the menace of Booth was fact or fiction, Lew did believe the other stories, about Booth's women. He recalled the recital of Alice and Dotty about the colonel's amorous quest to Zinzin the other night—in the black Mercedes which almost smashed into Lew's jeep wagon. Booth spoke freely of his physical needs, a new woman every month. He had lately been seen with a slender secretary from the Japanese embassy.

Lew drove on to the Utility Authority. This government agency was housed in a modest, three-story office building which Old Number One owned and, in the Kalya custom, leased to his own government at $25,000 a year. It stood next door to the First Methodist Church, a gift of the leading communicant, Old Number One, who retained the deed to the land.

The Utility Authority, Lew knew, was the only government

agency not operated by The Family patronage system. The reason was that Old Number One demanded running water, sewage and electrical service, and he knew that he would have none of the three if The Family administered the agency. A government post in Kalya was a reward for being born into the right family, and once a man or woman obtained the title of office, his duties were deemed to have largely ceased. The system worked smoothly for such departments as the Foreign Ministry, Treasury, Taxation, Education, Customs, Justice and Agriculture, but plainly it could not produce kilowatts or water from the tap. Accordingly Old Number One hired a West German concern to operate Ft. Paul's basic utility services under a long-term contract.

Old Number One made only one stipulation. Since there was an acute water shortage because of inadequate storage facilities, the Utility Authority was required to shut off water mains to most city clients at 10 P.M. each night. This replenished the special reservoir which served, on an around-the-clock basis, the Palace and its showplace lawn, embassy row and Founders House, Kalya's one luxury hotel. The German firm disapproved of this discriminatory practice, but Old Number One was adamant. So the valves at the Ft. Paul water works were adjusted every night at ten o'clock and all but the few favored taps went dry.

In contrast to the slack atmosphere in other government buildings, the Utility Authority's connoted efficiency. The air-conditioned reception room had pale green walls and upholstered benches with copies of European magazines. Lew asked the pretty receptionist, a Kalya girl wearing a crisp, white shirtwaist, for Lincoln Beach.

"He's in billing," she said. "Third floor, second door on the right." She did not ask his name or business, for she could not relay the information in phoneless Kalya.

The second door on the whitewashed third floor corridor had a glass panel with the legend "Lincoln Beach, Chief Billing Division." Lew knocked.

"Come in."

The man who rose from behind a neatly arranged desk was quite young, perhaps twenty-six to thirty, thought Lew. His face was a rich, dark brown and there were little creases about his brown eyes as though he laughed a good deal. He was smiling now.

He wore a tan summerweight suit, snugly tailored to fit. The white shirt had button-down collar tabs and his narrow tie was of sedate red and black stripes. Lew had the impression he was meeting a junior executive in an American metropolitan area, a man fresh from the Ivy League.

"I'm Link Beach." His accent was American.

"My name's Lew Corleigh. I'm with the Peace Corps."

When they shook hands, Lew snapped his index finger against Beach's as the grip finished. Beach smiled.

"You've been here a while, I see. Sit down, Mr. Corleigh." Beach indicated an office armchair. "Don't tell me we've misbilled you over at Peace Corps headquarters."

"No," said Lew. "This is personal. I just wanted to meet you."

Beach laughed. There was a deep, friendly ring to it. He settled into his desk chair and tapped at the desk blotter with a letter opener.

"That's a new angle around here," he said. "Most people who come in here want to fight. The other day a Fizi came in, waving our bill in one hand and a knife in the other. It was a hairy time, especially since the old guy couldn't read the bill."

"You must get all kinds," said Lew. "No, this is personal. Here, I'll just give you the message."

He took Osterlord's note from his wallet and handed it to Beach who read it twice. "You can trust him," he read aloud, "Jim Osterlord."

Beach apparently uncertain of what to say, looked at Lew for a moment. "Well," he said, "what can I do for you?"

"I'm not sure," said Lew. "The reason I'm here is just curiosity, I guess. Jim and I were talking politics up in Zinzin the other night. I claimed there was no opposition to Old Number One and The Family and I couldn't understand it. Jim said I didn't know what I was talking about. Then, after we gassed a little more, he just wrote out that note and handed it to me."

"I see." Beach glanced sharply at him, then went to the door which apparently connected with another office. He turned the key in the lock.

"Where did you go to school, Mr. Corleigh?" He had lowered his voice.

"Call me Lew."

"All right, Lew."

"I went to Penn State," said Lew. "That's in . . ."

"I know where it is," interrupted Beach. "I played football—you know, soccer—for Cornell, and we played Penn State there once."

"How long were you in the States?"

"Six years," said Beach. "Two at Andover and four at Cornell. Of course, I got started late. I was twenty-two when I started college. I've been back here, let's see, about two years now."

"You sure haven't lost your accent. You sound like New York or someplace around there."

Beach laughed. "You mean I don't drop all the last syllables like we do in Kalya. Where are you from, Lew?"

"Evanston, outside Chicago. I've been over here almost two years. But you do sound like an American. Beach isn't one of The Family, is it?"

Beach shook his head. "No. I was named and raised in a Lutheran mission school, the one near Loli. I was a Mola boy. My father was killed in a fight with a government soldier who came to collect the rice tax, and my mother took me to the school. I saw her only twice after that. She's dead now." His voice took on an edge. "We don't live long in Kalya, you know."

"How'd you get to the States?"

"Scholarship," he said. "I spoke good English, growing up at the mission, and I studied hard. Still, it wasn't easy for me in the States. . . . Well, Jim Osterlord—now there's a bright guy—thinks there's some political opposition in Kalya, and you don't, huh?"

"That's right," said Lew.

"And Jim thinks I can enlighten you?"

"Well, that's what I assumed. Look . . . Link . . . this is nothing special. Just Peace Corps curiosity, I guess."

"The Peace Corps is doing a fine job here," said Beach. "It's trusted, which is more than you can say for a lot of my countrymen." He cast another appraising look at Corleigh. "Is Jim right? You can be trusted?"

"Sure."

"What's your particular job with the Peace Corps?"

"I'm something called a volunteer leader," said Lew. "That's an uptown phrase for truck driver. I drive the jeep wagon back and forth to Zinzin, delivering supplies and bringing back . . . well, complaints, mostly."

"Oh." Beach showed interest. "Zinzin. How often do you make the trip?"

"Once a week round-trip," said Lew, "as long as my kidneys hold out."

Beach got to his feet and walked around the desk. "What are you doing tonight, Lew?"

"Nothing. Why?"

"Okay," said Beach. "How about meeting me about nine in the Ginger Baby bar? I'll be in one of the back booths." He grinned. "Not many people will see us there and it's got the loudest jukebox in town. All right?"

"Okay," said Lew. "I'll see you there at nine."

4

The Ginger Baby bar, on a side street of downtown Ft. Paul, was a refuge for Peace Corps volunteers careworn in the service of humanity. It was a smoky den squeezed between a combination barbershop and Lebanese jewelry store on one side, and the grandiloquently named Elite Dry Cleaning and Photographic Supply Shop on the other. When Lew arrived at nine o'clock, it throbbed with rock-and-roll music, muddled English and shouted tribal expletives. Two girls, one a heavy-lidded African and the other a fading ash-blonde from Switzerland, tended the long mahogany bar under hooded amber lamp bulbs. A reclining Eurasian beauty, clad in a leopard skin, was painted on a wall mirror above the rows of liquor bottles. A wide-bladed ceiling fan revolved in creaky protest, faintly stirring warm, thick odors of human perspiration. On a tiny, darkened dance floor, three couples were doing the highlife, the slow West African shuffle which The Family performed with hauteur and young tribal Kalyans with uninhibited zest.

A slim Peace Corps youth, who wore sideburns and played the bull fiddle in a local jazz combo, nodded to Lew from his seat at the bar. His stool was next to one occupied by a Chinese-Negro girl who wore a set, petulant smile and a vivid yellow gown which exposed one shoulder. Her bare arm was draped around the back of the volunteer's neck.

"Goals Two and Three," said the youth to Lew. Peace Corps Goals Numbers 2 and 3 dealt with the cementing of friendship between volunteers and the residents of the underdeveloped countries in which they labored.

Lew grinned. "The best way," he said.

Down the bar two inky tribal girls, both wearing large gold earrings, flanked a drunken Scandinavian and vied for his next purchase of the tea which the bar girls drank from whiskey glasses. Three tribal men, wearing clean white shirts, argued hotly in the Nano tongue. The coin-operated jukebox blasted a wild guitar-and-drums recording while a young Negro at a side table played a noisy but professional accompaniment on a trumpet. Four patrons, mixed as to color, sex and age, beat time by hammering beer bottles on a table. The Ginger Baby bar was swinging early tonight.

In the rear were four booths with high wooden sides which screened the occupants from the rest of the establishment. Lew found Lincoln Beach alone in the last booth. He was clothed in the same tan suit with a button-down white shirt and striped tie. He smiled broadly in greeting and they shook hands with the Kalya snap of the index fingers.

"I'd have asked you to come to my apartment," said Beach, raising his voice to be heard above the din, "but Colonel Booth's boys are nosy when it comes to the visitors of some of us. In here, if we're seen, we could have met by accident."

Lew ordered a straight Scotch. He never drank water anywhere in Kalya unless he knew it had been boiled. The waitress shoved the tip, a Kalya dime, into a crevice of the green brassiere which she wore above her bare midriff. Corleigh and Beach leaned toward each other across the table in an effort to create a tunnel of communication in the Ginger Baby's clamor.

"So you want the political lowdown?" said Beach. "Why?"

"As I said, plain curiosity. When Jim told me there was opposition to The Family, I couldn't believe it. After all, I've been here almost two years and I keep my ears open."

"I see."

"The Kalya government," said Lew, "seems pretty bad to me,

inefficient, on the take, and murder on the tribes. I just wondered whether any Kalyans feel the same way I do. You, for instance."

Beach took out his wallet and fingered Jim Osterlord's note. "Does this mean what it says?" he asked.

"It does. My hand is inside," said Lew, using the Kalya phrase for the pledge of his word.

Beach nodded, satisfied, put the paper away, took a swallow of his drink, and then looked Lew in the eyes.

"I think," he said slowly, "that my country's government is phony as an American three-dollar bill. It's as corrupt as hell, far worse than your most crooked city or state machine, and remember this is a government for a whole country. It's rotten, it's slovenly and it's on the take from top to bottom."

Beach leaned closer to Lew and rubbed his glass in a circle of moisture on the table.

"Let me tell you my story," he said. "As I said, I was raised in the Lutheran mission at Loli. They were good people, and I was a fairly smart kid, so I learned and got good marks. But I knew instinctively that all the Christian morality was a bomb as far as Kalya was concerned because even a moron could see that the rules of the game in Kalya were a lot different. First, you had to case The Family and play the palship bit with some important members of it. That way you might get a government job—a few tribal men did. If so, you had it made for life. You never had to work, not really, and you could palm a lot of government graft on the side. The only alternative was a life of hardship and sickness in some stinking village. There was only one way to become a big-shot and every kid in school knew it. So honesty, hard work, self-reliance and all the other old virtues that the Lutheran missionaries taught might be all right in some far-off dream land like America, but they were actual liabilities here.

"Then I got that six-year scholarship from the African American Institute, two years at Andover and then four at Cornell." Beach smiled in memory. "Oh, sure, I saw your lousy segregation and a couple of times when I was refused service in a restaurant, I was so mad I could have slugged the guy. But I saw something else in the States too. I saw that the missionaries had something, that if a man worked hard and saved his money and was pretty smart, he could get ahead, easily if he was white. With a Negro, it took more doing, but he could. What it really took was work and brains. That was a revelation to me, a real deep one, and when I realized its full meaning, it really shook me up. The whole system was different from the one in Kalya. I could see what a country could be when people produced instead of sitting around on the take, doing nothing."

"You'd make a good walking ad for the U.S. Chamber of Commerce," said Lew.

"Like hell I would." Beach shot a finger at Lew. "You know something? I don't like your country. It's a white country and you think you're superior to the black man. Man, you've got fifty years of revolution on your hands before you learn—if you ever do."

"Do I act like I think I'm better than you are?" Lew tried to keep his tone conversational, but he could feel his temper rising. "After all, I'm sitting here because I want to learn from you."

"The Peace Corps is different," said Beach. "Most of you come from the top ten per cent of tolerant whites. Let's not kid each other, okay?"

"Oh, come on, Link. The Peace Corps draws from every level in the States."

"Maybe," said Beach. "I'm just telling you what I see and feel. I admire the American system, but not the people who run it. . . . Anyway, by my senior year at Cornell, I'd decided to come home and set up a business for myself and stay away from the government."

"But you didn't do it," said Lew.

"No, I didn't. My first days back here were a terrific shock. I found that I would have to bribe a half dozen juys just to get into business—to get financing, to get a license, to rent quarters, to drive a car. Hell, the whole deal was riddled with graft and hot money, and the apathy and laziness it produced as a by-product were appalling. Then I realized that, like it or not, I'd have to work inside the government if I was going to do anything to help change the system. So I looked around, found that the Utility Authority was the one agency being run on an honest basis. I went to the German fellow who runs the Authority and applied for a job. He took a liking to me when he found I meant business, and here I am."

The trumpeter was now parading about the back of the room. The noise was shattering and Beach, with a helpless hunch of his shoulders, had to suspend his talk. When the clamor abated somewhat, he continued in a loud voice as though addressing a deaf man.

"Let me tell you what I found when they put me in charge of billing," said Beach. "I found that a couple of hundred members of The Family hadn't paid a utility bill in months and some actually never had paid a water or electric bill at all. That's hard to believe, but it's true. Oh, they were billed all the time, they just never came across. So, I sent out letters to all the delinquents, warning that unless back bills were settled in thirty days, their water and lights would be turned off. God, did that bust open a hornet's nest! The Family was outraged that anyone would have the audacity to ask them to pay up. You know Bill Fess, the commissioner of agriculture?"

Lew nodded. "I hear he's even stooped to robbing lepers now." Lew related Roger's story about the theft of fingerlings destined for the leper colony's fish pond.

"I believe it," said Beach. He was angry now. "He's a crook. Anyway, one day at a cocktail party at Founders House, Fess confronted the German who runs the Utility Authority. Fess had run up a bill of about a thousand dollars on utilities, and he told my boss he'd gotten a letter demanding payment. In a loud, insolent voice that everyone around could hear, Fess said that if his water and lights were turned off, he'd have the German thrown out of the country. The boss didn't put up any argument there, but the next day he told me to go ahead and pay no attention to Fess's threats.

"So I wrote to Fess, Colonel Booth and all the other Family dead-beats, telling them they had only ten days to pay up or lose service. Booth came to my office and raised unshirted hell. That guy can be ugly when he's crossed."

Lew thought of Booth's motorcycle slamming into the tribal boy and Booth's contempt when Lew asked whether the boy would be taken to the hospital. He thought of the road incident near Zinzin. The security chief obviously was not revered for gentleness of spirit.

"A couple of days before the deadline," Beach continued, "the boss was summoned to the palace. Old Number One asked him what was the idea of cracking down on The Family. The boss said he couldn't run an agency with unpaid bills and if he couldn't collect, then he'd quit and tell the foreign press just why he'd done it—tell them the whole story. Old Number One backed down then.

"You see, Old Number One needed the service and he knew no Kalyans could run the utility lashup. Also he knew the director wasn't bluffing. So he gave him authority to go ahead with the crackdown. Fess, Downing and a whole list of characters settled just before the deadline. The only holdout was Hulbert Booth who owed us a little more than four hundred dollars. When he didn't pay, we shut off his water and lights. He was sore as hell, but two days later he came in and forked over the cash. But he still hates my guts."

Beach drew a copy of the *Daily Voice* from his coat pocket and pointed out a headline on page one: "Rice Shortage Hits Ft. Paul." Lew read the story which said that a longshoreman's strike in the United States had stalled shipping and prevented rice imports from reaching Kalya.

"That's what this damned corrupt system has done to my country." Beach almost yelled it. "It has so demoralized the tribal people that they won't even raise enough rice any more. This could be the richest rice-producing country in Africa, but who's going to plant rice when The Family comes along and steals it all through some phony tax levy? My God, a rice country importing rice from the United States! It's humiliating."

There was a lull in the Ginger Baby bar. The jukebox had ceased its amorous thunder for lack of new coins and the ambling trumpet player had subsided. Beach lowered his voice.

"The corruption has got to end," said Beach. "This could be a great country. We've got to work and build it, not with a lot of Marxist hot air, but with hard labor and an honest government. But we can't do anything until Old Number One either dies or is gotten out of office. The old guy has done some good, sure, building roads, appointing a few decent tribal officials like Steve

Muo up in Zinzin and getting foreign business outfits in here. But he's part of The Family and raised in the system himself. If he doesn't let The Family plunder, they'll find a way to ditch him. He's over seventy now and he can't last forever. The next election is the year after next. We've just got to field an opposition candidate to the Democratic Justice party. And if they rob us at the polls, revolution is the only alternative."

Beach smiled sourly. "The worst of it is your aid programs. The U.S. is pouring millions into this country every year, but most of it merely helps to prop up The Family. If it weren't for U.S. dough supporting Old Number One and The Family, we might have a chance to get rid of the regime. USAID is feeding corruption. Don't your people understand that?"

"Some do," said Lew. "I know one district AID official who thinks the whole thing is an awful waste. He's got a term for it —'Wawa,' meaning 'West Africa Wins Again.'"

Beach grinned. "You're talking about Forrest Stevenson, I'll bet. He's a shrewd old bird, but he's mostly talk. He won't stick his neck out. Still, it's too bad nobody at USAID listens to him."

"You said 'we' had to put up an opposition candidate," said Lew. "Who's 'we'? Have you got some others, some kind of organization?"

Beach studied Lew's face for a moment, then drained his glass. "Let's have another," he said. When the waitress, sullen and sleepy-eyed, brought the drinks, she dropped the tips into her green brassiere again and asked: "You want girl hyah?" Beach shook his head and the waitress shuffled off, heavy on her heels in the manner of tribal women accustomed to carrying headloads.

"I can't tell you about the others," said Beach. "Opposition is dangerous in Kalya. But don't worry. I'm not alone." Beach was silent a moment. Except for the tiny smile creases about his brown eyes, Beach's face was as smooth as a boy's. Yet Lew could feel that the guileless exterior was deceptive. There was a ruggedness and a commitment about him, a sense of force. "Don't forget," Beach continued, "that we've got about two hundred Kalya men abroad at American and European universities. They all talk politics. They discuss their country and they correspond between schools."

"But aren't most of those fellows members of The Family?" asked Lew.

"No, about half are tribal boys. Fortunately the scholarships are given by foreign foundations mostly, not by Old Number One's government. And then too, a few of The Family boys are coming around to our side. They realize the system's got to be changed."

"But what about the opposition right here in Kalya?" asked Lew.

Beach shook off the question. "That's our business." He jerked a thumb over his shoulder. "You talk too much in this country and you're liable to land in Kpali." Beach toyed with his glass, then spoke as though a random thought had just occurred. "Of course, we need help. We need help from people who sympathize with us and who aren't afraid to take a few risks."

He offered no further explanation. There was a clutter of movement in the Ginger Baby. A jungle band replaced the jukebox each night at ten o'clock and the band members were assembling behind the dance floor. A huge woman, as loosely ample as a bundle of wash, seated herself on a stool and inspected her musical instrument, a gourd enclosed in a network of nut shells. Two elderly gourd women took seats beside her and four men, their faces blank, thumped tentatively on jungle drums. After the erratic, preliminary sounds, a surge of rhythm flowed from the band. The beat of deep drums mingled with the rattle of shells on shaking gourds.

"A few people who don't mind taking risks," repeated Beach, raising his voice.

"Meaning?" asked Lew. He could feel a challenge in Beach's direct, fixed gaze.

"It's hard to get the word around in Kalya," said Beach. "If we had a man who traveled a lot, say on the road to Zinzin, maybe he could carry messages for us sometimes. . . ."

Beach had averted his eyes now and was studying his glass. Lew wondered. The offer may have been guarded, but it was plain enough. Suddenly Lew realized that he was not at all sure of his ground. He had come here, he told himself, propelled by curiosity alone, but now he was being beckoned toward something he didn't really understand. What did he actually know about this man who dressed like a junior executive, but who talked revolution? A man who would use a U.S. citizen for his own purposes, but who obviously had no love for the United States? Lew had taken him on faith because of Jim Osterlord. But how knowledgeable was Osterlord? After all, Jim was just another Peace Corps volunteer with a mania for building. Maybe there was a whole intricate web of Kalya politics that neither he nor Osterlord understood. How could he be sure Beach was what he said he was, that he didn't have his own power ambitions as selfish as those of The Family? Lew's instinct told him to be cautious.

"The Peace Corps," Lew said, "is forbidden to get mixed up in politics. That's the rule in every country."

Beach eyed him speculatively for a moment, then burst into laughter. "You really mean that, don't you? The innocents abroad. My friend, I don't know about other countries, but the Peace Corps is the greatest revolutionary force in Kalya."

"How do you figure that?"

"You're the whole climate of revolution for the tribes." Beach ticked the fingers of his left hand. "First, the Peace Corps is the only organization in the country that's incorruptible. Just as a simple example of honesty, you're a tremendous force for change."

Lew said nothing and Beach went on. "Second, you live with the people outcountry. The tribes know you're different from the other foreigners and The Family. They know you're not here to exploit them, but to try to show them a better way. You don't even try to shove a strange religion down their throats like the missionaries do."

"I suppose that's right, but . . ."

"The Peace Corps," interrupted Beach, "is the only group that the tribes will trust to hold their money. They know you won't eat it. Am I right?"

"That's true," said Lew. He had started to say more, but checked himself. It was apparent that Beach was building an argument toward a definite proposal to Corleigh. The oblique reference to message-carrying on the Zinzin road was obvious enough, and Lew was sure Beach intended to make it more direct. What should his response be? He shied intuitively from taking an active part in any plan that Beach might be hatching. A Peace

Corps volunteer had no business meddling in a country's internal politics, regardless of the rights and wrongs of it. In addition to the rules, it was common sense. Lew felt increasingly nervous and wondered whether he had made a mistake in coming here. Osterlord's note portended more than he had realized. And what was Jim Osterlord's role in this?

"The Molas and the Fizis and the others know a Peace Corps man can't be bought by anybody," continued Beach. "They know you're in Kalya just to help them and for no other reason. Isn't that right?"

"Well," said Lew, "they were suspicious in the beginning, I hear, but now, yes, I guess they do feel that way."

"And every tribal man with any sense knows that the only way to change his lot is to break the grip of The Family." Beach was plunging on as though he were aware of Lew's qualms and of the necessity to overcome them. He was almost shouting again now to be heard above the pulse of the jungle rhythm, and the cords of his neck were distended. "He knows, or he thinks he knows, that the Peace Corps is on his side, against Old Number One and The Family. So, my friend, you're helping to bring on a revolution in this country—whether you like it or not. You're already up to your neck in this thing."

Lew, uneasy, thought for a moment. "You're probably right, Link," he said slowly, "but you're talking about indirect effects. That's a lot different from a fellow like me taking an active part in some sort of plot to overthrow Old Number One. That's your business, not the Peace Corps'."

"You're quibbling, Lew, and you know it." Beach leveled a finger at him. "You remind me of a fellow who runs all over a ship warning the passengers it's about to sink, and then refuses to help man the lifeboats."

"That's not the same thing," said Lew. The analogy seemed inexact. Maybe he thought the ship might sink some day, but thus far he hadn't warned anyone, not even himself. "All I know is that if I took messages to Zinzin for you, I'd be messing in local politics, and the Peace Corps rules say no."

"Suppose I sent a personal note to Jim Osterlord, just friend to friend?" asked Beach. "Would you take that up for me?"

Lew hesitated. "Oh sure, I guess so. I'm only an errand boy

anyway. The best thing I do is carry letters back and forth. Personal notes between you and Jim would be just regular delivery stuff, I guess."

Beach smiled. "You're not sure about me, are you, Lew?"

"Well, frankly, I'm not sure about everything involved here. I never paid much attention to politics back home, but I know enough to realize there are wheels within wheels in any country."

"There is also right and wrong," said Beach. "And if you think The Family's right, you're wrong."

Lew bridled. "I never said The Family was right."

"But you refuse to help fight it," said Beach. "I've misjudged you. You're not another Jim Osterlord after all."

"What Jim does is his business," said Corleigh. "I think my position is pretty clear. I'm an American in a foreign country and I could do a lot of harm if I started meddling in things I don't understand."

Beach leaned across the table and pointed a finger at Lew's chest. "Just why are you in the Peace Corps, Lew?"

Lew hesitated again. He didn't want to falsify. "A lot of mixed motives, I suppose, but I do want to do some good, help people lead a little better life—if that's possible."

"And what's the road to the better life?" asked Beach. "Making a few improvements, distributing textbooks and teaching rote English? Or is it a real attack on the underlying problems, graft, corruption, extortion?"

"Both," said Lew. "But the attacking is up to you. You're the Kalya man."

Beach hesitated and the throb of the music took over. The splash of shells on the gourds had a harsh, primitive sound to Corleigh. Beach leaned still closer across the table and rested his weight on his forearms.

"I'm talking like this, Lew," he said, "because I think I can trust you. Man, you repeat anything I've said here and it's Kpali for me. The fact is, Lew, we're hard up for help. Hard up? We're desperate. I feel this thing so strongly, it's tough to take when you adopt the attitude you do."

"Look at it my way, Link. For one thing, it's against the rules. For another, I'm not sure of everything involved, even if I were willing to ignore the rules."

Beach looked at him sternly. "What you're really saying is, 'If The Family robs and exploits the tribes, that's none of my business.'"

"But it is, huh?"

"You're damn right it is," said Beach. "Otherwise you're just playing Peace Corps patty-cake over here."

Lew was surprised to hear Beach use the same phrase that Jim Osterlord had. "And how about our example for honesty and hard work?" he responded.

"Example isn't enough," said Beach. "Not in Kalya. The Peace Corps talks a lot about 'involvement.' Maybe you ought to find out what it's like to become really 'involved.'"

Lew grinned. "You sure keep pushing, Link. . . . Let me think about it a while. After all, Kalya's not going to collapse tomorrow."

Beach nodded. "You're right. It certainly isn't. It won't fall apart until at least the day after tomorrow." He scanned Lew's face again. "Whatever happens, you're not going to mention our talk or my name, are you?"

Lew put out his hand and shook Beach's. "I told you before. My hand is inside."

"That's good enough for me," said Beach. "Maybe we can talk again after your next trip to Zinzin."

They shook hands once more and Lew left the back booth. The Ginger Baby was steaming toward its Friday night crescendo. The dance floor bulged with Africans and Europeans, all swaying in frenetic, self-absorbed motions for which partners were but forgotten accessories. The beat of the native gourd-and-drum band thudded with the power of a sledge hammer. The fat tribal woman, her face wet with sweat, leaned far out from her stool and shook her shell-laced gourd ferociously. She stared with glazed eyes at the buttocks of one dancer as though he were the only person on the floor. The other dancers watched her hypnotically while the drums pounded an accompaniment like pulsing blood. A haze of smoke obscured the dim lights. The bar was now three deep and Lew nodded to several volunteers, including a woman teacher, as he passed. The Peace Corps youth with the sideburns was clutched in a wobbly embrace with the Chinese-Negro girl who wore the off-shoulder yellow gown. Peace

Corps Goals Number 2 and 3 were being pursued with visceral enthusiasm. Friday night at the Ginger Baby wouldn't end until dawn.

"Oh, Red!"

Lew caught a flash of white from a corner table near the door and he turned to see Rachael Frisson motioning to him with her ivory cigarette holder. She wore a glove-tight green dress and a matching bandeau of bright green silk about her spire of hair. The white man sitting beside her had delicate features and waved hair and, as Lew walked to the table, he noted the man held his cigarette with a droop of the wrist.

Rachael introduced the man as an officer of the Belgian embassy. Lew found his handclasp a limp one.

"We just stopped in for a quickie before the party at the Fesses," said Rachael. Her dress was deeply V'd and her lips were freshly crimsoned. Lew, although accustomed to Rachael's dramatic hairdos and clothes, found her suddenly unnerving. His hands felt awkward at his sides.

"Join us, Red?" There was a throaty sensuousness in the invitation.

He shook his head, too quickly, he felt. "Thanks, Rachael, but I've got a date," he said and he wished he had.

"I wondered why you were leaving so early," she said. "That couldn't have been a girl with you in the back booth?"

"No," said Lew. "I just ran into a guy who wanted to beat my ear about nothing much."

"Another time, Red," she said. She waved her holder dismissively, but her eyes held his with a questing look. Lew felt vaguely unsettled and annoyed that the Belgian was there. He fumbled his good-nights, and no sooner was he outside the bar, than he wished he were inside again.

He drove to the Peace Corps hostel through a muggy night that kept his shirt clinging damply to his back. The hostel, on the fringe of Ft. Paul, was a cracked-cement and stucco edifice that had housed the Ethiopian embassy in the building's better days. The largest offices had been converted to dormitories, one for women and one for men, where outcountry volunteers could stay in double-decked bunks for one dollar a night.

Corleigh and three other volunteer leaders lived permanently

at the hostel and waged a losing fight to protect their own
supplies from the forays of hungry visitors. One refrigerator bore
a hand-lettered sign: "This box is off limits for transient PCVs,"
but the notice proved merely inciting to men and women forag-
ing for beer and sandwiches in early morning hours. The men's
dormitory on weekends was a snarl of knapsacks, laundry bags,
sweat socks and smelly shirts, while the women's dormitory
resembled a tenement on wash day. Lingerie, cotton dresses
and stockings were strung from bunks and window frames in an
intricate maze. Sleep was improbable on weekends for all but the
most insensate visitors, for the simmering nights brimmed with a
chaos of noise: grunts, muffled oaths, the padding of bare feet,
the splashing of water from the hostel's always inadequate "night-
storage" tank, brushing of teeth and the intermittent loud talk
of late returners.

It was Lew's practice on weekends to sit on the second floor
balcony, try to fall asleep in a chair and hope that he would not
be routed by a downpour. The balcony proved only slightly less
uncomfortable than inside the hostel, for it overlooked a Fizi
complex of tin and corrugated zinc shanties in which all-night
movement appeared to be the rule. Babies cried, dogs growled
and old men crouched in disputatious palavers as they drank
palm wine. The hostel's windows were protected by steel rogue
bars anchored to the moldy cement, but this did not prevent an
occasional Fizi, when the hostel finally slumbered, from prying off
the bars over a window and making off with a haul of radios,
watches and purses.

Tonight the balcony had but one occupant in the canvas deck
chairs. It was Roger, the lord of the lepers. He had draped his
bony frame between two chairs, but he sagged in the middle and
his feet hung over the side of one chair. He corkscrewed back
into sitting position when Lew appeared.

"My favorite truck driver," he said. "Some night, huh? It must be
ninety still. I feel like a wet tent."

They sat in soggy silence for a few minutes. Then Lew said: "I
was telling a guy today about Fess swiping those fingerlings from
the leper pond. That's the lowest steal yet."

"Oh, I'll get some more somewhere." Roger appeared unconcerned.

Beach was still much on Lew's mind and he was puzzling over what his course should be. "Roger, don't you think the Peace Corps ought to fight The Family where we can? Why should we play their game without protesting?"

"Who are you going to protest to?" asked Roger. He sighed. "I went through all that. No, our job is to help where we can. That's all we can do."

Lew slapped at a mosquito, made the kill and inspected a dab of blood on his forearm. "But examples will take a couple of hundred years to change anything."

"And how long do you think Africa has been here?" countered Roger.

"Yeah, but changes of other kinds are coming fast everywhere, even here," said Lew. "Look how different the country is since they built the road to Zinzin ten years ago. Unless we try to change the system, I mean the government, working here is like trying to dip out the ocean with a sand-pail."

"I don't believe in messing in politics," said Roger emphatically. "We'd just get thrown out of the country, and a fat lot of good that would do. Then who'd take care of the lepers?"

Roger was off on a monologue about the latest developments at the leper colony. Several more cases had been arrested by treatment with the solfone class of drugs contributed by Baptist societies. Roger had gotten one toeless man to raise turkeys and two boys had started to dig a well.

Lew began to nod as Roger talked and soon Roger's low voice took on a lulling, dreamlike quality. Lew could see Lincoln Beach's angry, smooth face in the smoky Ginger Baby bar, and from the Fizi tin-hut encampment below came the sound of old men's voices. Lew pictured himself flying from Kalya less than ninety days hence, and he thought of a soft hotel bed in Paris and the click of women's high heels on the boulevards. Then he remembered the onslaught of rain the other night at Zinzin and he realized, sleepily, that soon the big summer rains would come—for good.

5

The sun glowed savagely hot in a colorless sky the next Monday morning as Lew Corleigh loaded the jeep wagon for his weekly outcountry trip. He heaved bundles of textbooks over the open tailgate and stacked mail, CARE packages and medicines beside them. Sweat beaded his arms and shoulders as he rolled three fifty-five-gallon drums of kerosene up a ramp and into position. Finally he loaded two cartons of yellow manila envelopes, the termination instruction kits for some sixty Group V volunteers along the road to Zinzin who would be ending their service in July and returning to the United States. Lew thought of his own termination envelope being prepared in the Peace Corps office above him and he calculated the remaining time as he did every morning: eighty-five days to go.

The loading operation took place in the clay-and-gravel parking area behind the garage building in which Peace Corps headquarters occupied the second story. Prudence Stauffer called to him from the balcony.

"Did you remember the kerosene, Lew?"

He held up a circled thumb and forefinger, then pointed to the drums inside the jeep wagon. She nodded primly and strode back into the office. She wore a simple cotton print dress and, as usual, her corn-colored hair was gathered into a tight bun. Lew grinned at the retreating figure. Little Miss Missionary was on the job.

Lew took a pencil from behind his ear and checked off items on the clipboard which he used to keep track of his chores. He placed a mark beside each notation until he came to the last one: "See Williams about Genghis for zz. vols." Oh, he'd overlooked that one. He couldn't drive into Zinzin without some report for Arlene, Arch, Cindy and the others. He thought of Lincoln Beach, his laughter and his remark that "you're already up to your neck in this thing." Beach's mocking challenge still nettled him this morning.

Lew climbed the stairs to the Peace Corps office and knocked on the door of the plywood partition which separated the Peace Corps representative's office from the rest of the staff.

Carter Williams, plump and dark-haired, wore a short-sleeved shirt open at the neck. His expression was one of tentative anxiety as though he expected bad news and would be happily relieved if disappointed. His quick-roving eyes played over Corleigh in the manner of a man who wonders what annoyances this new courier brings. They exchanged opening pleasantries.

"Moses Harter, the school principal at Zinzin, is giving the PCVs trouble again," said Lew, "and they wanted me to report to you." He sketched the affair.

Williams clicked open a penknife and began digging at his nails as Corleigh talked. Williams had come to the Peace Corps in hopes of snapping the tedium of business routine in Philadelphia, much as a man idles over the Sunday newspaper travel sections and daydreams of strange lands. His chief motive was foreign travel and he had been irked to find that his Peace Corps stretch would be spent in but one country. To his Ft. Paul post he brought the attitudes of his Philadelphia insurance adjusters firm. Most human grievances, he believed, were matters meriting instant sympathy and indefinite postponement. Experience taught him that settlement, while often inevitable, could be obtained on easier terms with the passage of time. Some problems, like vintage wines, mellowed with the years and at long last reached the stage where they could be savored as ripened memories.

"Your Genghis Khan," he observed, "is certainly a bad apple.

Unfortunately he's not alone. His kind makes our job very difficult over here."

"I think he's worse than the others, Mr. Williams," said Lew. "If he's allowed to keep on getting away with his deals, it'll sabotage all our work up there with the Molas."

"I suppose so." Williams sighed as he inspected his newly excavated nails. "Bad for volunteer morale."

"That's the least of it," said Lew. Williams' failure to grasp the deeper issue troubled him. "The volunteers up there think it's time that the staff took some action."

"Action?" Williams appeared hurt. "What kind of action?"

"They think you ought to lodge a protest with Commissioner Downing," said Lew.

With the air of a man being put upon unnecessarily, Williams reached into his center desk drawer and took out a folder. He riffled the sheets within. "Here are protests on the activities of various principals and Kalya officials that I've filed with Downing. There must be fifteen or twenty of them. To my knowledge, he acted in only one case, and that was against a woman teacher who wasn't a member of The Family."

"But this is different, sir," said Lew. A faint flush came to his cheeks. "Here's a guy who makes the poor tribal kids pay for free textbooks and then pockets the money. And we carted all those books up there. If the Peace Corps doesn't go to bat against Harter, then we're going to get the reputation with the Molas of condoning The Family's robbery."

"I know, I know," said Williams. "It puts us in a bind. I don't like it."

"The way the volunteers look at it," insisted Lew, "if the tribes turn against us, then we lose all our influence and we might as well pack up and go home. What purpose would there be in staying?"

Williams shifted uneasily in his swivel chair and looked reproachfully at Lew. "But we're here only at the invitation of the host government. We can push Old Number One's people only so far."

"But the PCVs don't think there's been much pushing."

Williams pointed to the folder. "I'd say fifteen or twenty filed protests indicate considerable pushing." He glanced swiftly at

Corleigh to see whether the sheer volume of protests had registered.

"Frankly, Mr. Williams, we were hoping this would be worth a personal protest to Downing in his office."

"You were, eh?" Williams frowned. Of the varied duties of a Peace Corps representative abroad, the care and support of volunteers rated priority status. Williams was envious of young Prudence Stauffer for the high esteem in which volunteers held her. It was no secret that many of them thought that Miss Stauffer, not Williams, should be the representative in Kalya.

"Perhaps you're right." Williams cogitated in silence a moment. "Well then, let's do it. You'd better come along to explain the situation to Downing. But you'll have to put on a dark suit and tie. He's a stickler for protocol."

Lew drove back to the hostel, put on a white shirt with tie, and donned his only suit. It had been months since he'd worn a tie, and his collar was damp by the time he returned to the Peace Corps office. He and Williams drove to Downing's place of work in the representative's new green jeep with the legend "Peace Corps No. 1" lettered on a door.

Kalya's compulsive campaign to construct ornate, modern government buildings had not yet reached the Department of Education. It was billeted in an old apartment house from which three tiers of balconies extended over the street level. The iron railings had rusted, staining the building with long, brown streaks. The reception room on the ground floor was populated by three lax Kalyans who sat at desks with covered typewriters. When Williams asked if Commissioner Downing was in, a large woman in a torn, smudged smock, looked at him blankly.

"I dunno," she said. "He t'ird flo'."

Corleigh followed Williams up a narrow, dusty stairway. The walls, whitewashed years ago, were yellowing. On the third floor, the door at the end of the short corridor was surmounted by a large sign, embossed with the yellow and red seal of Kalya. It bore the inscription: "J. Richardson Downing, Commissioner of Education, Department of Education, Republic of Kalya." The piquant mulatto girl at the reception desk was chewing gum and reading the *Daily Voice*. Williams bowed and asked for Downing.

"He in conference, Mist' Will'," she said, "but I tell him."

She thrust her head through an inner door and said something in a muffled voice.

Williams and Corleigh seated themselves on a hard bench and Williams said in a low voice, "That's protocol. He'll keep us waiting fifteen minutes."

Approximately a quarter of an hour later, the inner door burst open and Downing rushed out with hand extended. No other conferees were in evidence. He was a tall, wiry, coffee-hued man, and he wore an orange shirt beneath a shimmering synthetic-fiber suit, flecked with scarlet threads, which seemed about to crackle as though electrically charged. His personality was similarly infused. He shooks hands with Williams with a loud snap of the index finger.

"A great pleasure, Mr. Representative," he cried. His voice had a shrill, nasal quality. "You don't come often enough."

Williams introduced Corleigh and the commissioner snapped off the special handshake with enthusiasm. "Every Peace Corps volunteer is my friend, my yes," he said. "Come in, come in."

In contrast to the somnolent, blighted appearance of the rest of the building, Downing's office bespoke a yearning for elegance. A brown carpet, of thick piling, covered the floor. An aging floor lamp, with the dangling tassels favored in other decades, stood beside his mahogany desk, which had paneled inlays of ebony. Several bookcases held paperbound official documents, including many publications of the United Nations. Framed honorary degrees from African institutions of learning hung on the walls. The desk had an in-and-out box, the bottom layer empty and the top compartment holding one booklet. A copy of *Paris Match* rested on the green desk blotter. Downing seized the booklet from the out box.

"Educational psychology," he said, rapping the booklet smartly, "that's what we need more of in Kalya. It's a new discipline, but it's proliferating, my yes. I hope to persuade the Prime Minister to let us include a modest amount for a chair of educational psychology in next year's budget. We know what we're teaching, but do we know the human dynamics of how to teach it? That's the question we pedagogues of Kalya must ask ourselves. The psychological climate is everything in the newly developing countries. Erudition is not enough, much as we may cherish its solace. Do you agree, Carter?"

The tumbling rush of words left Lew baffled, but Carter Williams smiled amiably. "You've got to keep abreast of the times," he said with noncommittal deference.

"My yes," replied Downing. "That's the error my good academic friends in Sierra Leone have fallen into. No psychology in the classroom. Here we have it intuitively in abundance, thanks to the challenge of orienting our tribal cultures to modern civilization. But we must structure it into formal molds so it can be weighed and evaluated. The teaching system that fears evaluation carries the seeds of its own destruction."

Commissioner Downing beamed triumphantly and then leaned across the desk and slapped his palms on the blotter.

"Enough theorizing," he said. "I can see by the gleam in your eye, Carter, that you're here on a practical mission. Always practical, the Peace Corps, my yes."

"It's the principal at Zinzin, Moses Harter," said Williams mildly. "Our teaching volunteers fear that some of his recent actions don't conform to your, uh, high standards, Mr. Commissioner. I brought along Lewis Corleigh, our volunteer leader who travels the road to Zinzin, to give you the details."

"I'm anxious to hear," said Downing. He leaned back, posed his fingertips beneath his chin in judicial fashion. Also, Lew noted, his face tensed and his eyelids narrowed.

Lew told the story of Genghis Khan's recent enterprises: the amorous proposals to Cynthia Fuller, the impending motherhood of the native second-grade teacher, the levy of a month's salary against the girl and the ten-cent fee on free textbooks.

"Disgraceful!" exclaimed Downing. "I refer, of course, to the imposition of a fee on the tribal children for free textbooks. As for Mr. Harter's romantic endeavors, I'm afraid, gentlemen, that's another matter. We're inclined to be more lenient in such personal affairs than our brothers of the West. My yes."

"I merely told you that so you'd get the whole picture," said Lew. "The real point about the teacher, Mr. Commissioner, is the way Gengh—Mr. Harter—forced a month's salary out of her for his own use. He claimed it was a new order out of Ft. Paul."

Downing frowned. "Are you sure you're not confusing it with the contribution of a month's salary which all government employees, teachers included, are privileged to make for the Founders Day festivities?"

Lew shook his head. The annual deduction of a month's pay, he knew, while officially ticketed for Founders Day, went to finance Old Number One's Democratic Justice party, the country's sole viable political organization, through which Old Number One and The Family gained re-election to the offices of Prime Minister and the legislature every six years.

"No," said Lew. "The girl already paid that. Mr. Harter claims she owed another month's salary under a new order from you. The girl only gets thirty-eight dollars a month. We suspect Harter has 'eaten' the money."

"Shocking!" thundered Downing, but his expression appeared rather unperturbed for one shaken by shock tremors. "Francine!" he called. The pretty receptionist appeared at the door.

"Get me the file on Moses Harter, our principal in Zinzin," he ordered. The girl smiled, dubiously, and withdrew.

"We can't tolerate such breaches of discipline," said Downing. "It's an outrage." He spoke for five minutes on the department's evolving, long-range, structured, mandatory and eminently successful program to set the highest ethical standards of any educational system in Africa. The girl reappeared.

"No way," she said. "Can't find Mist' Hart'."

"Someone must have mislaid the file," said Downing in the aggrieved tone of a man who seldom finds such flaws in his efficient empire. "Well, gentlemen, I'll study the records when they're located. I'm truly sorry we can't settle this right now."

He smiled apologetically, and Lew could not help admiring the polished play-acting. Lew knew and so did Carter Williams that the Kalya Department of Education had no personnel files. A Peace Corps volunteer, at Downing's behest, had spent six months in the building, attempting to compile teacher and employee records. The undertaking failed miserably, chiefly because none of Downing's underlings could be persuaded to take an interest in such a dreary chore as record-keeping and secondarily because the intricacies of an alphabetical filing system proved too much for the three civil servants assigned to the task.

"I thank you again, gentlemen, my yes," said Downing, rising and terminating the interview. "My own communications to such outcountry towns as Zinzin are not always reliable, so I appreciate all the information the Peace Corps can give me. And, never fear Carter, Mr. Harter will be dealt with in the most unmistakable terms."

They left the building unnoticed. The three attendants on the ground floor were engrossed in captious bargaining with "Billy Number 15," official, legal name of the most industrious of the city's omnipresent Mandingo traders. The Mandingo businessmen were all licensed as Billies Numbers 1 through 20 for a variety of peddling and shopkeeping enterprises—Billy Number 4, for instance, was the owner of the Elite Dry Cleaning and Photographic Supply Shop next to the Ginger Baby bar. Most of the Billies were incensed currently because Billy Number 15 had somehow cornered the supply of new Japanese transistor radios, over one of which he was haggling with the educational employees.

"Downing will never do a thing about Harter," said Williams as they drove away. The thought did not appear to distress him. "Still, it will give me more leverage for the next complaint." He shot an appraising glance at Corleigh. "I hope you'll tell our Zinzin people that I tried."

"Sure," said Lew. He had the impression that Williams was more concerned with the appearance of his mission than with its results, and the thought depressed him. Official Kalya's obsession with form to the exclusion of substance was contagious.

At Peace Corps headquarters, Lew changed into khaki pants and polo shirt, hung his dark suit in the textbook storeroom and made a final check of the jeep wagon load. It was noon now and he'd be pressed to make Zinzin by tomorrow night. As he settled behind the wheel and buckled the seatbelt, he noticed a long white envelope on the floor boards by the clutch, out of line of casual sight. His name was typewritten on it. When he opened it, he found a smaller envelope addressed to James Osterlord and a typewritten note: "Dear Lew, I'd consider it a great favor if you'd deliver this letter for Steve Muo to Jim Osterlord. Thanks. L." A letter, obviously from Lincoln Beach, to Steven Muo, the district commissioner at Zinzin. So Muo and Beach were working together in the underground or whatever it was. From what Jim Osterlord had said and Beach's complimentary remark about Muo, that figured. But delivering a personal note to Osterlord, as he'd promised Beach he'd do, wasn't quite the same thing as carrying a message destined for Muo. Beach obviously had gone beyond the boundaries of their small understanding. In essence Lew would be delivering a letter from one foe of The Family to another. He felt uneasy. He was being drawn—unwilling?—into some kind of organization, an underground, a cabal, or just what was it? He sat for several minutes, eyeing the letter and pondering his course. Finally, still uncertain, he placed the letter in the glove compartment and snapped the catch. He had a day and a half to decide what to do.

A massive black cloud blotted the eastern half of the sky as he drove north toward Zinzin. Overhead the sun burned with unyielding brutality, but flashing strings dangling from the cloud indicated that, off to the east, Kalya's outcountry rain forest was being drenched with water. In these days of the small rains, prelude to the torrential summer floods from the sky, a traveler could never be certain where the rain would fall. All afternoon the eastern cloud flanked the bouncing jeep, threatening ominously, yet never releasing its dark burden.

The macadam road ended fifty miles from Ft. Paul just beyond the entrance to the largest of The Family's rubber plantations, this one jointly owned by William Fess, J. Richardson Downing and a member of the Itambel board of directors whose name Lew could not recall. The rubber trees stood in stately rows, each trunk bearing a wired wooden bowl to collect the dripping latex juice. The orderly lines of trees, so strangely disciplined for Kalya's unruly bushland, stretched for miles along the paved road like soldiers on a parade ground. Then the macadam ended, the rubber trees straggled into heavy bush and the rolling, jungled hills began. About every half hour the jungle came to an abrupt halt, as if by command, to reveal a village of circular mud huts, dormant in the flooding sun which seemed to shine by special permission of the vigilant black cloud to the east. At most of these villages Lew made his routine stops to deliver supplies to lonely Peace Corps teachers who were distressed that he must hurry on without the usual quota of gossip. He was late arriving at Loli that night, too late to visit Forrest Stevenson, and he ate and slept in the mud-stick home of Susan, who was her chipper little self again, popping with good humor, now that Lew had repaired her refrigerator by his mechanical wizardry—turning the big box upside down. Susan had only one complaint, that the *Volunteer*, official house organ of the Peace Corps, painted Peace Corps accomplishments in too rosy a light. Lew agreed, as he had with a hundred other volunteers, that the publication erred on the side of cheery optimism.

The black cloud vanished the next day and the rutted road threw off dust like a dog shaking itself. Each rare passing vehicle trailed a powdery funnel and by mid-afternoon Lew was splotched with grime as the dirt mingled with the moisture of his body. Heat enfolded him like a warm, soggy blanket and he longed for the shower hut at Arlene Offenbach's.

He drove at last into the outskirts of Zinzin, but it was a Zinzin he had not seen before. The main road, usually clogged with aimless humanity, was deserted. Not a single person walked the road and even the scrawny dogs and stiff-legged goats had disappeared. Shutters were closed on the mud-stick huts. No women husked rice or squatted over feeble fires. Zinzin seemed a ghost town, broiling in abandoned decay. The huts cast round, fat shadows in the oppressive first twilight and the only sound was the crunch of the jeep's tires on the baking soil. Lew turned into the Lutheran compound, equally forsaken, and parked the jeep behind Arlene's house. It too was shuttered. He went to the back door and called, "Bock-bock."

Arlene opened the door at once, yanked him in by the arm and closed the door quickly behind him. The kitchen was dark and Lew stood for a moment while his eyes adjusted to the lack of sunlight. Arlene's breathing was heavy.

"The devil's dancing," she whispered.

"Oh, I should have guessed."

She shushed him and led the way to the small living room. Several thin rays of light, in which dust shimmered, pierced the room from the corners of the bolted shutters. They sat down in silence. The house was stiflingly hot.

Almost every Kalya tribe had its town devils. The ritual of their rare dances was similar, but that of the Mola tribe was the most rigorously observed. The devil danced, upon orders from the paramount chief, only in times of peril. In the primitive Mola litany of

joy and disaster, the devil danced when catastrophe impended
and the jungle gods must be propitiated. He danced when
famine threatened, when drought seared the cassava, the plantain
and the rice, or when an individual had so transgressed the rules
of the secret Golo or Mata societies that ruin for the entire town
could be anticipated from avenging deities. When the devil danced,
every person must withdraw inside his hut, close the shutters and
keep babies and animals within. It was taboo to watch the devil's
sacrament and, it was believed, anyone who peeped through a
window would be struck down, if not at once, within a few days.
In the rigid canons of Mola demonology, even the devil's attendant could not look upon the dancer. This small boy must keep
his eyes averted as he reverently brushed dust from the devil's costume with a palm frond whisk broom. Music was provided by a
jungle band, men on the wooden drums and women on the
shell-laced gourds, but the group must play with backs to the devil.
Mola lore was filled with stories of drummers who inadvertently
saw the devil and died in agony within a few hours. In Zinzin, as in
other Mola towns, the hour when the devil danced was an hour
of silent terror.

As Lew and Arlene sat in the gloom, he could hear the throb
of the drums and the chainlike rattle of nut shells against the
gourds, a juiceless sound that spoke to its listeners of death.
The rhythm was steady and deep. The chanting beat swelled
slowly, almost imperceptibly, in pitch. The music was lonely
and implacable, so primitive that it seemed to match the course
of blood from a pounding heart. The rhythm had the throat of evil
and even civilized men could not shake a nameless feeling of
apprehension when they heard it.

"It's spooky, isn't it?" said Arlene.

"I'd like to say no, but I can't." Lew found himself answering
Arlene's muffled voice in kind. "How long since it started?"

"About twenty minutes."

"Then we've got about another hour," said Lew. "I've heard a
devil dance twice, but I've never seen one."

The pitch of the drums and gourds was rising, and now, suddenly, the wail of a woman pierced the chant. It was a desolate
cry, half of ecstasy and half of fright, and it trailed away into a
moan as though from an injured animal. That would be the lead-

ing gourd woman, thought Lew, informing the devil that his incantations had unpenned the dread of the unknown which the rites demanded. By custom the drummers and gourd women remained stationary while the devil danced the length of a town's main road. The rhythm notified the shuttered huts of the devil's progress by ever-mounting intensity in pitch and volume.

"He's coming closer," said Lew.

He moved to a window and bent over toward the crack through which fading sunlight came.

"You're not going to look?" Arlene sounded frightened. "Please don't, Red."

He turned toward her. "You don't really believe that stuff about being struck down, do you, Arlene?"

She brushed nervously at her upswept hair with the comb at the crest. "Of course not," she whispered. "Don't be silly. It's just that I think as long as we're here, we should honor the customs of our neighbors. We'd want them to do the same in the States."

Lew grinned in the half-dark. "Is that the real reason? You're sure you don't believe in the punishment for watching?"

"I just don't like the idea," she said defensively.

Lew reached over and patted her arm. "Look, Arlene, I'm going home in exactly eighty-four days, and I'm going to see one devil dance before I go."

"I don't think it's right," she protested.

"Maybe not, but here goes."

Lew turned back to the window and put his eye to a broad crack between shutter and window frame. The laterite road, perhaps fifty yards away down the slope of the hill on which Arlene's house rested, was as deserted as when Lew drove into town, but a small cloud of dust far to the right indicated that the devil was on his way.

Slowly a huge figure, a kind of grotesquely padded scarecrow, came into view. The devil wore an enormous bundle of thick fibers of the type tribal women used for weaving baskets. He was dressed in layers, perhaps seven or eight of them, and each layer overlapped the one beneath. His legs and arms swelled to great size and his body had an elephantine girth. His straw headgear was heavy and conical in shape. In front of his eyes stretched a narrow band of glittering material not unlike the spangled plastic used to make children's toys. This visorlike band protruded from the matting, giving the devil the appearance of a spaceman encased in a pressure suit of some ludicrous home-made design. Beside the straw figure walked a small boy, naked save for a loincloth, who brushed at the devil with a bundle of palm fronds. The boy's posture was peculiar, for he had to lean away and avert his head so as not to look upon the forbidden. Thus some of his attempts at brushing were mere wild slashes at the air behind him. Lew's first impulse was to laugh aloud.

But something in the movements of the devil suppressed the laugh. The dancer's first steps when he came within Lew's view amounted to a kind of shambling run. The devil turned in a slow circle, his arms and legs flopping as though he were a giant puppet on a string. He lurched left and right, waved his weird headgear foolishly. He was disjointed and seemingly erratic in his shuffling, and yet there was a taunting arrogance about his movements as though he were mimicking the panic that would befall any person who failed to heed the barbaric warnings of the dance.

Then he spun like a top and careened toward the side of the road in a skidding slide. He halted abruptly, stood ominously still for a moment, and then began a slow, measured tramping with his hidden feet. The tread increased with the rising pitch of the far-off rhythm and soon he was dancing feverishly, pounding the road and stirring a whirlpool of dust. He writhed like a grotesque, straw-encased cobra. He raised his huge, padded arms imploringly and his head shook like that of a lunatic. There was a frenzy to the dance now. He swung wildly in weaving gyrations. An arm swept out unexpectedly and sent the attendant sprawling in the dirt. The boy picked himself up, dazed and terrified, and groped about for his palm fronds. The devil whirled, cut and plunged with incredible speed for one so bulky. On and on went the dance in the heavy, lowering twilight. As Lew watched, fascinated, he felt a peculiar mood of evil encompassing him. The dancer seemed possessed of a lonely, heedless power. Lew wanted to turn from the window, but he could not. The fury of the dance, compounded in apprehension by the silence of the dancer, proved hypnotic. Lew started when Arlene spoke.

"What's he doing now?"

"He's . . ." but Lew failed to answer. The devil suddenly went limp, as if destroyed by his own violence. He stood slack, with the conical headpiece drooping, like a battered scarecrow in supplication. Then he resumed the first shambling, flapping, chaotic motions and shuffled out of view down the road.

Lew turned to a chair and sat down heavily. He felt exhausted.

"What was it like?" asked Arlene in a low but excited voice.

"I can't really say," replied Lew. "I don't know why, but it gets you. I can see why the Molas would be scared stiff."

The drums and gourds began to diminish in volume. They faded quickly, then suddenly ceased after one wild, upbeat, stricken note. The devil's dance was over. Lew realized that he had watched it for almost an hour.

"You can open the shutters now," he said. "When the drums stop, that means the devil has disappeared into the bush. It's kind of an all-clear."

Arlene opened the shutters and they both looked out. Up and down the road there were the small noises of huts coming to life. A few people emerged cautiously, and then slowly the children, the goats and the dogs came forth. The road gradually filled with people and animals, but there was a muted quality about the town in these last few minutes of dusk. People stood in small, hushed clusters and files of men could be seen winding toward the big palaver hut.

"They're frightened," said Lew, "and they're trying to find out what it means."

"Well, what is it all about?"

"I haven't the foggiest." Lew tried to allay her anxiety. "Let's drive over to Alice and Dotty's. The gang will probably head there."

They were nearing the cluttered household of Alice Franklin and Dorothea Wyzansky when Lew remembered that he'd forgotten to take his shower. He grinned at Arlene. "I bet I smell like a goat," he said.

"You're right," she replied. "You do."

The Peace Corps clan gathered in an atmosphere of simmering speculation. Arch Lettermore, in a flowered sports shirt and tattered shorts, greeted them at the door with a glass of rum and water for each. The chubby Negro was grinning. "Man, oh man, what a show," he said. "That devil is Sammy Davis, Jr., in a portable hay mow."

"You mean you saw him, Archie?" asked Arlene.

Lettermore put a finger to his lips and motioned his head toward the kitchen where the houseboy, in his soiled Sweet Briar sweatshirt, was padding softly about. "Don't let on to Joe-Joe," whispered Arch.

Ted Kramer turned from the window with a perplexed look on his chalky, pimpled face. "They're all milling around and talking to each other like they're not sure what's up," he said.

Dotty and Alice emerged from the kitchen along with fragrant fumes of stewing lamb. Dotty's white cotton shift was stained and her uncombed hair trailed flying wisps. Alice peered through spectacle lenses that showed flecks of grease. She wore an unpressed blouse and below her dirty blue jeans her ankles were still white with calamine lotion in memory of the driver ants.

"After that blowup," said Dotty, "you're all invited to stay for lamb stew. We figured you'd be around. Cripes, what a performance! I mean I've still got the shivers." She lighted the lamp, dispelling the deepening shadows.

Alice plopped onto a sofa. "Those drums." She grimaced. "Did you bring our termination kits, Lew?"

Corleigh nodded and Arch promptly did a whirling, pounding dance. "The termination frug!" he shouted. "Anybody can watch."

Cindy Fuller came out of the bathroom. She wore a gray cotton dress, freshly laundered, and her hair was tied with a soft rose ribbon which matched her lipstick. Lew knew she was the prettiest woman he'd seen all day. She smiled affectionately and waved to him.

"What's it all about?" asked Lew.

"Who knows?" said Kramer. "This is the first time the devil has been on the streets in the year I've been here."

"Doesn't anybody know?" asked Arlene. She still looked worried.

"Not us, honey," said Dotty. "I mean, we just work here."

They all talked at once. Arch said it was a charity ball for

Genghis Khan, devil's division. Ted said the devil danced as a warning to Dotty and Alice for repulsing the advances of two Ft. Paul members of The Family. Alice wondered why the devil hadn't borrowed Jim Osterlord's motorbike and done a modern dance on wheels. Cindy said the ceremony probably had some deeper meaning that concerned them all. The excited voices collided and sentences were lost.

Then they became aware that Joe-Joe was standing silently in the kitchen doorway. He was kneading the bottom of his Sweet Briar sweatshirt with nervous hands. The chatter died away.

"Da devil dance fo' bush school," he said.

"What do you mean, Joe-Joe?" asked Alice, speaking slowly and spacing her words.

The boy shrugged and rolled his eyes. "Bush school one time, da's all."

"But they had bush school last winter," protested Cindy.

"Devil, he want Golo boys, you see, teach'." Joe-Joe waved to the east toward the high bushlands.

"I go home now," he said and he walked to the door, his bare feet slapping on the cement floor. He slipped out, closed the screen door quietly behind him and was swallowed by the night.

"Now what the hell does that mean?" asked Kramer.

No one knew, but all speculated aloud at once.

"Where's Osterlord?" asked Lew at last. "He ought to have the word."

But it was an hour later, after a third round of drinks, before they heard Osterlord's "bock-bock" at the door. His creeping thatch of black hair had grown even longer since Lew had seen him last week. He accepted a rum-and-water without comment from Arch and seated himself outside their circle as though he might be tainted by overly intimate contact with his fellows. With his olive complexion, his shirt made of tribal country cloth and his aloof frown, he did seem a man apart.

"Well, what's your guess, Mr. Mola?" asked Kramer.

"About what?" Osterlord showed no interest.

"The devil, tongue-tied," said Dotty irritably. "Cripes, don't act so haughty. I mean you might need us sometime, maybe."

"Maybe," said Osterlord without conviction.

"Seriously, Jim," said Lew, "what's your theory about all this? We can't figure it out."

"I've got more than a theory," said Osterlord.

Arch Lettermore jumped up and did a swift, spinning dance, imitating the devil, in front of Osterlord. "Okay, man, talk," he said, "or I'll humbug you good."

Osterlord smiled indulgently at Arch and sipped his drink. He questioned Alice. "Do I get invited to dinner too?"

"Of course, silly," said Alice. "Now quit being so mysterious."

"I'm not trying to be," said Osterlord. He stretched out his legs. "But this thing is no joke. It's another of Genghis Khan's crafty gambits." He paused and this time they waited for him without heckling.

"A couple of weeks ago," he said, "Genghis told Cindy that he might have to close the school for three weeks because of the pressure of his 'law business,' as he put it. Cindy told me about it. Right, Cindy?"

She nodded. "Law business," she said with a sniff. "He got his certificate as an attorney by giving the chief justice five head of cattle. He's never seen a law book in his life."

"But there's money in lawyering," said Osterlord. "The Molas love litigation. Look at that case of Mrs. Stevenson down in Loli. Anyway, I told Steve Muo about Genghis's plan to close the school. Steve got sore and told Genghis he couldn't do it. They argued and Genghis got ugly. He claimed Muo had no authority over him as school principal and he could do as he damn well pleased."

"I didn't know Muo cared much about the school," said Lew.

"Steve's a proud Mola," said Osterlord, "and he's especially proud of the government school since the Peace Corps teachers came in. He thinks the kids are learning and he's determined that all the Mola young ones should learn to read and write at least."

They were all quiet now, listening. Arch hunched forward, elbows on his knees. Dotty smoked rapidly, scattering ashes over her dress and the floor.

"Anyway," continued Osterlord, "yesterday Genghis came to Muo and said a session of the Golo bush school would take place at once. Muo said that was against government regulations, that bush school could only take place during the winter vacation. Old Genghis accused Steve of being a traitor to tribal traditions and he left in a nasty mood. Steve went to see the paramount chief and claimed that Genghis was violating the government's agreement with the tribe. But the old man refused to interfere. He contended he'd delegated his bush school authority to Genghis. Steve thinks Genghis has something on the paramount chief. Maybe he's slipping him money or something. Then, suddenly, it was announced this afternoon that the devil would dance."

Osterlord paused a moment. "It's an obvious warning from the devil that nobody is to interfere with the Golo school. According to the word being passed now in the palaver hut, all the boys will be taken to bush school in a couple of days."

"But it's all so confusing," said Arlene. "What power does Moses Harter have over the devil?"

"He's a powerful man," said Osterlord. "He owns half the town and almost everyone's in his debt one way or another."

"Jim, who is the devil?" asked Lew. "Do you know?"

Osterlord nodded. "It's supposed to be the deepest secret in the tribe, but the way I get it, he's Genghis Khan's nephew, that runty little guy who works at the clinic. He's a mean one."

"Why, he isn't more than five-feet-two," said Cindy. "I'd think he'd be buried alive in all that straw."

"It takes an awful lot of straw to make a straw man," intoned Arch.

"Imagine that ugly little pipsqueak scaring anybody," said Dotty. "Cripes, I mean I feel better already. He's nothing but a paper devil."

"For us," said Osterlord, "but the town's frightened. The thing even got to Steve Muo. I went to see him right after the dance and he's in a funk. Steve likes to believe that he's shed the old fears and taboos, but deep inside, he's still hooked. He won't admit it, but he's afraid of the devil too."

"The way you make it sound," said Ted Kramer, "this is a simple power fight between Genghis and Steve, the bad guy and the good guy."

"That's right," said Osterlord, "and it looks like Genghis has won this round. My guess is that Steve won't have the stomach to interfere any more, unless somebody can stiffen him. I feel sorry for the guy."

"You mean our school will have to shut down for a month?" asked Cindy.

"That's about the size of it, Cindy."

"It's a bloody, cryin' shame," said Alice. "We'll all go nuts, sitting around this hole with nothing to do for a month."

"Wawa," cried Dotty.

"Wawa," chorused Arch, Ted and Alice.

The session turned into a hubbub of exasperated complaints and denunciations of Genghis Khan. Alice set out the lamb stew, fresh bread from the Mandingo bakery, sliced pineapple and coffee. They all served themselves, buffet style, in assorted plates and crockery, and they ate from their laps amid frustrated lamentations of their lot.

Lew thought of the letter in the glove compartment of the jeep. He had been undecided whether to deliver it, but this new, cunning strategy of Moses Harter offended his sense of justice. Genghis Khan, Lew felt, had to be curbed somehow and Peace Corps rules made in Washington seemed frail and irrelevant here in Zinzin. Genghis Khan had made the decision for him. Lew went outside, found the letter and then seated himself in a corner next to Osterlord. He handed the letter to him.

"It's addressed to you," he said, "but Link Beach gave me a note indicating it's really for Steve Muo."

Osterlord glanced sharply at Lew, then showed a small, crooked grin. "So Link hooked you into helping The Forge, huh?"

"The Forge. Is that what they call it?"

"That's what they call it," said Osterlord enigmatically. He studied Lew's face between mouthfuls of stew. "How'd you like Link Beach?"

"Okay," said Lew. "He impressed me as a real guy who thinks his country's in one hell of a mess."

"He's the man who knows," said Jim. "I'll take the letter to Steve in the morning. Why don't you come along and meet him?"

"It's a deal. Save a bed for me at your place tonight."

Osterlord left immediately after dinner and then Cindy announced that it was time for her to go to the night-school class she taught. The others loudly deplored her departure. The clan obviously was set for a long night of rum, moralizing, indignation and self-pity. Lew excused himself and left with Cindy.

Cynthia Fuller's night class for adult beginners' English was held in a room of the mud-stick government school. When they arrived, the kerosene lamp already had been lighted. Five men and one woman clustered about a rough board table. They sat on hard benches in the flickering, yellow glow of the lamp and they were bent over little paperback cartoon books of English conversational phrases.

Cindy introduced Lew as a Peace Corps friend. They all bowed to him, but Lew noted that the usual wide Mola grins were missing. There was an air of apprehension in the room. Cindy called the roll, a list of twenty-two tribal names. Sixteen pupils were absent.

"This is our worst attendance so far," she said. "Where is everybody tonight?"

The six Africans looked at one another with lowered heads, like children unwilling to tattle on a fellow pupil who has violated class rules. There was no reply.

"I see," said Cindy in a kindly voice. "Well, we'll just go ahead as though nothing had happened. Oon, you begin reading on page thirty-one, please."

Lew recognized the man at the end of the bench, a huge Mola with bulging muscles under his clean, white shirt, as Oon Gilli, the neighbor of Arlene Offenbach and the worker on Jim Osterlord's road. Gilli grinned sheepishly, placed his finger on a line of print and read slowly: "This is my house. My house has windows, a roof and two doors. My house is a small-small house." He read with painful care, each word isolated in nervous uncertainty, but he finished with a proud grin and turned around toward Corleigh to accept the plaudits of the visitor as well. Lew nodded and waved to him.

"Very good, Oon," said Cindy. "You made only one mistake. The word is 'small,' not 'small-small.' In speaking, 'small-small' is an expression we use here in Kalya. But the real word is just 'small.' "

Gilli's face was blank, and the other five showed equal lack of comprehension. Cindy carried the kerosene lamp to the tiny, cracked blackboard and wrote the word "small" in large chalked letters.

"Moona," she asked the woman, "what word is this?"

"Small-small," came the prompt reply.

"No," said Cindy patiently, "it is 'small'—s-m-a-l-l." She wrote "small-small" on the board and pointed to it.

"Pimo," she asked, "what word have I written here?"

Pimo, a man with grizzled hair who was missing two front teeth, gazed intently for several seconds. "Small-small," he said.

"Good, Pimo." She pointed to the one-syllable "small," and looked at Gilli. "Now, Oon, what word is that?"

"Small-small," replied the big man, quickly and triumphantly.

"No." Cindy's voice was soft. "It is simply 'small.' The other word is 'small-small.' This one is 'small.'"

"Don' be vexed wid me, teacha'," said Gilli.

"I'm never vexed with you," said Cindy, "but you must learn the difference. Do you all see it now?"

There was no reply, only cordial but uncomprehending neutrality on the faces of the Zinzin adult night class. Patiently, almost tenderly, Cindy Fuller spent five minutes explaining the difference. At last, she handed the chalk to Pimo and asked him to identify the two words.

"Dis one he small," said Pimo, whistling slightly through the space where his teeth were missing. He looked long and hard at the hyphenated word. "Dis one he small-small," he said. He said it cautiously, putting the word on probation for the moment.

"Exactly," Cindy's voice glowed. "Now, do we all understand?"

The six heads all bobbed and there was a shine of recognition in several pairs of eyes. Cindy returned to the table with the lamp.

"We have made progress," she said. "Progress, that means we have improved, we have learned something. Now we know which word is 'small' and which word is 'small-small.' So we say that in our lesson tonight, we have made progress. Prog-gress. Repeat it after me, class. Prog-gress."

"Prog-gress," they chorused.

Lew sighed. He had followed the laborious exercise so intently that he, too, felt drained by the class's effort. There was no breeze and the murmuring Zinzin night lay heavily on the schoolroom. The humidity was thick and sticky.

"So what kind of progress have we made tonight," asked Cindy, "large or small?"

"Small-small," cried Oon Gilli.

A roar of laughter convulsed the little class. Pimo beat his hands on the table. Moona shook her head to and fro and laughed deep in her throat. One man shouted with glee and another began alternately clapping and pointing at Cindy. Gilli beamed a hero's triumph. Oon Gilli had scored total victory in the most revered of all Mola forms of humor—humbling a supposedly superior intelligence of the West. Cynthia Fuller, the great teacher from America, had been gloriously outwitted by a tribal student. Gilli's name would be sung in the streets of Zinzin tomorrow and the whole town would know that Cindy Fuller had been bested. There would be a special satisfaction too because Miss Fuller was a Negro and therefore endowed with certain nameless knowledge that no white man could ever acquire. To humble such as Jim Osterlord or Arlene Offenbach was a precious accomplishment, but to outpoint Cynthia Fuller or Archibald Lettermore was to ascend to ecstasy. It was a full ten minutes before the class settled down. Each time Cindy tried to resume the lesson, a new mocking howl would thwart her. The rout of the West had to be rolled upon the tongue, tasted, relished.

Cindy took the ribbing gracefully, smiling at each sally. Lew found himself swept up in the glee, his sympathy with the class. He laughed so hard, he had to rub his damp eyes with a handkerchief. By the time the class finally resumed, all eight people in the room were welded by a common bond. The terror of the devil's dance was forgotten and the remainder of the adult English hour sped away on wings.

The concentration was sharper now, a new zest to the learning, and as Lew watched from the humid gloom at the rear of the mud-stick school, he felt a tingle of pride in Cindy, in the Peace Corps and, yes, even in his country. Somehow, he thought, this was good. He couldn't explain why, and perhaps no English learned here tonight would ever benefit the six eager Molas. Yet in some deep, ancient way, a human link was being forged.

Lew was glad, after all, that he'd selected the Peace Corps, and he wished he could bring all his cynical friends from the United States to sit in Cindy's African class for a night.

"Good night, small-small teacha'," cried Oon Gilli as class terminated, and the eight people laughed again as they went out into the night. Lew thought of his new acquaintances and then of the marauding Genghis Khan and, for the first time, he became deeply angry at the scheming school principal with his intricate, devil-dance strategy to advance his own interests to the detriment of the town.

He sat with Cindy in her neatly scrubbed and dusted house and they drank iced tea by the light of the stuttering kerosene lamp.

"Isn't it queer," she said. "When Oon showed his wit after that painful 'small-small' business, I was so proud of him, I almost cried. For the first time in my life, I was actually happy to be made fun of."

"I know," said Lew, "and I was on their side. I wanted you to get your nose rubbed in it, but good. Do you mind?"

"Of course not." She eyed him reflectively and sipped at her tea. There was silence a moment and then she said: "Red, you're courting me, aren't you?"

"That's an old-fashioned word," he said, "but yeah, I guess I am. But the devil dance cheated me out of the dinner you promised me."

"I'll make that up on another trip." She drank the tea and did not look at him. "Red, I thought about you all week and I decided something. I don't want you to court me or make love to me."

"Oh." He waited.

"What was the name of that country club near Evanston that you and your folks belong to?" she asked.

"That's a strange question. The Skokie at Glencoe. Why?"

"You couldn't take me in there, could you?"

"The hell I couldn't." He bristled. "I could take you anywhere I wanted to."

"But would you want to?" Her eyes were still on the glass of tea. She spoke quietly.

"Yes, I would." A blurred vision of the clubhouse, dotted

with white, hostile faces, swam into his mind. He felt vaguely defensive.

"You may think so, but I don't really believe you would." She was calm and there was no animosity in her tone. "Red, I'm awfully lonely here. I guess all the women are. I want to love and be loved, but . . ."

"But . . ."

"Oh, I don't know." She sat stiffly and she kept her face averted.

"But I don't appeal to you. That's what you mean, isn't it?"

"Oh, act your age, Red." She looked him full in the eyes this time and her attitude was that of a reproving schoolteacher. "If you don't know how attractive you are, I'm not going to swell your head by telling you."

"Thanks."

"Don't put on that hurt air. It doesn't become you."

"But," he protested, "last week you sounded as though you'd made up your mind."

"And this week it's different? Well, it is. Last week you said we were both four thousand miles from home. And we are, you know. Now, be honest. Do you think we'd be sitting, talking like this, in Evanston or Atlanta?"

He thought for a moment. "Maybe and maybe not, but hell, Cindy, we're in Kalya and we've been here almost two years. We've both learned a lot."

"Knowledge doesn't have anything to do with it." She brushed nervously at her hair. "Oh, Red. Can't you understand?"

"No, I can't." He tried not to sound petulant. "If the idea's revolting to you, well, that's it."

"Revolting?" She put her hands on his shoulders and turned him toward her. "Look at me. Do I look like a woman who's revolted? It's just that we're both going home in three months, Red, and . . . well . . . I'm just not going to get involved now."

She dropped her hands to her lap and sat studying them. Over her shoulder Lew could see the photographs of her parents and the rosewood and ebony African carvings. What was she trying to tell him?

"I guess I'm just mixed up, Red," she said. "I'm not as invulnerable as I may seem."

At the moment she did seem fragile and helpless. She was thin beneath her trim gray dress and the rose ribbon in her hair gave her a childlike appearance. He felt a rush of tenderness for her and he drew her to him and kissed her. She did not resist.

"I'm fond of you, Red," she said. "The other night you said you really didn't know or understand Negroes until you came over here. Well, the same goes for me with whites. Over here, I've learned to understand. Alice and Dotty are riots, aren't they? Arlene is sweet and idealistic. I don't care much for Ted Kramer, but I admire Jim Osterlord even if he is withdrawn and patronizing to the rest of us. I hope I can be their friend always, but especially yours, Red."

"You want me just as a friend?" His voice sounded as though he were abused.

"Not 'just' a friend. A friend, period. Is that so little a thing? I think it's a great deal."

How many men over the centuries had been shelved by women who wanted them as "friends"? There must have been millions. And he'd bet not one of them liked it.

"But why? You didn't sound like that the other night."

She looked at him gravely. "I told you I'm vulnerable sometimes. Do I have to spell out why? . . . No, I don't. You understand as well as I do."

"Maybe so." He smiled. "I guess you hurt my male ego. You know you're spurning me."

"Spurning you? It's just the other way around. I'm saying you're the kind of sweet person I'd like to have as a friend all my life. I'd like to think we could get together back in the States and share our memories here." She smiled. "Although not at the Skokie Country Club, if you don't mind."

"I suppose I have to accept," he said, "but I don't have to be taken. You're just a woman who's found a new excuse to retain her virtue."

Her slow smile spread. "Pretty good act too, isn't it? Better than the devil's dance. I scared you."

"Small-small," he said, and they both laughed.

The sense of affection and well-being that he'd experienced

in the schoolroom gradually settled on him anew. "I admire you, Cindy," he said. "You're what a volunteer ought to be."

"Thanks, pal." She pumped his hand with mock masculine heartiness. "Then it's buddies."

"Buddies," he said. They laughed again, but over her shoulder he could see the mosquito netting draped above her bed and he felt a stab of regret. God, this could be a lonely country sometimes.

They talked for an hour of the Peace Corps, Genghis Khan, Oon Gilli and the unknown rites of the Golo bush school, and when he got ready to leave, she kissed him on the cheek.

"You know something?" She tilted her head and eyed him speculatively. "There was a moment a while ago when . . . if you'd hauled me into the bedroom, I would have gone."

"Now you tell me." Why did she have to say that? "I'm not the type, I guess."

"I know. That's why I like you."

Jim Osterlord was snoring when Lew reached his house. Lew undressed in the dark and climbed between damp sheets on the spare bed. He was irritated and restless, and his thoughts of Cindy grated like sandpaper. Then he thought of her standing patiently and proudly while the adult night class hooted its glee over the small-small victory. He knew the scene would remain in his mind for many years. When he finally fell asleep, it was in a mood of gentle melancholy. He dreamed that he was seeing for the last time a pleasant town where he had lived and where warm memories clung to every road, bush and tree.

6

It was mid-morning as Lewis Corleigh and James Osterlord drove toward the district commissioner's building in the Peace Corps jeep wagon. Already the heat welled about them like that from a giant oven. Languid dogs sought the haven of storefront shadows and the throngs of directionless humanity moved in Zinzin's streets with an ageless torpor. Lew drove slowly, his hand never far from the horn. Osterlord, dressed in khaki shorts and his thick country-cloth shirt, waved abstractedly to native friends. He was intent on his explanation to Corleigh.

"They've got Steve in a box," he was saying. "The trouble is that the district commissioner doesn't have many powers. He's supposed to be the government here, but just what that involves is left kind of vague, probably intentionally so."

"As Maureen Sutherland would say, the job's 'unstructured,'" said Lew.

"You said it. Steve is supposed to have the last word on everything, but when the town gets in a real hassle, like this thing of Genghis trying to shut down the school, the people revert to tribal custom. They like Steve, but they're scared stiff by the town devil—and that bastard, Genghis, has the devil sewed up and the paramount chief along with him."

"You're gabby this morning, pal," said Lew.

"If you're going to work with The Forge," said Jim, "you've got to understand the background."

"I never said I would," protested Lew.

"You brought Link's letter."

"That's because of Genghis and the school—"

"Right," Osterlord cut in. He grinned and raked a hand through his disheveled mop of hair. "And what's wrong with Zinzin is what's wrong with Kalya. That's why you ought to know what's behind the deal here."

Osterlord had begun the explanation back at his house while smoking his acrid, after-breakfast Mola cigar, and after dispatching Freddie, the houseboy, on his daily errands. Much of the history of Zinzin and the Molas Corleigh already knew, but Osterlord was determined to repeat the story with particular application to his friend Steve Muo.

For centuries, he said, Zinzin had been the ruling seat of the Mola tribe. Here sat the paramount chief and two of his subordinates in the Mola chain of authority, a clan chief and a town chief. Long before the birth of Christ, they had dispensed justice under rude, unwritten tribal law, set the annual rice levy, arbitrated the interminable disputes which so enchanted the litigious Molas and provided for the instruction of the young through the secret Golo and Mata societies. They were at once the civilian chiefs and the guardians of the Mola religion, a simple form of animism.

The Molas lived in precarious balance with the land, but they also developed some industrial arts. When the first white explorers came many years ago, they found an advanced iron-working community with smelters and forges and proud artisans skilled in their use. Later, with the influx of mass-produced trade goods, the iron art fell into decay and only a few withered old men could now remember the days of the forge and the bellows.

The Mola chiefs ruled wisely or foolishly, benignly or malignantly, according to the man, in the manner of rulers of all ages and continents. Some Mola chiefs, corrupted by Arab traders, sold their people into slavery across the Atlantic. With the later advent of The Family's government in Ft. Paul—the Vinings, the Fesses, the Booths, the Downings—new Mola chiefs were seduced by handsome gifts from The Family and they acquiesced when forced labor was thrust upon the Molas. The people worked on Family farms and plantations for pittance wages and came to accept their harsh, impoverished lot as a way of life sanctioned by their chiefs.

Then along came a young man named Steven Muo, son of a late clan chief and thus presumed to be deft in the skills of politics and palaver. Muo joined Old Number One's Democratic Justice party and voiced his allegiance to Ft. Paul. At the same time, he became a forceful wrangler in the palaver hut and he began to espouse a strange, new doctrine—that the Molas actually could influence their destiny through the ballot. Old Number One, bending judiciously with the democratic winds sweeping Africa, had opened the vote to all adults in Kalya. Now the Molas, argued Muo, should vote as a bloc, ready to support their friends and defeat their enemies, so that Ft. Paul could never take the tribe's faithfulness for granted. Elders muttered uncertainly over this advice, unsure as to just what a vote meant or what it might achieve. But the young flocked to Muo's leadership and, suddenly, on the eve of the last national election, the realization hit Old Number One that a political threat had risen in remote Zinzin.

Accordingly, Kalya's patriarch moved swiftly and, in the opinion of Ft. Paul's embassy row, cannily. He appointed Steven Muo the government's district commissioner for all the high bushlands of the Molas, the first tribal man in Kalya to hold such an important post. In Ft. Paul, where astonishment and consternation swept The Family, the Canadian ambassador was heard to remark at a reception one night: "Old Number One has improved on the Americans' political motto. With him, it's 'If you can't lick 'em, join 'em to you.'" In time The Family's fears were allayed and members became convinced once more of their leader's shrewdness. For Muo safely endorsed all The Family candidates for Parliament in Mola territory. Family candidates won with only the usual token opposition tolerated by Democratic Justice leaders in Kalya's one-party regime. District Commissioner Muo, they said, was only a figurehead, a man of limited intelligence whose talents provided no real threat to the system. If you wanted to do business in Zinzin, they whispered,

Moses Harter was your Family man, the subterranean but actual power in Mola land.

The government invested the new commissioner with the façade of authority. The old mud-stick building was razed and in its place was erected a fine, four-room concrete structure with cool floors of figured tile, metal screens and an imposing red tile roof. For once Moses Harter, the contractor, did not chisel on the specifications. He did not have to. The profit allowed by Ft. Paul was bountiful. The new building crested a small hill on the main road. Flowers bordered a pebble walk in front and from the flagpole flew the red and yellow banner of Kalya.

"When Steve finally realized they had him set up as nothing but a figurehead," said Osterlord as they drove toward the building, "he got sore, but good. That's when they started the underground and named it The Forge in memory of the old iron-working days. Now comes its first big test."

Corleigh parked in the curving gravel driveway, then turned to Osterlord as he switched off the ignition key. "Jim, level with me. I know you're working with The Forge or whatever they call it. But do you belong to it?"

Osterlord paused with one tanned leg thrust out of the jeep. "Red, for a smart guy, you ask too many questions."

A tiled corridor led to the commissioner's office. The door was open. The room's simple furniture consisted of a metal desk with kerosene lamp, several chairs and two filing cabinets. On the wall, behind the desk, hung the seal of Kalya between two crossed Mola spears, fashioned in the old days when smiths plied the iron trade.

Commissioner Muo rose to greet them. He was a stocky man of solemn mien reflecting no fixed age. The face was pure Mola, strong-featured, prominent, wide nose and cheekbones, the skin a smooth, deep black. His wiry black hair was close-cropped. He wore dark trousers with a neatly laundered short-sleeved white shirt which exposed thick, heavy arms. Chest muscles bulged under the shirt.

Osterlord introduced Corleigh as a Peace Corps courier. Muo gripped Lew's outstretched hand with unexpected pressure. They ended the clasp with the Kalya snap of index fingers.

Osterlord handed Beach's letter to Muo and spoke rapidly in

Mola. The commissioner, frowning, read the letter slowly, then reread it, his lips moving as he did so. Muo spoke briefly to Osterlord in Mola. Jim, in response, closed the office door. Muo sat down, indicating chairs for the two Peace Corps men.

"Mist' Beach say you carry lett' for us?" Muo directed the question unsmilingly at Corleigh.

"Well . . ." Lew hesitated. If this was the moment of decision, he was unready for it. He turned to Osterlord. "Tell him about the rules," he said. "You know, about not meddling in Kalya politics." What had started as simple curiosity seemed to be propelling Lew toward an unknown destination—and faster than he cared to go.

Osterlord addressed Muo in Mola and a full exchange followed. Muo glanced appraisingly at Corleigh several times. At last Muo nodded and spoke to Lew in his truncated English.

"What you t'ink Mose' Hart'?" he asked. "He vex you?"

"He vex me plenny," replied Lew.

"Bad man. He eat da money. He close da school." Muo voiced his English in a deep, singsong cadence. "Hart' humbug Mola man an' Peez-kor too. Ever't'ing in Zinzin chac-la." Muo paused, then added contemptuously, "Hart' no Mola. He Fam'ly."

The commissioner fell silent and fixed Corleigh with an expectant, unwavering stare. The case had been presented to the jury with overwhelming evidence for conviction and the prosecuting attorney was waiting confidently for the verdict. Corleigh looked beseechingly at Osterlord, but Jim's only reaction was a tight smile.

"Eh, man," said Muo. "You say you pineapple. Let see yo' juice."

Corleigh frowned, puzzled. The idiom was new to him.

"Put up or shut up?" he asked Osterlord.

Jim nodded, still with the small, taunting smile.

Lew felt himself being drawn irresistibly to this stolid tribal man and to his alliance with Lincoln Beach, whatever it was. There was more than impulse, he told himself, for he trusted Jim Osterlord and Jim obviously was partially committed, perhaps totally. Besides, the alternative, a flaccid neutrality in the face of Genghis Khan's depredations, was an odious one. He thought of the devil's dance and he thought of Cindy and her adult pupils huddled about a kerosene lamp. If the Peace Corps meant anything . . . Lew felt exhilarated by what he was about to say.

"All right," he said. "I'll do what I can. But let's be careful. Christ, if Williams ever found out . . ."

"We could really blow it," finished Osterlord. He spoke to Muo again in Mola. Muo nodded vigorously.

"Good. Finish palavah one time," he said.

The question was closed. Lew had agreed to aid an organization aligned against The Family, something called The Forge, and he experienced an odd sensation of relief at his enlistment.

That issue settled, Muo turned quickly to the problem of Moses Harter. He spoke of his dilemma in halting, painfully chopped English. A law of Parliament, initiated by Old Number One, expressly provided that Golo and Mata bush schools could be held only during the long winter vacations of the government schools. Now Moses Harter defied that law for private gain, and the dance of the town devil had so terrified the community that no one in Zinzin would dare protest. Lew noted that Muo spoke of the devil with awe in the manner of a man who glimpses the truth but cannot bring himself to know it fully. Several times Muo interrupted his English to talk with Osterlord in Mola. One long, troubled silent period was followed by a flood of words in the Mola tongue.

"He's decided there's only one thing to do," said Jim, "to go down to Ft. Paul and lay the case before Old Number One, charging Genghis with breaking the law."

Muo nodded assent. "Maybe no way," he said darkly.

"But he's got to try," added Osterlord. "The only thing is, he hasn't got any way to get down to Ft. Paul."

"How about his car?" asked Lew. Zinzin boasted two private passenger vehicles, Harter's new red Mustang and Muo's 1955 model Chevrolet.

Muo smiled for the first time. "Eh, ya. Dat t'ing chac-la."

"The generator doesn't work," said Jim, "and the differential's kaput. Also there's no tread left on the rear tires. Outside of that, it's a real go-go rig."

"How about the money bus?" asked Lew.

Muo stood up and pulled at his pants pockets. They contained two coins which he juggled in his hand.

"Jeez, man," said Jim, "the bus costs twenty-eight bucks a round trip. That's two weeks' salary for a commissioner."

"Well?" Lew could sense what was coming.

Osterlord spoke to Muo again in Mola and Muo's solemn features brightened.

"You could take him down at night," said Jim. "If you leave right after dark, you could make it by dawn to Ft. Paul."

"Hell, Jim," objected Lew, "that's two strikes on me to start with."

Williams had forbidden Peace Corps drivers to carry other than American citizens since the death last year of a Lebanese merchant in a jeep accident. The rule against making the Zinzin–Ft. Paul trip at night was unwritten but firmly cemented by common consent—and common sense.

"That road's hairy enough in the daytime," said Lew.

"No problem, Red." Osterlord's tone was that of a sergeant giving orders to a new recruit.

Osterlord and Muo had another exchange in Mola and then the commissioner shook hands with both Americans.

"He'll be at my place a little before seven tonight," explained Osterlord. "That'll give you about ten hours of darkness. Ought to be enough. You can spend the day sleeping."

Lew was surprised and mildly resentful at Osterlord's failure to consult further Lew's own wishes, and he recalled the first time he'd had the same reaction. It was almost nine years ago when he'd received his first orders as an Army private. Now, as then, he wondered just what he'd gotten himself into.

At Osterlord's house, Freddie gave them the latest news. The houseboy, fresh from his errands in town, said Friday would be the last day of government school. All boys under sixteen years of age would go to the Golo bush school on Saturday, perhaps for a month, perhaps longer. As always, the site of the jungle encampment was secret. It was taboo to search for the location, and the few uninitiated who trespassed on sacred Golo terrain never returned to tell about it. There was other gossip. A young girl had seared her arm badly over a cooking pot this morning and it was rumored that she had inadvertently seen the devil for an instant yesterday. The terrified girl denied it, but she refused to go to the clinic for treatment of the burn. Some said that proved her guilt and Freddie agreed.

"She see devil small-small one time," he said, nodding his head knowingly.

Lew spent the remainder of the morning trying to sleep. The effort was unsuccessful. Two flies circled his head and if he pulled the sheet over his face, the heat proved intolerable. Even lying naked beneath the sheet, he became drenched with sweat. He dozed once, but sat up with a start when he realized, from somewhere in his subconscious, that he had forgotten to take his weekly dose of chloroquine that morning. He fumbled in his medical kit while recalling Ted Kramer's serious attack of falciparum malaria last fall. Lew found two tablets, then went to the kitchen and washed them down with water from the crockery filter, a standard item in Peace Corps households. When he returned to bed, sleep was impossible and he read through a month-old copy of the overseas edition of *Time*, two tattered copies of *Look* and a soiled brochure entitled "Reptiles of Kalya," prepared by the Peace Corps' first staff physician in Kalya four years ago. Lew was edified to learn that his prime enemies in the poisonous snake world were vipers, cobras and black mambas in that order of virulence. He had yet to see a viper or a cobra, but he still remembered, with a chill, the mamba he had encountered on the bush trail.

He finally fell asleep in early afternoon and dreamed of a bustling European city that he supposed was Paris. The figure 83, his remaining days of service in Kalya, flashed on and off from a huge electric sign near a boulevard café where he sat. Every other table was occupied by sleek, stylish women. All the faces, soft and luminous, were turned toward Lew and on each was written a subtle invitation. He awakened to find Jim Osterlord shaking his shoulder.

"Freddie's fixed some country chop," said Jim. "Steve will be here soon."

The houseboy was dismissed right after the evening meal. Muo arrived on foot a few minutes later with the first screen of darkness. Muo stowed a cheap, frayed suitcase in the rear of the wagon and then, at Jim's suggestion, he crouched on the floor-boards between the front and rear seats.

Lew threaded the jeep slowly through Zinzin's streets, which were as choked with people and animals as a morning market. Fires smoldered beside mud huts, and kerosene lamps in the Lebanese stores threw fragile spears of light to the roadway. The congestion thinned as the jeep moved to the outskirts of town and far off to the right, on a slight incline, Lew could see a small amber glow where Cindy Fuller taught her night English class. He could imagine her black hair tied with a rose ribbon and her patient ways as she instructed Oon Gilli and the grizzled Pimo. Lew brooded over the picture and he felt both tender and sad.

Beyond Zinzin the high bush vaulted into the jagged night shapes of the forest trees, the red oaks, the limbas, sapelli and mahogany. The stars were out, the oppressive humidity of daytime had lifted and the air had a sharpness refreshing to the skin. From the jungle came the plaintive call of the black kite, roosting after a day of scavenging. Otherwise the bush was silent, and the metallic banging of the jeep filled the night.

Lew braked to a halt under a tall dabema tree which spread its leafy crown so widely that the stars were blotted from sight.

"Come on up front," he said to Muo. "It'll be okay now."

Muo settled gratefully into the cushioned seat beside Lew and watched closely while Lew showed him how to buckle the seat-belt. Muo unclasped and fastened the buckle several times, then pulled the belt tight with a grunt of satisfaction. The commis-sioner lit a cigarette and smoked in silence while the jeep wagon began its long, lurching journey to the capital.

Through the night Muo alternated between dozes and wrench-ing efforts at conversation. Aware of Lew's difficulty in under-standing him, Muo spoke slowly and tried vainly to pronounce each English syllable. He praised the Peace Corps, spoke with admiration of Jim Osterlord and told of his vow to break The Family's throttling grip on the life of the Molas. By unexpected questions, Muo revealed flashes of knowledge about the world beyond Kalya which surprised Corleigh. Muo seemed to know as much about Europe and America as he did about his own country.

"Where Harvar'?" he asked once after a long period of silence during which the jungle seemed to slide past like darkened, camouflaged ships at sea.

"Harvard?" repeated Lew. "That's at Cambridge, right next to Boston in the state of Massachusetts."

"Oh, Bost'? Dat place da Pres'dent Ken-ned-y!"

"That's right, Steve." Lew glanced at his seatmate. "What did you think of Kennedy?"

"He hero. He mah fren'. I cry dat time he shot. Hear radio in Leban' stoah. I go home and cry one long time dat night."

There it was again, that bewildering African affection for the slain American president. Lew had heard similar stories throughout Kalya. In the most isolated hut villages, men and women could remember where they were and what they were doing the night they heard the news from Dallas. Many said they cried, even as Lew did when he left off throwing a football behind the fraternity house at Penn State and went to his room to be alone. What was the puzzling human chemistry that linked the black men of Africa to that poised, brittle, witty, urbane young white man from Boston? In the movie theater in Ft. Paul, Lew had heard cheers and strangled wails when Kennedy's face appeared on the screen in an old news clip. In a Loli hut he had seen Kennedy's picture framed in fresh flowers, and at Kpapata a desiccated crone gained queenlike renown because of her boast that a grandson in Guinea had voyaged to America and seen John Kennedy's grave. Kennedy had been killed almost three years ago, but his name and face lived in Kalya as though touched with magic.

"Jim Ost'lor'," said Muo. "He go Harvar' too. He like son da Ken-ned-y."

Lew eyed Muo in pleasant surprise. "That's what the people in the Dominican Republic called the Peace Corps," he said, " 'the children of Kennedy.' "

"For true?" Muo repeated the phrase several times, testing it for rhythm. "Da chil-dren da Ken-ned-y." He appeared to like the sound and he smiled briefly at Corleigh, rumbled a contented growl and fell asleep again.

The journey seemed endless. At night the jungle appeared to enfold the road as though in an effort to make it captive. The conical bug-a-bug mounds sat like giant dunce caps, fey guardians of the shadows. The high bush leaned toward the car, silent, opaque, the heavy shapes walling off the sky so that only a thin river of stars was visible above the road. The jeep's generator was faulty and the headlights shone dimly no more than fifty feet in front of the car. Thus Lew failed to avoid several large depressions and once the front end slammed into a hole with such violence, Lew feared the axle might crack. He reduced speed after that and calculated he was barely maintaining the thirty miles an hour average necessary to reach Ft. Paul before daylight. He halted once to pour gasoline into the tank from the emergency can he carried at the rear of the wagon. Then the jarring ride began again and his back ached, telling him that his kidneys were rebelling once more.

The stilled bush had an ominous quality in the hours after midnight, but occasional flashes of movement disclosed its hidden life. Once Lew saw two shining pinpoints of light to his left and then a vanishing form that had the imprecise outline of a leopard. Several times a free-tailed bat fled through the fringe of the headlight's beam, and once he glimpsed a lion monkey on a tree limb.

When the jungle would end abruptly, signaling another roadside enclave of darkened huts, the sky spread suddenly above as if through opened doors, revealing whole cities of stars and a sliver of pale moon. Once, when Muo was awake, Lew gestured toward the sky and remarked on the beauty, but Muo gave no sign of shared appreciation. Africans, Lew had noted, rarely spoke of the majesty of their land and its heavens. Perhaps life was too harsh, too close to the bone of want for the nurture of pleasing imagery.

They saw but one person along the road during the night, an old man squatting beside a hut. Only three vehicles passed them, a food truck and two passenger cars. The night stretched like a long, lone ribbon, the road a prisoner of the jungle. The first gray of dawn limned the eastern horizon when they reached the paved section leading the last fifty miles to Ft. Paul.

Steve Muo came awake with the increase of speed on the smooth macadam. Lew pressed the accelerator and rolled along at fifty miles an hour.

"That's better, huh?" he said. "We ought to make it in little more than an hour now."

Muo stretched and lit another cigarette.

"I give Ol' Num' One plenny humbug dis day," he said. His jaw set in anticipation.

"I'm with you . . ." Lew began.

There was a roar to the rear and a man on a motorcycle was beside Lew in quick blur. The rider swept a hand to the side. Lew slowed down and stopped on the dirt shoulder.

"Boot' man," whispered Muo. He averted his face toward the right window and threw out his cigarette.

The cyclist came to the car beside Lew's open window. He wore black pants and puttees and a white shirt with an insignia on the right sleeve. Lew knew that he was one of Colonel Hulbert Booth's men, but the interception surprised him. The security police patrolled the paved section of the road as an extension of their mission to protect Old Number One's person, but Lew had no idea they were on duty at such an hour.

"You break speed," said the elite policeman.

Kalya had no posted speed zones outside the city of Ft. Paul and, so far as Lew knew, no legal limits. "I was only doing fifty," he said. "Anyway, there's no traffic."

"You bust da law," said the officer. "What you do heah dis time?"

"Peace Corps emergency," said Lew.

"Eh, ya." The policeman leaned his elbows on the car door and grinned. "What you keepin' fo' me, man?"

"I never pay dash," said Lew. "We're not allowed to."

The man's face hardened. "Who say 'dash'?" He nodded toward Muo who was still half-turned away. "Who yo' fren'?"

"He's from outcountry," said Lew. "His stomach hurtin'."

The officer leaned into the car to get a better view of Muo. He frowned for a moment, then withdrew his head. He motioned them down the road.

"I let you go one time," he said. The tone was unfriendly. "You go slow, Peez-kor fellah."

Lew started the jeep again and drove toward Ft. Paul at a sedate thirty-five miles an hour. In the rear-view mirror, he could see the motorcycle, its headlight on low beam, following them.

"He Fam'ly," said Muo with distaste. "He want five dollah."

"I know," said Lew, "and he can wait for it until hell freezes over."

"Dash!" Muo spit out the word. "Dat Boot', he take two dollah ever' five. Boot', Fam'ly, dey vex me plenny." Muo clenched his fists and sat rigidly, staring ahead.

The cycle followed them steadily, maintaining an even interval, past the ordered rows of plantation rubber trees, past the sleeping villages and past the tin shanties which marked the outskirts of Ft. Paul. Dawn spread its hushed orange-gray patina as they entered the city, and the motorcycle veered off on a side street. Then the upper rim of the sun appeared beside the looming bulk of Founders House, and the first fingers of the day's coming heat probed the jeep's open windows. Muo indicated a street and then a house, and Lew stopped the car in front of a sagging wooden structure. Two Africans were sleeping on a narrow porch. Lew recognized the building as tribal rooming house where accommodations could be had for forty cents a night inside and fifteen cents on the porch. A refuse dump beside the paintless house exuded a stench of decay, and a mottled cat poked warily amid the rusting tin cans.

Lew let down the jeep's tailgate and dragged out Muo's dented suitcase. The two men shook hands, Muo said his thanks and then walked up the creaking stairs to the porch. Lew stood a moment, wondering, after Muo disappeared into the house. Was this stolid, inarticulate man to be a new force in Kalya? Muo impressed him as a man of sincerity and determination, but one of limited resources; a man who seethed under the callous rule of The Family but who had few tools with which to fashion his anger into action. Old Number One held the vast power skein of an entrenched autocracy. Steve Muo seemed to hold nothing but his frail, battered suitcase in a cheap, odorous rooming house. Yet, perhaps, working with Lincoln Beach in The Forge . . . The Forge? Just what was it, anyway? Lew had pledged his help, but for what? A series of protests? An election battle? A fight to rally the tribes in redress of wrongs? Revolution? Lew drove to the hostel in a mood of restless doubt. In the Kalya vernacular, he had put his hand inside, but inside what?

The hostel had the stillness of early morning when Lew

parked the jeep and walked wearily into the kitchen. He had
been on the road almost twelve hours. His muscles were stiff with
fatigue, his stomach felt bloated and his head ached. The thought
of breakfast was unappealing and he contented himself with a
glass of pineapple juice. In the room where the volunteer leaders
slept, there were the heavy breathing sounds of slumber. He undressed quickly, slid into his bunk and was asleep within minutes.

When he awoke, it was night again. The other men had finished
supper and left, so he ate alone in the kitchen, munching on
cold chicken, fried plantain and sliced bananas. Arthur, the houseboy, sloshed about the kitchen sink and placed dishes in the
drying rack. Lew could see they were still covered with a film of
grease. Arthur loved music with his work and from the hostel
record player came the muffled, erotic pleasurings of Eartha Kitt.
The room was moistly cloying and there was the smell of rain in
the air. Arthur, returning from a trip to the garbage can outside,
brought news.

"White fellah outside want palavah you," he said, gesturing
toward the rear of the house.

The man standing under the twisted whismore tree wore gray
slacks and a madras jacket. His tie was knotted despite the
burdensome evening heat. The tan of his face extended over his
brow to thinning brown hair. He wore black-rimmed spectacles
and he moistened his lips with his tongue as he put out his hand.

"Mr. Corleigh? I'm Bruce Kellogg. Political officer at the embassy."

Lew tightened. Like other Peace Corps workers, he bracketed
U.S. embassy officials with foreign members of the diplomatic
set, all to be dealt with politely, warily and as infrequently as
possible. The enameled niceties of embassy row were a long way
from the cutlasses, charcoal fires and shrunken breasts of outcountry.

"Glad to meet you," said Lew with less than complete honesty.

"I just wanted to get to know you," said Kellogg with cheery
informality. "Since I had a free night, I thought I'd drop by."

"Sure. Well, come on in."

"Oh," said Kellogg, "this is all right. It's hot enough out here."

"It's a little hard to talk here though." Lew pointed to the Fizi
encampment. The tin and zinc shacks framed a medley of noises.

Dogs growled, babies whimpered and the old men were growing
querulous over their palm wine.

"Frankly," said Kellogg, licking his lips in an odd, slow motion,
"I'd just as soon try it here. I wanted to talk to you privately."
He nodded toward the house.

The embassy man offered Lew a cigarette and when Lew declined, he lit one and leaned against the yellowish brown trunk
of the ancient whismore.

"What can I do for you?" asked Lew.

Kellogg's easy smile seemed to take note of Lew's guarded tone.
"I know the Peace Corps doesn't care to mix too much with us
white-collar types," he said. "By and large, I think that's a healthy
attitude. After all, you're here to help the people, and we're here
to keep Washington on the old policy-straight-and-narrow. Two
different jobs, what? I can't say we have the best of it either.
Sometimes I envy you characters the simple life."

Lew tensed. The simple life of flies, tainted fruits, smelly latrines
and tepid water trickling out of oil drums? He waited without
comment. Kellogg inhaled deeply and blew a smoke ring.

"My particular job as political officer is gathering information.
Here in Ft. Paul, that's easy enough, but outcountry, it's something else. I'll level with you, Mr. Corleigh. Outcountry we know
next to nothing. You know the communications problem, what?
And for a white man like me—not being Peace Corps—to gain
anything significant by traveling—well, you can appreciate my
problem."

"Yeah," said Lew unsympathetically. We've all got a problem,
mister, he thought. "I suppose it's rough."

"That's why I came to you," said Kellogg. "You travel the road
to Zinzin. Pretty often, don't you?"

"Once a week round-trip."

"That's what I was told. To come to the point, Mr. Corleigh,
I hear there's some kind of political trouble up in Zinzin, and I
need your help. What can you tell me about it?"

Lew frowned. What he thought he knew, he wasn't sure of yet.
And what he surmised, he wasn't about to disclose to a stranger.

"Have you got some kind of credentials?" asked Lew. "A card
or something?"

Kellogg pulled a wallet from his jacket pocket and flipped open the card section. There was a laminated State Department card, with photograph, identifying Bruce Kellogg as an embassy officer.

Lew still stalled. "How do I know you're not CIA? . . . We're not supposed to talk to the agency."

"Central Intelligence?" asked Kellogg. "Well, you don't, I suppose. I assure you I'm the embassy political officer. You'll just have to take me on faith, Lew."

Corleigh noted the casual switch to his first name as well as the fact that Kellogg evaded the question. His feeling of random antagonism sharpened.

"I'm sorry," he said. "I'm afraid I can't help much. There is a squabble on up there, all mixed up with tribal stuff, and it's hard to straighten out. I really don't have the pitch on it yet."

"Oh, come off it, Lew. After all, you make Zinzin once a week. There are seven Peace Corps people up there and you must get some pretty reliable information from them."

"Look, Mr. Kellogg," said Lew, "even if I did have the right dope, I couldn't go around blabbing it. You know as well as I do that it would compromise the Peace Corps in Kalya if word got around that we reported what we heard to the embassy."

"I agree," said Kellogg. He blew another smoke ring. "There are, however, times when any sound practice must be breached out of necessity. What?"

Lew said nothing. Kellogg, leaning against the tree, was studying his face. From the hostel came the sibilant enticements of Eartha Kitt and in the Fizi squatters' camp a child squalled.

"Lew," said Kellogg, "I don't believe you're quite as naive about the Zinzin situation as you pretend."

"Meaning?"

Kellogg moistened his lips with the circular movement of his tongue. "Well," he said with exaggerated casualness, "I think if I had driven a district commissioner to Ft. Paul last night, I would have talked quite a lot of politics."

Lew started. "Where did you hear that?"

"It's my business to hear things." Kellogg's smile was not without pride.

Let's see, thought Lew, only Jim Osterlord, Steve Muo and himself knew . . . or, perhaps, that motorcycle security man? The cop had looked across at Steve once. Yes, that must be it. The

Family's intelligence net was operating. But how did the word get from Colonel Booth and his men to the American embassy? Lew eyed Kellogg closely. If he weren't a CIA agent, he gave a good impersonation of one. Lew felt cornered.

Kellogg watched him a moment, an amused look on his face, then straightened up from the tree trunk and took a step toward Corleigh.

"I understand," he said. He adjusted his eyeglasses on the bridge of his nose. "I know how you feel about breaking rules, and if it's policy not to report to the embassy, well, that's it."

"I guess that's the way it has to be," said Lew, relieved.

"A Peace Corps volunteer should always obey the rules," continued Kellogg. He paused. "And by the way, Lew, isn't it an infraction of your rules to ride a Kalya national in a Peace Corps vehicle?"

Anger flashed over Lew. "Yes," he said. He felt if he said more, his temper might flare openly.

"Well, think it over," said Kellogg, again with the catlike lick at his lips. "There are times when a man owes a duty to his country, what? If you decide to help, drop by the embassy. Tomorrow, if you wish."

The embassy officer snapped a mock farewell salute to Corleigh and walked out to the roadway. The madras jacket melted into the night and Lew realized, with a start, that he had been suavely threatened with blackmail. If Kellogg had still been there at the moment, Lew would have hit him.

7

Lew Corleigh's anger had subsided by the next morning when he parked the jeep behind Peace Corps headquarters but, in a fit of introspection, he puzzled over his own reactions. He had talked freely of politics to foes of The Family—to Steve Muo and Lincoln Beach—yet he had refused to talk to an officer of his own embassy. Could that be justified, he wondered. He had bridled at Kellogg. There was something about him, a tacit assumption of authority, perhaps, or that curious habit of moistening his lips, which offended Lew. And the bald reference to violating Peace Corps vehicle rules was Lew's first taste of blackmail. The memory again infuriated him.

"By the look on your face," said a small, brisk voice, "a penny for your thoughts would be a bargain."

He had almost collided with Prudence Stauffer in the office doorway. Her freckled arms were loaded with books and her Kalya-woven handbag dangled from a hand. As usual, she wore no make-up and her plain little face was fixed in its sober, work-aday expression.

"Sorry, Prudence," he said. "I guess I'm not awake yet."

She clutched the books to her thin bosom and frowned at him. Lew noted the prim line between her eyebrows and her determined manner of cocking her head. Prudence Stauffer, staff member, was about to interrogate a volunteer. Duty summoned. Volunteer morale came first and one had to express an interest in each man and woman. Lew grinned in anticipation.

"How are things in Zinzin?" Prudence asked.

"You sound as if you really wanted to know," he said lightly.

"Of course I do." By way of proof, she placed the books and handbag on the reception desk and stood waiting, an intent expression on her face. Her small chin, too pointed for grace, thrust forward.

"Prudence," he said, "why don't you shake that bun out of your hair? We need a little glamour out here. Why go around looking like an old maid mission-school teacher?"

"Here to work," she said. "Not here to flirt."

"Hey, honey, that almost rhymes."

"Stop it, Red," she said severely. "Want to know what's going on in Zinzin."

Lew sighed. "Plenty. Frankly, the joint's a mess. Genghis Khan is on the rampage again. He's going to close the school and yank all the boys into the bush. And the devil danced, the town is scared stiff and there's all hell to pay."

"Really!" Prudence folded her arms and planted her feet wide apart. "Hope you're going to tell the rep?"

Lew flicked his shoulders. "Oh, I'll fill him in, but there's not much Williams can do. We made a personal complaint to Downing the last time I was down. You know Downing. He couldn't care less."

"Hate it when the PCVs can't operate," she said. "Something ought to be done."

"Hell, honey, it's the system. Unless somebody breaks the hold of The Family on the tribes, we can't do much. It's the same old story."

Prudence pursed her lips and cocked her head again. "Not sure that's the answer. We've just got to work harder."

"And flirt less, huh?" Her look of utter concern matched her rooted stance. Lew grinned. "You try too hard, honey. Why don't you undo that bun, and I'll take you out on the town some night?"

"You're impossible." She gathered up her books and bag and

strode to the door. Then she paused, turned around and surveyed him seriously. "You're a good worker, Red. Maybe I will one night. . . . We'll see."

And she clicked the door sharply behind her. Lew turned to find Carter Williams standing in the doorway of his own office.

"That's one date I'd like to see," said Williams. "I don't think that woman has been anywhere for fun since she arrived in Kalya."

"Any sacrifice I can make for staff morale," offered Lew.

"Ready for extra duty, huh?" Williams smiled briefly, then erased it. "Step into my office, will you, Lew? There's something I'd like to discuss with you."

The Peace Corps chief closed the office door behind them, indicated a chair for Corleigh and settled himself somewhat awkwardly in his swivel chair. He squared a memo pad on the desk blotter and cleared his throat. Lew could sense that what Williams was about to say was offensive to him, a breach in office tranquillity.

"I got a call from Ambassador Milbank this morning," said Williams. All American agencies in Ft. Paul were connected to the U.S. embassy by special field telephones, the only phone system in Kalya. "He was a bit perturbed, for Milbank. He said he understood the Peace Corps was meddling in internal politics in Zinzin and he wanted a report."

Williams' plump face showed worry lines. He clicked open a penknife and began digging at his fingernails.

"Of course, I told him I'd have to wait until you came in." He darted a swift glance at Corleigh, probing his face for reaction. "Just what is the situation up there?"

"Genghis Khan again," said Lew promptly. "Same thing we went to see Downing about, only worse." He recounted the recent incidents.

Williams' frown deepened. "That sounds farfetched, a man going to all that length, devil dance and all, just so he can practice law," he said.

"You've got to know old Genghis," countered Lew. "Besides, this is basically a struggle between Harter and Muo over the whole system. It's The Family against the Molas."

"Where is Muo now?" Williams eyed his nails as he asked the question.

Lew sensed at once that Williams had been informed of Muo's night journey in a Peace Corps vehicle. The embassy's intelligence lines apparently extended into Colonel Booth's office, or that of Old Number One, perhaps both. Was Bruce Kellogg, the man in the madras jacket, the link? Lew was troubled, but he realized this was no time to be evasive.

"I brought Muo down in the jeep night before last," said Corleigh. "I suppose you already know that?"

Williams nodded.

"I know I wasn't supposed to," said Lew, "but Muo had to put his case before Old Number One, and he had no other way to get down."

Williams tapped the desk with his penknife and when he spoke, he ignored the rules infraction. Lew was grateful for the lack of reprimand.

"I just don't like this business generally," said Williams. "It's one thing to protest to Commissioner Downing on a strictly educational matter, but this bush school thing is pure tribal politics and the Peace Corps should stay out of it. Definitely out."

"But it's all one piece, Mr. Williams," protested Lew. "If the school closes, that means the Peace Corps teachers aren't working. And all so Genghis can line his own pockets."

"I don't see how you can be so certain of that," said Williams reproachfully.

"Jim Osterlord knows Zinzin politics inside out," said Lew. "I'll take Jim's analysis any day. Also, Steve Muo impresses me as a real honest guy who's just trying to give the kids the schooling they're entitled to."

"You may be right." Williams wore the harried look that indicated his abhorrence of problems not susceptible to postponement. "Still, I'm afraid you and the other PCVs may have gotten in over your heads." He paused and looked bleakly at the telephone. "I'm under instructions to call the ambassador back. Could you wait outside a moment?"

The phone exchange took only a few minutes, then Williams came out of his office. "He wants to see you right away," he said.

Lew pointed to his khaki pants and sports shirt.

"Don't worry about that," said Williams. "Milbank isn't Downing. No stupid rules over at the embassy about how people dress, thank God."

The United States embassy, largest but least pretentious on embassy row, spread over a small hill not far from the ornate Founders House hotel. Shining with new white paint outside, it was a citadel of cool, crisp cleanliness inside. The woodwork glistened, the floors had a mirrorlike polish, and not a stain or blemish, so prevalent in even the newest Kalya government buildings, marred the walls. The chancery, a wing attached to the big house where the ambassador lived and entertained, reflected subdued efficiency. Window air-conditioners purred and the tattoo of the electric typewriters was muted. Young women flashed smiles at callers from their metal nests of filing cabinets, message baskets and neat-looking desks. Kalya, with its smudged face and lethargic pace, seemed a world removed. The ambassador's secretary, a sleek but overweight girl, escorted Lew to the inner office.

Willard Milbank, a lean, fiftyish man who Lew knew was a career foreign service officer in his first ambassadorial post, stood at the door to greet him. He was in shirt-sleeves and his manners were equally informal. He gripped Lew's hand with friendly pressure and his smile was a pleasant balance of heartiness and diffidence. He pronounced Corleigh's full name twice and when he inquired about Lew's health, the interest seemed genuine. Lew's wariness dissipated. By the time they were seated he had decided he liked the ambassador.

"I feel grateful for the chance to talk Kalya politics with a Peace Corpsman," said Milbank. "The Peace Corps really knows this country much more intimately than I do—or any of my staff, for that matter. Oh, we know the palace politics, but when it comes to the tribes and the people, we're just not in the same league with you fellows."

He turned his swivel chair slightly, stretched out his legs and folded his hands at his waist. The movements had a leisurely, amiable quality.

"Of course, our missions are quite different. You're here to help the people however you can. My job is to keep a finger on all the U.S. agencies here—there are too many of them, if you want the truth—and make sure we're all pulling in the same direction. And that effort is a pretty simple one, really. It's just to make certain that we keep Old Number One and his government inside the U.S. ball park."

Milbank apparently detected Lew's surprise at his use of the familiar designation for the Prime Minister, for he smiled at Lew as though sharing with him all the overtones of shrewdness, chicanery and guile with which the appellation for Alexander Vining was freighted in Kalya.

"We all know how much it means to keep Old Number One on our side," he continued, "and away from the fire-eaters and the Marxists. So far, we've been doing pretty well. There's not a single Communist bloc aid project in Kalya." He motioned his head over his shoulder. "Actually, the Soviet ambassador had to wait a whole month for his last private appointment at the Palace." Milbank grinned, relishing the diplomatic rebuff.

"So now, this Zinzin business," he said. "The Palace seems upset about some kind of political hassle up there and it has the idea the Peace Corps has gotten mixed up by taking sides. I'd like a frank report from you. Let's just take our hair down and level." He grinned. "No worries about bugging in this embassy. Frankly, in Kalya, I don't think they'd know how."

Corleigh, relaxed, told the story from the beginning and recounted candidly the circumstances under which he brought Commissioner Steven Muo to Ft. Paul.

Milbank nodded. "I gather Muo got in to see Old Number One yesterday afternoon. That's why the old man was so upset, I guess. But now, on the central point, aside from your driving Muo down here, has the Peace Corps become involved in this skirmish?"

Lew thought quickly of Beach, Muo and The Forge, of his own promise of aid and of Osterlord's obvious deep commitment to the cause of opposing The Family. He hesitated. He did not want to lie, even by implication, on a matter of this importance, and he was irritated by his sudden, sharp sense of divided loyalty. The ambassador had a right to the truth. On the other hand, he had given his word to Lincoln Beach not to talk.

"Well, not really, I suppose," he fumbled. "Osterlord is a close adviser to Muo and, of course, Jim hates everything Genghis Khan is doing to the town. There's no question where the sympathies

of the other six Peace Corps people lie. They're all against
Genghis. That goes for me too, Mr. Ambassador. But so far, nobody has done anything openly that I know of—except for Muo's
ride with me."

"That ride seems to rile Old Number One, for some reason,"
said Milbank. "How he found out, I don't know."

Lew told of being stopped by a security motorcycle patrolman.
Milbank nodded. "Well, of course," he said, "that must be it.
Personally, I don't care for Hulbert Booth. He's an ugly customer
and his men, as he boasts, have a thousand eyes. Still, Old Number
One is accusing the Peace Corps of interfering in Zinzin politics
and we can't afford to alienate him on a matter of such—well,
of such fringe concern, if I may put it that way. I'm afraid I'm
going to have to insist that all the Peace Corps people up there
keep their hands off this fight."

Lew bit his lip. He could envision the hooting reaction in Zinzin when he brought this embassy order. Alice and Dotty would
shriek "Wawa," Ted Kramer probably would get drunk and the
depth of Cindy's dismay would unnerve him.

"But Mr. Ambassador," he pleaded, "how about the school?
The Peace Corps is under contract to teach. The new Kalya law,
ordered by Vining himself, says bush schools can operate only in
the winter vacation. So, actually, Genghis Khan is breaking the
law. Why are we doing anything wrong if we try to keep the school
open?"

Lew thought Milbank's quick glance was an approving one.
The ambassador tugged at an ear lobe as he pondered a moment.

"I suppose you're right," he said, "and maybe that ought to
be my line with Vining. All the Peace Corps is doing is insisting
that the school remain open and that the law be upheld. Yes, I
think that's it."

Milbank paused. "But is that really all that's involved up there?
I had an idea from various things I've heard that at least some
volunteers were into something a bit deeper than that."

Lew stiffened. "I'm not sure what you mean."

Milbank eyed him directly. "Lewis, do you know a man named
Lincoln Beach?"

The abruptness of the question startled Lew. He felt his cheeks
flush. "Well . . ." he began limply. "Well, yes, I do. Yes."

The ambassador studied him for a moment, then rose to his
feet. "Could you come with me? There's something I think you
ought to see."

Lew followed Milbank out of the office and down the hall,
past the nests of stenographers and the rattle of typewriter keys.
Milbank knocked on a door, then opened it without waiting. It
was a small, bare office and the man behind the desk was last
night's hostel caller.

Milbank said simply: "Mr. Corleigh, this is Bruce Kellogg, our
political officer. He has something quite interesting to show you."
The ambassador left, closing the door behind him.

Kellogg's smile was the same bland, neutral one. "We meet
again, what?" he said.

Lew, recalling the threat of last night, tensed and said nothing.
A blue business suit had replaced last night's madras jacket. Kellogg lit a cigarette, then stepped to one of three filing cabinets
against the wall. A drawer, pulled out, had a red tag on the front
with the word "Open" in black letters. Kellogg flipped through
manila folders and extracted two of them. He seated himself again,
put on his black-rimmed spectacles and opened one of the folders.
He leafed through a typewritten sheaf of papers.

"These are a few notes on your friend Steven Muo that the
ambassador thought you'd be interested in," he said. He licked
his lips in the cautious, circular motion. "I won't bother you with
a lot of this stuff, what? But here's one paragraph I'd like to quote.
'In April 1964, Muo went to Ghana, ostensibly for a personal
visit with relatives of his wife, but while in Accra, he attended
a political workshop run by Peking-trained African Communists.'"

Kellogg peered at Corleigh over the rim of his glasses and blew
a smoke ring which floated lazily across the desk. Corleigh found
himself tensing even more. He said nothing. Kellogg opened the
other folder and studied the first sheet.

"This one has a few more entries," he said. "It concerns a
young man I think you know, Mr. Lincoln Beach of the Utility
Authority. Let's see now, while a student at Cornell, he attended
a number of meetings of the Progressive Strike-for-Freedom movement, a Communist-oriented civil rights group." Kellogg flipped
several pages and paused at a paragraph which Corleigh could see
had been marked with red crayon in the margin. "Beach also made

two trips to New York City and each time he conferred with known Communists in Harlem. There's a third, perhaps significant, item here. Beach once signed a petition circulated by JUDO, the Junior Union to Defy Oppression, urging disconnection of utility lines in the name of civil rights protests. JUDO, as you may know, is organized and run by Communists."

Kellogg smiled again with a flicker of pride which Lew found annoying. The officer took several rapid puffs on the half-finished cigarette, then ground it out in an ash tray.

"The ambassador thought you ought to have that information, what?" he said. "My own feeling goes a little further. In light of what you've just heard, and I assure you it's accurate, don't you think you have an obligation as an American citizen to tell us what you know?"

Lew had had an urge, suppressed though it was, to be totally candid with Ambassador Milbank, but with this man, he felt no such compulsion, citizen or not. Something about Kellogg made him want to remain shut like a clam after prodding.

"You ducked last night when I asked you whether you were CIA," said Lew. "Personally, I believe you are. There's an explicit Peace Corps policy, laid down at the start under Kennedy, against reporting to the CIA."

"But none against associating with Communist sympathizers," said Kellogg. He paused. "Also, Mr. Corleigh, when it comes to Peace Corps policy, you don't always abide by the rules, do you?"

"That won't work," snapped Lew. "I've already told the rep and the ambassador about bringing Muo down."

Kellogg sighed. "Why you'd rather fence with me than be co-operative, I don't know, but let me be perfectly straight with you. We know that the skeleton of an organization, unfriendly to the government, has been put together in Kalya. Now our concern is not with any legitimate aspiration for reform, God knows, that's probably needed here, what?" Kellogg shook his head wearily, in the manner of a man who wonders if the world will ever yield a just share of its fruits to the poor and the humble. "But we can't afford to see any group—government, anti-government, pro-African unity, or whatever—slip into Communist hands. If that happened, and your bit of information could have helped prevent it, you'd reproach yourself for a good many years, I think."

"What, specifically, do you want to know?" asked Lew.

"Anything you know about the underground and its members and objectives," said Kellogg. "We're not asking you to take any action, merely to help us piece out the pattern. It may be a good thing for Kalya and it may be a bad thing. Assessment comes later. Our job right now is just to get the facts."

Lew shook his head. "I really don't know anything, Mr. Kellogg—nothing definite, anyway. And if I did, I'm not sure . . . I'm no spy. I'm a Peace Corps volunteer."

"You're an American first, what?" said Kellogg coolly.

"Well, let me sleep on it," said Lew. "I'll keep my ears open on the next trip to Zinzin, and if I find out anything firm . . . well . . . we'll see."

"You're a stubborn man, Corleigh." Kellogg licked his lips once more. "I find it strange that a man has to sleep on the simple question of whether or not to give legitimate information to his own government."

"Well, that's the way it is." Lew felt confused. "I'm not too sure of myself when it comes to politics . . . wheels within wheels and all that."

Kellogg seemed to soften suddenly. He stepped around the desk and put a hand on Lew's shoulder. "It's all right," he said gently. "I know you'll do the right thing. Come see me next week."

Lew walked back toward Milbank's office, but the abundantly fed secretary said the ambassador had no further demands on his time. Lew left the embassy far more perturbed than when he had entered, and he failed to see the approving looks he received from the bank of female stenographers. "Maybe we should have joined the Peace Corps," said one girl, watching his exit. The others giggled.

Corleigh was a troubled man. What was he supposed to do now, he wondered. He walked slowly through the lush embassy grounds, with its sapelli trees, twittering birds and African gardener who sweated, hatless, as he mulched a flower bed in the oozing heat of late morning. The information about Beach and Muo had startled Lew. He liked Ambassador Milbank and his impulse was to help him. On the other hand, he intuitively distrusted and resented Kellogg.

And, he wondered, just how had Bruce Kellogg learned that

Lew knew Lincoln Beach? Of course, the Ginger Baby bar had been crowded that night, but who besides the waitress had seen the occupants of the back booth? He recalled seeing Rachael Frisson as he left and he remembered her knowing comment. He couldn't have been with a woman, she had said, or he wouldn't be leaving so early. Had Rachael seen Beach later at the back table? If so, whom would she have told and why? Rachael was well acquainted with such members of The Family as the Fesses, and Lew knew she coveted her social contacts with Kalya's upper stratum. She enjoyed the stilted afternoon teas and the contrasting all-night, uninhibited parties.

As he left the embassy gates, a blue Sunbeam convertible sped by on the street. Something clicked in his memory. Two weeks ago, late one night in downtown Ft. Paul, he had seen Rachael Frisson in a blue convertible. She had worn a shimmering strapless white dinner gown and her hair was piled theatrically high. She had waved to Lew, and he noted that the driver beside her was Major Felix Booth, the brother of Hulbert and the deputy director of the elite security police. The little major drove with one hand and the other was draped possessively about Rachael's dark, bare shoulders.

8

The money bus veered into the dusty hostel driveway and shuddered to a halt. It was Saturday afternoon and Lew was at the door calling futile instructions to Arthur who was supposed to be weeding the flower bed, but who was leaning on the hoe handle with a borrowed transistor radio pressed to his ear.

A thicket of heads protruded from the bus and then, to his surprise, Lew saw Cynthia Fuller descending from the vehicle. She carried a large knitted tote bag and when she shook her cotton dress, dust particles shimmered in the sunlight. She smiled when Lew took the bag from her, but she seemed tired and listless.

"What are you doing here?" he asked.

"I came down to get a real shower bath." The effort at banter was forced. She shook her head. "Not really, Red. It's a mess up there. The school is closed and the whole town is scared. We're all in a funk. Even Jim, for the first time since I've known him, is beat."

"I'm not doing much better down here."

"No? Well, I just had to do something. I thought I could see the rep and try to get some kind of staff opposition going against Genghis." Her shoulders sagged. "Can't say I have much hope though. Well, anyway, I can lay in my supplies. I haven't been down in two months."

As she mounted the stairs to the women's dormitory, Lew realized that he felt as cheerless as Cindy. The embassy files on Lincoln Beach and Steven Muo perplexed him, nagged at him. A gray film beclouded what had seemed a clear-cut choice. Maybe somehow he should get to know both Kalya men better. As he puttered in the kitchen while Cindy bathed, he wondered what she'd think of Beach. He trusted her intuition, especially with Kalyans. Slowly an idea took shape.

When Cindy came in to raid the refrigerator for a snack, she looked more like her old self. She wore freshly pressed jeans, her hair was tied with a rose ribbon and her white blouse showed that she had used her old hand iron before leaving Zinzin.

"I've got an idea," he said.

She grinned. "The last time you had an idea, I almost got manhandled in my own house."

"No," he said, "this is pal stuff. Look, you're beat from all that ruckus in Zinzin. You need a night out on the town. Why don't I get a date and we'll make it a foursome?"

"Four? That adds up to three. Can't you count?"

"No, no. I'll get a good-looking guy for you."

"What color?" she asked, narrowing her eyes suspiciously.

"You're always worrying about non-essentials," he said. "Let's see, if you're coffee with cream, he's chocolate."

She smiled. "Well . . . and what's his name?"

"Lincoln Beach. You must have heard of him. He went to school in the States and he works at the Utility Authority. A real brain. We throw in his looks in the bargain."

"All right. I guess I have to trust you . . . buddy."

A drive to Beach's office sealed the arrangement. "She's a knockout," promised Lew.

"So I should take your word," Beach parried, "when you're not sure of mine?" Lew nodded. They both laughed. It was more of a problem to persuade Beach that he and Lew had nothing to lose by being seen publicly together. The Family and the U.S. embassy already knew they were friends, Lew argued as he described some of the events since he returned to Ft. Paul. Besides, the Peace Corps was supposed to socialize with inhabitants of the host country. Didn't The Family fraternize with some Peace Corps people?

Why not act casually and naturally? Beach pondered a while, but at last assented.

Lew found Prudence working alone in the Peace Corps office. She was writing reports and there was a dab of ink on her freckled nose. "Tonight's the night," he said. She made polite excuses, but he insisted. It would be a foursome, he said, with Lincoln Beach, whom Prudence said she knew slightly, and Cindy Fuller. That would make two Peace Corps volunteers in the party, and Prudence had an obligation to sustain their morale, didn't she? When she finally yielded, Lew found her embarrassed blush beguiling.

It would be a big night, the Saturday dinner dance on the Founders House roof. Beach had been there a number of times, but for Lew and the two Peace Corps women it would be a first. Cindy hurriedly went into town to shop for a new dress at the Belgian-owned store patronized by expatriates and members of The Family. She found but one to her liking in the slim stock, a sleeveless pink linen import from Italy.

Cindy was standing somewhat apprehensively, smoothing the dress, when Beach arrived at the hostel and was introduced by Lew.

Beach bowed from the waist. "A real pleasure," he said. "Now I'm sure Lew can be trusted."

"He can?" Cindy's brown eyes were alight. "With what?"

"With accurate descriptions of women," said Beach, grinning. "He said you were a knockout."

"Oh." Cindy obviously was as pleased with what she heard as with what she saw. "He said something interesting about you too, but I'll never tell."

Lew laughed. "Well, we got over the first hurdle without busting any shins. Let's go."

The three drove in the jeep to Prudence Stauffer's house, a streaked cement building several notches below the standard enjoyed by other staff members. When Prudence came out on hearing the car stop, Cindy gasped in dismay and scrambled out of the car.

"Oh, no, Prude," she cried.

"Oh, my goodness," said Prudence.

"Such profanity, ladies," said Beach.

Both women had purchased the same pink, sleeveless sheath. They hugged each other, and Lew thought Prudence might burst into tears before they all laughed.

"It's my first new dress in two years," wailed Prudence.

"Mine too."

"I'll go change," said Prudence.

"You will not," said Cindy. "We're something new—integrated twins."

Prudence thrust out her little, pointed chin. "Well, if you don't mind, Cindy, I'm game."

"Mind?" echoed Cindy. "It's a riot. Come on. We'll have a ball."

And then Lew saw that Prudence's bun had vanished. Her light blonde hair was shaken out full in a delicate wave. Her lips had color for the first time, a pale lipstick that blended with the dress. Prudence sat in the front seat with Lew.

She flicked a hand at her hair. "Like it?" she asked timidly.

"It's great. A smash." He grinned. "No Miss Missionary tonight."

The Founders House roof drew the elite of Ft. Paul on Saturday nights. A cool breeze sifted past the huge stone urns, splashed with tropical flowers, which bordered the roof. The canopy had been rolled back tonight, and the stars winking across the sky seemed to be reflections of the nest of lights in the city below. At this height, the stains, odors and excrescences of Ft. Paul were blotted from the senses. Not a zinc shack nor a refuse dump could be seen, and the city was wrapped deceptively in a soft, jeweled cloak.

The waiters, mostly tribal men, wore gold-trimmed monkey jackets. Silver tableware glittered on white linen and from the busy bar came the tinkle of glasses. A seven-piece orchestra, its members dressed in dinner jackets, played highlife music.

The crowd was thickening as Lew's party was escorted to a table overlooking the city. Ft. Paul's cosmopolitan night set formed a wide spectrum of race, color and nationality, from the milky blondes of the Scandinavian embassies to the blacks and tans of Kalya's Family. The dance floor already exhibited a full racial mix and all did the highlife as somewhat haughtily interpreted by The Family. The dancers moved in a slow, serpentine

circle about a lone performer who would then tap someone in the
ring to succeed him as the centerpiece. The steps of the dance
were small, precise ones, while hips and shoulders weaved in sensu-
ous abandon.

The dining crowd, its conversational hum now approaching the
music in volume, included embassy employees and members of Ft.
Paul's large expatriate community. Lew noted the city's leading
Lebanese merchant, several West German and Japanese importers
and Horace Magruder, a bluff, hearty American who was operating
director of Itambel, the Italian-American-Belgian consortium. With
Itambel's huge investment in iron ore mining, Magruder was
the most influential industrialist in Kalya, a man who reputedly
could get Old Number One's ear at any hour.

Kalya government officials, synonymous with The Family, were
out in force for a night of living it up. There were Downings,
lesser Vinings, Fesses and Booths among others. Lew saw Colonel
Hulbert Booth, a bulge under his white jacket, sitting at a table
with his petite Japanese woman of the hour. In the colonel's party
was Rachael Frisson, hair swept high. She was flourishing her
ivory cigarette holder and she was seated next to Major Felix
Booth, a little man who grinned constantly with a proud expanse
of teeth. Lew pointed out Rachael to the others.

"Takes her partying seriously," said Prudence.

"Goals Two and Three, you know," said Cindy with a touch of
acid.

Beach shook his head. "I hear she's out a couple of nights a
week with The Family. That's not my idea of what the Peace Corp
is supposed to be doing here."

"I don't like it either, Lincoln, but I understand it," said Cindy.
"After all the discrimination at home, Rachael's the kind who
wants to fly high over here. She's in the top social circle now and
she loves it."

"The Family and the Peace Corps don't mix." Beach's smooth,
brown face was set in disapproval. "If she wants to live it up,
there are plenty of other people to do it with."

"You don't dig her," said Cindy. "You went to Cornell. Rachael
comes from Baton Rouge. That's different. In Baton Rouge they
treated her third-class. Over here, she's going to go first-class all
the way, believe me."

Beach nodded grudgingly. "I hate to say anything good about The Family, but at least they don't discriminate on color."

Not quite true, thought Lew. The Family's men were free to take women of any race or hue, which many did enthusiastically. The Family's women, however, lived by a strict social code. They could mix with African men, but the girl who dated a European or an Asiatic quickly became an outcast.

"Still," said Beach, "Miss Frisson ought to pick her friends with more care. The Family corrupts everybody, Peace Corps included."

"I don't like her taste in men," said Lew, "but you've got to admit she's a looker."

There was something else about Rachael, he thought. He recalled her frank look of invitation at the Ginger Baby bar and he remembered what several Peace Corps friends had said about her; that she flirted with white men and then, when they were sufficiently aroused, she'd reject their advances with a laugh. She was a strange one, he decided.

The waiter came for drink orders, and when Prudence, her brow knitted, ordered palm wine, the others burst into laughter.

"Palm wine at Founders House!" hooted Beach.

"For God's sake, Prude," said Lew, "this is a night out. You're not trying to make character outcountry. You're partying."

"All right, then," she said. "A daiquiri."

The others ordered Scotch and by the time they were ready for dinner, a third round was on the table and the party was gathering steam. Beach danced with Cindy and then led Prudence, her cheeks glowing, out to the floor for the highlife circle. Cindy and Lew remained seated.

"I like him," said Cindy. "Thanks."

"I'm your new buddy, remember? Anything for a friend in need. Now, will you do me a favor?"

"Sure, Red. What?"

"Link wants me to do something for him," said Lew, "but frankly I don't know him too well. Kind of size him up for me, will you? You know, fish around—background, character, all that?"

"I'm not very good at that kind of thing."

"Cindy," he said, "you're good at anything you do."

"Well, I'll try. But I've got to warn you. Right off, I think he's smashing."

Lew got his own chance with Beach when the women went to the powder room together. The two men exchanged small talk and then Beach provided the opening.

"Steve tells me you've decided to help us," he said. "Is that right?"

"It is," replied Lew, "within limits. The politics is your business, but keeping the school open at Zinzin is ours, so I suppose . . ."

"Same thing." Beach waved a hand in deprecation. "If you're going to help us, don't start quibbling about terms. Steve likes you. More important, he trusts you as he does Osterlord."

"Steve and I were both Jack Kennedy fans, I discovered," said Lew. "By the way, Steve was low on cash. Did he find a way back, or is he still here?"

"I gave him some dough. He's still here. He didn't make much hay with Old Number One. He'll tell you about it. I told him we might meet him around twelve at the Ginger Baby. Okay?"

"Sure," said Lew, "if the girls are willing." He leaned across the table. "Listen, Link, something is bothering me. Before I get too deep into this thing, I'd like an honest answer from you."

"Shoot. I'll answer anything except questions about my love life."

"Well," said Lew, "I told you that some people already know we're friends, and . . . well, I heard a story that when you were in the States, you spent quite a bit of time hanging out with left-wingers, and . . ."

Laugh lines crinkled about Beach's brown eyes. "What you're trying to ask is: Am I now or was I ever a member of the Communist party? No. Next question."

Lew hesitated. "The story is you had some meetings with Communists while you were a student at Cornell. . . ." He found his inquiry distasteful.

"The story?" Beach's eyebrows arched. "Talk with Communists? Sure I did . . . and with right-wingers, eggheads, Democrats, Republicans, the works. I was there to learn. I talked to everybody. Look, Lew, I don't know what this is all about, but I don't mind saying what I believe. I came to the conclusion that Marxist theories would never work in our tribal setup. What we need here is work and education and training, but mostly work. We need investment, a government we can trust, financial stability."

He gestured toward a nearby table where members of The Family were laughing and drinking. "They don't put their money back into the country. They stash it away in Swiss banks . . . millions. All they do in Kalya is rob it blind. That's the system I want to break. The hell with Communism. The only 'ism' I want here is workism. Anything else, Senator?"

Lew grinned weakly. "Yeah, there is. There's a report you signed a petition for a Communist-run outfit called JUDO." He looked directly at Beach, but he felt embarrassed.

"Oh, for Christ's sake!" Beach rapped his glass on the table. "Yes, I did. So what? They were ganging up on freedom riders that summer in Alabama. I was a sophomore and ready to do anything in reprisal. I found out later that the JUDO line was pure Chinese Communist. And the purpose was pretty wild—something about tapping fire hydrants and disconnecting power lines." Beach studied Lew's face for a moment. "Say, just who's been feeding you all this, anyway?"

"A guy who thinks you're not a proper playmate for me," said Lew.

"Bruce Kellogg?"

Lew tried to conceal his surprise.

"Sure," said Beach. "Kellogg, the what-what man. He's the big CIA agent here."

"CIA?"

Beach laughed. "Oh, sure. Everybody in the know in Ft. Paul knows that. This isn't a very big city, Red. Well, next time you see your Mr. Kellogg, you tell him I'm something new in international politics—a capitalistic revolutionary." He laughed again, then grew serious. "You didn't talk, did you?"

"I told you my hand was inside," said Lew.

The women returned, laughing self-consciously at the condescending stares their identical dresses evoked from women diners. "They think we're either going steady or else advertising the new line from Italy," said Cindy.

Lew danced with Cindy and then with Prudence. The drinks had made Prudence giddy and somewhat befogged. She tucked her head on Lew's shoulder during a rare slow dance tune that relieved the frenzy of the frugs, monkeys, highlifes and twists. "I'm not much of a drinker," she said.

"It's that missing knot in your hair," he said. "You feel un-balanced without it."

"Lew," she whispered, "I don't feel right here. You'll use up half of your monthly subsistence on one dinner. And all these people spending money like water when half of Kalya is trying to get enough to eat—and the other half is sick."

"Give up, puritan," he said. "You can't save humanity just by staying home Saturday night."

"Don't care," she said. "Feel out of place here."

Back at the table, Lew said: "Prudence thinks we're hurting the Peace Corps image here. As soon as we eat, I move we go on to the Ginger Baby. That's more our style."

Beach hoisted his glass. "To the Ginger Baby!" They all drank to it and when they finished, Prudence said: "But I've never been there either." She hiccoughed and they laughed. Then the waiter arrived with thick slabs of roast beef.

"If your conscience bothers you, Prude," said Cindy, "just leave yours for me. I haven't had a decent piece of meat like this in two months."

They ate with scant interruption for talk and were well into the peach parfait, served in tall, silver-plated goblets, when they found Colonel Hulbert Booth looming over the table. His white dinner jacket fitted smoothly save for the mound under his left shoulder. The thin mustache seemed oddly out of place in his rough features. An observer's eye quickly left his face to take in his whole body. He was a powerfully built man and his stance was the confident one of long authority.

"Good evening," he said. The voice was deep but devoid of warmth. "All the world-savers are here together tonight, I see."

Corleigh and Beach rose stiffly, but Booth motioned them to sit. Beach introduced the two women.

Booth bowed. "I know you both by reputation. Ah, three Peace Corps apostles and . . ." He looked at Beach. ". . . a servant of the people."

"Just a bill collector, Colonel," said Beach coldly.

"So you are." Booth's formal smile evaporated. "A dedicated clerk. Kalya could use more of them." He turned to Lew. "You've been traveling in interesting company recently, Mr. Corleigh."

"Thanks."

"But you must watch your speed," said Booth, "when you have passengers in your jeep." His face was fixed in the set smile again. "The Peace Corps assumes its own risks in its service here, but there's no sense endangering the lives of others, is there?"

Lew said nothing.

"Drivers who are careless about their passengers," continued Booth smoothly, "sometimes meet with unfortunate accidents themselves."

"What's that supposed to mean, Colonel?" asked Beach.

Booth did not bother to turn toward him. "I was addressing Mr. Corleigh. Unfortunately, despite his service here, he still isn't acquainted with all our Kalya customs. I understand he doesn't have many weeks to go before returning home, and we wouldn't want those final days marred by some regrettable accident that could be easily avoided."

"Thanks for the advice, Colonel." Lew tried to keep his voice under control. "I try to obey the rules."

"All of them?" Booth let the question hang for a moment, then bowed to the women. "A pleasure, ladies. I must get back to my guests."

"Bastard!" growled Beach when the colonel was out of earshot.

"I think he was threatening you, Red," said Prudence. "What for?"

"Oh, we had a run-in once over a kid he ran down with his motorcycle," said Lew. "Booth talks a tough game."

"He likes rough games with the women too," said Cindy. She recounted the experience of Alice Franklin and Dorothea Wyzansky for the benefit of Prudence and Beach.

"Enough of Booth," said Beach. "Let's pay the check and hit the Ginger Baby. That's more our speed."

On the way out, Beach walked with Corleigh. "That was a real threat, Red," he said in an undertone. "You've heard of being 'boothed'? If I were you, I'd be on my guard."

"Oh, he wouldn't dare harm an American, especially Peace Corps."

"The word was 'accident,'" reminded Beach. "Just pay attention, that's all." He paused. "By the way, if you intend to ask Steve about attending a Chinese Communist workshop in Accra a couple of years ago, don't bother. He did, but it didn't make a dent on him. Steve isn't a theorizer. All he wants to do is bust Moses Harter's hold on Zinzin and run an honest show up there."

"You're two steps ahead of me," said Lew.

"And why not? I knew Bruce Kellogg long before you did." The exchange nettled Lew. Beach not only had curiously ready answers—he had them before the questions. Lew thought of Kellogg's red-marked file papers and then of Ambassador Milbank, a reasonable man, and he wondered. . . .

The Ginger Baby throbbed with the beat of the jungle band, the Swiss and African barmaids worked feverishly to supply the shouted requests for whiskey and the smoke was so thick the eyes smarted. A polyglot crowd babbled in a hash of languages and the Ginger Baby's predominant odor was a sharp fusion of perfume and perspiration. The human press along the mahogany bar included some Peace Corps people.

They found Steve Muo sitting alone in a back booth. He was drinking the native Kalya beer whose taste, Lew long ago decided, was not unlike ginger ale spiked with detergent. Muo sprang up and gave the Kalya handshake elaborately to Cindy, Lew and Beach in turn. He bowed gravely at the introduction to Prudence.

"Eh, ya," he said, indicating the table. "One big fight to keep dis place."

They all crowded into the booth with Muo. Prudence tried to order Coca-Cola, but the others noisily insisted that she have another daiquiri to match their Scotch. The waitress, shuffling on her heels tribal fashion, brought the drinks and dropped the money in the crevice of her soiled green brassiere.

"A toast," said Beach. They raised their glasses. "To the Zinzin school—and down with Moses Harter!" They all drank, but Prudence brushed her chin while raising her glass. The rum drink splashed on the table.

"Oh, dear," she said. "I'm getting squiffed."

"I'm seeing double myself," said Cindy. "Everywhere I go, I see my pink dress twice."

Steve Muo examined both dresses, feeling the texture. "Eh, ya. Peez-kor, huh?"

Cindy giggled. "You think it's a new uniform, Mr. Muo?" He nodded seriously.

The talk bubbled on, but beneath the gaiety, Lew could sense that Muo's mind was elsewhere. Apparently Beach sensed it too.

"Tell them about your conference at the Palace," said Beach. Muo frowned and Beach added a few words in Mola.

"No good," said Muo. "Ol' Num' One, he say I boss da gub'ment. Mose' Hart', he boss da school."

"But how about Harter putting on bush school this time of year?" asked Lew. He spoke slowly. "He broke one of Vining's own rules. Bush school is supposed to be in the winter."

Muo nodded vigorously. "I tell him dat one time but . . ." He struggled for words, then appealed to Beach in Mola. They spoke at some length.

"He told me yesterday," explained Beach, "but I wanted to get it straight again. It seems that Old Number One agreed that the new law had been violated, but he said that since the paramount chief had approved the bush school, there must be some special extenuating circumstances. Vining said he didn't feel justified in overruling the paramount chief without more information, and he could not spare the time now to go up to Zinzin and inquire personally about the facts."

"But Muo's his government man up there," protested Cindy. "Why doesn't he take Muo's word about it?"

Muo, comprehending, shook his head. "No way," he said bleakly. "Hart', he Fam'ly. I Mola."

"It's the old story," said Beach bitterly. "When it's the tribes against The Family, The Family always wins. Old Number One just wants to keep Steve in office as a figurehead."

"Rotten," said Prudence, triggering a blast of angry inveighing against The Family and the system. When it died down, Cindy said she had an idea.

"It came to me while I was talking to the rep this afternoon," she said. "Williams keeps complaining that the Peace Corps can't get mixed up in Zinzin politics."

"Yeah," said Lew, "and he's taking a lot of heat from higher up."

"Yes, but we've got a contract to teach school," said Cindy. "Now listen. The school is closed and the principal is absent. When the principal's absent, as his assistant, I become the acting principal. Now suppose, as acting principal, I post a notice at the school saying it will remain open and that the examinations in July will not make allowances for any absences. In other words, I just go ahead as if Genghis were sick, out of the country or something."

"But every kid who's in bush school and misses the work will flunk the exams," said Lew.

"Sure," said Cindy. "And when the parents realize that, how many do you think will put up with bush school as against having their kids stay behind a grade?"

"Plenty," said Lew. "The devil has scared the bejesus out of them. And besides, you think that isn't getting mixed up in tribal politics?"

"It is not," replied Cindy. "It's just doing our duty to the school and to our contract."

Lew remembered that Ambassador Milbank had taken kindly to the line that the Peace Corps was within its rights and its obligation in trying to keep the school open. But what about the people of Zinzin?

"Cindy," he said, "you'll be talking to empty classrooms."

Beach thumped his glass on the table. "Wait a minute," he said. "I think Cindy's right. Oh sure, it probably won't bring the boys back from the bush, but it will set the stage for next time. If every boy in town fails to get promoted, Harter will have one helluva time getting away with anything like that next year, especially if the town finds out he just did it to line his own pockets."

"And don't forget the girls," said Cindy. "If we keep the school open, they'll pass and the boys won't."

"I'm for it," said Beach. He turned to Muo and went into a long explanation in the Mola tongue.

"Eh, man, da' good." Muo flashed a rare smile at Cindy and tapped his head. "Peez-kor teach' plenny heah. We vex ol' Hart' one time." He chortled and took a gargantuan swallow of beer.

"You going to tell the rep?" asked Lew.

Cindy shook her head. "This is just a routine matter of school administration," she said. "We don't bother Carter Williams with every little detail."

"It's a great idea," said Beach. "And it has nothing to do with Steve. He's out of it entirely. Man, that will really put Old

Number One on the spot." He rubbed his hands together, called the waitress and ordered another round.

When a new daiquiri was placed before Prudence, she stared at it dully, then turned to Lew.

"Red, I'm sorry," she said, "but I have to get out of here or I'll be sick." The color left her face.

"I'd better take her home," said Lew. The others made sounds of commiseration. Prudence stood up, gripped the edge of the table and smiled wanly.

"Guess missionaries and booze don't mix," she said. She waved a dignified farewell, and Lew found it difficult not to laugh.

Outside the bar, Prudence planted her feet firmly apart and drew several deep breaths. "Better now," she said, ". . . I think."

On the short jeep ride home, she sat rigidly and stared straight ahead. "Feel . . ." she began, but finished with a burp. At the house, she led Lew silently into the living room, then said in a small voice: "Think I'll be sick now. You wait here."

While she was in the bathroom, Lew made two cups of instant coffee in the kitchen. She was still pale when she returned, but she looked gratefully at the coffee and began to sip it.

"Some party girl," she said. "Ashamed of myself."

"Forget it," said Lew. "It happens to the best of boozers."

She smiled faintly. "You're not put out, Red?"

"With you? Never. It just proves you ought to get out more. You've got to learn to unbend now and then."

"I do?" She looked in dismay at a splotch on her new dress. "Think it proves that as a glamour girl, I'm a bust."

"Pretty nice bust," he said. It wasn't exactly luxuriant, he told himself, but it was trim and appealing.

They sat on the flowered muslin couch and talked of Cindy, Link Beach and Steve Muo. She asked where he'd met Beach, and he said guardedly that Jim Osterlord had urged him to meet him sometime and he'd done so.

"What do you think of him, Prude?"

"I think," she said, "that he's one of the finest men in Kalya. I just wish he had some influence in the government."

They talked of the Zinzin school and Moses Harter.

"Prudence," he said, "let me ask you something. Suppose there was an underground in Kalya shaping up against The Family.

I don't know that there is, but let's suppose it. Then would a Peace Corpsman be justified in trying to help it? I mean, just as a hypothetical case."

She toyed with the coffee cup for a moment. "Don't think there's any blanket answer to that, Red," she said. "It depends on what kind of underground and what kind of help. I'd say that was something he'd have to decide for himself."

"But it would be taking sides in Kalya politics," he said, "and that's against policy."

"Matter of degree," she said. "When a Peace Corps teacher walks into a classroom, that minute, whether she knows it or not, she starts taking sides. Every educated tribal person means one more threat to The Family's monopoly."

"Link Beach said practically the same thing the other day," observed Lew.

Prudence's look was a quizzical one. "He did? Well, I'm not surprised. He's the best proof of what we're talking about."

Prudence wore her most serious look. Color had returned to her cheeks. Her new hairdo hung over one eye, she had kicked off her shoes and there was the splotch on her dress. She reminded Lew of a little girl after her first dance. Prudence seemed small and defenseless, and Lew felt a protective urge.

"Tired?" he asked.

"No. Thinking. I always look solemn when I think."

He put an arm around her. "Thinking about what?"

"About Zinzin and Kalya," she said. She moved her head onto his shoulder. "Nothing's simple, is it? We denounce Old Number One and joke about him, but he does run this strange country. He insists on public education for all tribes, and he builds roads and offices and he tries to develop Kalya with companies like Itambel. But then there's the graft and stealing and The Family looting the tribes. But how would you or I—or even Link Beach— rule a country where the people still cower when an old straw devil dances? I don't know. Everything's complicated, isn't it, Red?"

"Even you." He ran a forefinger around her small, prim mouth.

"Me?"

He folded her against his chest and kissed her. The moment their lips touched, she quickened. Her mouth pressed roughly against his. Her slight breasts thrust against his chest and her hips arched toward him. She gripped the back of his neck so hard, he could feel the sharp edge of her fingernails. Her hunger startled him and Lew found himself responding with a tight embrace. They clung together for a long while. Then the tenseness eased and she nuzzled his neck with her mouth.

"Even you," he repeated.

They kissed again. This time the embrace was a tender one with the small, awkward ventures of discovery. She sighed and looked up at him.

"Wanted you to kiss me for a long time," she said.

"You could have let me know, Prude."

"But I'm such a plain one, Red. I didn't think . . ."

"Too much thinking," he said. He kissed her and again he felt the quick press of her arms.

"I thought there was something going between you and Cindy," she whispered.

Her shyness flattered and amused him. How could he answer truthfully, or did he have to?

"We decided to be friends," he said. "It's lonely for a girl in Zinzin—and for a guy driving the Zinzin road, for that matter." He paused. "I don't know. Too complicated maybe. White man, Negro woman, all that. Anyway, I admire her and like her, but . . ."

"But?"

"Well, we never made love, if that's what you're getting at." She kissed his cheek. "You didn't have to tell me that, Red."

"I wanted to," he said.

She drew back and looked at him intently. "Can I be your girl?"

Again that sober, concentrated look of hers somehow amused him. "Anything for staff morale," he said.

"Well, can I?"

"You look like you're proposing to merge a couple of railroads." This time he laughed. "Okay, it's a deal."

She stood up, straightened her dress, looked at him gravely and then walked to the kitchen, her stockinged feet padding purposefully. When she returned, she had two small glasses with a pale liquid.

"Palm wine," she said. "Feel better. We're going to have one drink to celebrate."

They touched glasses. Prudence drank hers with a frown. Lew couldn't decide whether she looked like a little girl swallowing medicine or a female executive about to sign a dubious contract. He grinned at her, but her eyebrows remained drawn together over a crease of tiny freckles.

"I'm not going to be plain any more," she said. It had the ring of a public announcement.

"Oh?"

"I'm not going to wear my hair in a knot any more. I'm going to wear lipstick at work—and I'm going to do something about my bust."

Her frown had the mark of high purpose, there was no banter in her tone, and Lew could contain himself no longer. He broke into laughter and his hand shook so much, he spilled the last of the palm wine. She stood quietly, her feet placed apart, until his laughter subsided.

"What's so gawd-awful funny?"

"You," he said. "You! Prudence, you're a character. I think you're the funniest, wackiest, gutsiest little dame I ever met."

"Thanks for the gutsy," she said stiffly, but she began to smile.

"You're so damned businesslike." He grinned and shook his head.

"I don't see any reason to be coy," she said.

"I think a guy could fall in love with you." He rose to his feet, drew her to him and kissed her seriously.

"That might be nice," she said. "I've never been in love, not really." She studied his face again, as though searching within him. Then she took his hand. "Right now, though, I'm sleepy. It's time for you to go."

"Go? Why? The night's still young."

"Not this night," she said firmly. "We've been to two parties and one palm wine celebration."

"You're getting stubborn, Prude."

"Always stubborn. That's one quality of mine you forgot to name."

She drew him toward the door. Her good-night kiss was a purposeful one. "Will you see me as soon as you get back from Zinzin?"

He grinned down at her. "Same night I get back."

Lew walked from the house, bemused and wondering, and he was fumbling with the jeep's ignition key before he realized that the night had grown sultry and that the heavy dampness had a threatening quality. The big spring rains would not hold off much longer.

It was Monday morning, and Lew Corleigh was pounding the road to Zinzin, when Prudence Stauffer ended a half hour's consultation with Dr. Sam Zerwick in his cramped office behind the beaverboard partitions at Peace Corps headquarters.

"And that's all there is to it?" she asked.

"That's all there is to it, Prudence." Zerwick slapped his knees.

"So all I do is take the pill? It's that simple? Are you really sure it's so safe? I don't want to be careless."

"Ninety-nine per cent guaranteed . . . if you follow the directions," he said. "Don't worry. I don't want any population explosion in Sam Zerwick's bailiwick." He tilted his great head. "It's none of my business as a physician, but as a close friend, Prude, I hope you know what you're doing."

"It's my turn to say 'don't worry,'" she said.

"I worry about all my patients over here."

She planted her feet wide and her little face wore its solemn look. "You see, Sam, I think I've found a man who might be for me."

"They all do," he said roughly. "That's not my concern. My province is the physical and mental health of the Peace Corps in Kalya. Frankly, I don't need another single god-damned woman coming in here, coiled as tight as a spool of wire, trying to make a full-time psychiatrist out of me—just because she's got the wrong man."

"But if he's the right one?"

Zerwick grinned. "In that case, a lot of other problems get solved. For your sake, Prude, I hope yours is the right man."

"Hope so too," she said. "Otherwise, I don't think Peace Corps Washington would approve of your—uh—instructions."

"The hell with Washington!" he glowered. "If I followed all its red tape, we'd really be fouled up over here."

Dr. Zerwick stood and patted her shoulder. "If he's playing games with you, you come and tell me—and I'll personally beat the bastard to a pulp."

Prudence smiled. "That's the nicest offer I've had all day."

"By the way, Prude," said Zerwick as he held the door open for her. "I like your new hairdo."

9

Cynthia Fuller tacked up two notices early Wednesday morning, one at the government school and one at the gas station at the Zinzin crossroads.

She had worked on the announcement while riding with Lew on the two-day trip from Ft. Paul. They had stayed overnight at Loli, Lew with Forrest Stevenson and his jittery wife, Grace, and Cindy with Susan, the Peace Corps teacher. On the long ride they talked of Prudence and Lincoln Beach. Cindy, reporting as promised, delivered her analysis of Beach: a dedicated, practical reformer, a gentle man with a tough core, unafraid if sometimes too excitable, intelligent, trustworthy and, as an afterthought, extremely attractive. He was her kind of man, she said musingly, and if given the breaks, he could be the sort of leader who could remake Kalya.

It had rained heavily Monday night and the jeep sprayed mud all day on the final leg to Zinzin. The vehicle became mired once and Cindy had to get out and help Lew put boards under the wheels to give the tires traction.

Zinzin steamed like a Turkish bath as Cindy posted her identical placards:

NOTICE

Classes at the government elementary school will start
again Thursday morning for all pupils. No allowances will
be made on the July semester examinations for absences
other than those caused by illness.

Cynthia Fuller
Acting Principal

The Mola translation underneath, lettered by Jim Osterlord, was
largely psychological in purpose. Few residents in Zinzin were tu-
tored in their language's written version, but Jim argued that the
dual announcement would add emphasis.

Whichever version took hold, the impact was formidable. The
school news became the sensation of Zinzin within an hour. The
word leaped from hut to hut as though on stabs of lightning.
Gabbling women gathered about the gas station. As they gesticu-
lated, their headloads of wash or vegetables bobbed precariously
like overripe blooms in a strong wind. Old men, heading toward
jungle clearings with belted cutlass, turned and streamed instead to
the palaver hut. The excitement of the adults infected small children who dashed feverishly through the streets, calling to one another and bawling the words "Peez-kor" over and over. Lebanese
merchants slouched dourly in the doorways of empty stores. The
women were too full of news and rumor for shopping. In the
open market, the shriveled crones called their prices in shrill dismay
at the lack of customers. Everywhere the argument raged. The
Peace Corps had defied the town devil and calamity would over-
take it. Perhaps all seven Americans, as well as the driver from Ft.
Paul, would be felled in one colossal, dreadful stroke. Dissenters
whispered that it was not the devil, but Moses Harter, whom the
Peace Corps was challenging. The dark-skinned woman from the
United States, Teacher Fuller, had no evil in her. She wanted to
teach the children. And hadn't Old Number One ruled that bush
school could be held only during the winter vacation? Still, the
boys already were at the Golo camp, deep in the jungle, no one
knew where. Only the paramount chief could summon them
home and the chief himself was officiating at bush school rites.

What would be the outcome? Speculation flew on dark and frightened wings.

Lew and Cindy watched and listened in town throughout the morning, then drove to her house for lunch. It was slightly cooler in her plastered mud living room with its hooked rugs, orange curtains, the photographs of her parents and the rosewood and ebony carvings of African faces. Lew sank gratefully into a chair. Four hours of a Kalya day usually crumpled his spirits as thoroughly as they soaked his shirt.

"Well," he asked, "what do you think?"

Cindy brought iced tea from the kitchen and they both drank deeply. "I'm just not sure," she said, "and I don't think they are either. From what I picked up, they're secretly glad somebody at last stood up to Genghis Khan. But also, I guess, they think we'll all be dead by tomorrow."

"I feel half dead already," Lew said.

"Bock-bock." The voice at the door was a commanding one.

"Come in," said Cindy.

The door was thrown open and Moses Harter strode into the small living room. Lew, who had seen him only in passing several times, was fascinated by the face. It was yellowing, almost Asiatic in complexion, and now the features, contorted by anger, seemed to emphasize the nickname the Peace Corps had pinned to him. He was a short, stout man. A scar on his cheek merged with heavy mouth lines which drooped like a tired mustache. Harter wore a wide-brimmed planter's hat which he did not bother to remove, dark trousers and a sports shirt which screamed in yellows and reds, the national colors.

"Miss Fuller, you will take down those notices at once." There was barely controlled fury in his voice, but the diction was precise. Harter had learned his formal English from The Family and he was proud of his enunciation.

"I am the principal during your absence," said Cindy, rising to confront him, "and I'm responsible for the education of the children."

"The school is closed." He glared at her and slapped his thigh for emphasis. "You are mocking one of the most sacred Mola traditions, the bush school." In his meticulous diction, the sibilants had a curious hissing sound.

"The law says bush school in winter vacations only," said Lew.

"The law!" Harter wheeled on him. "I know you. You're that Peace Corps truck driver."

Lew grinned in spite of himself. "Touché. That's me, all right."

"What do you Americans know about law?" Harter asked, his tone heavy with contempt despite the precise diction. "You riot and you murder and you spit on black men."

"And we whip Miss Fuller so hard, she can't even teach in a closed school, can she?" asked Lew.

"Never mind the sarcasm, Red," said Cindy. Her peremptory tone surprised him. "I'll handle this myself." She folded her arms. "Now, Mr. Harter, when you're ready to return to your job as principal, and open the school, you may issue such orders as you please. Until then, I'm in charge."

Harter shot a finger at Cindy and Lew tensed, fearing for an instant that Harter might strike her.

"You fly mighty high, Miss Fuller," he said. "You vex me."

"That's an obvious understatement," said Cindy calmly.

"Shut up!" Harter raged. "I may not have gone to some fancy American college, but my little finger knows more than your head does."

"I never questioned your shrewdness, Mr. Harter," she replied, "nor your capacity for harming the people of this town."

Harter held Cindy with a look of hatred through half-closed lids, and Lew remembered that he was watching not only a man whose authority was challenged, but one whose advances had been repulsed by this poised young woman from Georgia.

"You are inciting my people to violate tribal tradition," railed Harter, "and you're not going to get away with it."

"And you're breaking the national law of Kalya," said Cindy. Her arms were still folded, her expression embattled. "They're not 'your' people either, Mr. Harter. You're not a chief, and you're not the government. Mr. Muo is the commissioner."

"Muo!" Harter spoke the name with contempt. "I'm the Prime Minister's man in Zinzin, and not Steven Muo or that humbugging Osterlord—or Cynthia Fuller either."

Cindy did not reply. The two stood in silent confrontation, measuring each other like two prize fighters before the final bell.

"I shall ask you still again one time." The sibilants whistled through Harter's fury. "Will you take down the notices?"

"No."

"Then," said Harter, "you are hereby dismissed as assistant principal."

"Oh, no," said Cindy. "My appointment comes from Commissioner Downing in Ft. Paul."

"We shall see." Harter turned to Lew. "And I warn you to stay out of this, Mr. Truck Driver—and that goes for your friend James Osterlord too. Before this is over, you will beg me, man, to hold my foot."

He turned abruptly and walked from the room. His departure was less than heroic, however, for in his angered haste, he brushed his wide-brimmed hat against the doorjamb and knocked the hat askew over one eye. He righted the hat with a final hostile glare and banged the screen door behind him.

"A man of undiluted charm," said Lew.

Cindy did not smile. Now that Harter had gone, her shoulders sagged and her combative shell seemed to dissolve. Her hand trembled as she reached for her glass of iced tea.

"I'm not sure how much more of his bullying I can take," she said.

They speculated for a few minutes on Harter's next move and then, by unspoken common consent, they rode the jeep wagon to the house of Alice Franklin and Dorothea Wyzansky where, they felt sure, the rest of the Peace Corps contingent would gather.

The big living room of the crisis household presented its usual face of neglect and disorder. The Scrabble board occupied its same spot on the cement floor and dust covered the litter of old magazines. Alice sat, as though dumped, on the tattered sofa, brooding through daubed spectacles. Only her plump legs showed change. They were no longer streaked with calamine lotion. Angular Dotty, in soiled shirt and blue jeans, sat at the other end of the sofa and scattered ashes on the floor from her cigarette. Through the kitchen door, Lew could see a pile of dirty dishes and he wondered whether Joe-Joe had worn his Sweet Briar sweatshirt to bush school.

The others were all there, even Jim Osterlord. Jim waved hello from his chair in a corner where he sat leafing through the begrimed stack of record albums and idly inspecting their titles.

"What's the latest bulletin from the front?" asked Dotty in the tone of a warrior resigned to defeat.

Cindy told of Harter's visit.

"The man has impeccable manners," added Lew.

"He whistles while he works," said Arch Lettermore. He grinned and mimicked Harter's speech with a series of exaggerated hisses.

"I think we've had it," said Ted Kramer. "Jesus, I wish I was Group V with only seventy-five days to go."

"Seventy-six," corrected Alice.

Further scattered comments were all those of the vanquished. The air of dejection was thick in the room. Even Arlene Offenbach seemed dispirited. The Lutheran mission school remained open, she reported, but the attendance was small and the two remaining girls in her fifth-grade class were so frightened, she had dismissed them for the day.

"Wawa!" groaned Dotty. Nobody laughed.

"Now listen," said Cindy, "we've got to quit acting like we're licked." For the second time that morning, Lew was impressed by Cindy's composed determination. "I'm not at all sure we'll lose," she said, "and even if we do this time, we've got to remember next year and the next. Some of us are going home soon, but Ted, Archie and Jim will be here for another year and Arlene for almost two years."

They looked at her in respectful silence.

"I told Genghis I wouldn't take down those announcements," she continued stubbornly, "and I won't. Now, let's just wait until tomorrow morning and see who shows up at the school."

"Cindy's right," said Osterlord from his corner. He brushed at his mop of hair. "You're here to teach school."

"All of us should be in class tomorrow morning," said Cindy.

"But the boys are all out in the bush, God knows where," said Kramer.

"There are the girls," insisted Cindy. "Some of them may show up and if so, we've got to hold class."

"You think there's much chance, Jim?" asked Arch.

"Some," said Osterlord. "And if there's nobody to teach, you might all spend the time improving your mind by learning Mola."

"Sarcastic louse, aren't you?" growled Kramer.

"No, just helpful," said Jim, rising. "Well, I've got to get back to the road. See you in Sunday school."

His departure was followed by the usual eruption of character dissection in which distaste and envy mingled in fairly equal proportions. Dotty ended it by asking, with a shrug, what one could expect of a snotty Harvard man. Then came more theorizing about Genghis Khan and when the group broke up, they all promised that they would be in class on time in the morning.

Lew, deciding to remain in Zinzin to witness the next round in the struggle, divided the afternoon between a soggy nap and a stroll through town to gauge the temper of the people. Zinzin seemed to be returning to its normal, torpid ways, although he noted that more people stared at him longer than usual and more naked little boys and girls trailed his steps.

One flurry of excitement came near evening. Moses Harter drove up to the gas station in his red Mustang, tore down Cindy's placard, shredded it and scattered the pieces disdainfully over the ground. A murmuring crowd collected and soon after, Jim Osterlord arrived on his motorbike with a duplicate sign. He tacked it on the wooden pillar near the gas pump, grinned at the gathering and rode away on his sputtering cycle.

That night a savage downpour bombarded the tin roof of Osterlord's house for more than an hour. The onslaught had a vicious intensity. Two big leaks opened in the living-room ceiling and Jim threw a protective canvas hood over the short-wave radio. Conversation was futile. The two men sat in damp isolation while the rain thundered on the roof with the force of mallets. Lew's clothing became limply moist and he wondered if all his remaining seventy-six days would be mildewed ones.

When the rain stopped abruptly, Osterlord lighted the kitchen kerosene stove and they sat beside it to dry out. The talk ranged over the Zinzin contest and when Lew found the proper opening, he told of his visit to the embassy and Bruce Kellogg's office.

"Balls," said Jim with a snort. "I've been all through that. That CIA stuff of Kellogg's is for the birds. I've known Muo and Beach for a year now, and if they're Communists, I'm a Buddhist Mormon."

"But Link admitted that the material on him and Steve was accurate," said Lew.

"Accurate in detail, sloppy in implication." Jim flung out a dismissive hand. "All old crap that doesn't mean a thing. Listen, you can take the whole CIA and stuff it. Look at the Bay of Pigs, the Dominican Republic and trying to bribe what's-his-name, the prime minister of Singapore, for God's sake. What has the agency done except pull one boner after another?"

"Kellogg is after me to tell him what I know about The Forge," said Lew.

"Did you talk?" demanded Jim.

"No, don't worry. I gave Link my word. Besides, I don't know much." Lew paused as he thought. "Still, Milbank has a point. Suppose you were the ambassador, and the Peace Corps began raising Cain with your policy?"

"I'd cheer them on," said Osterlord. "It's simple. We're here to help the Molas. The Family is robbing them, so we do what we can to stop the thieves."

"I know, I know." The theme had a timeless cast.

Jim eyed him closely. "Quit stewing, Lew. You're in this thing now. It's Muo and the rest of us against Genghis."

"I know that too," said Lew, but as he prepared for bed he felt the press of opposing forces as though he were locked in a slowly closing vise.

The stuttering short-wave radio awakened Lew the next morning and he squirmed uncomfortably between the damp sheets. Then he sat on the edge of the bed and listened to Osterlord. The words sounded strange.

"The leftover grapefruit is still rotting," Jim was saying. "The pineapple is ripe. Nothing settled. Please report crop conditions at the market. . . . Sure, sure. He's still in bed. Why not?"

"Hey, Red!" Osterlord yelled. "Prudence wants to talk to you."

Lew rubbed at sleepy eyes as he seated himself at the microphone. "Good morning, Prude," he said. "My, you're looking pretty today."

"Liar," said Prudence, "but it's nice to hear. When will you get back? I miss you."

"Probably not until Saturday. There's a lot doing here. I'll see you Saturday night, I hope. Here's Jim again."

"That's all from Peace Corps Zinzin," said Osterlord. "Roger . . . over and out."

Osterlord, bare save for khaki shorts, scratched at his tumble of uncombed hair. "What the hell was that 'pretty' bit?" he asked.

"I always sweet-talk the ladies," said Lew. "And what was all that citrus garbage you were talking?"

"Prudence and I have a little code when things get hairy."

"A code?" repeated Lew. "What kind of code? What were you saying?"

"Nothing much. Just a lot of yak." And Osterlord went out through the kitchen to take his morning outdoor shower in the trickle from the oil drum.

With Freddie away with the other boys at bush school, the breakfast was dismal. Jim opened a can of tuna to go with the melon, powdered milk and burnt toast. Lew tried to eat the fish, but his stomach rebelled. The first whiff of Jim's sulphurous native cigar did not help. Osterlord, not bothering to clear the dishes from the table, wheeled out his motorbike from its place near the door.

"Come on down to the road," he said. "We ought to make time today in spite of the rain. We're on an incline now."

But Lew was delayed for almost an hour. When he tried to light the kerosene stove to heat water for shaving, he found it wouldn't work. After lengthy, helpless tinkering, he decided a fuel line was plugged. He poked at it with a broom straw and finally opened a passage through the encrustations of grease and rotting food particles. Then he couldn't find Jim's pocket-size mirror and he nicked his chin while shaving by the reflection from a tin can.

The jeep's motor, moist from the night's rain, was sluggish in starting, and by the time Lew got underway on gummy, slippery roads, he was a coil of irritation. He headed for the government school.

The muddy school grounds were deserted save for two cows grazing in islets of grass in the soccer field. The zinc roof glistened under the full morning sun and the CARE kitchen threw an oblong shadow. Lew parked the vehicle and walked around to the front of the mud-stick school building.

Cindy and the four other Peace Corps teachers stood under the portico by the main doorway. There were no children to be seen nor any of the Kalya teachers.

"We lost," said Cindy.

Lew looked at his wrist watch. It was 9:30, an hour past the time when classes began.

"Not a kid showed," said Kramer, "and none of the Kalya teachers."

"There's the devil to pay," said Arch Lettermore, "but I guess ol' Genghis Khan already paid him."

Alice and Dotty leaned glumly against the building. "Welcome to the wake, Red," said Dotty. "Cripes, I mean you can buy this hole cheap today."

Alice glared at her roommate. "And if you say 'Wawa' just one more time, I'll scream."

"Really, didn't anybody show up?" asked Lew.

Cindy pointed over his shoulder. He turned to see three small girls, dressed in neat cotton school smocks, standing about a hundred yards away.

"They started across the field," said Cindy, "but then a woman ran after them and apparently warned them not to come any closer."

One of the girls waved and Lew could hear faint giggling. The volunteer teachers waved in reply.

"How about night school last night?" asked Lew.

"Only Oon Gilli and old Pimo came." Cindy shrugged. "Oon said our attendance was small-small."

Suddenly Cindy began to cry. She put her arms against a portico post and buried her head in them. Her shoulders heaved beneath the fresh gray dress and she wept with little choking sounds.

Ted Kramer patted her back. "Come on, Cindy," he said, "we'll figure out something." The others stood silently, too embarrassed to look at her.

When the sobs diminished, Alice rooted in her handbag for a hankerchief. Cindy dried her eyes with it.

"Thanks," she said. "I'm all right now. I'm sorry I . . ." She turned and looked at her notice posted on the door. "You might as well take it down, Dotty."

Cindy declined a ride. Instead she walked away alone, her head bent, across the wet soccer field.

Lew drove the others to the Franklin-Wyzansky house, then went on to Jim Osterlord's road project. The jeep sloshed through the puddles of Zinzin's streets. Some people stared at him, but Lew had the impression that others looked away when he passed.

Osterlord's road had been pushed almost a mile beyond the sluggish creek where Lew had seen the crew installing an oil-drum culvert two weeks before. The road now ended on a slight hill, a reddish slash into the towering, matted bush where the foliage shone moistly from the night's rain. There was no work gang in evidence, only Jim standing by his motorbike and Oon Gilli, shirtless, leaning on a long-handled spade. The heat in the narrow jungle cut had a clammy closeness.

"What's up?" asked Lew.

"That god-damned Genghis," said Jim through set teeth. "He came here early this morning and shanghaied the whole bunch to work on his farm."

"But how could he get away with that?" asked Lew.

"Oon tells me he made a speech in Mola and said they'd all be paid from the money collected by the Peace Corps. Genghis told them that both Muo and I had agreed to it."

Osterlord's words had an angry rush.

"Hold it, Jim," said Lew. "Slow down."

Osterlord ignored him. "Oon refused to go. Said he didn't believe him. So Genghis cursed him and said, in effect, that he'd get his. Right, Oon?" Osterlord spoke swiftly in Mola and Gilli nodded his head in assent.

"The crummy bastard!" shouted Osterlord. He swept his hand at the road which snaked back toward Zinzin. "But he's not going to stop me. By God, he's not. Listen, Red, you ride Oon home and then come right over to Steve's office. I'll meet you there."

Osterlord started the motorbike with a fierce kick of his leg, gunned the throttle and went slithering toward Zinzin in a spray of mud. Lew realized that Jim had not even bothered to ask about Cindy and the school.

Lew found Jim and Steven Muo in Muo's office talking heatedly in Mola. The commissioner shook hands with Lew.

"How do, mah fren'," he said gravely. "Bad news."

"I'm telling him Genghis has gone too far," said Jim. "Steve has got to crack down on him."

"How?" asked Lew. The question had been puzzling him since he left Jim at the road.

"He's got to go over to Genghis's farm and order him to release the men. And I mean, right now."

"No way," said Muo. He gestured helplessly and then pointed to the crossed Mola spears on the wall. "Ol' days no mo'ah."

"Order him in the name of the government," said Osterlord. He repeated the sentence in Mola.

Muo shook his head. "He Fam'ly," he said. "An' road is Peez-kor. No gub'ment."

The talk went on. Osterlord, outraged over the road and insisting on action, finally grew provoked with his friend. Muo, at first stubbornly, then sulkily, argued that he had no weapons with which to contest Moses Harter. His heavy-muscled torso seemed to shrink under the pressure of the dilemma and several times he looked pleadingly at Corleigh. He was a frustrated man and defeat was written on his broad, black face.

"No way," he said finally. "Eh, ya. Ever't'ing chac-la. We write lett' one time to Link Beach. Maybe he know."

Osterlord reluctantly agreed, muttering over the waste of valuable days. He wrote in English while he and Muo jointly composed in Mola. In essence, the letter outlined the impasse at Zinzin and asked Beach's aid in formulating a plan to oppose Moses Harter.

"You're not making enough of the school," offered Lew.

"What about the school?" asked Jim. He was chewing on a pencil.

"Not a kid showed up this morning," said Lew. "Cindy cried. They all figure they're licked."

"Oh." Jim impatiently jotted a few lines in the manner of a man being forced to deal with trivia.

"Your road isn't everything, you know," said Lew.

Osterlord flared. "Except for this building and the CARE kitchen, it's the only damn thing built in this town in five years."

He sealed the letter in an envelope. Lew folded it into his wallet.

"I've got to hit the road," Lew said. "I'll see you next week. Let's hope Link can come up with something."

Gloom enveloped Lew's round of four Peace Corps houses for the mail pickup. Cindy said she had no heart for writing home. Her face seemed drained. He found Arch and Ted pitching pennies in the shade of their house and arguing peevishly about religion. At the Franklin-Wyzansky house, Alice handed him one ink-smeared envelope, reported spiritlessly that Dotty had gone back to bed. At this last stop, Lew saw a knot of people gathered at the Oon Gilli hut adjacent to Arlene Offenbach's house. Arlene came down the gummy hillside road to meet the jeep. She appeared distraught as she stopped him some distance from the mission compound.

"They've brought Morfu's clothes," she said in a tight voice. Lew saw that she had been crying.

"When?"

"Just a few minutes ago. Maybe you'd better talk to Oon and his wife. I just can't take it any more."

Lew left the jeep and slogged up the hill, his heavy GI work shoes sucking at the mud. Oon Gilli squatted on his haunches beside his hut, his head drooping. Mrs. Gilli huddled at the hut's entrance. Her expression was blankly sorrowing and her hands kneaded a boy's khaki shorts. On the ground lay a ragged T-shirt, a matchbox and a piece of blue-black iron ore. Several neighbors, including a bare-breasted young woman and an old man with wrinkled shanks and leg sores, stood awkwardly a few feet away.

Mrs. Gilli looked bleakly at Corleigh and pointed to the piece of iron ore. "Teach' Full' gib Morfu one time," she said. Her dry eyes held a look of desolation that made Lew want to turn away.

He went to Oon and squatted beside him. "Bush school," said Oon in a strangled voice. He raised his head and looked at Lew for understanding.

Lew nodded. He had sensed it and now he knew. In the ancient Mola ritual, the dumping of a boy's clothes and belongings at the hut door of his parents meant that he had died in Golo bush school. There was never an explanation. Identity of the Golo tutors remained unknown and when the boys returned from the bush, newly initiated into the secret society, their lips were sealed. In the old days, the deposit of clothes signaled that the boy had been selected for human sacrifice by fire. Now, since the government edict banning religious killings, there was no way of knowing.

Oon dropped his head again and Lew studied the strong face

with its heavy Mola features. Was Oon thinking what he was? The sequence of events was too striking to be mere coincidence. Oon had continued to attend Cindy's night class. He had protested the dispatch of his son to bush school. Then, this morning, he had refused to follow the road gang which deserted Osterlord's project to work on Harter's farm. The time interval indicated that Harter could act swiftly and that the bush school site was not far away.

"Moses Harter bad man," Lew whispered.

Gilli swung his head sharply toward Corleigh. His look was one of startled, shared recognition, but it fled almost at once. In its place came an expression of haunting fear.

"Eh, ya," said Gilli. He shot another glance at Lew, unfriendly this time, and quickly rose and stalked into his hut.

Arlene came hurrying from her house, bearing a metal pot and two china mugs. She bent over Mrs. Gilli.

"Here's some iced tea," she said. "It's nice and cool."

Mrs. Gilli accepted a mug and sat sipping the liquid. Her eyes were blank beneath the bright green band wrapped about her head. She rubbed her bare toes against the piece of iron ore.

"Morfu good boy," she said.

"I know," said Arlene. "Miss Fuller said he was the smartest in her class."

Mrs. Gilli set the mug on the ground, took her son's frayed T-shirt and spread it tenderly across her knees. She muttered something in Mola and then began to moan. The sounds were low, private ones, and she swayed slightly, oblivious of the people around her.

Arlene put her head at the hut door and called softly to Oon Gilli. There was no response. She patted Mrs. Gilli's shoulder, but the woman did not look up. The neighbors drifted away, one by one.

Arlene took Lew's arm and walked with him down the hill to the jeep. They stood by a fender in the brutal midday sun and Arlene began to sob.

"I'm frightened, Lew," she said. She held his arm tightly.

"It's that maniac, Harter," he said. "Oon knows it too, but he's afraid to admit it."

"We're all afraid," said Arlene. "I'm not sure I can stick it out here. I don't know, Lew, suddenly it's all so strange and so . . ." Her voice caught in another dry sob.

"Come on, I'll drive you over to Alice and Dotty's. It'll do you good to have some of your friends around."

She shook her head. "No, I'll stay." She smiled once, then turned and picked her way up the mucky slope toward her mud-stick house.

Lew's last sight of the mission hilltop as he turned the jeep around would remain with him for years. The Gillis' circular hut stood alone in the brilliant sunlight, its brown thatched roof casting a thin shadow. In the doorway slumped the figure of a woman, a boy's shirt spread over her knees and at her feet, crumpled khaki shorts, a mug and a lump of iron ore. Overhead, against the blank, blue sky, a single hooded vulture soared on immobile wings.

The old mood of depression settled on Lew as he drove toward Loli. The school was closed, Steve Muo seemed undone, Zinzin was in the clutch of fear and Morfu Gilli, the boy with the bright eyes and the finely chiseled features, had died somewhere in the tall bush that walled the unfinished road of Jim Osterlord. There was the hot urge to fight back, but how could they contend with a man whose allies were superstition and dread and a tangle of Golo rites, dancing devil and jungle murder? Lew could imagine trying to explain it all to his father back in Evanston, and he wondered whether even such a knowing man as Ambassador Milbank would understand. Only Lincoln Beach, of all the people he knew, would fully comprehend, but could even Beach find a way?

The mood persisted throughout the drive to Loli and even the thought of a night of air-conditioned comfort in Forrest Stevenson's trailer home did not lift the cloud of despair. At his first Loli stop, at Susan's, he called "bock-bock" several times before he realized she was not at home. A packet of letters, bound with string, rested on the sill behind the screen door.

When he turned back toward the road, about a hundred yards away, he saw a motorcycle beside the parked jeep and a security patrolman looking in the front window. He was surprised, for ordinarily Booth's men seldom ventured beyond the paved section of the highway which ended fifty miles from Ft. Paul. As

Lew walked toward the jeep, the officer saw him, grinned and waved a companionable greeting.

"All okay," the man called. He kicked his motor into action and racketed away toward the center of Loli.

Lew tossed Susan's letters into the mail sack on the rear seat and settled into place preparatory to starting the car. As he did so, he sensed a flow of movement on the floor board to his right.

Then he saw it. The head was long and narrow, and in the open, bluish-white mouth a partially protruding tongue wavered like a tiny pendulum. Behind the head curved a dark loop. It was a black mamba, perhaps six or seven feet in length.

In one motion Lew grabbed the door handle, thrusting it downward, and threw his body to the left. At the instant his right foot was jerked from the floor board, the snake struck in a downward lunge. Lew felt nothing and he hoped blindly, in his flooding panic, that the fangs had broken harmlessly against the heavy leather of his GI boots. He lurched from the car, slammed the door and, in a flash, remembered gratefully that all the windows save the one at the driver's seat were up. He walked quickly, trying not to run, to the rear of the jeep wagon. As he bent over to inspect his right shoe, he found that his hands were shaking. There was no new mark on the shoe. Then he saw two small moist spots, about a half inch apart, low on the right leg of his khaki pants. He looked quickly at the sweat sock beneath, but the wool was fuzzy and soiled and he could see nothing. Pulling down the sock, he inspected the skin just above the shoe top. He thought he saw them: two tiny red dots on the skin.

A wave of fright rolled over him and in vivid, scattered fragments, he remembered what happened when a black mamba bit. If the fangs reached bare skin and injected venom, two drops could be fatal within an hour, frequently within as little as twenty minutes. A man's breathing quickly became shallow and he died with terrible, gasping struggles for air. The mamba's venom, he knew, poisoned the nerve centers controlling the lungs and the lungs shortly collapsed. At the same time, the heart beat wildly, for the poison paralyzed the inhibitory nerves which regulate the heart's pumping. Lew felt his own heart racing, whether from fright or venom, he did not know.

A shivering convulsed his whole body. He put a hand on a

rear fender to steady himself. He must think clearly, swiftly. He seemed to sense a tingling on his lower right leg, but he could not be sure. He thought he'd seen the fang marks on his leg, but again he could not be absolutely certain. Where was the medical kit? Just inside the tailgate, squeezed behind the spare tire. The mamba must still be on the front floor board. Gently, with trembling hands, he turned the handle which rolled down the rear window. He reached over the tailgate, grabbed the medical box, tugged feverishly to free it. The box stuck for a moment, then came loose. Lew quickly rolled up the window again.

Now, what were the instructions? First, inject one ampule of 10 c.c.'s of the bivalent serum into his leg approximately at the spot where he'd seen the two red marks. But now he couldn't see them, or could he? For God's sake, quit shaking, he told himself. Think. Next? What was next? He couldn't remember. His mind, curiously, could envision the entire page of Sam Zerwick's medical manual in the section on snake attacks, but the words below the first instruction were illegible. Oh God, what was that second step? Two minutes must have passed already.

At that moment he heard a soft plop. He moved back instinctively and, under the car, he could see a long, black rope wriggling from the road. The mamba, having crawled out the open front window, vanished into scrub foliage at the road's shoulder.

The snake's departure seemed to unlock Lew's memory. Second step, inject another ampule of serum heartward of the bite, on the upper leg if the snake struck at the foot. Lew let down his trousers and underdrawers and jabbed the needle into his thigh. The final step came easily, for he and other volunteers had joked about it often. The last 10 c.c.'s were to be injected into a buttock. He reached into the kit, then felt another surge of panic. There was no third ampule. He fumbled frantically amid bandage rolls, chloroquine tablets and bottles of aspirin.

He stood still for a moment, riven with fear. Had he or had he not been bitten? Slowly he pulled up his drawers and pants and fastened his belt buckle.

Suddenly his strength drained from him like water rushing

through a broken pipe. Lew fainted. The last thing his mind told him was that his head struck the tailgate as he fell, blotting out the flash recollection of a uniformed security patrolman riding away from the jeep on a motorcycle.

10

Lew awoke to find himself in a strange room. The walls were painted a soft pink, he lay between fresh sheets and through an open screened window, he could hear the shouts of children at play. He stirred and looked about him. Next to him was another bed, similar to his, with a white coverlet tucked neatly in place. A mirrored dresser held a row of bottles and a large hairbrush, and on the walls were two framed Andrew Wyeth prints of New England autumn scenes.

Lew was pleasantly relaxed and his limbs felt buoyant, as though he were floating. Only the muggy heat and a small, dull ache at his right temple marred a sensation of mild euphoria. He raised a hand and felt a bandage and a swelling above his forehead. Then he remembered the rear end of the jeep and an opened medical kit.

He threw back the sheet and sat upright to examine his right leg. It appeared normal and he sank back again, sweating slightly, while memories of the jeep and the mamba marched in swift sequence. He knew he had fainted and struck his head on the tailgate, but what then? He could remember tiled walls and a hover of faces, Forrest Stevenson's among them. Then he saw Sam Zerwick and a worried look on Prudence's little freckled face and he had fragmented recollections of a long ride on a mattress.

The door opened a few inches and he saw Prudence looking at him with a frown of concern. He waved to her. "Come on in."

She came to the foot of the bed. "Well," she said, "looks like I've got a live man in my house."

"Your house?"

She nodded. Her hair was combed out full and softly waved. She wore a white sweater and green pleated skirt. Her lips had color. In the crease of her frown, Lew could see a splash of freckles. He felt good.

"Wha' hoppened?" he asked.

"You tell me," she replied. "Susan came walking home five days ago in Loli to find what she thought was your dead body lying behind the jeep. There was a medical kit on the ground and a couple of used-up snake-bite ampules. Did you think a snake bit you?"

"I thought so, but I wasn't sure." He related the whole incident for her.

"Well, it didn't," she said. "The fangs went through your pants, but just barely. There were several tiny dried crystals of venom in the fabric. You must have pulled your leg away just as the snake struck."

"I did," said Lew, "but I could have sworn I saw two marks on my leg. Jesus, then I fainted—like an old lady."

Prudence sat on the edge of the bed, caressing his forehead, and told him what occurred after Susan found him. When Susan saw the expended ampules, she found where he had injected himself, but could discover no evidence that the fangs had reached him. She waited until she could hail a passing money bus. Several passengers helped her bring a mattress from her house and the bus carried Lew to the four-room Episcopal hospital at Loli. A Dutch doctor examined him and decided Lew had suffered a concussion. Forrest Stevenson notified Peace Corps Ft. Paul via a USAID dump-truck driver. Sam Zerwick and Prudence Stauffer arrived in Loli in late afternoon of the second day. The Peace Corps physician agreed with the Dutch doctor that Corleigh probably would recover from the concussion without permanent damage. Lew, she said, had quite a few conscious

periods and he had joked with her and Dr. Zerwick. Yesterday
they'd put him on a mattress in the specially padded physician's
jeep and brought him down to Ft. Paul.

"Yeah," he said. "I guess I do remember most of that, but I
don't remember talking to you."

"Once you said I was cute, but that's as far as you'd commit
yourself."

"So?" He grinned. "Who says I didn't know what I was doing?
Hey, what day is this?"

"Tuesday," she said. "Almost dinnertime. Going to have
chicken broth, poached eggs on toast and grapefruit juice."

"Can I get up?"

"Sam says it's okay," she replied, "until you start feeling dizzy
or weak. Then back to bed."

Lew wore his pajamas to the dinner table and found that
neither he nor Prudence was embarrassed by his attire. She joked
about his five days' growth of beard, a rusty stubble that tickled
his jaw.

"You look like either Van Gogh or a buccaneer," she said.
"Not sure which."

"It's funny," he said, "but I feel at home here."

"Never had a man around the house before," she said. "I like
it."

When they finished eating, Lew broached the subject that had
been bothering him since he awakened. "Prude, I'm convinced
Booth's security cop, the one I saw standing by the jeep, dumped
that mamba into the car. I suppose you think I dreamed it?"

She shook her head. "No, I believe you."

"But why? You wouldn't think Booth would try to get me just
because I brought Steve Muo down to Ft. Paul once?"

"Maybe," she said. "He did threaten you at Founders House
that night. But my guess is that the officer was in Zinzin and
after all the commotion there, he trailed you down to Loli. You
see, Harter and others of The Family have gotten the idea that
you're the chief culprit in the Zinzin trouble."

"How do you know what happened in Zinzin?"

"I talk on the radio to Jim Osterlord every morning, remember?" She rattled the dishes as she cleared the table. "But a lot
of people in Ft. Paul know now too. Moses Harter came down

the day before yesterday and saw Old Number One. Apparently he accused the Peace Corps of making trouble in Zinzin and demanded that Old Number One put a stop to it. The embassy's all upset and the rep's in a stew too. Williams puts on a pained look, as though it were all started just to bug him."

"Wait'll I tell him about Booth's man putting a mamba after me."

Prudence paused in her table tidying. "I'm not sure I'd tell him, Red."

"Why not, for God's sake? I might have died."

"Know it. But how can you prove anything? You knocked yourself out and then went into a coma. People will say you were seeing things."

"But you believe me," he protested.

"Sure." She stooped and kissed his forehead. "But I'm not sure other people will. . . . Well, you don't have to decide right now. It's time you got back to bed."

Lew did feel weak, his legs watery, as he walked the few yards to the bedroom. It was a relief to get back between the sheets and within a few moments, he was asleep again. When he awakened, it was dark in the room and he had only half the bed. Prudence lay beside him, her legs pressed against his and her chin resting on his shoulder.

"Some hospital," he said. "Some nurse."

"Awful glad you're here," she said. "It was a close one."

He moved on his side and put his arms around her. She snuggled closer and he could feel the warmth and the smoothness of her skin.

"Do you always sleep in just your panties?" he asked.

She shook her head in the crook of his arm. "Just wanted to feel close to you."

"New health measure, huh?" he asked.

He held her tightly and she murmured an objection. "Lie still, Lew. Sam Zerwick says you should take it easy."

"I feel okay. Don't worry. This time I won't faint."

"Sure?"

They laughed and she kissed him. Their embrace was one of questioning, and later she did not protest when Lew slid off her briefs and his pajamas. They made love, tenderly at first and then passionately, and in the long, lulling aftermath, he wondered at her intensity and at the fresh candor of her desire.

"I think I am your girl," she whispered. Then they fell asleep and this time, Lew slept soundly until morning.

He stayed at Prudence's house three more days. The headache slowly dissolved, his strength returned and he shaved himself while she sat on the edge of the bathtub and watched him as seriously and as intently as a child. He discovered that he did not want to leave and he secretly hoped that he might have a small relapse that would provide an excuse for staying.

"You suppose this is what being married is like?" Prudence asked once.

"If so," he replied, "it's not such a bad deal."

"I like Maureen Sutherland's word better," she said. "You know, t'riffic."

Sam Zerwick, beaming and mock truculent, called each day. He said he wanted it clearly understood that he had prescribed Prudence's house as the ideal recovery ward. "Williams made some sniffling objection," he said, "and I dared him to stay just one night at that noisy barracks of a hostel."

Lincoln Beach came for a long visit while Prudence was at work at Peace Corps headquarters. After listening to Lew's description of the Loli incident, Beach said he agreed with Prudence. It would be wiser, he said, for Lew to keep his belief about Booth's security patrolman to himself. The story would seem far-fetched to those unacquainted with Booth's methods.

Lew belatedly remembered the letter from Muo, found his wallet and gave Beach the note. Beach shook his head as he read it.

"I've got no plan for them—not after Harter came down and made some kind of deal with Old Number One," he said. "We're too small and we're not ready yet. The Peace Corps is the only muscle in Zinzin. If you can't keep Harter in line up there, nobody can—not yet."

"We tried Cindy's scheme and we lost," said Lew, "but good. Morfu Gilli dead and Jim's road stopped completely."

"The Peace Corps has one more trump card," said Beach.

"What's that?"

"Moses Harter owns two houses that the Peace Corps rents in Zinzin," said Beach.

"Yeah, Jim told me. The one Cindy lives in and Jim's. Some kind of dummy arrangement, isn't it?"

"Right. The Peace Corps could put the squeeze on Harter by canceling the rentals."

Lew thought for a moment. "I'm not sure it would accomplish much. Still, I hate to see Genghis raising hell with the Peace Corps and making money out of it too."

Beach nodded. "This is a long battle." He eyed Lew's head at the spot where Dr. Zerwick had placed a fresh, smaller bandage. "Have you still got doubts about being with us, Red?"

"You kidding? Booth tried to kill me." Lew could see the bluish-white open mouth of the mamba and the tiny, flickering tongue. He shivered.

"Now you know how it feels," said Beach.

They talked at length of Cindy, and Beach wanted to know every detail of her confrontation with Moses Harter. He beamed admiringly when Lew described her unruffled poise.

"A great girl," said Beach. "Kalya could use her full-time, believe me."

"How about you?"

Beach laughed and shook his head. "She's going home with your group. How many days now?"

"My God, I'd forgotten," said Lew. "Let's see, it's sixty-something. Yeah, sixty-eight."

Lew went home to the hostel the next morning, a Friday. The dormitories were in their customary state of soggy disorder. Arthur was still leaving greasy dishes in the drying rack, and somebody had made off with Lew's mosquito netting and a packet of stainless-steel razor blades. The Fizi squatters behind the house cackled their discontent at one another. The day stewed like a pot of malodorous vegetables. Within an hour Lew was as testy and limp as the other volunteer leaders. The weekend was worse, for it rained with battering ferocity each afternoon and the visiting Peace Corps teachers from outcountry tracked mud through the kitchen and sat like sodden lumps about the record player.

Lew was glad when Monday morning arrived and he could

leave for the Peace Corps office and his neglected paperwork chores. Carter Williams was waiting for him. Williams guided Lew into his office by an elbow, inquired solicitously about his head injury and insisted that Lew sit in the more comfortable swivel chair.

Williams said he wanted a full report, so Lew talked for an hour, describing the events at Zinzin and Loli. But, heeding the advice of Prudence and Beach, he did not mention the Booth security officer. Williams slumped in a side chair and fretfully scraped at his fingernails with a penknife.

"I can't understand how that snake got in the jeep," he said. He darted a glance at Lew. "Do you think somebody put it there?"

"Search me. Maybe I left the front door open." Lew felt his voice lacked conviction. He knew the door was closed tight when he returned to the jeep. "It wouldn't be the first time a mamba crawled into a car."

"Well, thank God it missed. You're one volunteer I wouldn't want to lose, Lew."

Williams jabbed at the desk blotter with his penknife, and Lew recalled the chief's frequent boast that there had not been a single Peace Corps casualty requiring a disability termination during his tenure in Kalya.

"That Zinzin business is a mess," said Williams. His plump face sagged as though under visible pressure. "Old Number One's on a rampage and, of course, the ambassador demands an accounting from me. I think Miss Fuller made a serious mistake in posting that notice about the school. I can't understand why she didn't clear with me first."

He sounded petulant and hurt. Lew passed up the obvious invitation to comment.

"She seems to be a sensible young lady," said Williams. "What ever got into her?"

"It seemed pretty logical, sir," said Lew. "After all, Ambassador Milbank himself said that keeping the school open was a legitimate Peace Corps concern."

"I know," said Williams, "but there are ways and there are ways. Miss Fuller took the most provocative course possible.

She must know of Moses Harter's closeness to Vining and of the delicacy of the whole situation."

Delicacy? Lew wanted to shout a rebuttal. How about Morfu Gilli, probably slain in bush school, and the impressment of Osterlord's work gang and a mamba planted on a floor board by an agent of Hulbert Booth?

"The PCVs are upset." Lew controlled his temper with an effort. "They were sent up there to teach and that tinpot dictator, Genghis Khan, knifes everything they try to do. You've got to understand how they feel, Mr. Williams."

"I do, of course." Williams paused and inspected his newly cleaned nails. "Lew, there's another matter I'd like to discuss with you. You've been a fine volunteer, one of the best. Also you've been through a harrowing experience, and we still aren't completely sure about that head bump of yours. You've only got a little more than two months until termination. I want you to take it easier on the last leg, so, with your permission, I'd like to transfer you to Kolamon."

"Kolamon?" The name dazzled. High in the mountains, Kolamon was the only posh Peace Corps billet in all of Kalya. The five volunteers there taught at the new teacher-training institute. An American foundation had granted funds to erect modern, stone buildings on a campus of rolling lawns and tigerwood and sweet cedar trees. The institute had electric lights, hot and cold running water and cozily furnished quarters for the faculty. Kolamon boasted Kalya's lone swimming pool. The mountain air was bracing and the rainfall moderate. The Peace Corps contingent, a breezy, insouciant lot, was dubbed "the jet set" by envious colleagues. Two romances in last year's departing group led to marriage, and this year three of the Kolamon teachers had applied for a year's extension of duty.

"Just the place for you," said Williams. "You might teach a history class, or, if you'd prefer, you could just act as a kind of administrative leader for these last two months."

At one time the offer would have been irresistible. But now Lew thought of Zinzin, of the cloud of dejection in the Franklin-Wyzansky household, of the rapacious Genghis Khan, of Steve Muo and Link Beach. No, it would be desertion under fire. And then there was Prudence, and Kolamon was two hundred miles away. . . .

"Thanks," said Lew, "but I'd rather stick it out on the Zinzin road. There's going to be trouble up there for some time."

"That's just the point. Let me be frank with you, Lew. Commissioner Downing and the Prime Minister have the idea that you're pretty deep into Zinzin politics." Williams shot an appraising glance at him.

"Me? Why me? I'm just a truck driver."

"I think they have the idea," said Williams, "that because you go back and forth between Zinzin and Ft. Paul, you've been instrumental in lining up this Peace Corps office against Moses Harter."

"I wish I had," said Lew.

Williams colored at Lew's rebuke. "Let's say you've become a symbol to them. So, it would take the heat off me if you'd consent to a transfer. A favor to me, in a way, but actually to the whole Peace Corps too."

"But that's chucking in the towel," said Lew. "I think we ought to stand and fight."

"And just how would you do that?" Williams sounded peevish. It was impossible to imagine Carter Williams flying battle flags.

"For one thing," said Lew, "you could cancel the rental arrangements on two Peace Corps houses that Harter owns up there —and move Cindy and Jim somewhere else."

Williams frowned. "I don't recall his name on any of the lease papers."

"No," said Lew, "because he's renting us Cindy's house and Osterlord's through a dummy name. It gives me a royal pain to think that guy gets about eight hundred dollars a year from the Peace Corps."

"Well, of course, it would require quite an investigation to get at the facts . . . and I'm not sure it would be a good policy anyway. . . ."

There was a knock on the door and the blonde volunteer receptionist entered, carrying a sheet of paper.

"This just came over from the embassy," she said.

Williams read the message, then looked at Corleigh with an

expression which managed to blend relief and anxiety simultaneously.

"I'm afraid it's a little late for any . . . er . . . rental retaliations," he said. He handed the paper to Lew.

PRIORITY
PECTO
CARTER WILLIAMS, REPRESENTATIVE
U.S. EMBASSY
FT. PAUL
KALYA

Startling demand from Prime Minister Vining that Peace Corps withdraw Zinsin. Ambassador Milbank advised to delay matter pending consideration here. Rush detailed report. PCVL Lewis Corleigh ordered Washington for consultation first available transportation.

Frank Sherrod
Deputy Director
Peace Corps Washington

Lew blinked and reread the last sentence. It was difficult to believe that he had been singled out by name in a Washington cable. "PCVL Lewis Corleigh" seemed to jump off the page at him.

"Me again," he said. "Jesus, you'd think I was trying to bomb the Palace or something."

"I told you that you've become a symbol," said Williams. "Vining and Downing have got the idea you started the whole ruckus. So I would surmise that Milbank named you in his dispatches."

"Well, what now? Why me?" Lew was baffled. If Washington wanted firsthand reports, why not Cindy Fuller or Jim Osterlord?

Williams ignored the question, went to his desk and rummaged in a drawer. "Let's see. There's a Pan Am jet tonight, I think. It stops at Monrovia and Dakar and then direct into Dulles at Washington. I'll have to work all day on my report. You can deliver it for me."

He found the airline schedule. "Yep, that's right. Ten o'clock from Vining Airport. You'd better get over to the Pan Am office. The girl will fix you up travel orders and a voucher for you." Lew left the office in a fog of speculation and plans. He picked up the ticket, round-trip economy class, packed a bag at the hostel and made arrangements for another volunteer leader to take over his Zinzin route. He had but one suit, so he borrowed another from his substitute driver. He paid a hurried visit to Lincoln Beach, then spent several hours in search of Prudence. He located her at the Ft. Paul headquarters of CARE, where she was trying to arrange food supplies for a new CARE kitchen built by Peace Corps teachers in one of the hut villages in her district. Prudence, both dismayed and excited over his trip, agreed to drive him to the airport.

Lew spent the remainder of the time writing out instructions for his substitute on the Zinzin route . . . Susan's balky refrigerator . . . eighty-seven, no eighty-eight, mail pickups with specific directions to Peace Corps houses . . . special supplies for Roger's lepers . . . best shower, Arlene Offenbach's . . . best overnight stop, Forrest Stevenson's at Loli . . . make sure Katherine and Barbara aren't skipping school at Kpapata . . . new rat trap for Arch Lettermore . . . most reliable informants on Zinzin, Cindy Fuller and Jim Osterlord. The list of instructions, crossed out, erased and revised, finally covered two dozen pages.

At nine that night he went back to headquarters to pick up Carter Williams' official report. The Peace Corps chief sat alone at a typewriter. He had a harried expression, his collar was open at the neck and a number of paper cups stood on his desk. The electric coffeemaker was simmering.

"I hate reports," he said. "After twenty years of them in Philadelphia, I thought I was off to a stimulating job in exotic Africa —but not to make out more reports."

"Wawa," said Lew.

"You can say that again." Williams folded a sheaf of papers and sealed them into an envelope, affixing a special layer of Scotch tape. He wrote "Confidential" on the envelope, addressed it to Frank Sherrod, and handed it to Lew.

"Nothing in there you don't know," he said. He pushed back his swivel chair and sighed heavily. "Lew, I think you ought to realize that your role has changed now. Here in Ft. Paul, we have our differences over policy and that's the way it should be. A passel of yes-men may be all right in the Army or Navy, but not the Peace Corps. We talk it out, don't we?"

Lew nodded and Williams smiled. "But in Washington, we have to present one front—the Peace Corps Kalya front. Essentially I say in my report that we should seek an accommodation with Old Number One on Zinzin. There's just no sense in jeopardizing our whole position here over one school and one road in one town. Do you agree?"

"It depends," said Lew, "on what the accommodation is."

Williams opened his palms wide in a gesture of assent. "Of course, of course. Let's just make sure that we don't become inflexible. The man of principle who won't bend a little can lose everything."

Lew, uncomfortable in shirt, tie and city suit, stood uneasily by the desk. "I'm just going to state the facts as I know them," he said.

"Exactly." Williams reached out and pumped Lew's hand. "Good luck, Lew, and when you get back, we'll have that nice billet at Kolamon waiting for you."

Williams escorted him through the darkened reception lobby. At the main door, he placed a hand on Lew's shoulder. "Be a team player, Lew." He paused. "As a personal favor to me."

"I'll do my best," said Lew.

Prudence was waiting in a staff jeep. They drove through Ft. Paul, rich in odors and rustling night sounds, past the clay bug-a-bug mounds and past the marshes where the mist hung low and bullfrogs croaked like despairing old men. Then came a rubber plantation, its orderly rows of trees in marching formation. Prudence parked at a darkened end of the airport lot and they kissed with a long embrace.

"Take care of yourself, Red," she said.

"I'm going to miss you, Prude." And he knew he would.

"Am I still your girl?"

"Sure. We drank palm wine to it. Remember?"

She took his face in her hands and gazed at him with her most concentrated, solemn look. Her chin was thrust forward.

"Lew, tell me something honestly—and don't laugh. Am I any good in bed?"

But he couldn't help laughing. There was such an intensity in Prudence and such . . . how had Cindy said it? . . . such vulnerability under that brusque exterior of the Peace Corps staff member. His laugh was an affectionate one, and he kissed her again.

"Good?" he repeated. "You're great. Thank God for lady missionaries."

He carried his old leather suitcase in one hand and held Prudence's hand in the other as they walked into the terminal. The bronze doorway plaque announced: "Alexander Vining International Airport. Constructed, 1953, in the administration of Alexander Vining, Prime Minister of Kalya, 1944– ."

All lights were on, shining in yellow pulses from the erratic airport generator. There was a welter of activity and the usual chaotic battles between passengers and the Kalya officials in their gray, baggy uniforms. Embarking fee, two dollars. Visa exit stamp, one dollar. Outgoing customs inspection. Ticket validation. Health-card stamps. A florid German businessman cursed, two bewildered Kalyan women wept, the incoming jet screamed and the loudspeaker fretted cavernously: "Mr. Frawley, Mr. Frawley, Mr. Frawley." There was no enlightenment as to what the unknown Mr. Frawley was supposed to do. A snarl occurred at the weigh-in scales when the clerk ticketed Lew's bag for Dakar instead of Dulles, and the head ticket agent had to be summoned to unravel the situation. The terminal windows, for some inexplicable reason, were all shut, and the barn of a hall steamed like a locker room. Lew's fresh shirt was streaked with sweat, and in the distance, he could hear the crash of thunder.

Lew and Prudence parted at the gate as other passengers filed in a long line to the high-tailed jet with its row of lighted windows like phosphorescent markings on a great fish.

"Stick up for the PCVs, Red," said Prudence.

"I'll try," he said. "Williams wants me to take his line—and urge that we make book with Old Number One on Zinzin."

She wrinkled her nose in distaste. "Carter hates trouble. If we can't work for the tribes, what's the use of staying here?"

"Right." He kissed her good-by. "If anything new happens up there, get word to me quick in the embassy pouch."

He was the last one on the plane. The engines shrieked, then leveled into a shrill, steady whine as the jet taxied to the end of the runway. When it slid into the sky, Lew could see the shimmer of Ft. Paul to his left and a straggle of street lights marking the beginning of the highway to Zinzin.

Lew's seatmate, a Louisianan with a purring drawl, talked of the oil boom in Nigeria. They were at thirty thousand feet a half hour later when Lew realized that somewhere beneath him stood the mud huts of Zinzin. He could visualize the group at Alice and Dotty's, stewing in their frustration, and he wondered if even old Pimo had showed up at Cindy's night class.

"Coffee?" asked the stewardess. Lew shook his head without looking up. He was thinking of Oon Gilli's wife, huddled at her hut door with Morfu's shirt spread across her knees.

11

Frank Sherrod, deputy director of the Peace Corps, tossed the packet of papers on his desk, lit a cigarette and leaned back in his chair. He shook his head, smiling in the manner of a man who does not quite credit what he has read.

"Your rep is some man for detail," he said. "Incredible stuff. A real bucket of eels."

Lew shifted in his chair. "It seemed familiar enough in Kalya, but walking across Lafayette Park this morning, I felt like it all happened on another planet."

Sherrod nodded sympathetically. "The jets cut time and distance, but they seem to widen the culture gap. It's hard to place old Andy Jackson's statue down there in the same world with the devil dance and bush killings."

"You're right." Lew was pleased at Sherrod's insight and astonished at his grasp of the details in Carter Williams' lengthy report. The deputy director had raced through some twenty pages in less than a quarter of an hour.

Lew's initial qualms had been substantial when he entered the graying twelve-story limestone building which housed Peace Corps headquarters. But soon after he entered Sherrod's fifth-floor office at 9 A.M., he had been put at ease. Almost at once the deputy loosened his tie and invited Lew to take off his coat. In the opening small talk Sherrod revealed himself as warm, friendly and perceptive about the problems of Peace Corps workers. He was a lanky man, probably in his early forties, Lew guessed, whose brown hair was crew-cut and whose eyebrows needed clipping. He had a disarming habit of mocking himself and his official position by a casual phrase and a deprecatory hunch of his shoulders.

Lew was grateful for the informal atmosphere, for he'd had only two hours' sleep at the Hotel Washington, across Fifteenth Street from the Treasury Building, following the jet's dawn arrival at Dulles Airport. Unable to do more than catnap as the plane crossed the Atlantic, Lew had rehearsed his story and had imagined himself dueling painfully with some obtuse Peace Corps official in an effort to explain the significance of bush school rites and Moses Harter's law practice. Now, with Sherrod, he felt his task already half completed.

"So much for Williams' view," said Sherrod. "Now I want to hear your story. Williams doesn't know Zinzin firsthand. You do."

"It's pretty long," said Lew.

"Never mind, I don't bore easy—except when I hear myself talking. We've got all morning. Shoot."

Lew related the whole, complicated tale. He even told what he had withheld from Williams—that he believed one of Colonel Booth's men had placed the mamba in his jeep with deliberate intent to kill him. He failed to mention only two essential facts, that Lincoln Beach and Steven Muo had formed an underground "Forge" to battle The Family and that Lew Corleigh and Jim Osterlord had pledged to help it.

Sherrod interrupted only for brief questions and when Lew finished, almost an hour later, the deputy director left his chair and stood for a moment by his window overlooking the courtyard between Connecticut Avenue and H Street. Then he sat on the sill and turned toward Lew.

"Now, first, Lew," he said, "I want you to get over any feeling of guilt about not talking to the CIA—and I agree with you, Kellogg sounds like an agency man. The CIA has instructed its agents not to pin down Peace Corps people for information. That's government policy. One major case of a volunteer spying for the CIA, and the revelation could ruin this organization abroad. So, forget it."

"Thanks," said Lew. "It's been bugging me. The guy made me feel kind of unpatriotic."

"Don't. And if Kellogg presses you again, tell him I ordered you not to talk." Sherrod paused and looked out the window again. "Now, about your story. It dovetails with Williams' in everything except the overtones. I can tell you think this Zinzin business is crucial to the Peace Corps and its aims. Williams, as I suppose you already know, definitely does not."

"Williams," said Lew, "doesn't think the school and the road are worth a showdown fight with Prime Minister Vining. The PCVs feel just the opposite. If we let Harter keep on terrorizing the town, we might as well pack up and leave."

"And if we don't . . ." Sherrod paused and glanced sharply at Lew. "If we don't, we get thrown out of Zinzin."

"We . . ."

"That's what it boils down to, isn't it? You've been called back here because Vining, or Old Number One as you call him, demands that the Peace Corps get out of Zinzin. Unless we make a swift 'accommodation' with him, to use Carter Williams' word, we either have to pack up voluntarily or be ordered out by the Kalya government."

"I guess that's about the size of it," said Lew. He felt outpointed. Sherrod was a man of direct mental processes.

"No, that's only part of the size of it." Sherrod dropped his smile and his tone grew brisker. "If we don't accede to Vining's demands on Zinzin, we risk being thrown out of Kalya altogether. And if the Peace Corps has to leave Kalya, we face a very ugly situation. The loss of Vining's friendship would have incalculable repercussions on our whole position in Africa. Had you thought about that?"

"Of course." Lew was irked. Sherrod's new tone sounded patronizing. "Every volunteer in Kalya has gone over that whole issue umpteen times. The trouble is, Mr. Sherrod, you're looking at this as a political power fight, but with the PCVs it's a personal, moral question between right and wrong. Genghis Khan is a crook who's determined to keep the old system of exploitation going. . . . No, it's worse than exploiting the Molas, it's almost slavery. On the other hand, Steve Muo is a decent guy who's trying to get a fair shake and a new life for his fellow Molas. So are we."

Lew's voice rose as he spoke and he finished a bit breathlessly. He could feel a flush in his cheeks.

Sherrod smiled. He left the window sill and seated himself again behind his desk. "How old are you, Lew?"

"Twenty-seven."

Sherrod ignored the edge of truculence in Lew's voice. "A fine age," he said. "When I was twenty-seven and an assistant professor at Williams, I made a speech asserting that the election of Eisenhower over Adlai Stevenson could mean the collapse of Western civilization."

"Meaning I'm still wet behind the ears, huh?"

"No, no," said Sherrod hurriedly. "You haven't let me make my point. Your generation, at least what I see of it in the Peace Corps, is a lot savvier than mine was. You have a depth of knowledge and a grasp of world affairs that we didn't. At twenty-seven, the typical Peace Corpsman is fully capable of making major decisions. That's why we have so many young staffers all over the world. That's why we brought you back here for a personal report —because we respect your judgment. I have to hand it to Sarge Shriver. He insisted that we always go straight to the volunteers for our information. In any other government agency, this Zinzin affair would have been handled exclusively by bureaucrats at the top. Not the Peace Corps. We want the facts from the men and women on the spot."

Lew was still miffed. "So why bring up my age in the first place?"

"Because I don't want you to think that we're going to disregard any of your views that may not coincide with those of Williams and Ambassador Milbank just because of your youth. We have an obligation to you. And you, Lew, have an equal obligation to us—to give us your best recommendations based on the widest possible look at the whole picture. And I repeat, the whole picture."

Lew relaxed. "Maybe I did misunderstand you. I guess I didn't make myself clear either. I said it was a basic moral issue in Zinzin and it is. But that doesn't mean we can't do some maneuvering of our own."

Sherrod tapped a pencil against his teeth, then grinned at Lew. "I'm listening."

"We're talking as though we didn't have a card left to play," said Lew. "But that's not true, Mr. Sherrod. The Molas love the Peace Corps in Zinzin. Well, maybe 'love' is too strong a word, but they do like us and admire us. They know we're only there to help them. The Kalya system has made them distrustful of everybody—even other Molas. They won't trust anybody except the Peace Corps with money or anything else. Sure, the devil, the bush school and Morfu Gilli's death have them all scared right now, but they'd raised Cain if Old Number One kicked the Peace Cops out of town. Frankly, I think Old Number One is bluffing."

"Really?" Sherrod seemed impressed. "You honestly believe the demand to withdraw from Zinzin was a bluff? After all, he cabled his ambassador here in pretty specific terms."

"I can't be certain, of course," said Lew, "but it's a distinct possibility, especially when you know the whole background of his troubles with the Molas and putting Steve Muo in as commissioner and all. Don't worry, Old Number One has got his problems too."

"He's got to keep his fences mended like any other politician."

"Right."

Sherrod tapped a piece of paper which was tucked into the corner of his desk blotter. "Ambassador Milbank apparently doesn't agree with you. In his cable here, he requests authority to ask Vining's terms for consenting to let the Peace Corps remain in Zinzin. If they merely involve a Peace Corps pledge not to interfere with Harter's operation of the school of which he's principal—and Milbank assumes that to be the case—he asks that he be empowered to give that pledge. Then he'd write off the incident as closed. Milbank says nothing about any possibility of a bluff."

"Apparently he doesn't mention Jim Osterlord's road either," said Lew. "Genghis Khan shanghaied Jim's whole work gang."

"Is the road so important?"

Important? Lew thought for a moment. Osterlord, of course, believed the Peace Corps world began and ended in his raw slash through the jungle. It wasn't of such towering significance, perhaps, yet . . . He could see Jim's cigar box with the nickels and dimes collected from almost every Zinzin hut. He could see Oon Gilli, grinning and sweating at the oil-drum culvert. And he thought of the pall of shattered dreams that would settle on the town if this road, like those before it, ended by going nowhere.

"Oh, hell," said Lew. "I guess you could prove that nothing we do over there is very important. All I know is that Jim's road would open a lot of new trade in Zinzin and it's the only major Peace Corps community-development project in Kalya. The people contributed the dough and the Mola men are working on it. It's the whole concept of self-help the Peace Corps is always talking about."

"Then it is important," said Sherrod. He paused for a moment. "If we accepted your theory, just how would we go about calling Vining's bluff?"

"Well," said Lew, "we ought to tell Old Number One flatly that Moses Harter is breaking the law by holding bush school this time of year. Also that he's guilty of forced labor of Mola men on his farm. Forced labor, hell. It's slavery in my book."

"And if, or perhaps I should say when, he rejects that position, then what?"

"Then . . ." Lew paused. He had told Carter Williams that in Washington he could just state the facts, but on the plane over the black Atlantic, he had thought of the arguments of Lincoln Beach and of Forrest Stevenson. He felt sure that they were right and he decided that if he were asked, he would state his conviction.

"Then," he said, "we could threaten to withhold all American aid money in Kalya. We're pouring about twenty million a year into the country. Old Number One would go broke in a couple of months without our dough."

Sherrod sat in silence, his eyes searching Lew as though seeking a new appraisal of him. "I wonder," he said slowly, "if you realize the implication of what you've said? That kind of threat could inflate this Zinzin business into a first-class international crisis. If it failed to work, we could lose one of our best friends in Africa."

"But," insisted Lew, "if we knuckle under to Old Number One without a fight, we'll lose the Molas. And that's the way to ruin the Peace Corps, Mr. Sherrod."

"We'd stay in Zinzin, but we'd lose our soul, huh?"

"Right." Lew could imagine the mood of contempt and dismay in the Franklin-Wyzansky household when the group gathered to hear word of a Peace Corps surrender. "You wouldn't have a nickel's worth of morale left in Kalya."

Sherrod rose, circled the desk and placed an arm about Lew's shoulder. "That's strong medicine, Lew, but I appreciate your candor. You lay it on the line as you see it, and we couldn't ask more of any volunteer."

"Well," said Lew, "I didn't think anything would be gained by hedging."

Sherrod shook Lew's hand. "We'll do what we can here," he said, "but you've got to realize that both State and the White House are into this now. We'll just have to see what develops." He picked up a slip of paper from the desk. "Now, let's see. You're to see the Kalya desk officer at State at one-thirty and then the deputy assistant secretary of State for African affairs at three-o'clock. Just level with them as you did with me. You'll find them both easy to talk to."

But Lew found Oscar Zimmerman, a foreign service career officer who headed the Kalya desk at the State Department, anything but easy. Lew was kept waiting a half hour in the aseptic little reception room which served the desk officers of three West African countries. Three secretaries worked at typewriters under fluorescent lights that bathed the room in a white glare. One woman kept glancing at the wall clock and then at Lew, critically, as though he were a bothersome snag in the web of world affairs. "He's running awfully late today," she said once. Then later: "Do you pronounce it Core-lay?" When Lew nodded, she frowned and made a mark on her stenographer's pad, then resumed her furious assault on the typewriter. If the written word could heal the wounds of mankind, this office was prepared to fashion a global poultice.

When Lew was finally admitted to Zimmerman's office, the desk officer gave him a swift, watery smile and simultaneously pressed a key on his phone box. "Hold all calls for the next twelve minutes, please, Florence," he said. He was a balding man whose blond strands of hair and eyebrows seemed to blend anonymously with his pale flesh. He glanced ruefully at a large stack of papers in his correspondence box.

"You're the devil-dance man, aren't you?" His tone was distantly polite, uninvolved. "I saw some of them during my tour in Kalya. Frightfully clumsy exhibitions. Can't say much for Kalya's art forms." Zimmerman flicked several pages of the sheaf of flimsies before him. "And you got bit by a mamba? Lucky to be here, I guess."

"No," said Lew. "It just missed. The fangs didn't get beyond my pant leg."

"Good show."

He may have seen some devil dances, thought Lew, but he has yet to encounter his first mamba.

"Well," said Zimmerman, "let's get down to the gut issue, as Teddy White likes to call it in his president-making books. Prime Minister Vining wants the Peace Corps to get out of Zinzin. You and the other Peace Corps warriors want to fight back. Is that right?"

"A bit oversimplified," said Lew, "but yes, I guess that's about it. You see, Mr. Zimmerman, all the volunteers in Zinzin feel that—"

"I've already read their side," Zimmerman cut in. "I don't like to be brusque, Mr. Corleigh, but we do work under time pressure here. I think we'll make faster progress if you'll just let me ask a few questions."

The telephone buzzer rasped twice. Zimmerman pressed a key. "I told you to hold the calls. . . . Oh, I see. Of course. Put him on." He held his hand over the phone's mouthpiece. "Congressman Taggard," he explained to Lew. "I'll try to keep it short." But Zimmerman listened for almost five minutes, interrupting only for an occasional "yes" or "I see." When he hung up, Zimmerman was plainly annoyed.

"Where Phil Taggard gets his information so fast is beyond me," he said. "Know who he is?"

"I think so," said Lew. "Isn't he the man on the House Appropriations Committee who gives the Peace Corps a hard time?"

Zimmerman nodded. "Now he's heard somewhere about this Zinzin business and he's concerned lest 'the kids,' as he calls you, are going to alienate America's best friend in Africa."

Lew was stunned. It had been little more than twenty-four hours since the Peace Corps cable arrived in Ft. Paul. How had a congressman learned of the affair so swiftly? Lew had a sinking feeling. Washington was the huge labyrinth he had feared, and already he felt lost in it.

"Back to the questions." Zimmerman spoke rapidly. "Mr. Corleigh, do you know how many times Kalya has voted at variance with the United States at the U.N.?"

"No, sir."

"Exactly four times. Four times in the twenty-one years since the U.N. was founded." Zimmerman held up four fingers. "And not one of those was on a substantive matter. And do you know why?"

"Well," said Lew, "I guess all the foreign aid money we dump in there might have something to do with it."

"That's the cynical view," said Zimmerman. His pale eyebrows lowered in reproof. "I don't minimize the power of the dollar, but I happen to know from my own tour in Ft. Paul that Prime Minister Vining is, by personal conviction, a dedicated friend of the United States. Now, Mr. Corleigh, if you have a close friend who means a great deal to your future, how often do you line up with his enemies against him?"

"Not often," replied Lew, "but if you're talking about the Molas, they're not enemies. They're citizens of Kalya who just want a fair shake."

"I'm talking about Communists," retorted Zimmerman. "If this government loses Vining, it might as well put up a welcome sign over all West Africa for the Peking 'technicians' who'll arrive by the planeload. . . . And I'm talking about Steven Muo and Lincoln Beach. I've gotten to know those two by reputation. They figure in at least a third of the reports that have come across this desk in recent months."

Lew was about to defend the two Mola men, but Zimmerman went on with another question. He fired a series of inquiries at Lew, all slightly rhetorical, all stressing the allegiance of Prime Minister Vining to the West in general and to the United States in particular. As Zimmerman talked, Lew sensed a growing feeling of oppression not unlike that which enveloped him frequently at twilight on the jungle road to Zinzin. The Kalya desk officer wasn't really questioning him. He was preaching to him, painting world policy as a great mountain range in which Zinzin was but a tiny fissure. Lew actually felt relieved when the secretary put her head in the door and said: "It's two-twenty. Your next appointment is waiting."

"I hope we can squeeze in another session before you leave," said Zimmerman with his wan smile. In shaking hands he managed by slight pressure to guide Lew toward the door. "Just remember, we've got to look at Zinzin in its proper perspective."

Perspective? thought Lew as he left. Zimmerman's view of the world was so wide that Zinzin became only a trifling blemish and Cindy Fuller, weeping at the doorway of the mud-stick school, but a vanishing speck.

Anthony Maggiore, the deputy assistant secretary of State for African affairs, was a radically different cut of man. He was a short, fat, effervescent second-generation Italian who saw Lew promptly at the scheduled time of three o'clock and who beamed when Lew called him "Mr. Maggiore."

"What a promotion!" he cried. "You're the first fellow since I took the oath to call me anything but Tony."

He seated Lew on a black leather sofa, offered him a cigar, lit one himself and began to bubble with small talk. "How I admire the Peace Corps," he said. "If I didn't have five kids to feed, I'd be there myself. Tell me about it. How's Kalya? And just where in the hell is this Zinzin that's got Old Number One so worked up?"

As Lew talked, Maggiore nodded happily amid a swirl of smoke that soon split about the room like vapor trails. Lew found himself going into details such as his night ride to Ft. Paul with Steve Muo and Cindy's confrontation with Genghis Khan.

"Great name, Genghis Khan!" exclaimed Maggiore. "I know the type. There was a sneaky son-of-a-bitch just like him when I was starting out in politics in Manhattan. The guy made a fortune out of painting contracts in my district before we trapped him. Hogan, the DA, got a conviction and put him away for ten years."

Lew's story about the mamba provoked the deputy assistant secretary to a fit of sympathetic wrath. "Why, of course, that goddamn security cop put the snake in there," he said. "Who could doubt it? If it had been me, I'd have rammed a fist down that Colonel Booth's throat." Maggiore bounced excitedly on the sofa as he threw a punch at a smoke wreath. "God, Lew, you take things too calmly. Anybody sics a poisonous snake on Tony Maggiore and he's going to spend the rest of his life running."

Lew, buoyed on this frothing sea of congeniality, soon found himself expanding on the policy significance of Zinzin.

"Sure, it's basically a question of right and wrong, Mr. Maggiore," he said, "but also it's the tribes against a corrupt government. If we cave in to Old Number One without a fight, it means the Peace Corps and the United States are casting a big vote for corruption."

"That's a point I'm glad you made," said Maggiore, but some of the enthusiasm seemed gone from his tone.

"Look, sir," said Lew. "I don't claim to be any great brain on foreign policy, but it seems to me that Zinzin is pretty much like the situation we had in Cuba, in Vietnam and in the Dominican Republic. We play along with a corrupt government and we don't pay enough attention to the poverty and the real grievances of the people until it's too late. Then there's all hell to pay."

"Now wait a minute," said Maggiore. "I'm not sure Kalya is really comparable. After all, we are working with the people. That's the whole point of the Peace Corps effort there."

Lew felt the sympathetic atmosphere contracting. "But the Peace Corps is only a drop in the bucket compared to our other programs there," he protested. "All our foreign aid money goes through government hands. It's a subsidy for Old Number One, and The Family oppression he tolerates can only lead to revolution. And when that happens, the Peace Corps and the U.S. will wind up out in the cold."

"Oh, come now, Lew." Maggiore laughed dismissively. "A revolution in Kalya? Let's be serious. The CIA has never found more than a glimmering of unrest there. A couple of Communist-oriented guys and that's it. I read most of the Kalya reports."

They talked until five o'clock, but Lew felt that his arguments were running downhill like water after a mountain storm. When he switched from the colorful particulars of the Peace Corps' clash with Moses Harter to the broader policy implications, Maggiore's interest dwindled rapidly. At the end, the deputy assistant secretary even used the same word Zimmerman had.

"I sympathize fully with the Peace Corps problem in the outcountry villages," he said, "but Zinzin is only one town on an awfully big globe. I think we've got to remember, Lew, to look at this thing in perspective."

There was a final spurt of geniality when Lew made his exit. "Save a bed for me at the hostel," said Maggiore. "I'm going to spend some time with the Peace Corps on my next visit to Kalya. We'll both ambush Hulbert Booth some day and fix his wagon for him."

At the door he pumped Lew's hand. "And don't worry. We'll do the right thing by the Peace Corps in Zinzin. Something can always be worked out. Give me a ring before you leave."

Lew felt frustrated and depleted as he left the State Department building and walked toward Peace Corps headquarters where he was to check Sherrod's office for tomorrow's schedule. Homeward-bound civil servants clogged the sidewalks, the rush hour traffic moved with its irritable, bleating medley of sound and Washington seemed to ooze bureaucracy at every pore. It was all so immense and yet so fragmented; so impenetrable, so opaque. It was as though human beings were streaming from the granite hives of government, leaving the long corridors, the desks and the duplicating machines to formulate their own inanimate policy for the nation overnight. Government had a million faces, and yet no face, and Lew felt that he was the only person in Washington that evening who cared about people who lived in towns like Zinzin.

At Sherrod's office Lew learned that he was to spend the next day in a series of meetings with Peace Corps staff members. He was descending in the elevator, walled in bleak thought, when he heard a familiar, gay voice. A hand clutched his arm.

"Lou-ou!" It was Maureen Sutherland, stretching his name into two syllables, each one a little gasp. She wore the dark glasses, her black hair hid half her face and she leaned toward him like a bending wand. "What a treat, baby!"

In the lobby she spoke through set lips, the phrases ejected with little explosions like seat capsules from speeding fighter planes. "I simply adored, you know, my stay in Ft. Paul and I can't wait for the next trip. How is the rep, and that divine Rachael Frisson? And Prudence Stauffer? Such a serious little, you know, plodder, that one."

"They're all fine," said Lew. He was a runner left at the starting line.

"What brings you to Washington? Oh yes, something sinister about Zinzin, isn't it? I think I'm supposed to sit in with you tomorrow with Frank or somebody. I'm dying to hear everything."

"It's quite a story." Rounding the first turn, a man had to use his elbows to gain running room.

"I'll bet it's fantastic." She fingered her dark glasses and bent her figure like a willowy question mark. "Africa is the most exciting place in the whole program and Kalya is, you know, incredible really. I'd give my last dime to get a cynic like Phil Taggard, that troglodyte, to live outcountry with the PCVs for a while, wouldn't you?"

Lew nodded. Maureen rushed past his forming reply. "But Taggard reminds me of something, Lew. I'm not sure the reassessment of kerosene refrigerators in Kalya will come out, you know, favorably for the volunteers. All the staff evaluations aren't in yet, but they don't look, you know, too good so far. Of course, it will all depend on Frank."

"I'd forgotten . . ."

"Of course, baby, with everything you have on your mind." They were heading into the last lap, he sensed, and he was hopelessly in the rear. "I'd love to have a drink with you, Lew. They've got the sidewalk tables set out Chez François. But I've got to dash. One of those frightful six-to-eight dos at the Gabon embassy. It'll be a bore, but I'm expected and I think Teddy and Joan will be there and you know . . ."

She offered her cheek and Lew, feeling slightly foolish, pecked at it. Maureen trotted off, her spike heels drilling at the terrazzo floor. Lew sighed. He had not only lost the race. He had been lapped.

That evening, in the vague, rootless mood that always settled on him in hotel rooms, he called his parents in Evanston. His mother, delighted to hear his voice, asked about his health, his girls and his work. His father, stuttering, wanted to know about his plans. Lew said he ought to hear any day now from his three applications for graduate school. His father said that sounded like drifting and, although Lew demurred, he privately agreed with him. Ever since Lew had decided against taking over the fuel oil business, his father acted as though his son had intentionally wounded him. Neither parent was surprised to hear that Lew was in Washington. They seemed to assume that flying missions by Peace Corps laborers were routine occurrences. Lew put down the phone with an empty feeling. Evanston was a page torn from a book, fluttering away like a leaf in the wind.

He fingered through the Washington phone directory, hoping a familiar name might jog his memory and produce an old friend. He did remember that a classmate from Penn State was working at the Budget Bureau and he found the name. But a call to the home number produced no answer. Then he went out, bought a fifth of bourbon and downed several stiff drinks while he read through the final edition of the *Washington Evening Star*. He ate alone at Costin's in the Press Building, feeling guilty at spending $6.95 for a steak dinner. With his Peace Corps per diem of $16, he knew, he would arrive back in Kalya broke. No more Founders House dinners for Prudence and perhaps not even a night at the Ginger Baby.

That night he sat on the canopied roof terrace of the Hotel Washington and nursed a brandy for more than an hour. The May night was silky, the sky was only partially overcast and he could see, far across the Potomac River, the flicker of the eternal flame at John Kennedy's grave. He could see, nearer at hand, the red lights atop the Washington Monument blinking their altitude warning to arriving aircraft. And over the roof of the Treasury Building, Lew could see the rear of the White House. Lights from the high windows silhouetted the circular balcony and probed into the magnolias, elms and white oaks on the back lawn.

Lew wondered whether the President behind those windows had ever heard of a town named Zinzin. He thought back over the talks that day, and with each recollected phrase or attitude he grew more depressed. These men in Washington thought only of Old Number One's professed allegiance to the United States, of the world's power alignment, of the sterile debates in the halls of the United Nations.

And perhaps they were right. Who was Lew Corleigh, a Peace Corps truck jockey, to tell the policy makers that a cluster of thatched-roof huts called Zinzin was worth a battle by the United

States government? Was it even worth a skirmish by him? If you couldn't fight City Hall, how could you face up to the huge, baffling bureaucracy of Washington? Perhaps the thing to do was just to answer their questions and go on back to Kalya, maybe even take Williams up on the Kolamon offer for the final weeks. A feeling of bitter melancholy closed about him. It was all too big, too formless, too far removed from the sights and sounds he knew. Did anyone in this city care about the Molas? Probably not more than a handful of men in government had ever heard of them.

Then, suddenly, beyond the night traffic hum of Washington, he could sense the sounds of Zinzin. He could hear old Pimo's cackle of delight when Oon Gilli cried "small-small" in Cindy's night class. He could hear the descending song of the coucal and the sputter of a Peace Corps kerosene lamp. He could hear the spades hitting rocks on Jim Osterlord's road, which now led nowhere in a steaming jungle, and he heard Steve Muo struggling to form the English phrases that might evoke help against the depredations of Genghis Khan.

It was so easy, he thought, in this Washington of the glib phrase and the pillowy decision-by-committee to forget the heart of the matter—the people. In Kalya it was a corrupt autocracy against the people, The Family against the tribes. His country and the Peace Corps had to side with the people or somehow the grand phrase "foreign policy" became a meaningless mouthing and somewhere, in a thousand Zinzins, the world would be lost.

As he brooded, that central thought became vividly clear, like a shaft of light in a darkened forest. He had said it before. He had heard it from others and he had toyed with the significance. But now he knew. And as he gazed out at the soft night, over the roofs and the billowing tree shadows of Washington, he resolved that he would not be diverted from this core of truth.

He drained the last of his drink. He took a final look at the mellow lights of the White House and he thought of Lincoln Beach's bursting, knowing laugh as he described the Peace Corps as "the greatest revolutionary force in Kalya." Then he thought of Prudence, her grave little frown, the spatter of freckles between her brows and her fiercely protective urge for the volunteers and their mission. "If we can't work for the tribes," she had said at the airport, "what's the use of staying here?" Link and Prudence were both right, Lew told himself, and he determined once more not to let Washington lure him from his new certainty. When he stood up and stretched in the night air, he felt confident and content.

12

It was two days and six conferences later, and a sudden rainstorm, unseasonably chill for late May, lashed downtown Washington. Lew stood at his hotel room window and watched the rain drive along Fifteenth Street in slanting sheets. Pedestrians ran for cover, a gust tore an umbrella from a woman's hand and the gutters became racing streams.

The sky's color, a pasty gray, matched Lew's own mood. His new resolve held firm. He had argued the case of the Molas of Zinzin before variously layered officials of the Peace Corps, the State Department and the Agency for International Development, but by a dozen hints and side remarks, he realized that Washington saw Zinzin as only a bothersome eruption on the shell of world policy. The irritation could be cured by the salve of words, and a young man who advocated drastic methods on behalf of a small, unknown African tribe was not to be taken seriously. "Corleigh is the kind of fellow who'd use radioactive cobalt to get rid of a wart," said Oscar Zimmerman at one meeting. Lew had the distinct impression that only his presence in the room prevented a decision to reject his pleas out of hand.

His gray mood was pierced by a clamoring of the telephone. He looked at the bedside instrument in surprise, for this was the first time it had rung.

"Lewis Corleigh?" asked a feminine voice. "Congressman Taggard is calling."

Lew waited a moment.

"This is Phil Taggard." The voice was thin and scratchy. Lew was taken aback. Somehow he had imagined that Taggard would crash like falling timber. "I'd like to discuss this idiotic Zinzin business with you, if you can spare a minute."

"Yes, sir. Would you like me to come up to the Hill?"

"No, the phone will be all right. Nobody has seen fit to cut me into these Kalya talks." Taggard's complaint had a whine to it. "However, I've learned enough from my own sources to get the picture. . . . No thanks to your Peace Corps people, I might add."

"I'd be happy to fill you in, sir," said Lew.

"No, you wouldn't." Taggard sneezed into the phone. "Pardon me. Damned spring cold. I get one every year. . . . Don't bother to be ingratiating, young man. Let's just get down to cases. As I understand it, you're urging that the United States threaten to withhold all foreign aid from Kalya unless Prime Minister Vining lets the Peace Corps have its way in Zinzin. Is that correct?"

"Yes, that's about it. You see, the Peace Corps up there has a contract to teach school and a fellow named Moses Harter has closed the school to further his own . . ."

"I know all the background," Taggard cut in. His cold seemed to exaggerate the flat, nasal tone. "I want to tell you what I just got through telling Frank Sherrod on the phone. If the Peace Corps falls for your ideas and persuades the White House to follow your line, I'll make it my business next year to cut fifty cents out of every dollar of Peace Corps appropriations. This is the most outrageous proposal I've ever heard in Washington in my sixteen years in the House. It bears out the prediction I made when this nutty Peace Corps notion first came up five years ago. I said then that if we unleashed a bunch of well-meaning kids to roam all over the world, the day would come when they'd get us into trouble up to our ass. And that's just what you're fixing to do right now."

Taggard paused for breath and Lew could hear him wheezing slightly. Surprisingly, there was no fury in the Utah congressman's attack. Instead he ticked off his complaints in a dry voice like an accountant reporting on the fiscal ills of a concern facing bankruptcy.

"The Lord knows I'm no champion of foreign aid," continued Taggard, "but to withhold it from our most loyal supporter in Africa is about the most preposterous, imbecilic suggestion of the decade. It makes about as much sense as going over to Red China and building a subway system for Peking."

The mention of Peking evoked in Lew's mind a picture of Genghis Khan's yellowing, Asiatic face as he stood in Cindy Fuller's house and upbraided her. Lew found, curiously, that Taggard's assault did not unnerve him.

"I don't think you understand, Congressman Taggard, the problem in Zinzin," he said. "We're there to try to help educate and better the Molas, but at the same time, they're being looted by the Kalya government. If we condone that, some day the Molas will come to hate us. The same with the other tribes. They deserve a better break—and we're trying to give it to them."

"Idealism," said Taggard, "doesn't make policy, young man. If we're going to wage a war on corruption, we'd kick half of the big cities of this country out of the Union, to say nothing of three or four states. But I don't propose to argue with you. I'm telling you. If the Peace Corps loses us the friendship of Alexander Vining, the Congress will chop the Peace Corps in half next year . . . and that's a personal promise from Phil Taggard."

"I can't agree with you at all, sir," said Lew. He hoped he did not sound as mired in defeat as he felt.

"That's your privilege," responded Taggard. He sneezed again. "I'd like to say I respect your judgment, but I can't. The idea of scattering a bunch of college kids around the world to reform it never made any sense in the first place—and this Zinzin is the proof of it."

"I'm sorry you feel that way." Lew was surprised at his own calm. He remained as unheated as Taggard. "I think Zinzin proves just the opposite. I wish you could come over and see for yourself."

"I certainly will if this sort of nonsense keeps up," said Taggard. "Nothing personal in this, Corleigh. I just refuse to sit by and watch the Peace Corps lose a whole continent for us."

Lew stood for a moment after the congressman's "good-by," staring at the phone and trying to sort out the medley of impressions.

The telephone rang again. The hotel operator said: "A party has been trying to reach you from New York for the last few minutes." Lew waited while another operator gave instructions. He heard coins clink into a box at the other end.

"My name is Armin Schaper," a man's voice said. "I tried to get you at the Peace Corps and they gave me your hotel. I'm calling from Kennedy International. I've got a message for you."

"Who from?" asked Lew.

"From a Peace Corps staffer in Kalya named Prudence Stauffer. I just finished two years as a volunteer in the Ivory Coast and I came through Ft. Paul and some other places on my way home. Miss Stauffer wanted me to call you as soon as I landed at Kennedy."

"Okay," said Lew. "You've got the right man. What's the word?"

"I'll just read it to you: 'Dear Lew. Harter still has the town terrorized. Now he's threatened Cindy physically. The school and Jim's road are still closed down, and clothes have been dumped at the hut of a second Golo bush boy. Stick by your guns. Love, Prude.'"

"Is that all?"

"Yeah. Listen, Corleigh, I don't know what this is all about, but they said you would. I would have called you this morning, but we had a seven-hour engine delay in Dakar."

"Sure appreciate it," said Lew. "Can I do anything for you?"

"Nothing, thanks. I'm just making connections to my home in Oklahoma City. God, this airport's a madhouse. I'm homesick for the Ivory Coast already."

"I know what you mean. You've got the re-entry shakes. . . . And listen, thanks again. That note was important."

Lew slumped in a chair and watched the rain drive into dancing pools on the roof of the Treasury Building across the street. Prudence's message seemed of a piece with the slate-gray overcast. She was not a woman to cry havoc or see a flood in every rising creek. Genghis Khan, poisonous in his contempt for the Peace Corps, apparently would not rest until it was driven out of Zinzin. And the disheartening thing about Washington, Lew thought, was that nobody seemed willing to take the time to understand. Even Anthony Maggiore, who brimmed with sympathy, grew uneasy when Lew tried to explain the stakes. Frank Sherrod knew the facts, but did he weigh their meaning? Lew ached to find someone who would listen and comprehend, or better yet, someone of influence who could be made to hear, see and feel the conflict in Zinzin as he and Prudence, Jim and Cindy did. Lew knew he had to do something more . . . soon . . . but what?

The famous names of Washington boiled in his mind like bubbles, winking in the light and then collapsing. He knew none of these men and he could imagine a barricade of secretaries in every office, all smilingly insistent that he should come another day. Then, as the names flickered and vanished, he thought of Emmett Shannon, the exuberant young congressman from Chicago. Shannon had lectured to Kalya V near the end of the Group's training at the University of California at Los Angeles. The congressman had sat up late that night, discussing the world with the recruits. If nothing else, Shannon admired the Peace Corps.

Lew called the congressional switchboard, got Shannon's office and made his request for an appointment with the secretary who answered.

"Tell him I met him when he spoke to the Peace Corps at UCLA," he said.

Lew was somewhat surprised after a moment to hear the congressman's voice on the phone. Emmett Shannon evidenced none of the guarded reserve to which Lew had become accustomed in Washington, and Lew liked Shannon's candid admission that he could not remember him.

"But if you're Peace Corps, I'm your man," said Shannon. "You got a problem?"

"Yes, sir, I do," Law replied. "I'm still on duty over in Kalya, Mr. Shannon, and I've been called back to Washington for, well, consultation they call it. We're in a jam with the government in a little town named Zinzin. It's kind of complicated and I'm having a helluva time making people here understand. I've just about had it, and, frankly, I could use some advice from you."

"That's what I give away free," said Shannon. "Well, let's see.

I've got a half hour before dinner. I may have to sign some letters while we talk, but come on up."

Lew found Shannon's office in the middle building of the three structures which housed members of the House of Representatives on Capitol Hill. The congressman sat at a littered desk near a window bay which was stacked high with books. Autographed pictures of fellow politicians and framed newspaper cartoons covered the paneled walls. An armchair housed a tangled heap of documents.

Shannon burst from his chair, surged around the desk and pumped Lew's hand. He had black hair, a pugnacious jaw with a deep cleft at the chin, and flesh so pink it might have been recently massaged. He was at once a fountain of words, and now Lew recalled that at the night training bull session, Shannon, irrigated by Scotch, had talked until 3 A.M.

"Sure," said Shannon, "I remember you now . . . Red Corleigh. You and the other guys kept me up half the night at UCLA. Great bunch. How's Kalya?"

"Not bad," said Lew, "until recently. Now we're in a rhubarb with the government, and Old Number One—the Prime Minister and boss of Kalya—wants to throw the Peace Corps out of that town I told you about on the phone, Zinzin."

"I want to hear all about it." Shannon seated himself again. He scratched at an ear with one hand and riffled a stack of papers with the other.

Lew related the whole episode, deleting nothing except his pledge to help Muo and Beach. Shannon interrupted constantly. Each event in Kalya reminded the congressman of an incident in his own political career which, apparently, had been a hectic melange of causes, feuds and forensic triumphs. Shannon's swift anecdotes all gave himself star billing and Lew recalled his lavish use of the pronoun "I" at the training session. Still, the young congressman's absorption with self had a boyish candor, and Lew found himself drawn to the life of Emmett Shannon like metal to a magnet. The man's energy was phenomenal. His body moved as restlessly as his mind and his tongue.

Lew's account of his two talks with Bruce Kellogg lit a fuse. Shannon responded like a string of popping firecrackers.

"That damn CIA," he said. "If I were President, I'd lock the door and throw away the key. The way that agency operates is a disgrace in a democracy. It gets away with murder—literally. I told the director the other day that I'm going on a one-man crusade to force him to account publicly to Congress. . . . Take the FBI. At least it tells us how much it spends and how many employees it has. So the Congress has some way to gauge the FBI's effectiveness. But the CIA operates completely sub rosa. Trying to figure out how good—or how bad—it is is like trying to catch a black cat at midnight."

Lew was baffled by the outburst. Then he recalled Taggard's vendetta with the Peace Corps. Did every legislator have his pet hate in Washington, a valve through which to vent his penned frustrations over the great bog of bureaucracy?

"Of course," said Lew, "I don't know for sure that Bruce Kellogg's a CIA man. That's just what everybody in Ft. Paul says."

"Sure he's a spook," said Shannon. "He's got to be. He reminds me of the character I met last year down in Brazil . . ."

The congressman was off on a story involving São Paulo, CIA intrigue, a female guitar player, bribery and a series of self-nullifying directives from Washington. Just before the denouement, Shannon abruptly derailed the narrative.

"Say," he said, "how about coming along with me tonight to the Jefferson Study Club and telling your story there? Ever hear of us? . . . We're the action liberals on the Hill. The Birchers call us left-wing kooks, and the White House thinks we pressure it too much. Nobody likes us but our constituents and our consciences. We were going to discuss anti-trust policy tonight, but I'd like to put you on too."

"You mean speak?" The thought conjured up a picture of a formal joint session of Congress with a chamber of legislators staring at Lew.

"Hell no." Shannon laughed. "We just sit around the table and shoot the breeze. You just tell your own story like you did just now. Nothing to it."

Before Lew could answer, Shannon had swept around the desk and clapped him on the shoulder. "You may make some time for yourself. And if you don't, at least you get a freel meal."

Fifteen minutes later Lew was in the Presidential Room of the nearby Congressional Hotel with a glass of bourbon and water in his hand and his mind in a mild state of shock. Shannon steered him by an elbow, introducing him to a ring of strangers. Of about twenty men present, Lew recognized only one, Senator Alvin Demarest of New Hampshire. Lew had seen the senator's picture frequently and knew him to be a member of the Senate Foreign Relations Committee. Demarest was an angular man with dark eye pouches and a long, shadowed face. There was an air of quiet brooding about him, and he smoked a pipe as though he had not quite learned how. He used three matches trying to keep it lighted during a brief chat with Lew.

The dinner talk around the long table centered on the parliamentary mechanics of Congress. Much of it Lew did not understand, for it featured obscure bills, legislative knavery and the occult trade jargon of Capitol Hill. One anecdote, which provoked great hilarity, was less arcane. Emmett Shannon told the story and starred himself. He had, said Shannon, given his word to the President that he would vote for a farm subsidy measure desired by the White House. But then a consumer's organization, led by irate housewives, stirred opposition to the bill in Chicago. Shannon began to suffer. He did not have a single farmer in his district, and a vote for the President's agricultural bill, he said, "would be like cheering for Nasser in Israel." Still, he had given his pledge to the President. Torn between self-preservation and the specter of presidential disfavor, Shannon said he "resorted to statesmanship"—and left town without telling his staff where he was headed. He registered in a Front Royal, Virginia, motel under an assumed name, and read committee reports for the three days the farm bill was debated in the House. His staff told him later that the White House had called frantically around the country in an effort to locate him. Although the bill passed by five votes, Shannon still was not sure how to handle the President. Should be plead amnesia, an ailing mother or an attack of hepatitis? Shannon gave a droll imitation of a man in political misery, and laughter again convulsed the Jefferson Study Club.

After a dessert of cheese and grapes, Shannon rapped on his water glass with a knife. "Before we get around to anti-trust," he said, "I thought we ought to hear in confidence from our guest, Mr. Lewis Corleigh of Evanston, a Peace Corps volunteer in Kalya. Lew told me his story this afternoon and, I must say, I was greatly distressed by what I heard. This is a story that, it seems to me, goes to the heart of what's wrong with our policies in the underdeveloped countries. Lew, why don't you just go ahead and tell it as you told it to me?"

Lew swallowed, then began haltingly by describing the relationship of The Family and the government to the tribes of Kalya. He fumbled for words at first, but once launched into the story of Zinzin, he found that his diffidence faded and the words flowed easily. Senator Demarest, sucking moodily on his pipe, took out a pocket notebook and began writing in it. Lew talked for almost an hour. When he concluded, the questions came from all parts of the table.

"I don't get the politics of it," said one congressman. "If Vining needs the Molas' support, why does he give the back of his hand to their leader, this fellow Muo?"

"Well," answered Lew, "you see, Moses Harter was clever enough to stage the devil dance, so the people think the closing of the school is ordained by the spirits. They don't blame Old Number One at all. So I guess Vining doesn't feel he's risking any loss of Mola votes."

"Does this man Harter have something on Vining?" asked another.

"Not that I know of," said Lew. "But Harter's part of The Family, and that's the way it is in Kalya. Old Number One lets The Family do pretty much what it wants."

"I take it you don't put much stock in the embassy's—or the CIA's—belief that Muo and what's-his-name are following a Communist line?" Lew was asked by one legislator.

"No, sir, I don't," he replied. "There just isn't any evidence of a Communist movement in Kalya. Beach calls himself a 'capitalistic revolutionary' . . . but it seems to me that the best way to insure a Communist push over there is for the U.S. to side with The Family against the tribes. Some day—I don't know when—the tribes are going to wake up and overthrow The Family. And if we aren't with them, they'll find somebody else."

The questions continued for an hour. What was wrong with the USAID program in Kalya? How long did it take for an untended black mamba bite to kill? What was the total U.S. commercial investment in Kalya? How did a kerosene refrigerator work? What did Lew think of the Peace Corps overall?

When the meeting finally broke up, without ever getting around to anti-trust problems, Lew wondered just what he had accomplished. The questions were all earnest ones, and members of the study group obviously took him seriously. No one had indicated boredom or sought to minimize Zinzin's importance as had some of the executive officials in downtown Washington. Still, what could any of them do about it?

"You made an impact," said Shannon with a parting handshake. "Good job. We won't let this thing drop. I'll be in touch before you leave."

Alvin Demarest asked Lew to remain a few minutes, and they seated themselves on banquet chairs in a corner of the emptying room.

"This whole thing intrigues me," said Demarest. He wasted a match on his pipe and gazed resentfully at the bowl. "It's a microcosm of our major dilemma abroad—the short-term advantage versus the long haul. I made no criticism of our policy of expediency in the first postwar years. We were fighting the cold war. But now we're in danger of not seeing the forest for the trees. We play to the rulers and we neglect the people."

"You don't think I'm overdoing the importance of Zinzin then?" asked Lew.

"No, I don't," said Demarest. His long, shadowed face had a somber cast. "Zinzin is a perfect symbol, and if we don't face the problem now, there'll be a hundred Zinzins to come."

Lew recalled his own resolve two nights earlier. "That's what I think," he said.

"You're right," said Demarest. "Somewhere along the line we've lost our perspective. What's the real purpose of foreign aid—more than a hundred billion of it since World War II? The purpose is to raise standards of living around the world, so that hungry nations won't be lured into a Communist militancy that threatens peace. That's what we want, peace. It's in our self-interest. But we can't maintain the peace merely by supporting any regime that gives lip service to our side. That may work for a decade or two, but in the long run, if we lose the good will of the peoples of the world, we lose the world."

Demarest paused and fussed with his pipe. This time he managed to light the tobacco and keep it burning. "I want to get back something precious that we've lost. I want people, when they think of the United States, to think of the Statue of Liberty—and not the Central Intelligence Agency. . . . We've got to recapture some of our early idealism. The Peace Corps seemed to do that. But Zinzin shows how the Peace Corps too can be sacrificed to expediency."

"I tried to say that downtown," said Lew, "but they kept repeating that one little school and one jungle road weren't worth losing our best friend in Africa."

"Vining isn't a friend," said Demarest. "He's a hired voice. The real friends of the future are those school children and the night-class students of Miss . . . what's her name?"

"Fuller," said Lew. "Cindy Fuller."

"Yes. Cindy Fuller." Demarest mused on the name for a moment and then rose from his chair. "Well, Lew, keep up the fight. You've got hold of something vital. Don't let go."

"I won't, Senator," said Lew, "but I feel kind of helpless. One Peace Corps truck driver doesn't carry much weight around here."

"But one senator occasionally does," said Demarest. "For what it's worth, Lew, I'm with you."

Outside, the rain had dissolved into a mist that muffled the city. On the cab ride down Pennsylvania Avenue, Lew could see the street lamps, glowing softly above wet posts. The city had a stillness, broken only by the chant of tires on the slick pavement.

What did the support of men like Shannon and Demarest mean? Shannon seemed volatile but erratic. He was attracted by the battle in Zinzin as an intellectual exercise, but Lew wondered if the Chicago congressman would ever do more than talk about it. Demarest appeared deeply interested and ready to help, but what could one senator do? Then Lew thought of the message from Prudence. He could see her serious little face—alight with affection for him now?—and he could feel the warmth of her body against his the night they slept together at her house. For the first time in his life, he realized, he missed a woman.

There was a note in his call box at the hotel from Frank Sherrod's secretary: "You are booked to return to Kalya on the 8 P.M. flight tomorrow from Dulles. Mr. Sherrod has scheduled a final conference in his office at 11 A.M."

13

The room telephone rang the next morning while Lew was knotting his tie before the mirror and puzzling, as he often did, over his face. It had the neutral familiarity, yet strangeness, of a face often seen in a railroad station, an elevator or a drugstore. The first sight of it each day usually evoked mild misgivings, but this morning he felt cheerful and he wondered why. The early sun, bathing the newly washed streets below, might be a partial answer but, he thought, it was probably the prospect of returning to Kalya that buoyed him. Prudence, the road to Zinzin, the jeep, the hostel, the great dabema trees . . . all wore the garments of home.

He picked up the phone in the confident manner of one who does not anticipate bad news.

"This is Horace Magruder." The voice had a bluff, hearty timbre. "I don't think we've ever met, but you may know the name. I'm from Kalya."

"Yes, I know you, Mr. Magruder," said Lew. "I saw you a couple of weeks ago at a Founders House dance."

"Oh, good. Listen, Mr. Corleigh. I'm down in the lobby and I'd like to talk to you. How about buying you breakfast?"

"All right. I'll be down in a minute."

Horace Magruder waited in front of the elevator. He was a man easily picked out in a crowd. He stood well above six feet, his shoulders were wide and his face had the tanned flush of the outdoors. His nose was striking. It was enormous, pitted and slightly crooked as though it had been broken once.

"Corleigh?" he asked. When Lew nodded, Magruder put out a large hand and buried Lew's in a grip that made the fingers ache.

"Coffee shop okay? It's not fancy, but we can talk there."

As they walked to the basement restaurant, Lew speculated on what might be coming. It had to be connected with Kalya politics, he felt, for the operating director of Itambel, the Italian-American-Belgian mining consortium in Kalya, would hardly waste his time in social chitchat with an ordinary Peace Corps worker.

When Lew ordered toast, coffee, bacon and two scrambled eggs, Magruder nodded agreement but told the waitress: "Just double that egg order for me."

"I believe in getting well fueled early in the day," he explained. His genial grin was appealing. "A lot of Americans don't eat much breakfast in Africa, but after twenty years in Kalya, I find I can take the heat much better on a full stomach. Now it's a habit everywhere I go."

Lew waited. Magruder folded his big hands on the table, and Lew noted that the backs sprouted a scrubby growth of black hairs. "So what do I want?" asked Magruder. "To be blunt, I'm here to lobby you."

"Me?" The word "lobby" had the sound of heavy artillery.

"You. You've become an important man, Mr. Corleigh."

"Call me Lew." Somehow, Lew felt, the abbreviated name might diminish the size of the expected barrage.

"All right, Lew. I was here in Washington on business when I got a call from our New York office. They have a report that the Peace Corps is threatening a major showdown with Old Number One over the closing of some school in Zinzin. Is that about right?"

Lew hesitated. "Well, Mr. Magruder, I was called back here by the Peace Corps. It's official government business, I guess, and I'm just not sure whether I ought to . . ."

"Never mind." Magruder gestured with open palms, signaling

that he wanted no confidences. "I think I know the score. If you'll permit me, just let me go ahead as though the facts were understood."

He paused. Lew found himself staring at the huge nose, and quickly shifted his gaze to his napkin.

"Lew," said Magruder, "let me give you my thinking about Kalya. I've been there, as I said, twenty years. I think I know it inside out, as much as any foreigner can. Now, first, I'm not going to shadowbox about my self-interest. Itambel has a three-hundred-million-dollar investment in Kalya, and in addition to a pretty big salary, I have a modest chunk of the stock. We've got one of the finest and most profitable iron ore concessions in the world. Our ore is incredibly high-grade, around sixty-eight per cent pure.

"Now, you know that Old Number One is friendly to us and to every foreign concession. All told, the American and European commercial stake in Kalya is well over a billion dollars, according to the latest figures. Also, as you know, there isn't a single Communist-bloc project in the whole country. Kalya is one place where our side doesn't have to worry."

The waitress brought the breakfast order and Magruder promptly attacked his plate of bacon and four eggs like a man who had fasted for a week. He ate in silence for a while, stoking his mouth with great portions, then gestured with his fork.

"We both know, Lew, that Kalya is a complicated country for foreigners. Nothing is simple there to the Western mind, and it's difficult to get a reasonable perspective from any one angle, either from mine, say, or from the Peace Corps'."

"I don't get you," said Lew.

"Well, for one thing," said Magruder, "USAID is a bust there. We're pumping in—what is it?—about twenty million a year in government aid. Three-fourths of that money is wasted. We're just turning the country into a big charity case. The Kalyans will stay on the dole as long as we'll dish it out."

The argument had a familiar ring to Lew. He had heard much the same thing many times from Forrest Stevenson in Loli. Magruder took a large swallow of coffee. The iron ore director was on his third cup.

"The trouble with AID," he continued, "is that it doesn't require much work by the Kalyans, and no sane man in Kalya is going to work if he doesn't have to—not until he learns to take pride in his skills and learns the nature of incentives. Now, the Peace Corps is different. You try to teach the people to help themselves. We do the same thing at Itambel. Sure, you're over there for unselfish motives, while we're there to make a buck, still . . ."

Magruder leaned back in his chair and began to probe his teeth with a toothpick. "Still, I don't believe, frankly, that motives have much bearing on results. We're teaching the Kalyans more trades and skills than the Peace Corps ever will. Have you visited the concession, Lew?"

Lew nodded. "I agree with you. You've got a great training program. It's impressive."

"Then you've got the picture," said Magruder. "We have Kalyans now who can repair trucks, maintain the loading gear and do some pretty fair carpentry and masonry work. In fact, I've got five good Mola men who run the whole water system on the concession. They keep the mains and pumps in good running order and they can plan new extensions. By contrast, I challenge you to find one decent plumber in all of Ft. Paul. Also, it's only a matter of time until we bring some of these tribal men up into management. A lot of them already are foremen on the work gangs."

"I won't argue with you on any of that," said Lew, "but what's it all got to do with me, Mr. Magruder?"

Magruder snapped his toothpick in two and leaned across the table. "Just this—and I think you can already guess what I'm about to say. I don't want you to do anything here that would upset the applecart in Kalya. I don't want the Peace Corps thrown out of the country, and I damn sure don't want Itambel thrown out either."

"Well then, let me level with you too, Mr. Magruder," said Lew. "The Peace Corps is in Kalya to help the tribes, but practically everything we try to do is blocked or sabotaged by The Family. I guess it's no secret that the whole problem has come to a head in Zinzin."

"No, it isn't," said Magruder. "But before you start advocating any big, rash moves here in Washington, I think you ought to realize everything that's at stake—for the United States and for Kalya."

"Look," replied Lew, "we're not on the same wave length. I can see your point, but the Peace Corps is trying to do something for the tribes. The Family doesn't give a damn about anything but itself—and Itambel inevitably has to take the side of The Family. Don't you have two members of The Family on your board of directors, and isn't one of them Old Number One's nephew?"

"That's right."

"And how much do they get paid for not working?"

"I won't pretend they work," said Magruder. "They each received five hundred shares of stock for nothing, and the stock is worth about one hundred twenty dollars a share on today's market. Also, they get three dollars and fifty cents a share dividends a year." Magruder paused, frowning. "Sure, it's a lousy system. Do you know we have to pay 'dash' every time we turn around, big bribes and little ones? We even have to slip money under the table to get our truck fleet inspected, for Christ's sake. Of course, we'd be a lot better off with a clean, incorruptible government. Any businessman who thinks otherwise is a fool."

Magruder's big nose seemed to shine like a light bulb. Lew smiled and said: "You're making a pretty good case yourself for a showdown, a lot bigger than ours in Zinzin."

"But don't you see, Lew?" said Magruder. "This is no time for a showdown in Kalya. The country needs a whole lot more education, more mechanical training and a growing tradition of self-government. Sure, Old Number One winks at the corruption. But he's a smart man, sometimes a really brilliant politician. He knows just how far he can go with The Family and with the tribes.

"And look how astute he's been with his African neighbors. With the leftists he's polite and friendly, but distant. He keeps on good terms with these new military bosses who've seized power all around him in the last year, but he lets them know there'll be none of that in Kalya. He's doing the best job in West Africa of yanking his country into the twentieth century. Believe me, he's the only man right now who can hold Kalya together."

Lew thought of what Prudence had said the night she became sick after the party at Founders House and the Ginger Baby. Could anyone else, she wondered, run Kalya as well as Vining?

"The main thing," continued Magruder, "is to bring along some responsible leaders besides Vining. But all that's a generation in the future at least. A revolution right now would be an unholy mess. Who knows what radicals might take charge? You get turmoil over there now and the U.S. can kiss Kalya good-by."

"Is there ever a right time for change?" asked Lew. "Won't you be saying the same thing twenty years from now?"

"No, I won't." Magruder tilted his head and gazed reflectively at Lew. "You've probably got the old, outmoded concept of big business, Lew. The piracy days are over. We know that for long-time profit, we've got to have a stable government and wide distribution of goods throughout a nation. We can't exploit a country and hope to survive in the midst of poverty. But believe me, Lew—and I say this with all sincerity—this is just not the time in Kalya. If you insist on bringing this Zinzin dispute to a head now, you're running the risk of having the whole West thrown out of Kalya."

Could that possibly be true, Lew wondered. Magruder was a powerful influence in Kalya, a man who had the ear of Prime Minister Vining. It was hard to imagine Old Number One ejecting Itambel which paid Kalya ten million dollars a year in taxes and strewed favors and money throughout The Family. Lew wondered how much Magruder had learned at the American embassy about the opposition to Vining. He chanced a query.

"Do you know Lincoln Beach and Steve Muo?" he asked.

"Sure. Why?"

"Some people around the embassy have the idea they're a couple of Communists."

"So I heard," said Magruder, "but I don't believe it. I don't doubt that those two would like to unhorse Old Number One some day, but they're no Communists. Sometimes the CIA overplays its information, maybe because it thinks that's the kind of simplistic politics Washington understands. No, I'm not the sort who sees Reds under every bed. But what I do fear is the Communists exploiting some major civil upheaval and making a real Marxist revolution out of it."

"You're persuasive, Mr. Magruder," said Lew, "but I don't think you understand the situation in Zinzin. If it were just a case of an ordinary school principal doing some petty thieving, the Peace

Corps people might be willing to go along. But this guy Moses Harter—we call him Genghis Khan—is a murdering gangster. Really, he's an evil man. The volunteers figure if they let him get away with it, we'll lose the whole ball game with the Molas."

"Then you picked the wrong man," said Magruder. "Harter is the one school principal in Kalya that Vining will back to the hilt—no matter what he does."

"Why?"

"Oh, come off it." Magruder looked surprised. "You mean you don't know?"

"Know what?"

"Harter is Old Number One's favorite illegitimate son. He's got three of them outcountry, and he'll do anything for them. But Harter is his pet."

Lew was stunned. "No," he said slowly, "I never heard that, not even from Jim Osterlord, one of my Peace Corps friends up there. Jim knows the town cold."

"Well, it's a fact," said Magruder. "Believe me, Lew, this is one you can't win."

Magruder paid the check and walked to the door with Lew. As they shook hands in parting, Magruder said: "Remember, Lew, we're on your side—for the long haul. But the time isn't ripe for any drastic stand in Kalya. Whatever you do here in Washington, for God's sake, be reasonable."

Lew went back to his room pondering this new development. Genghis Khan the illegitimate son of Old Number One. . . . Could that be true? If so, why hadn't Jim, Steve or Link told him about it? Still, it would be foolhardy for Magruder to lie about such a relationship. In the small world of Ft. Paul, it would not take the Palace long to trace—and retaliate against—the originator of false gossip of such personal nature. No, thought Lew, the story was probably true. If so, a lot of other factors began to make sense: Old Number One's stubborn refusal to entertain any complaints against Harter, Steve Muo's seeming reluctance to challenge Harter publicly, Genghis's own wealth and arrogance, and the physical danger to those suspected of opposing Harter. Colonel Booth's protection of Vining's person extended to members of the Vining family, and the black mamba indicated his zeal for the job.

Lew thought again, with a shiver, of the snake on the jeep's floor board.

Then Lew realized that he was more shaken by the talk with Magruder than he would have cared to admit to him. Once again a film of doubt clouded his resolutions. Lew liked Magruder, his frankness and his common sense. The mining director's persuasive talents were as forceful as his physique. And another thing. Magruder's assessment of Old Number One's political skills, and Kalya's dependence on them, meshed with that of Prudence. Nothing was simple, she had said that night at her house.

He sat by the window overlooking Fifteenth Street and tried to read the morning *Washington Post,* but the march of the day's news did not divert his mind from the dilemma of Zinzin. As he had talked to Senator Demarest last night, his course seemed clear, direct. Now he wondered again. He sat for an hour, trying to chart his own way through the conflicting views of Magruder, Demarest, Shannon, Zimmerman and Maggiore. He realized with dismay that he had wavered between doubt and certainty ever since the night, a month ago, when he made up his mind to help The Forge.

Now, unexpectedly, he recalled what his staff sergeant in Germany had once said. The sergeant was a skinny, pinch-faced, taciturn man from the hills of Kentucky who had plunged through France with Patton's tanks in World War II and then had fought in Korea. "Only two things count in combat," he had said, "you and your outfit. Everybody else is the son-of-a-bitchin' enemy." The comment, long forgotten, brought an odd kind of comfort to Lew now. Washington and the U.S. embassy in Ft. Paul could debate the intricacies of high policy, but what counted for Lew Corleigh was the Zinzin Peace Corps outfit of four women and three men, and their mud-stick school and jungle road. He couldn't let them down. The view might not have the breadth of Senator Demarest's global concepts, but it had the gritty feel of reality. Lew could see Zinzin. He could smell it. He could hear it. He knew Cindy Fuller and Jim Osterlord, and he could feel intuitively the poignant grief of Morfu Gilli's mother, huddled at the door of her hut. The seven Peace Corps workers were his outfit. He had to do what he could for them.

He arrived at the office of the Peace Corps deputy director

shortly before eleven o'clock and found that Frank Sherrod's secretary had his airline tickets ready for him. He also found, somewhat surprisingly, that his final talk with Sherrod would be a private one.

Sherrod's greeting had the same informal, friendly and low-key flavor that Lew had come to associate with the lanky official. Sherrod's coat was draped over the back of his chair and his tie was loosened at the neck.

"How'd you make out at the Jefferson Study Club?" he asked. He cocked his thick eyebrows and his grin was a knowing one.

Lew was confused. "Well, I . . ."

"That's okay, Lew," said Sherrod. "This isn't the Army. A volunteer is free to talk to anyone he wants to. As a matter of fact, considering the heat we're getting from Phil Taggard, I'm just as happy you told your story to some of our friends."

"But how'd you find out?" asked Lew. "I didn't know I was going myself until dinnertime last night."

"Everyone in Washington has his private operatives," said Sherrod. He paused for effect, smiling. "I ought to make it mysterious, but the truth is that my secretary's brother is the administrative assistant to one of the congressmen who was there last night. Small town, Washington. In some ways, not much bigger than Ft. Paul. We all get the word, sooner or later."

The phone rang. Sherrod picked up the receiver with a look of annoyance. Instantly, however, his manner changed. He straightened in his chair, cradled the receiver against his shoulder and—unconsciously, Lew thought—began tightening the knot of his tie. Sherrod tensed as he waited.

"Good morning, sir," he said into the phone after a moment. He bristled with attention. "Yes, sir, he is. . . . All right. I'll put him on."

Sherrod held out the receiver to Lew. "It's the President," he said. "He wants to talk to you. I'll wait outside."

Lew took the phone in a state of quasi-shock.

"Lew Corleigh?" The voice had the enfolding supplicatory tone Lew had heard scores of times on the radio in Africa. It was at once commanding and placating. The door closed as Sherrod left the room.

Lew gulped. "Yes, sir, Mr. President."

"Say, young fellah, what's this business you've gotten me into over there in Kalya? Some town called Zinzin. They had to rustle me up a special map into the situation room, so we could find the place."

"Yes, sir," said Lew. "It's about three hundred miles from Ft. Paul on the road we built for Kalya about ten years ago." Lew felt a stiffness in his fingers, and realized that his grip on the receiver was absurdly clawlike. He tried to relax.

"Alex Vining is giving my people fits over there," said the drawling voice. "He's a foxy grandpa, that one, but I need him on my side. . . . Now, Lew, give me a quick rundown. What the hell's the situation over there?"

"Well, Mr. President . . ." Lew hesitated. His hand was still too tight on the phone. How could he squeeze the whole story of Genghis Khan, the devil's dance and Golo bush school into a compact, logical statement?

"Easy, son. I've got a few minutes. Let's just hit the high points."

Lew tried. He compressed the long story into a short one of about three minutes, but he faltered several times, repeated himself needlessly, and when he finished, he felt he had failed to convey the significance of the clash in Zinzin. Here, speaking to the President in Washington, such things as Osterlord's shanghaied workmen and Genghis Khan's levy of a textbook fee seemed not only remote, but somehow trivial.

"So, Mr. President," he concluded, "we feel that this Moses Harter is a symbol of The Family's abuse of the tribes all over Kalya, and if we don't pitch for the Molas, we might as well all come home."

"Let me get one thing straight, Lew." The voice was more insistent now. "You think we ought to threaten to cut off foreign aid unless Vining lets the Peace Corps reopen that school and that road in Zinzin?"

"Yes, sir," said Lew. "We figure the Peace Corps has a lot of unused leverage there now because we're popular with the people." He was hurrying too much, he realized. "And Old . . . Mr. Vining . . . well . . . I think he's bluffing. He can't afford to lose the Peace Corps or USAID either."

"Mmm." There was silence at the other end for a moment.

"We'd be shoving in a lot of chips. You got any compromise suggestions for me?"

"No, sir." Lew thought of his Peace Corps friends, his outfit, in Zinzin. "I think we've let Moses Harter and The Family use us enough as it is."

"All right, Lew," said the President. "I appreciate what you're up against. Now you just go on back to Africa. We'll do the best we can for you. Tell Sherrod I'll be in touch with him later. And good luck to you. I'm mighty proud of the Peace Corps."

"Thank you, Mr. President. Good-by, sir."

Lew was still shaken when Sherrod returned to the room. "That was pretty sudden," he said. "I guess I got kind of confused. . . . I wish I could have explained it better."

"Forget it," said Sherrod. "He just wanted to get a personal feel of the thing through you. He's probably got a file a couple of inches thick on Zinzin. He's a very thorough President, this one."

Lew rubbed his ear, still thinking of the voice from the White House, dropping final consonants, entreating, insisting, subtly appealing for personal loyalty. "He asked me if I had any compromise ideas. I told him no."

Sherrod smiled as he loosened his tie again. He tilted back in his swivel chair and put one foot on a desk drawer. "Lew," he said, "I know you don't like the sound of the word 'compromise.' "

"Sometimes you have to go half-way," said Lew. "But I can't see how a compromise could work in Zinzin. What would it be?"

Sherrod shrugged. "Search me. But compromise is the essence of politics, especially with this man in the White House. What we call 'foreign affairs,' that big mouthful, is just politics away from home. Washington and Ft. Paul aren't much different when it comes to dealing government to government." He placed his hands behind his head and gazed at Lew. The look was a friendly one. "This thing has to be settled soon, and as you can guess from that call, it's going to be a White House decision. Don't expect too much, Lew."

Lew frowned. "The President said he'd do the best he could for us."

"He will. But don't forget the pressures on him. He looks at

that map in the situation room and he sees all of Africa, not
just your town of Zinzin. And then, I happen to know that Phil
Taggard's bugging him too. Taggard cuts some ice at the White
House. Outside of the Peace Corps and a couple of little nit-
picking issues, Taggard votes the administration way most of the
time. The President doesn't like to lose Taggard's influence on
other matters." He paused. "And now, of course, Demarest and a
couple of other Jefferson Study Club men will be putting on heat
from the other side. The old wheels within wheels. Well, we'll just
have to wait and see."

"I hope my coming here hasn't made trouble for you," said Lew.

"So what if it has?" asked Sherrod. "The day a volunteer can't
come into this office and speak his piece, that day I quit the
Peace Corps. No, I'm glad you made your pitch. It needed saying."

"But it won't get anywhere, huh?"

"Maybe." Sherrod smiled again. "And then again, maybe not.
Well, I guess that's it. Can we do anything for you before you
take the plane tonight?"

"Yeah, I've run out of dough. That sixteen bucks a day doesn't
go far in this town."

"The secretary will get you an advance." Sherrod rose and held
out his hand. "All I can say is what the President told you,
Lew. We'll do our best. If the decision were mine, I'd give
Genghis Khan the works." He sighed. "We meet his kind all over
the world. And it's a kind I don't like, to put it mildly."

They shook hands and Lew left. Except for the details of departure, his mission to Washington was over. And, thought Lew,
not a day too soon.

14

The jeep slid around the curve like a water bug, the rear wheels slipping to the side. The rain fell in a blank torrent. The windshield wiper fanned feverishly, but water followed each sweep of the blade, seemingly flushed by a giant hose. Steam fogged the inside of the jeep's windows, water seeped through the cracks and dripped on Lew's trousers. He was driving at less than ten miles an hour, but he could see only a few yards ahead. Brick-red water filled the ruts of the road, and the jungle on either side of the highway could be distinguished only by its slightly darker shade. The rain merged the towering dabemas, the African pines and the sipo mahogany trees into indistinct walls. The big rains had come to Kalya with supernatural ferocity as if determined to wash the land and its people away forever.

It was mid-afternoon and Lew judged he was only a few miles from Zinzin, but the town seemed an ocean distant. He had left Loli soon after breakfast under black skies. The rain began almost at once and the already gummy road turned into a series of muddy rivulets. He had spent seven hours navigating a stretch that he usually covered in less than half the time.

Now, ahead of him, he saw the dim outline of another vehicle halted in the middle of the road. As he braked to a skidding stop, a huge African in the uniform of the Kalya Army came to the side of the jeep. Water streamed off his face and his gray shirt and pants were sodden. Lew rolled down the driver's window.

"Eh, ya," said the army non-com. "Road chac-la. Wat' much deep." He held the palms of his hands about two feet apart.

"Okay," said Lew. "I'll be with you."

He took his heavy poncho from the rear seat and squirmed into it, then pulled on a rubber rain hat. The instant he stepped from the jeep, water began to run down his neck under the poncho. The sergeant led the way up the road, trying unsuccessfully to keep to the muddy ridges. Both men slipped into the ruts and splashed mud up to their knees. The rain stung Lew's face.

Ahead were two sedans and a flimsy money bus in which several passengers were dimly visible behind the misted windowpanes. The vehicles were in a line, the money bus first, and Lew saw why they had stopped. The road dipped low at this point and a rusty river, several feet deep, surged across the highway.

"Jeep help one time?" questioned the soldier.

Lew nodded. Peace Corps jeeps were equipped with a heavy cable and revolving drum just behind the front bumper. If Lew could drive the jeep across, he might manage to pull the other cars to the higher ground on the other side.

The soldier, a brawny giant, guessing Lew's thoughts, waded into the rushing water and pushed his way to the deepest part. He gestured, indicating the water's level about midway of his thighs.

"I guess I can make it," Lew shouted. But if the engine flooded, he thought, and the water continued to rise, he might wind up owing the United States government a jeep.

He returned to the Peace Corps vehicle and drove it cautiously past the other cars. The gears were in four-wheel drive as they had been since the rain began. Lew drove the jeep into the water. All went well until it reached the bottom of the depression, then the wheels spun and the jeep refused to go further.

The sergeant became an instant commander. In a furious burst of speech, half Mola and half chopped English, he routed people out of the three cars. They numbered eight persons, two of them women, and none had raincoats or other protective clothing. The soldier herded his reluctant troops into the reddish water to the rear of the jeep. They all pushed. The deep tire tread caught hold, Lew eased the accelerator down, and slowly the jeep moved forward and upward.

While the Kalyans scuttled back to the shelter of their vehicles, Lew turned the jeep around so that the front bumper faced the waiting cars. He and the soldier blocked the front and rear wheels with logs. Then the soldier took the heavy iron hook and walked back across the newly cut river, the cable unwinding as he went. He hooked it to the front bumper of the money bus, then rousted out his troops once more. Inside the jeep Lew started the mechanism which operated the winch. The cable strained, the people shoved the bus and the Kalya driver accelerated slowly.

The bus made it to high ground, then the process was repeated with the two other cars. When all three were safely past the deep water, the money bus driver started his motor again and waved out the window. The big soldier ran to the front of the bus, unloosed a stream of Mola invective and held up two warning palms.

"Peez-kor numba' one," he yelled to Lew.

The soldier ordered one of the bus passengers to descend and hold the iron hook while Lew operated the winch. When the cable was rewound on the drum, Lew turned the jeep around. The sergeant motioned the jeep forward with a sweep of his arm.

Lew lowered the window and shouted through the pelting rain. "Thanks, man."

The giant grinned. "Peez-kor!" he yelled. He waved a huge arm while water poured off his face. His uniform was glued to his body.

The jeep took the lead of the bedraggled caravan, sliding toward Zinzin at ten miles an hour. Under his poncho, Lew could feel water oozing over his belly. He was soaked, dirty, tired and, he realized, happy. The soldier was a Mola. This was Mola land. Ahead lay Zinzin and seven Peace Corps friends. Lew Corleigh was coming home again.

His two days in Ft. Paul, after returning from Washington, had been a blur of anger, frustration and elation. The elation came first. Prudence had met him at Vining Airport and he could still feel the hunger of her welcoming embrace. They talked in spurts, interrupting each other, as if they had been separated for months. At first she refused to credit Lew's story of talking to the President. Then she made him repeat it three times while she picked analytically at each phrase for its portent for Zinzin. Prudence served a cold lamb dinner by candlelight, they both drank rum and afterward their lovemaking was an ebullient, newly burnished one of reunion. Lew did not get back to the hostel until dawn.

Thus he was brittle from lack of sleep when summoned to Carter Williams' office in mid-morning. The conference lasted most of the day, with Williams eliciting every nuance of Lew's meetings in Washington. The Peace Corps chief, wrapped in a petulant air, complained that Lew had exceeded his prerogatives in making policy recommendations, and he took umbrage at Lew's appearance before the Jefferson Study Club. When Williams finally said, "It looks as if you intentionally tried to make trouble for us over there," Lew lost control of his temper. Williams became withdrawn and sulky in turn and demanded that Lew accept a transfer to Kolamon. Lew retorted that he would resign from the Peace Corps first. While they shook hands at the end of five hours of inconclusive talk, their manner was excessively formal and the parting was abrasive.

Lew was turning now from thoughts of Williams to more pleasant ones of Prudence when the first huts of Zinzin appeared through the misted windshield. The rain had slackened somewhat, but it still slanted steadily from the east. The huts looked like the debris of a great flood, forlorn relics of a vanished populace. No people or animals were to be seen. Water ran everywhere in red streams, eroding the soil and pouring the rusty sediment off the embankments into the road. The sky was a black blanket overhead, and all of Zinzin seemed awash. Still, Lew felt a welling anticipation within him and an eagerness he had seldom felt when returning to his old home neighborhood in Evanston.

He decided to pass the Lutheran mission—Arlene's shower held no appeal today—and head directly for the house of Alice Franklin and Dorothea Wyzansky. He hoped the gang might be gathered there, and he yearned for a thick towel and dry clothes. He drove the jeep almost to the front door, then ran through the rain, holding his small suitcase under his poncho.

Lew yelled, "Bock-bock," but anxious to get under a roof, he opened the door without knocking.

"We're raided!" It was a high feminine voice that trailed off into a giggle.

The room was shadowed despite the wan light of a kerosene lamp on the central coffee table. At first Lew could see no one. When he put down his suitcase and pulled off his rain hat and poncho, a pool of water formed at his feet.

Then he saw Dotty Wyzansky coming toward him. She appeared unsteady on her feet and she held a glass in her hand. She wore old blue jeans and an unwashed shirt, one tail of which hung down over the front of the jeans. Her sallow face had a vapid, mocking grin.

"Welcome to the nut house." She slurred the words. "The great diplomat returns from Washington! Have a drink, Red, and tell us about life in the big city. Did you get laid by a white girl—for a change?"

Lew eyed her guardedly. Dotty stood with uncertain stance before him, bony and thin, and she waved her glass back and forth under his nose.

"What are you drinking?" he asked.

"Gin," she said. "Straight gin. I mean, you wanna make something of it? Huh? Do yah? Well, say something, Redhead. Don't just stand there. Preach me a sermon or something. Cripes, I mean you always were a stinkin' moralizer, weren't you?"

"I could use a towel," said Lew. He felt uncomfortably defensive. Handling male drunks had never been his forte, and the female variety always unnerved him. "If I can use your bathroom, I'd like to change into some dry clothes."

"Alice!" Dotty shrieked it as a command. "Bring his lordship a towel. On the double now. Chop-chop. Don't keep the great white hunter waiting."

"Will you shut up?" Alice appeared in the dim doorway of her bedroom. She stood with folded arms, a small, squat figure. Wisps of hair fell over her spectacles, and she was not smiling. Even in the half-light, Lew could see that her cotton smock was wrinkled and soiled.

"Hi, Red," said Alice. She jerked a thumb at her roommate. "She's been on the stuff for three days."

"And I'll be on it for fifty-six more," said Dotty. She flourished her glass at Lew, then shuffled to the tattered sofa, her sandals slapping on the cement floor. "I mean fifty-six lousy, bitching days to go—and every one a monsoon." She lit a match and held it unsteadily for a moment, trying to mate it with the end of a cigarette. Then she sank onto the sofa and flicked the match on the floor.

Lew, his eyes accustomed to the gloom, looked about the house. The floor apparently hadn't been touched by a broom since he last saw it. The record albums were scattered about, one shoe and a brassiere lay against the wall, dirty glasses covered the coffee table and, through the kitchen door, he could see dishes piled in the sink. There was a clammy, moldering atmosphere about the house, and on the tin roof the rain beat a sullen tattoo.

"There's a towel in the bathroom, Red," said Alice. "You're lucky if it's dry. It's been raining here for a week."

He carried his suitcase to the bathroom, his shoes squishing and his pants cleaving wetly to his legs. The Franklin-Wyzansky bathroom contained two pails of water, a rickety washstand and a towel rack. Bodily functions were performed in the outhouse. As Lew closed the door, he noticed that one of the pails was placed under a leak in the roof through which water dropped with the beat of a metronome. When he undressed, he discovered that both towels on the rack were limp and gray. Lew fingered them with distaste, then decided to dry himself with a T-shirt from his suitcase. While he dressed in fresh clothes, Dotty carried on a shrill monologue in the living room.

"Rain, rain, go away," she chanted, "Peace Corps ladies want to play. . . . Hey Red, can you cook? I mean you've been scrounging meals here for two years. Nobody cooks here any more. We jus' open cans, fifty-seven varieties. One for each day still to go—and one lef' over. I mean hung over. Hey, hey, what do you say, let's all jump into the hay."

"Shut up!" shouted Alice. "If you don't, Dotty, I'll brain you, so help me."

"Shut up, yourself, fatso," said Dotty. She paused, then added with authority: "Alice Franklin, you humbug me. You're a slut."

Oh God, thought Lew. Next thing, they'll be heaving things at each other. He squared his shoulders in his fresh polo shirt and walked into the living room. Dotty was slumped in the sofa with her feet on the coffee table. She held a shaky cigarette and the ashes dripped on her shirt.

"Knock it off, Dotty," said Lew. "Act your age."

"I am," said Dotty. She giggled. "I'm twenty-five and never been kissed. But I've been laid. Yes, indeed, Red. I mean by better men than you. But you do all right, don't you, Redhead? First Cindy, and now the little missionary in Ft. Paul. Changing your luck the African way, back-assward, or inside out or something . . ."

"Stop it!" yelled Alice. "For God's sake, stop it."

Dotty peered somberly at her roommate without hostility. "I guess I will," she said. She took her glass and walked, teetering, to the kitchen. "What Mrs. Wyzansky's favorite daughter needs is another little shot of gin. Just a small-small gin, Mama dear."

Alice shook her head. "She started Saturday night with Ted Kramer and neither one has stopped yet."

"Ted too?" asked Lew.

Alice nodded, eyeing Lew through her thick spectacles. "They got plastered here, and Arch tells me that Ted's still at it. . . . Red, I'm telling you, it's one God-awful mess up here."

Dotty padded back into the room, holding her tall glass. It was half filled. She stood facing Lew, took an enormous swallow, then stared at him defiantly.

"Does it rain in Washington?" she asked. "It rains here, Mr. Big Wheel Diplomat. Rain, rain, all the day, and the Peace Corps gets no pay."

Dotty took another large swallow of the gin, choked, spit some of it out and wiped her mouth with the back of her hand. "Cripes, that's good."

She glared again at Lew, walked carefully to the coffee table, set down her glass, then marched to her bedroom with long, measured steps. After a moment, they heard her flop on her bed. Alice went to Dotty's room, peered inside, then closed the door.

"Out like a light," she said, "and not a century too soon. . . . So, now let's have one in peace ourselves."

Save for the small noises of Alice making drinks in the kitchen and the drumming of the rain, the house fell silent. Lew listened a moment, cocking an ear. The rain had changed tempo. The fierce drilling had softened. Lew knew the rhythm. The rain would stop now within a few minutes. But would the house ever dry out? Moisture seemed a living thing here. His chair was damp, the walls dripped and there was an unattended leak near the scattering of record albums. Night was closing now, and Lew turned up the kerosene lamp.

Alice brought the drinks, gin-and-water with squeezed half limes, and sat on the torn sofa from which the batting hung in long, gray strings. Over Alice's shoulder, Lew could see mildew on the bindings in the Peace Corps book locker. Alice huddled in the sofa, a lump of a girl, and Lew felt a twinge of sympathy for her.

"Where does Dotty get the booze money?" he asked.

"We're paid one hundred fifty-seven bucks a month, don't forget," said Alice, "and outside of food, what's to spend it on? Oh, Dotty's okay. She never drank much before. She's just had it here, that's all. Now, Ted Kramer, that's different. You know Houhab, owner of the biggest Lebanese store? Houhab has him on the cuff for a couple of hundred dollars, according to Archie. Ted's been drinking for a couple of months, ever since the first trouble with Genghis."

"Fill me in, Alice," said Lew. "It's been three weeks since I was up last."

Alice wriggled forward on the sofa, so that her feet touched the floor, and brushed the hair away from her glasses. "Same thing," she said, "only worse. They dumped the clothes of another kid at the door of his hut. The boy was Pimo's nephew, you know, that nice old man with bad teeth who went to Cindy's night class. He kept going when everybody else, even Oon Gilli, had quit. The same day Genghis warned Cindy she'd be hurt unless she quit holding night class. So . . . nothing's really changed. The boys are still in bush school. The school's shut tight, there's nobody to work on Jim's road, and none of us has a damn thing to do except sit around and try to keep dry."

"Where is everybody tonight?"

"I don't know." Alice shrugged. "They don't come around much any more. Like I said, Ted's on the bottle. Archie plays solitaire or goes over to Arlene's for gin rummy. Cindy went down to Ft. Paul once. I think she's hooked on some Kalyan who works at the Utility Authority. Jim . . . well, you know Jim. God knows where he hides out. He's got that country wife at night, and

Archie says Jim's keeping busy drawing plans for that water system he's always talking about. . . . A water system yet!"

"And you?" asked Lew.

Alice colored. "Oh, I read a lot," she said. "I don't know, Lew, I can't stand this place any more. It was bad enough when I could teach during the day. Now . . . oh well, fifty-six days to go. At least that's what the calendar says." She pointed to the Canada Dry calendar, where red slashes marked each box through the current date, May 29. Alice smiled. "I cheat. I cross off the day first thing in the morning, but of course that day isn't really over at all, is it?"

The rain stopped. They finished their drinks and Lew had another while Alice prepared the supper. Dotty was right. They had chicken-and-rice soup from a can, tuna fish from a can, instant coffee from a jar. Only the bread, made at the Mandingo bakery, and the pineapple were fresh.

Alice asked about Lew's trip to Washington, and he told her everything he could remember. She did not seem particularly interested. She brightened only when he mentioned his encounter with Maureen Sutherland.

"That would really tie it," she said, "if they took out our refridges. But I bet they will. I can feel it. Wawa!"

"Maybe they will," said Lew, "but on the other hand, Washington may put some pressure on Old Number One for the school. Of course, I'm not very confident. Still, there's a chance."

"In a pig's eye," said Alice. "Why kid yourself? Anyway, I don't care. All I want to do is get out of this dump and get on the plane for home."

They spent an hour doing the accumulated dishes of three days. Lew washed while Alice piled the dishes in a drying rack and lamented the absence of Joe-Joe, who had not been seen since bush school started. Alice explained that she had refused to wash dishes unless Dotty helped, and since Dotty indignantly insisted that she was no houseboy, the job went undone. Sam Zerwick's repeated warnings that decaying food bred disease in Kalya were ignored in the Franklin-Wyzansky menage. Lew left soon after emptying the dishwater. The last sounds he heard were Alice's good night and gurgling snores from Dotty's bedroom.

Jim Osterlord was not at home when Lew arrived. The house

was as clammy as Alice and Dotty's, and Lew spent the rest of the evening holding his sheets in front of the kerosene stove in an effort to dry them. The tactic worked, and by placing his poncho over the mattress, he made a bed reasonably conducive to rest. He soon fell asleep, but he awoke twice during the night with a dull ache in his shoulder blades and groggily cursed the dank mattress.

He was puttering about the stove and feeling miserable early the next morning when Jim Osterlord returned. Jim's heavy leather work shoes were caked with mud, but his clothes were fresh and dry.

"Hi yah, Red." Jim spoke as though Lew were a permanent resident.

"And hello to you," said Lew. "Your country wife must have a dry hut."

"I brought her a hand iron," explained Jim. He went immediately to the short-wave radio, clicked on the battery power and began twisting dials.

He raised Prudence's oddly metallic voice in Ft. Paul and reported laconically that there had been no change in Zinzin. Weather report: sun out briefly, but sure to rain again soon. Then Lew took over the microphone. No word from Washington, said Prudence. She told him she missed him dreadfully. Lew said he missed her too. She echoed the thought, urged him to hurry back. Lew signed off reluctantly and saw Jim watching him with a half smile.

"Sounds like you've got a city wife," said Jim. "Good broad. You could look a lot further and do a lot worse."

"Thanks. From you, it's a compliment."

"Well, I know more about her than you think," said Jim.

"Oh?" Lew waited, but Jim went to the kitchen to finish making the breakfast Lew had started. He set the table, put out the eggs, bread and coffee.

"Now," said Jim. "Give me the word. What happened in Washington?"

Lew talked for an hour while Jim clouded the sour room with smoke from his Mola-made cigar. Osterlord wanted to know just who attended the Jefferson Study Club—he followed U.S. politics closely—but through most of the recital, he sat with a tight, cynical smile.

"Balls!" he said when Lew finished. "Washington won't do a thing, zero, period, nothing. You watch, the next thing will be an order from Williams, telling us to shut up and quit interfering with Genghis—or worse, get out of town."

His attitude irritated Lew. "Why the hell don't you get your hair cut?" he demanded. The black mop now curled around Osterlord's ears. "You don't even look Arab any more. You remind me of some phony Hindu fakir."

"I'll make you a deal. The day my men come back to work, that day I'll hand you the scissors and let you hack it all off."

"A pleasure," said Lew. The rasp in his own voice annoyed him. It's this cruddy weather, he thought. He was getting just like the rest of them. Everything seemed to grate on the nerves.

"I hear you're drawing plans for a water system," said Lew, making an effort at a normal conversational tone.

"And how." Osterlord's face brightened. "Steve's helping me. I'm not kidding, Red, if we don't get kicked out of this town, Muo and I are going to start on the water system as soon as I finish the road."

With no prompting, Osterlord launched into an exhaustive description of water towers, mains, taps, connections and pumps. He seized a sheet of old wrapping paper, roughed out a map of Zinzin and diagrammed the water system on it. He showed Lew the top shelf of his book locker, now filled with volumes and pamphlets on engineering, hydraulics and plumbing.

"I borrowed them from Itambel," he said. "They've got a pretty good engineering library up at the concession."

"Where's the dough coming from?" asked Lew. "It'll cost a small fortune for tanks, pipes and all that."

"The Forge!" Jim leaned across the table conspiratorially. His eyes gleamed. "The Forge is going to get a lot bigger, baby. Steve tells me they've got one guy in parliament now. We can put on the heat through The Forge, and through the Molas, and get some Kalya tax money. It's due, man. Outside of the commissioner's building, Old Number One hasn't spent a nickel up here."

Jim rambled on, gesturing with his cigar, caught up in his

grand dream of public works. Lew marveled at his enthusiasm, and then he thought of the women and children from Zinzin's mud huts, carrying water in battered oil tins. The water was fetched from the fetid streams in which garbage, human feces and the snail incubators for the schistosomiasis parasite mingled indiscriminately. It required a formidable wrench of the imagination to envision a man like Oon Gilli turning on the faucet for running water in his mud hut. Osterlord was afloat in fantasy. The Zinzin he imagined was a generation away. It was time to remind him of the realities.

"Meanwhile we've got the rains, Genghis Khan, no school and no road," said Lew.

"Yeah." The glow faded from Jim's face. "Genghis, that arrogant bastard. He's running clients through that magistrate court like it was a mill. Every once in a while he dashes off to bush school. And when you see him on the street, he gives you one of those cocky sneers of his."

"Hey, that reminds me," said Lew. "When I saw Horace Magruder in Washington, he said the reason we'd never have a chance against Genghis is that he's a bastard son of Old Number One. Did you ever hear that, Jim?"

"Of course," said Osterlord. He eyed Lew in disbelief. "Don't tell me you didn't know that? Hell, that's common knowledge in Zinzin."

"I don't get it," said Lew. "We've been talking about that guy for months now. You could have told me—or Steve or Link or somebody could have."

Osterlord's smile was patronizing. "Listen, Redhead, we assume you know something about this country after all your time here. Am I supposed to run a nursery school for retarded Peace Corps characters? After all, you got here a year before I did."

Lew bristled. "Can the snotty act, Jim. . . . It's damn strange I never heard about Harter. Him being a pet son of Vining's explains a lot around here."

"Live and learn, kid," said Osterlord, and he left the house without further comment.

The abrupt departure left Lew in a waspish mood which persisted during the two hours he spent drying out yesterday's clothes on a line strung in front of the kitchen stove. He was about to start on the mail pickup rounds, preparatory to the drive back to Ft. Paul, when Osterlord returned to the house with news.

Lew, Jim said, was marooned in Zinzin. Jim seemed to relish Lew's dismay. The road to Loli, said Osterlord, was washed out. The place where Lew had hauled three vehicles across yesterday was now an impassable, raging river. As though to punctuate the news, the rain suddenly thundered anew on the roof like an exclamation point. Both men had to raise their voices almost to the shouting level.

The next days limped by in the deluge. Lew had felt the special stimulation of a homecoming upon driving into town. Now the feeling eroded like the flowing, brick-red earth of Zinzin. Water ran everywhere, incessantly, ruthlessly, gullying the banks, undermining embankments and swirling ankle-deep in the undrained streets. The rain beat on the thatched roofs until the huts resembled wretched, weeping toadstools. The great trees drooped, the nearby jungle became a sinister, wet mass, and Lew wondered where and how the Golo bush boys survived there. Few people ventured into the streets, although an occasional Mandingo, a green or blue cloth clinging to his ribs, could be seen striding regally through the downpour. Inside the Peace Corps houses, every object became wet, new roof leaks developed by the hour and the air held the rotting odors of a swamp. Despite the rain, the temperature hovered around eighty-five degrees and each human body seemed to stew in humid misery.

As Lew went from one house to another, he found his old friends snapping at each other or morosely nursing their despair. Ted Kramer, although he had quit drinking, had now developed malarial shivers and he spent his day wrapped in blankets which he periodically dried before the kerosene stove. His religious arguments with his roommate grew ill-tempered, and Arch, with a sneezing cold, preferred to sulk over gin rummy. Lew played with Lettermore all one afternoon. Since shuffling the limp cards was impossible, they merely shoved them around the table before each deal. Arlene Offenbach moved from her house to the Lutheran school dormitory, the only half-dry place on the compound. Lew visited her but briefly, for she sat all day with the Kalya teachers, mending rents in the children's clothing. The always tidy Cindy Fuller now began to neglect her appearance. She had lapsed into a despondent mood and spent her time reading by her stove. She chatted affably enough with Lew, but she did not ask him back and he had the impression that she wanted to be alone.

The Franklin-Wyzansky household was a morass of ill will. Alice had begun hiding the gin from Dotty, and when Lew appeared at noontime, Dotty was raging after her roommate with a broom. When Lew suggested—tactfully, he thought—that she might better use the broom on the floor, Dotty turned from her quarry and began to berate Lew as a meddling moralizer who sponged his meals from them. Of the whole Zinzin contingent, only Jim Osterlord remained his constant self. Lew seldom saw him except at breakfast, for Osterlord spent his days at a drawing board in the commissioner's office and the nights with his succulent young country wife. Lew did not know where she lived, but he hoped, for Jim's sake, that the hut was dry.

The rain ceased with a startling flood of silence on Lew's third night in Zinzin. He lay awake for a while, then went to the door and looked out. The sky arched in flawless clarity and not a cloud obscured the bright field of stars. The next morning the sun rose with its old blastlike fervor and soon the jungle smoked with steam, and the earth began to suck up the pools of water which shimmered by the hundreds throughout Zinzin.

Lew and Jim felt so good, they shook hands like long-separated friends, teased Prudence on the short-wave and attacked a breakfast of grapefruit, chicken, plantain and coffee. Jim had just lit a malodorous cigar when a woman's voice called, "Bock-bock," at the door.

Cindy Fuller burst into the room. The rose ribbon was back in her hair and her white cotton dress was newly ironed.

"Guess what?" she cried.

"Genghis cut his throat," said Jim.

"Not that good, but good," said Cindy. "School reopens tomorrow. The boys are all coming back today from bush school. And the work gang will be back at your road, Jim, as soon as it's dry enough to continue."

"You're out of your ever-loving mind," said Jim.

"I am not." Cindy sat down breathlessly at the table. "Give me a coffee, huh? I'm so excited. But it's God's honest truth."

"Calm down, honey," said Lew. "Just give us the facts, ma'am."

"Genghis just came to my place," she said. "He was all smiles and politeness—if you can dig that—and he apologized for getting angry at me. He said that school would reopen tomorrow and that the workmen would come back to the road as soon as you're ready for them, Jim—honest. He said Old Number One—the Prime Minister, he called him—sent in orders by messenger this morning."

"Messenger?" asked Jim suspiciously. "What do you mean? Nobody could get through from Ft. Paul on that road."

"Old Number One had the man flown up to the mines in the Itambel helicopter," said Cindy. "And then he came down a couple of hours ago in an Itambel truck. The road to the mine is open."

"I know the Itambel road is open, but there's something fishy," said Jim. He eyed Cindy through the cigar smoke like a hostile witness. "It sounds too pat, the whole thing."

"I believe Harter," said Cindy. "After all, why would he come around and confess to me that we'd licked him—because that's what it is for him, a real defeat." She turned with a broad smile to Lew. "You did it, Red. I don't know what you said in Washington, but they got the message. You know Old Number One would never have caved in without some pressure from Washington."

"I don't believe it," said Osterlord.

But it turned out to be true. All that day the boys of Zinzin straggled back from bush school in ones and twos, all cloaked in a proud, secretive air. The Kalya teachers showed up suddenly at the government school and began brooming the walls, straightening the benches and sweeping out puddles of water. Jim talked to the driver of the Itambel truck, a Belgian, and learned that he had driven an emissary of the Prime Minister down from the mining concession before dawn. Steve Muo made it official. He said he had received written orders from the Executive Palace, via the messenger, to make sure the school reopened.

The news rippled through town under the beneficent sun. The toothless crones grinned as they cried their market prices. Customers flocked to the Lebanese stores, the women cackling and gabbling. A youngster in tattered khaki shorts showed Lew an ugly gash on his leg and pointed proudly toward the jungle. He had the mark of the bush upon him. Old men gathered at the circular palaver hut to debate the big news. The fever of good will burned off the black mood of the Peace Corps contingent. Arch Lettermore, wearing a wide smile and a Lincoln University T-shirt, went about town, spreading word that a victory celebration dinner would be held at six o'clock at Alice and Dotty's.

But the troops began gathering at the Franklin-Wyzansky household an hour earlier and when Lew arrived at the appointed hour, the party was well under way. His first surprise came at the door. Dotty met him at the door without a glass in her hand. She appeared pale and drained, but no longer dispirited, and for the first time since Lew had known her, Dotty wore a dress that had been newly laundered and ironed.

Lew was greeted with a whoop of delight. Arlene rushed to him, threw her arms about him and kissed him full on the lips. Ted Kramer, wan and pasty-faced, with a blanket draped over his shoulders, slapped Lew on the back. Cindy yelled the Mola word for hero. Alice thrust a roll of paper into the hands of Jim Osterlord, then took one edge of the roll and marched across the room, unfurling a huge paper banner with the crayoned legend:

BETTER RED THAN DEADSVILLE

"Now, Archie!" commanded Dotty.

Arch Lettermore stepped forward with simulated solemnity and handed Lew a glass.

"Straight rum," he said. "Drink!"

Lew took a swallow while the others, save for Dotty and Ted, raised glasses in salute. Arch flourished a sheet of paper and then began to intone in his most pronounced North Carolina drawl.

"Testimonial award to Lewis N. Corleigh, Peace Corps volunteer leader, Republic of Kalya . . . ahem . . . whereas . . . whereas the undersigned would rather be Red Corleigh than residents of the Deadsville decreed by Genghis Khan, Esquire . . . And whereas the said Lewis N. Corleigh never burned a draft card, having evaded service in Vietnam by prior gold-bricking in the United States Army . . . And whereas PCVL Corleigh's amatory powers overcame the stubborn defenses of Miss Prudence Stauffer, a dedicated Peace Corps staff member . . ."

"Hurrah!" shouted Alice and Dotty.

"Even if he couldn't make time with Miss Cynthia Fuller, the luscious, brown queen of Zinzin," added Arch sotto voce with a mock leer.

"Pour it on, Archie," yelled Ted.

Lew, standing self-consciously before the gathering, noted that the room was clean for the first time in his memory. The records were neatly stacked, the floor was swept clean, the shoe and the brassiere were gone and no dirty glasses covered the coffee table. And Alice wore a fresh dress. Lettermore continued:

"And whereas Lew Corleigh survived an attack of a vicious mamba . . . And whereas in commemoration of his courage, the Honorable Dorothea Wyzansky and the Dishonorable Theodore Kramer have agreed to go on the wagon for fourteen days, count 'em, fourteen . . . And whereas Lewis Corleigh undertook a confidential and vital mission to Washington . . . And whereas he presented the case of the people versus Moses Harter with sagacity, audacity and no doubt duplicity . . . And whereas his mission was crowned with success beyond the wildest hopes of any living person . . .

"Now therefore, the undersigned grateful members of Peace Corps Zinzin do hereby confer on Lewis N. (Red) Corleigh the first annual Martin Luther King civil disobedience award . . ."

"No racial commercials," shouted Ted.

"Silence, Whitey," ordered Lettermore. "You're lucky this isn't a Black Muslim meeting. . . . If I may be permitted to continue without further interruption from the cheap seats. . . . The first annual Martin Luther King civil disobedience award in honor of the first man in history who ever brought the Mola tribe anything better than leg sores."

Lettermore bowed formally, his abundant stomach creasing at the middle, and handed the typewritten sheet to Corleigh. The assemblage cheered. "A toast to Red," cried Arlene, and all drank again save Ted and Dotty, who raised glassless hands aloft. "Speech," said Cindy and everyone echoed the command.

"I'm overwhelmed," said Lew, "and deeply touched. I shall treasure this award in whatever graduate school will accept me. That's about all, except I sure hope it isn't premature. Thank you."

"No Wawa this time," said Alice.

Arlene kissed him again. Cindy kissed him to cheers, Dotty and Alice did likewise. Then Arch gave Lew a French embrace,

loudly smacking him on each cheek. Ted Kramer and Jim Osterlord shook hands with him and Jim said, "I'm sorry I shot off my
mouth this morning, Red."

The party promptly moved into high gear. The rum and gin
disappeared rapidly. Arch led a snake dance while Ted, clutching
his blanket about him, brought up the rear. Arch did the monkey
and the frug with Alice, and soon everyone was dancing. The sun
slid into the high bush, but the heat remained intense. Jim said
the place was beginning to "smell like a locker room," but nobody
minded.

Arlene became frisky on more rum than she could handle. Once
she mounted the coffee table and did a wild solo dance, jerking
her arms upward and gyrating her hips. "Take it off," yelled
Ted, whereupon she removed first her necklace and then her shoes.
But she ignored all further disrobing demands from the males.
Lew loudly recalled Osterlord's promise to let his hair be cut if
the work crew returned to his road project. Jim protested that
the men had not showed up yet, but the party overrode his ob-
jections. Alice threw a sheet over a chair and Arch pinned Osterlord to it while Lew lopped off half the black tangle with a pair
of scissors. Everyone cheered. More drinks were passed to salute
the barbering. The record player clamored rock-and-roll guitar and
drum combos, Ted Kramer did a shaky Indian war dance with
his blanket and Dotty beat time on a dishpan.

By eight o'clock Cindy was delivering a saccharine speech on
the glories of integration to which no one paid any attention,
and Alice raced about the room, emitting grunts and spluttery
sounds which were supposed to imitate Jim on his motorbike. Arch
did better with an imitation of Moses Harter, hissing his sibilants
and making lustful gestures at Cindy. By nine o'clock the din
began to subside. Osterlord and Arlene were locked in an embrace in the corner, oblivious of the suggestions for superior tech-
niques of dalliance. Dotty and Ted held hands on the disin-
tegrating sofa, while Lew, Arch and Cindy helped Alice serve the
spaghetti and meat balls buffet supper.

The food further quenched the fading fires of liquor, and soon
after the watermelon dessert, the party broke up.

"My gosh," said Alice, "I got so excited, I forgot." She crossed
the room to the Canada Dry calendar, took the red crayon which

dangled by a string, and crossed out another date box. "Only fifty-three to go," she said. Nobody cheered.

"Get to school on time," commanded Cindy.

Arlene and Jim were the first to leave. Both were somewhat bemused, and Jim clearly was embarrassed. "Lucky stiff," growled Ted Kramer after they had gone. "Only guy here with a country wife to cheat on." But the aura of good will prevailed, and when Lew rode Cindy, Arch and Ted to their homes in the jeep, they all sang "We Shall Overcome," and Arch thumbed his nose when they passed Moses Harter's house, a concrete structure almost as large as the commissioner's building.

"Ain't victory sweet," were Arch's parting words.

Lew rode alone then to Osterlord's house in a mellow mood. The stars were bright as diamonds overhead, a breeze rustled the tops of the dabema trees, the warm, caressing air had lost the punishing heat of daytime, and Lew wished that Prudence were there. In the town, a solitary dog barked, and in the high bush beyond, the Kalya night made its murmuring sounds.

15

Lew drove the road to Loli the next afternoon in an exuberant mood. His head ached slightly from the celebration, despite two aspirin, but he did not mind. The sun burned brightly for the second day, there were no cloudy threats of rain and the soft condition of the roadbed moderated the jarring of the jeep's chassis. Some potholes were still half-filled with water, but there were no impassable stretches. Where the surging muddy stream had been four days ago when the jeep winched three cars to high ground, there was now only low, tranquil water.

The sun was coasting down in the west like a great orange balloon as Lew turned off the main road and headed across the parkland to Forrest Stevenson's trailer home on the knoll. Both Forrest and his wife, Grace, came out to meet the jeep, and Geronimo bounded toward the vehicle in frantic starts and stops, barking his own melodrama.

Grace Stevenson worried her greeting as though Lew were still the comatose patient she had seen at the time of the mamba incident. She inspected his forehead and held his hand tightly.

"Are you all right?" she asked, somewhat as if she hoped he might not be. "I told Forrest I wasn't sure we'd ever see you outcountry again."

"I feel great." Her tremulous concern made Lew realize how good he did feel. "Maybe a bit hung over. We had a big victory party last night."

"Victory?" Forrest Stevenson's pale blue eyes were questioning. The U.S. AID official wore his usual expression of weary resignation. He stood thin and weatherbeaten in the shadows of the lowering sun.

"A big one," said Lew. "I'll tell you about it."

The air of the expanded metal trailer was deliciously cool after the ovenlike heat of the road. The window air-conditioners purred their pledge of comfort. Lew showered in the little metal stall, and when he appeared in clean clothes, Forrest was ready on the aluminum-fitted porch with a frosted mint julep.

"So let's hear about the victory," said Stevenson. His tanned face folded in the gentle smile. "I've almost forgotten how you spell the word."

Lew told of Harter's call on Cindy and of the Peace Corps celebration. Grace Stevenson, nestled in her chaise longue, asked repeated questions about the party, savoring the gossip, until her husband put in a mild dissent.

"Please, Grace," he said. "A party's a party. I want to hear more about Vining and Harter."

"There isn't much to tell," said Lew. "School started with a bang this morning. The kids showed up early, all jabbering and chasing around the soccer field. The classes were full, and even Dotty looked happy to be back at work again. Jim's road is still too muddy for work, but the men all showed up this morning ready to start. If the rains hold off again tonight, he's set to go tomorrow."

Stevenson shook his head and fingered his julep with a delicate, blue-veined hand. "Something about that story doesn't add up," he said. "I can't imagine that cutthroat Harter being magnanimous in defeat. It's out of character. There must be some hidden agreement we don't know about. What, for instance, has Washington done, precisely?"

"I don't know," said Lew, "but it had to be some kind of strong pressure on Old Number One. We talked to Prudence Stauffer this morning on the short-wave, and she said Williams told the staff the school was reopening today. He got the word from Ambassador Milbank who'd been over to see Vining yesterday. What the exact pitch is, Prudence doesn't know."

Stevenson frowned as he stretched his legs and took another sip of his drink. "My instinct tells me to look for Wawa," he said. "I can't believe Old Number One, as flinty as he can be, would give in just because Milbank waved a cable at him."

"I don't think there's any Wawa here, Forrest," insisted Lew. "We won, period. It shows that the Peace Corps has some muscle in this country. Now if Williams would only use it once in a while."

"Tell me about your talks in Washington," said Stevenson.

Lew's account was interrupted from time to time by Mrs. Stevenson, who wanted to know what the women wore, how Washington looked in May and, longingly, what the society columnists were saying. When her husband chided her for getting Lew off the track, she turned peevish, and Geronimo, for no discernible reason, raised his head from his paws and growled at Lew.

"You mean you actually recommended that foreign aid be cut off for Kalya if Old Number One refused to play ball?" asked Stevenson. "You're a gambler, Red."

"No, I'm not," said Lew. "I just took the line you're always preaching."

"Fine friend you are," said Stevenson. "You travel four thousand miles just to try to do me out of a job." But his smile was an approving one.

"I don't know who generated the heat," said Lew. "Maybe it was Senator Demarest or somebody else in that Jefferson Study Club. All I know is that we won. And that's what counts."

"Don't be too sure," said Stevenson. He looked at Lew, but his misted blue eyes seemed centered on a point beyond. "I think I'll keep my fingers crossed." He paused, then added irrelevantly: "June's a strange month in Kalya. Do you know we could have a semi-drought right in the middle of the big rains? It has happened, more than once."

"What's that got to do with anything?" asked Grace.

Stevenson sighed. "Nothing, dear, nothing."

Mrs. Stevenson turned to Lew. "It means another night of dreary philosophizing and talk, if you want to know. If it isn't raining outside, we're flooded with big, vague thoughts inside."

The dinner was a joy, from the imported Polish ham to the chocolate mousse, and when the houseboy cleared away the dishes, Grace Stevenson retired to bed with a paperback thriller whose cover sported a man wearing dinner jacket and black gloves and holding a smoking revolver. Soon the ancient Mola warrior arrived to patrol the grounds with his bow and arrow.

Lew declined the offer of brandy, but Stevenson refilled his own tumbler twice during the night. They talked until midnight, of African and American politics, the future of the AID program, Vietnam, astronomy, the Peace Corps, the sexual practices of The Family, the Davis Cup, the trouble with women, Hulbert Booth, German shepherds and the Aswan dam. Only when Lew went into his second round of yawns did Stevenson suggest that it was time for bed.

The next day's run to Ft. Paul was an easy one despite the sun, now baking in a hazy sky for the third successive day. The water had evaporated from the road now and on some flat stretches, the jeep even raised dust. Making his routine mail pick-ups, Lew was pleased to find that at Kpapata, both Katherine and Barbara were in school. The only complaint came from Bart, the spindly man with the beatnik chin whiskers, who said the spellers Lew brought up on the last trip were useless. They were meant for American kids, he said. What boy or girl in this village knew what a power mower, a supermarket or a ping-pong ball was? Bart put his question resentfully, seeming to blame Lew personally for the provincial outlook of the samaritans who shipped American textbooks to Africa.

That evening Lew stopped at the hostel only long enough to shower and change clothes. Prudence met him with a hug at the door of her house. She was wearing the sleeveless pink sheath on which she had splurged for their party at Founders House.

"Bet they're gung-ho now in Zinzin," she said.

"You look great," he countered. He had never seen her look so attractive. Her eyes were alight, her hair waved softly from her forehead and a timorous smile told him that she coveted, but was unsure of, his approval.

Inside the house, she perched on his lap, cradled his head and kissed his lips, his cheeks, his eyes. "One for each day," she said. "You've been gone six days."

"What's for dinner?" he asked.

Prudence slapped him lightly on the chin. "At a time like this you ask?"

"You didn't understand," he said. "What I mean is, will it keep? I thought if we mixed a drink and then moseyed into the bedroom . . ."

"Oh!" She bounced off his lap and went to the kitchen, returning with two glasses of rum on ice. She marched past him, holding the glasses high in front of her. "This way to paradise," she said. Then she laughed, quickened her step, and Lew followed her into the bedroom.

It was the third time they had made love and now, knowing each other, there was no awkwardness, no embarrassment. But there was something else, Lew thought, something he never felt before. It was not just that Prudence was happy and abandoned. There was a frolicking, rowdy manner about her. She rolled, squirmed and pawed at him, and occasionally she gave a low laugh of pleasure. There was joy, there was freedom and there was candid, animal exulting. He had once known a girl who cried afterward. Prudence, instead, rubbed her nose against his and laughed.

"Why didn't you tell me it could be such fun?" she asked.

"You never asked." He propped himself on an elbow and studied her little face with the splash of freckles between the eyebrows. "You know something?"

"What?"

"I think I'm in love with you," he said seriously.

"You think? Why, you conniving seducer." She pounded on his chest with her fists. "You mean you lured me to a fate worse than—and only *thought* you were in love? You're a rat." And she mashed his mouth with a kiss.

"God, you're rough," he said.

She sprang out of bed, grabbed the bath towel from the floor, draped it about her hips and began to dance about the room.

"I'm rough," she cried. "I'm tough. Maybe he loves me and

maybe he doesn't. He doesn't care. He has taken me. What shame. What shame."

Then she stopped twirling, held one end of the towel over her breasts and looked at him with wide eyes.

"Red," she said. "I'm happy. I'm awfully happy."

And so, thought Lew, was he. When in his life, he asked himself, had he ever felt so alive, so exhilarated, so full of himself and a woman? He looked at her soberly, half in wonderment, and he knew at that moment that he wanted to marry her.

During dinner she played melodic string music on the record player—"Just like at the Plaza," she said—and not until the after-dinner coffee did the talk turn to Zinzin. He told her about Stevenson's doubts that a valid triumph had been won.

"Just don't know," she said. "Williams acts odd around the office. He says Old Number One gave orders to reopen the school, but when you ask him what Washington did, he gets vague. Don't know if he knows anything more or not."

"Well, I guess we'll find out sooner or later," said Lew. "Meanwhile I'm going to quit worrying. A guy mixed up with a dame has better things on his mind."

"Sorry to hear about Dotty and Ted drinking," said Prudence. "Thank the Lord there's none of that in my district. Some teachers get discouraged and down in the dumps, but about all they do is mope around the house."

"Oh, Dotty's okay. She's just one of those dames who should never have joined the Peace Corps. She hasn't liked it from the start."

"Ought to weed 'em out in training," said Prudence. Her tone was again the efficient one of the staff member. "But I guess it'll get worse, now that the Peace Corps is expanding so fast. Don't think that's right. I like quality, not quantity."

"Me too," said Lew. "That's why I picked you."

She frowned. "Not much of me, is there? Lew, be honest with me. You sure you're not disappointed that my bosom is so . . . well . . . so kind of minor?"

Again her sober, intent look amused him. "Quit being so anatomical," he chided. "Too much scientific inquiry is bad for romance."

She would not be diverted. "Guess you do like me. You seem

to—sometimes." She cupped her chin in her hands and sighed. "Still, I wish I were built like B.B. or Gina, somebody lush like that. . . . No, that's self-pity. We've all got to do the best we can with what we haven't got."

"Prude," he said, "you're a puritan with yearnings to be a houri." She grinned. "You can't even pronounce the word right."

The banter continued, then trailed into serious musings about Zinzin, The Family, the Peace Corps. It was midnight before Lew left for the drive to the hostel.

The next morning at Peace Corps headquarters, Lew was called into Carter Williams' office at exactly 8 A.M., the starting hour for work of the Ft. Paul staff. The Peace Corps chief, his irritation with Lew now dissipated, was back to his normal, anxiously pliant self. Now that matters were settled in Zinzin, he said, the idea of transferring Lew to Kolamon could be shelved. Lew thanked him, reported on the reopening of the Zinzin school and asked what Washington had done to make Prime Minister Vining change his mind.

"I just don't know," said Williams. He toyed with his penknife and avoided looking at Lew. "The ambassador hasn't seen fit to tell me. I can only assume that my suggestion was followed and that Vining was assured the Peace Corps would cease . . . well, meddling . . . in tribal politics up there."

"Has there been some order like that?" asked Lew. "Nobody has told us anything."

"No," said Williams. "Still, that would seem to be taken for granted, wouldn't it? I do hope there will be no further trouble-making by our people in Zinzin."

"Trouble-making?" Lew was becoming exasperated with Williams again.

"Well," said Williams, "you did drive Muo down to Ft. Paul, and Miss Fuller did post a notice that was somewhat inflammatory, to say the least."

Lew was not disposed to argue the point. They had, he thought wearily, been over that ground before. His talk with Williams ended, as usual, indecisively, and Lew had a hunch that the Peace Corps chief was withholding information from him.

The bulletin board disclosed one topic that had not been mentioned. A typewritten sheet was tacked prominently in the middle:

FROM: Carter Williams, PC Representative
TO: Volunteer leaders

    1. Please make inventory of all volunteer kerosene refrigerators in your area by June 15. List type, brand name, age, together with name and duties of volunteer in whose house refrigerator is located.

    2. Prepare brief estimate of your own as to probable effect on PCV health and morale should refrigerators be removed.

Lew groaned. Jesus, he thought, that again. A picture of Maureen Sutherland flashed in his mind. She had become synonymous in his mind—unfairly, he conceded—with the kerosene boxes. He could see her dark glasses and creamy complexion, and then he could see himself wrestling Susan's refrigerator, turning it upside down in the house at Loli. The two pictures became confused, and Maureen's chic figure seemed to decorate the door of Susan's faulty refrigerator.

He sought out Dr. Sam Zerwick as one rebel against constituted authority seeks the company of another. The physician was alone in his cubicle, making out his monthly report on the afflictions of his Peace Corps charges.

"Red!" Zerwick cocked his head and peered through his enormous lenses. "Did you see that god-damn notice on the bulletin board?"

"Sure did." Zerwick's menacing tone heartened him. Lew could anticipate the forthcoming verbal explosion as he would the arrival of an old friend.

"Washington's out of its cotton-picking mind," said Zerwick. It was less a comment than an eruption. "If they take those boxes away from outcountry, I'm going to cable the Surgeon General and demand an investigation. You were in Washington last week, Red. Don't they have anything better to do than to nag us about refrigerators, for God's sake? A bunch of brainless, tinkering incompetents, if you ask me."

Lew grinned. He felt much better. "Maybe a Senate appropriations hearing is coming up—or Phil Taggard's on their backs."

"So what?" Zerwick yanked off his glasses and flourished them.

"They stick me out here in one of the most primitive medical areas in the world and tell me to keep everybody healthy. Then, by God, they undermine me with a lot of infantile nonsense. No refrigerators!"

"I agree," said Lew. "Of course, it does look like Washington has gone to bat for us up in Zinzin."

"That's another mistake," said Zerwick. "Why do we go sticking our noses into that? This is Kalya. Let the Kalyans run it."

Lew was surprised. "Now wait a minute, Sam. That's our hassle up there. You know how The Family screws the Molas. We're trying to stop it."

Zerwick shook his big head, blew on his glasses and slowly polished them with a tissue. "Man has been exploiting man since we came down out of the trees," he said. "In Kalya, if it wasn't The Family, it was somebody else. And now here we come, a bunch of would-be reformers, trying to impose our brand of morality and culture on people who don't want it. God-damn it, this is Kalya— not the United States. I think you're all lunatics, batting around in Kalya politics."

"So what are you doing here?" asked Lew. "I notice you try to put some order into that scummy Ft. Paul hospital. Aren't you doing the same thing? And isn't that progress?"

"Progress!" roared Zerwick. "Red, you get the hell out of here before I throw something at you."

Lew backed out the door, grinning. Zerwick was better than a liver tonic. His blustering gave tone to the muscles.

Lew crossed the reception lobby, heading for the workroom of the volunteer leaders. Rachael Frisson stopped him. The tall Negro girl with the imperious carriage handed him some papers from a stack she was carrying.

"Your forms for the refrigerator survey," she explained. "I had them run off on the mimeograph."

"I'll get a hot reception with these outcountry," said Lew. "I might as well be selling cemetery lots."

"The kids wanted it tough when they came in, didn't they?" she asked. She wore high heels, a vivid green dress that hugged all her curves, and her hair was piled regally high.

"We all learn," said Lew. He knew Rachael's views and he did not care to contest them this morning.

"I wanted to talk to you anyway, Lew," she said. "How about coming to my place for dinner tonight?"

"Well . . ." he hesitated.

"Oh, don't worry," she said. "I know about you and Prudence. I don't mean alone. I'm having a dinner party. There are some interesting people you ought to meet—especially after your trip to Washington. You're a celebrity now, you know."

Perhaps he was, in a restricted Ft. Paul sense, thought Lew. Rachael probably never would have thought of inviting him if he weren't. Or was there some special purpose here? He was suddenly intrigued.

"Check it with Prudence, if you like," she said with a patronizing smile. "I know how it is with twosomes."

"Never mind," replied Lew. "I'm not married. What time should I show?"

"Sevenish," she said, meaning almost eight, he surmised.

But Lew did feel a bit guilty and he drove by Prudence's house that evening to tell her where he would be. Prudence simulated a pout, but actually she was as curious as Lew about the invitation, and she exacted a promise that he would tell her who was there and what was said.

Rachael Frisson lived in a style which the Peace Corps would deem incompatible with her mission of succor. She had a four-room unit in an air-conditioned apartment house built the previous year by an Italian construction firm. The building had a spacious lobby, marble facing on the walls, and was the only structure in Ft. Paul, aside from the Executive Palace and Founders House, with an elevator. The tenants were either foreigners or high officials of The Family. There was a long waiting list of prospective occupants and residence there had become a coveted form of government patronage. Rachael's ability to lease a unit there indicated the degree of her acceptance in the Ft. Paul social community.

Lew had expected flair in Rachael's apartment, but he was unprepared for the decor which fairly shouted at him when he entered. The living room was done in stark contrasts of black and white. The walls were white, the thick, wall-to-wall carpeting a midnight black. A long divan was upholstered in a creamy white material, and the adjacent end tables, resting on carved jaguar legs, were of ebony. Two chairs, with enormous backs at least six feet tall, stood against the wall like inky sentinels. Around the room on bookcases and cabinets rested dark carvings of African busts. In the dining room beyond, Lew could see white linen draping the table, which was set with a sparkling array of silver and glassware.

Nor was Lew prepared for the prestigious character of the guests. There was Colonel Hulbert Booth, the usual chest bulge under his tailored dark suit, with his Japanese companion, a delicate woman who appeared almost doll-like beside her huge African escort. There was the Commissioner of Education, J. Richardson Downing, chattering with pseudo-profundity. His wife was a tall woman, more brown than black, whose effortless grace of manner showed a long acquaintance with Ft. Paul's cosmopolitan social life. And, to Lew's surprise, in a corner with drink in hand, stood Horace Magruder of Itambel. His wife had his same outdoor tan and she radiated the kind of confident, if surface, geniality that Lew associated with the women golfers at the Skokie country club back home.

The best-dressed man in the apartment was the elderly houseboy, a short, emaciated man who was as black as the ebony carvings. He wore white suede shoes, white knee-length stockings, white Bermuda shorts with pleats, white silk cummerbund and a white short-sleeved shirt with black monogram at the breast pocket. He glided impassively about the room with a silver tray laden with drinks.

The houseboy's sartorial splendor made Lew feel self-conscious about the lack of crease in his own dark suit, but there was no Peace Corps dowdiness in Rachael's garb. A white net strapless gown, seemingly held up by imagination alone, cut sharply in the rear to her lower back, exposing a smooth expanse of taffy skin. Her hair curved high, like an arbor over a gate, and at her ear lobes were tiny pearls. The soles of her spike-heeled shoes were gilt-trimmed.

After the introductions, Lew found himself in a corner faced by the imposing bulk of Colonel Booth. Both men were drinking Scotch-and-water. The security chief's mustache was clipped in a precise line. His smile was expansive and almost affable.

"I was sorry to hear about your encounter with a mamba," said Booth. "In Kalya, the jungle is always near."

"Snakes sometimes crawl into cars on their own," said Lew, "but not often." He looked squarely at Booth. "I think this one was helped."

"You do?" Booth frowned sympathetically. He raised his drink and with the movement, Lew could see the leather of his shoulder holster beneath the coat. "I didn't know the Peace Corps had enemies. After all, you're men of peace, as the name states."

"But if somebody pushes us around, we're liable to fight back," said Lew.

"No need of that in Kalya." Booth's smile spread to his ears, and Lew noted for the first time that the colonel's face was almost rubbery in its flexibility. "Of course, there was a little trouble up in Zinzin, but as I understand it, that's all settled now. And you'll be going home soon, with the thanks of Kalya as a memory."

Lew was glad that Rachael touched Booth's elbow and steered him away. It was difficult to keep up a pretense of amiability with a man he felt like hitting.

The cocktail hour fattened itself to two, and it was well after nine o'clock when the houseboy motioned them to the glittering table with its elegant settings. They ate by the light of tall candles and below them, through the window, Ft. Paul shimmered like sequins. Rachael served a Pouilly Fuissé with the fish course and a bordeaux with the roast beef, and Lew realized he had not feasted so well since the night at Founders House. Rachael was an urbane, even somewhat regal, hostess, and the houseboy moved about as though on silent roller skates. Lew's mission to Washington was the chief conversational fare. Everyone, save perhaps the Japanese woman, knew the background.

"It is unfortunate," said Commissioner Downing, "when the strictly pedagogical problems reach the higher political, not to say international, levels. The statesmen tend to lose sight of the child at his school desk, my yes."

"Well, in this case, Mr. Commissioner," said Lew drily, "the child wasn't at the desk. The school was closed."

"Exactly." Downing beamed and gestured with his fork. "The problem had proliferated, if I may say, beyond the educators. It had become tangled in the intricate web of politics. We must learn, my friend, to evaluate and process these matters at the proper, discreet level, my yes."

"With all due respect, Richie," said Booth, "that was not the case in Zinzin. The Peace Corps, as wonderful as it may be for our people, got in too deep up there. Foreigners just don't understand how to handle the tribal people. We do. That's the essence of the matter."

"Of course, you know from personal experience," said Lew. "I understand you called on some of our Peace Corps workers up there."

This oblique reference to Booth's amorous assault on the Franklin-Wyzansky household brought a surprised flash of hostility to Booth's eyes, but he quickly regained his composure.

"Yes," he said. "I do know the situation at first hand. Dealing with the tribes requires much background that some of our foreign friends just cannot acquire in a short time."

"Agreed, Hulbert," said Downing. He crackled with enthusiasm. "The tribal culture is complexly structured, as we educators know. The place to solve Zinzin's classroom problems is among the pedagogues of Zinzin, my yes."

Booth seemed as impatient with Downing's cluttered rhetoric as Lew was. The security chief turned to the rest of the table.

"Remember," he said, "that outside of Ft. Paul, Kalya is still largely a primitive land. It takes a genius like Alexander Vining to hold it together. I think the Peace Corps sometimes misses that point."

"I'd disagree there, Hulbert," said Magruder. He spoke with a casual firmness that indicated his status and lengthy dealings with The Family. "The tribal people aren't that primitive. They're merging quite well into the modern age. You've all seen what fine mechanics and foremen the Molas and the Fizis make up at the concession."

"And the women are such rapid learners," said Mrs. Magruder. "They run our commissary completely now, and most of the nurses at the Itambel hospital are Mola girls."

Booth nodded at her. "I understand. Still, outcountry is in a state of transition. The strong hand of authority is still needed, and when a situation does arise, such as that in Zinzin, well, then, compromise is the democratic way, isn't it?"

"I never in my life argued against compromise," said Magruder. His huge, pitted nose, oddly, seemed to emphasize his sincerity.

"Men of reason and good will can always work something out. It saves time, nerves and sometimes lives."

Booth tilted his head toward Corleigh. "But I'm not sure our good friend here understands the art. If I'm correctly informed, the reason he was summoned to Washington was that he and some of his Peace Corps colleagues weren't too interested in reaching an understanding."

"All we wanted to do, Colonel," said Lew, trying to keep the irritation from his voice, "was make sure the school stayed open. That's what the Peace Corps is here for—to teach."

"You see!" exclaimed Downing triumphantly. "At heart, it was a simple question of educational orientation."

Booth looked impatient again. "Richie," he said, "you went to too many teachers' colleges in too many countries."

"Not as many as Mrs. Booth did," said Mrs. Downing softly. "By the way, Hulbert, how is Matilda?" She had the deceptively innocent look of a woman who has just told her favorite enemy that the new dress flatters her.

The Japanese lady colored. Magruder inspected his napkin. Booth cleared his throat as if a bone had suddenly lodged in it.

"Better, thanks," said Booth. "I'd hoped to have her here to-night."

Rachael Frisson's smile was one of bliss as she savored the false-hood. Everyone at the table knew that the sexually acquisitive colonel had not slept at home two nights in succession for the last five years and, further, that a healthy Matilda Booth was more than content with her towering Senegalese gardener.

Over the liqueurs, there was talk of U.S.-Kalya relations, more talk of Zinzin and somewhat veiled references by Magruder and Booth to the need for mutual understanding and agreement. Lew was prepared to leave with the others, but Rachael said it was his duty as acting host to stay behind and help straighten up.

"I lied," she said when her guests had left and the houseboy had departed for the night. "I really wanted to talk a while." She kicked off her gold-trimmed shoes and lit a cigarette in the long, ivory holder. "Take off your coat, Red. Let's relax."

She put some Erroll Garner records on the hi-fi set, offered him a Scotch which he declined, then made one for herself. She sat down beside him on the white divan.

"You used to go with Cindy Fuller in Zinzin, didn't you?" she asked.

"That was B.P.," he said. "Before Prudence."

"Kicks before duty," she said. "A change of color is nice now and then, isn't it?"

He felt uncomfortable. "I didn't look at it that way. Cindy's okay, period."

"Don't be square, Red. We're not kids. Why fake it? You know black and white can be kicky."

"So it seems by the look of this apartment," he said.

"You like it?" asked Rachael. She inhaled slowly through the ivory holder. "Cindy knows her way around. Now I hear that she and Lincoln Beach are getting cozy."

"I don't know about cozy," said Lew. "They've been out together, and I hear she came down once to see him. It's okay with me. They're both tops."

"She's all right," said Rachael, "but he isn't. That Beach is a born trouble-maker."

The remark aroused his old suspicion that it was Rachael who had told one of The Family, probably Felix Booth, of Lew's first meeting with Beach at the Ginger Baby.

"I'll buy him any day over your friends, the Booths. Hulbert, the enforcer. Trouble-making? How about being 'boothed' and carted off to the prison camp at Kpali? Jesus, you can have that guy."

"Most of those stories are just rumors, peddled by people who don't know him," she said. "The Booths are one of the oldest and most sophisticated families in Kalya. The men are gentlemen, especially Hulbert and Felix. Hulbert has been educated in the States and in England too. Why the Peace Corps prefers to spend its spare time with ignorant Molas and Fizis rather than with Family people like the Booths, Downings, Fesses and Vinings is beyond me."

There was a natural hauteur and arrogance about Rachael, Lew felt. With her long ivory holder, clinging white gown and bare shoulders, she seemed less a Lena Horne, whom she resembled, than an authentic member of some proud African aristocracy.

"For my money," said Lew, "most of the The Family are pirates, and some of them, like your pal the colonel, are cruel as hell."

"They represent law and order," said Rachael stiffly. "You

can't govern a lot of shiftless tribes without stern measures now and then."

They argued over The Family and the tribes. For Rachael, The Family represented stability, culture, civilization, and no reasoning of Lew's could sway her.

"You don't get the point, Rachael," he said. "This whole Family government is corrupt from top to bottom. God, even the Mandingo Billies have to pay dash to get peddlers' licenses."

"The Family is no worse than a lot of city bosses back in the States," she flared.

"Yes, it is," retorted Lew. "Here, it's the whole national government."

"There's only one difference," she said. Her voice rose, blotting out the soft piano music on the hi-fi. "Here, Negroes are running the show instead of whites. That's why you get so righteous about it."

"Oh, come off it, Rachael," he said. "The Molas are black too. The Peace Corps isn't helping white people in Zinzin, or anywhere in Kalya. Race doesn't have a damn thing to do with the Zinzin trouble. Ask Archie or Cindy."

"Oh, I know all about Zinzin, no thanks to you." Rachael was angry now. She turned off the record player, lit another cigarette and waved the ivory holder at Lew. "I know all about it, and I thought right from the start that everything could be straightened out, if there was just a little give on both sides. After all, nothing much is involved except one small school. All that was needed was a decent compromise."

"Compromise?" repeated Lew. "What's all this talk of compromise? People have been hinting at it all night. There's no giving in. The school's open and Jim's road is going ahead. The Peace Corps won."

"Oh?" Rachael studied him archly. "Compromise, in case you don't know it, is what reasonable people always arrive at." She paused, inhaled deeply through the holder. "In fact, I got an idea and so I went to the embassy and talked to Bruce Kellogg about it."

"That's against policy," he said. "Kellogg's CIA."

"Oh, he is, is he. Who said so?"

"Everybody," said Lew. "So what's the idea?"

"That happens to be my business, not yours," she said.

The exchanges grew more acrimonious and even less informative, and in a few minutes, Lew rose to leave. Rachael promptly dropped her combative armor. She stood up, unpenned a soft, lazy yawn and stretched with sinuous movements of shoulders and hips.

"You're some character, Red," she said. "With you, a girl's perfectly safe. No passes. No propositions."

"Well . . ." He was at a loss for words.

"Prudence wouldn't like it," she said. "But, of course, what a girl doesn't know can't hurt her, to coin a cliché."

He ignored her smile of invitation. "I've heard stories about a woman," he said, "who flirts with white men and then, when they make a pass, she laughs in their faces."

"You're not talking about someone I know?" There was no animosity in her tone. Instead, she seemed amused.

"I'm talking about compromise," he said, "and those who won't be compromised."

She crossed her arms. "You don't like me, do you, Red?"

"Put it another way, Rachael. I don't understand you."

"Well," she said, "I understand you. And you know something? What I understand about you, I don't like."

And on that unequivocal note, they parted.

16

The moon etched the rolling hills in delicate lights and shadows as Lew drove up the parkland road from Loli. He was late arriving at Forrest Stevenson's trailer home, for his routine chores along the road from Ft. Paul had been augmented by two clerical assignments. He was required to distribute more termination instruction sheets for Group V and to fill out inventory blanks on the kerosene refrigerators. His Peace Corps friends hooted their derision at the inventory. In Kpapata, Katherine and Barbara were so indignant, they threatened to leave the country the day the refrigerators were removed. Bart, of course, accused Lew himself of proposing a ban on the iceless boxes just to make Bart's life miserable. Strangely, once again no rain fell. Along the highway, passing vehicles raised funnels of dust which coated the leaves of the jungle walls.

The frail Mola warrior in loincloth and yachting cap, bow in hand and quiver of arrows on his back, patrolled the Stevenson grounds. Within the house Geronimo barked his distracted alarms, and Forrest Stevenson stepped into the moonlight carrying an unneeded flashlight.

"You're just in time, Red," said Stevenson, "I was about to turn in for the night."

"You were right about the weather," said Lew. "Fifth day without rain."

Stevenson looked up at the sky, arching in starlit splendor, studied the motionless leaves of the dabema, then fingered the air like a man testing the weave of a fabric.

"It may go another week or ten days," he said. "It's the 'little drought' we sometimes get in June. We had one in fifty-seven that lasted three weeks before the big rains came back."

There was a note of fatigue in his voice and his fragile shoulders seemed to sag as he led Lew into the house. The German shepherd rushed Lew's legs, slobbering affectionately over the khaki pants. From the main bedroom, Mrs. Stevenson called a faint "Hello."

"Geronimo woke her up," said Stevenson. He turned on the floor lamp beside the big easy chair, invited Lew to sit, then fetched him a bottle of Heineken beer from the kitchen. Stevenson remained standing, his hands in his trouser pockets. His tanned face, showing the grooves of age beneath the pale, blue eyes, looked weary tonight, Lew thought.

"What's the word in Ft. Paul?" asked Stevenson.

"Not much new," said Lew. He grinned. "The Peace Corps still holds Zinzin with no counterattack in sight."

"Oh?" Stevenson went to a little desk against the wall, found a sheet of paper and handed it to Lew. "I've got bad news for you, Red. This came up late this afternoon by USAID truck."

Lew put down his beer, took the paper and read:

U.S. AID MISSION
FT. PAUL
KALYA

FROM: Mission Director Kalya
TO: District Supervisor Loli

1. Institute property survey and preliminary plans for construction of five USAID elementary schools and one secondary school in Mola territory surrounding Zinzin. Work will start immediately rainy season ends.

General contractor selected is Moses Harter, Zinzin. We are allotting $30,000 per school and $40,000 for the high school. All U.S. materials to be supplied by this office. Remaining materials to be procured locally by Harter.

Your immediate job is to identify sites and begin alteration of basic AID school designs as per requirements of each location.

2. USAID is taking over construction of Zinzin border road, 11.4 miles, begun by Peace Corps with local contributions. Contractor for this job will also be Moses Harter who assures this office he has ample local labor supply. Estimated cost $34,200.

Lee R. Knopf
Director Kalya

The shock for Lew was a physical one. Dazed, he read the directive slowly a second time. Then, as he handed the paper back to Stevenson, he could feel the anger and resentment flooding through him.

"God Almighty," he exclaimed. "That's a one hundred per cent sellout."

Stevenson nodded, and the old, sad look clouded his eyes. He walked to the chaise longue and sank into his wife's favorite nesting place.

"I can't believe it," said Lew.

"I can," said Stevenson. He held out his palms in a gesture of helplessness. "I warned you. . . . Wawa!"

"It's insane," said Lew. He felt betrayed, outwitted. The fact that his foes were anonymous fed his anger. "Genghis Khan the contractor! Jesus, he'll eat half the money."

"Not quite. On the grade schools, he's allowed three thousand dollars legitimate profit per school." Stevenson's words were muffled in weariness. "Then he'll chisel about five thousand dollars each on the specs, maybe ten thousand on the high school."

"And the road!" said Lew. "Over thirty thousand bucks, when Jim was figuring on doing the whole thing for less than three thousand."

"Now Harter gets that much a mile, most of which he can eat." Stevenson paused with a small, bitter smile. "Let's face it, Red. By Kalya standards, these contracts will make Harter a rich man for life."

"Wait'll they hear in Zinzin," said Lew. He winced at the prospect. After the victory party and Lettermore's award to him, Lew had become the symbol of a supposed Peace Corps triumph. Now, in defeat, he would be the scapegoat, taking the brunt of their despair. He felt cornered. The injustice of the contracts enraged him.

"Who the hell could have fallen for a phony deal like that?" he asked. "Who cooked it up? Talk about feeding the mouth that bites you!"

Stevenson rubbed his chin and gazed mistily at the ceiling. He thought for a moment, then said bleakly: "I think it's obvious. They listened to you in Washington, but they weren't impressed. So they gave Milbank the green light to work out what he could with Vining. And, of course, any swap that would benefit Old Number One's pet bastard would be appealing, to say the least."

"I wonder." Lew recalled Rachael Frisson's enigmatic reference to her "idea" and to a talk she had with Bruce Kellogg at the embassy.

"What?"

"I don't know," said Lew. "There was lot of talk about 'compromise' at a party at Rachael Frisson's. Horace Magruder was there, and so were Downing and Hulbert Booth. They all talked like they knew something."

"Well," said Stevenson, "the idea for the exact terms of the deal could have come from any one. Now you know your price for reopening your school in Zinzin—about seventy to eighty thousand dollars in Moses Harter's pockets."

"But Genghis himself said that Jim's work gang would return to work under Jim," protested Lew. He felt an urge to pick at the nauseating compact, hoping that somehow it might crack apart if only they probed it long enough.

"Only for a few days," said Stevenson. "Harter obviously knew the deal was cooking. It would appeal to his peculiar, malicious sense of humor to throw Jim a bone and then grab it back again."

Lew fixed Stevenson with a look of challenge. "What are you going to do about it, Forrest?"

"Me? . . . Why, I'll do what I'm ordered, of course."

"Good God," said Lew heatedly. "You're going to take that lying down? What about the Molas? What about the Peace Corps? For that matter, what about the U.S. taxpayers? They're being taken—but royally."

"They've been had before," said Stevenson. He shrugged in resignation. "It's not my decision. I just work here."

"I don't get you, Forrest," said Lew. He had always deferred to the older man's world-weary attitude, but now he felt an urge to goad. "You know this is a stinking deal. You despise it—and yet you won't do a thing to block it."

"Just what would you suggest?" Stevenson lay back on the lounge, his lids half closed.

"Well, for one thing, Genghis is a lousy contractor. Most of his houses start falling apart in a couple of years. You could at least put up an argument for another builder."

"Lew, Lew," said Stevenson, shaking his head, "this trade has the imprint of Washington on it. The policy boys figure they're playing for big stakes in Africa, and a few thousand dollars vanishing under the table is chicken feed to them. The fact that they don't know how to play the game is immaterial."

"But," insisted Lew, "every time they okay a deal like this, they dig themselves deeper into the sand. Those are practically your own words. I've heard you argue that way a dozen times if I've heard you once."

Stevenson nodded. "I sure have. There are two things wrong with this settlement—or appeasement is more like it—and lining the pockets of a hoodlum is the least of the two. A USAID-built school requires practically no self-help by the Molas. It's just another charity handout which breeds the desire for more. We might as well put them on the dole and be done with it."

"Then, for God's sake," exploded Lew, "why don't you try to bust it up?"

"Idealism is a luxury of the young." Stevenson gestured limply with a blue-veined hand. "And busting is a job for the fit. I spent thirty-five years trying to buck the system out here. Now I'm fifty-eight years old—and, my young warrior, I've had it." Stevenson drew a line at his throat. "Up to here, I've had it."

There was silence, broken only by the thumping of Geronimo's tail. The animal seemed to be applauding his master's sentiments. When Lew started to speak, Stevenson broke in.

"And don't bother to upbraid me for acting in self-interest, either," he said, this time with a flicker of emotion. "I'm not anxious to lose my job. I admit it. If there were a chance of stopping this shabby contract, I might try it. But in this case, no. . . . No more shattered lances for me, Lewis. I've got enough to fill a junk yard."

He sank back into the cushion, thin, delicate, aging, and Lew felt compassion for him. Lew could feel his own anger, simmering in frustration, and he wondered if these combative juices would seep away with the years as Stevenson's had. In Forrest Stevenson was he seeing the Lewis Corleigh of three decades hence? The possibility depressed him.

Stevenson heaved himself off the chaise longue. "Well, that's enough mischief for one day. I'm going to bed. Yours is ready for you, Red. Good night." And he walked off to share the bed of a woman whose malaise with Africa was confined to the continent's physical perils.

Lew sat alone in the big chair for a while, pondering, speculating, worrying, and when he went to bed, he fell asleep with a picture of Cindy Fuller's "small-small" night class in his mind and the hum of the AID-supplied air-conditioner in his ear.

The next day's ride to Zinzin was a joyless one. Heat swathed the abandoned bug-a-bug mounds, dust drifted inside the jeep and the road's potholes jarred Lew's backbone. Caustic Peace Corps comments on the refrigerator inventory along the route put him in a vile mood. Between stops, the new "arrangement" tormented him, and he dwelled cynically on all the men in Washington who had offered sympathy and aid for Zinzin— Shannon, Demarest, Maggiore, Frank Sherrod. Had a single one raised his voice? The nearer Lew drew to Zinzin, the more he dreaded to face the Peace Corps settlement there.

The feeling deepened when, on the outskirts of Zinzin, he met Jim Osterlord turning out of a side road on his motorbike. Jim flashed a smile beneath his crash helmet and waved the jeep to a halt. Osterlord appeared oddly jubilant.

"Hey, Redhead!" he yelled. "Come on up to the house. I've got great news, pal . . . best yet. Come on!"

Osterlord sputtered off, gesturing for the jeep to follow. From time to time, he turned to grin at Lew. When they arrived at Osterlord's house, Jim slid off the cycle and threw his helmet high in the air, catching it with both hands on the fall. He grabbed Lew's suitcase from the rear of the jeep and hustled into the house, tugging at Lew's elbow.

"Hallelujah, man!" Jim cried. "We've got it made . . . but good. Jeez, what a break! Wait'll you hear the news."

"Wait'll you hear mine," said Lew. "I've got news that stinks."

If Osterlord caught Lew's sour retort, he gave no indication of it. Jim tossed the helmet into a corner, lit a native cigar, hooked his thumbs in his armpits and puffed out a strangling cloud of smoke.

"Take a look at your new water boss," he said proudly. "This morning an official of Itambel drove in to see Steve." The ordinarily laconic Osterlord was afire with words. "He's got a beaut of a plan for a Zinzin water system. Now hear this!"

Jim stabbed the air with his cigar. His olive face glowed at the cheeks. "Itambel, under Magruder's orders, is going to take Steve and myself—and the four brightest Molas we can find around here—up to the concession for a three-month training course on how to build a water system. They're going to train us on the layout they built there a couple of years ago, and show us how to construct one like it in Zinzin. Also how to maintain it."

"Where's the dough coming from?" Lew tried to sound only normally curious, but already his mind was forming a triangle of suspicion: Vining to Magruder to Harter. And Rachael perhaps?

"Itambel promises to supply the pumps, steel and pipe for the water tower and the big mains, and even lend us trucks to haul supplies." Jim spoke rapidly, feverishly. His long-cherished dream had become an imminent reality. "All the town has to do is put up enough money to pay for connections, pipes into the huts and fixtures. Steve is sure he can collect the money. Man, what a break. . . . And we never even asked 'em. We never thought of it. They came to us."

Osterlord paced the room. Lew had never seen him so ebullient.

Jim had cast off his taciturnity like a bird sheds the dun feathers of winter for the plumage of spring.

"Listen, Red," he said, "we figure it'll take us two years to build the system. My time's up next summer, but I'm going to ask Williams to let me extend for a year . . . . It will be the first waterworks in Kalya outside Ft. Paul. How about that, baby?"

"What about your road?" asked Lew. The higher Jim's spirits soared, the more depressed Lew felt.

"The rains will still be on during some of our training at Itambel," said Jim. "Afterward, I can finish the road while Steve works on the prelim stuff for the water system. No sweat." Osterlord studied his cigar, his thoughts obviously enmeshed in blueprints of hydraulics and highways.

"You're not going to work on the road at all," said Lew.

"Why not?"

"Because they've decided in Ft. Paul," said Lew, "that the Peace Corps isn't going to finish that road."

Osterlord stopped his pacing. "What are you talking about?"

"Your road," said Lew. He detested this chore. "Listen, Jim, I hate to do this to you, but as I told you, I've got bad news. The road to the border is going to be completed under a USAID contract."

"You've got to be kidding." Osterlord sat down in a wicker chair facing Corleigh. The hair-shearing at the party had been a mistake, Lew decided. Jim's erratically bobbed hair now gave him the ludicrous appearance of a lackey in an old knighthood-era movie.

"I wish I were," said Lew. He summarized the AID memorandum and his discussion with Stevenson.

"Genghis!" said Osterlord. "But they're out of their minds. He'll steal them blind. And not only that, there's no self-help on these AID projects. The Molas won't learn a damn thing about building a school."

"I know," said Lew.

"But nobody clued me in," Jim protested. "When did all this happen?"

"Apparently just yesterday. But, of course, when Genghis called the kids back from bush school, he knew the kind of a deal that was in the works."

"Balls!" said Jim. He pondered a moment, brooding over his cigar. "But at least the Molas will get some new schools. They can sure use them."

"Sure," said Lew, "but look at the swag Genghis hauls down. It's big-time stuff for him, and it's corrupt as hell. In return for reopening the school, Genghis gets school and road contracts worth about seventy-five grand. Ambassador Milbank can call that compromise if he wants to. For my money, it's a sellout."

"Ditto." Jim frowned. "Still, you got to admit there'll be new schools. That's something."

"For how long?" asked Lew. Jim's indignation appeared to have ebbed already, and this irked Lew. "The way Genghis builds, the damn things will crack up in a couple of years."

"Oh, give 'em five," said Jim. He grinned. "But, man, our water system will last a hundred years. And, believe me, it will be an all-Zinzin project. We'll have every guy in town working on it." The gleam of the master builder was in his eye again.

"Jim," said Lew, "you're being bought off. Somebody hooked Itambel into the Zinzin deal by telling them how much you and Steve wanted a water layout. So, while you're up at the concession for three months, Genghis chisels on the school and road specs with nobody around here to check on him. Without Steve looking over his shoulder, Genghis will steal the pants off the USAID people."

"Oh, come on, Lew," said Jim. "That's too devious a plot. The water system hasn't anything to do with the schools."

"You think not? So why was Magruder giving me a lot of vague 'compromise' talk the other night in Ft. Paul? Compromise is for reasonable men, he says. . . . Listen, you know how close Itambel is to Old Number One. Vining can double their taxes any year he wants to. So what's maybe fifty grand in pipes and pumps against millions in taxes?"

Osterlord shook his head, blinking in the cloud of cigar smoke. "I don't believe it," he said. "Your imagination is working overtime."

"You mean you don't want to believe it," said Lew. He was losing patience with his friend. "Why don't you face it, Jim? You're nuts for building—anything—and everybody knows it.

Also, you're like that with Steve Muo." He held up crossed fingers. "So, they get you both out of town. It's simple."

Jim bridled. "Even if it's true, which I don't believe, look at all the improvements—schools, a road, the water system."

"You've got a construction complex, pal," said Lew. "Water on the brain is more like it. I never thought I'd hear you making apologies for Moses Harter."

"I'm not," insisted Osterlord. "I'm just saying that if there is a deal, better they build something than eat the money."

"What Genghis will swallow in the next year, he can live on for the rest of his life. . . . But you don't see that. You're the one who accused me of not seeing what went on around me in Kalya. Now who's the guy with the blindfold?" The taunt came out on impulse. Osterlord's posture of superiority on Mola lore and politics had long chafed Lew. "Well, I've got to go over to Alice and Dotty's and break the news."

"They'll love you for it," said Jim. He bit his lip. "I suppose I'd better let Steve know."

"Yes, I suppose you'd better." Lew walked to the door. Fuming now, he turned back to Osterlord. "By the way, Jim, whatever happened to The Forge?" Then he slammed the screen door behind him.

The weekly arrival of the Peace Corps jeep in Zinzin was an event as newsworthy as the docking of the mail boat at a jungle river outpost. Word always spread swiftly through Zinzin, and any deviation in Lew's accustomed rounds provoked perturbed speculation among the Peace Corps teachers. In case of doubt, they usually converged on the Franklin-Wyzansky abode, clearinghouse for all Peace Corps information. This evening Arlene Offenbach met Lew at the door.

"Why no shower?" she asked. "I had the towel and soap laid out for you."

"I ran into Jim," he said, "and we went to his place."

Everyone, even Joe-Joe, was present. The houseboy stood in the kitchen doorway, in drooping shorts and Sweet Briar sweatshirt, the toes of one paddlelike bare foot scratching at the other shin. Joe-Joe's return from bush school appeared to have had a salutary effect on the house, for the big living room still seemed reasonably tidy following the frenzied cleaning for last week's celebration.

"Did Jim tell you about Itambel?" asked Alice.

Lew nodded. He could sense the tingle of high spirits in the room, and it made him feel even more disheartened over the news he bore.

"Jim's going ga-ga," said Alice. "If Old Number One made him Zinzin water commissioner for life tonight, he'd take it."

"Cripes," said Dotty. "I mean you'd think he'd found a way to irrigate the Sahara."

"Man," said Arch, "you started it all, Redhead. Ever since you went to Washington, we've had nothing but good breaks. Even the rain stopped."

Ted, no longer swathed in his blanket, held up two fingers in a "V" sign, then Cindy said: "Don't stop now, Red. What else you keepin' for us?"

Lew felt a small, dead weight in his stomach. Telling Jim had been one thing, but now facing six people, he felt like an executioner. He walked to the torn sofa and sat down heavily between Dotty and Ted.

"Everything's changed," he said. "I guess I should turn in Arch's award. I . . . well . . . it isn't worth a damn now."

Cindy's hand went to her throat. "You mean . . . not the school again?"

"No, no," said Lew. "The school's all right. In fact, that's just the trouble. You're going to have six new ones between here and Loli."

"So, that's bad?" asked Alice.

Then Lew told them, as briefly as he could, adding his own surmises and those of Forrest Stevenson. He found it difficult to look about him, and when he finished the only sound in the room was a faint, muffled rustling in the back wall.

"Rats!" said Alice hollowly. "Archie, you promised you'd get rid of them for us."

"I'll come over tomorrow with the traps," said Arch. He said it as if he expected his efforts would be futile.

There was a long silence, then Dotty said: "I've got to say it. . . . I mean Wawa!"

"Double whammy Wawa," said Lettermore. "Imagine! Ol' Genghis comes out smellin' like a rose. . . . Seventy-five grand!"

Ted groaned. "And Dotty and I promised to stay on the wagon for two weeks."

"You'd better!" flashed Cindy. "We've got school to teach. Remember?" She crossed the room and kneaded Lew's shoulder gently with her fingers. "Don't take it so hard, Red. It's not your fault."

But Lew sensed there was more irritation than sympathy for him in the room. Even among people who should know better, the courier of bad tidings was to some extent blamed for the event. But further, Lew felt guilty. He had failed in Washington and he had no excuse. Somehow, if he had just made a more eloquent plea, it might have turned out differently. He had failed the Molas. Worse, he had let his own outfit down. He became aware of the cloying heat in the room. God, didn't this country ever cool off?

"Well," he said, "I've got the termination skeds for the Group Fivers." He went to the jeep, returned with a manila envelope. He handed sheets of paper to Alice, Dotty and Cindy.

"Williams," he said, "lists some of the things here that you'll be asked in the final interview."

Dotty rattled her paper in a palpable attempt to turn their minds from Genghis Khan and his sudden riches. "Oh, this is really something," she cried. She broke into sharp, cynical laughter.

"Listen to this," she said, "and I quote: 'PCV Dorothea Wyzansky. Termination interview, 10 A.M., July 23, Peace Corps office, Ft. Paul. Dear Dorothea, Perhaps you would be good enough to give some thought to the general subject matter that will be covered in your interview. As you know, the questioning is not designed to evaluate you individually, but to help the Peace Corps plan for the future,' etcetera, etcetera, blah, blah. Now, Number One: 'With reference to your experience, do you think the primary beneficiary of your service has been (a) Kalya, (b) certain Kalya individuals, (c) the United States, (d) international understanding in general, (e) the Peace Corps, (f) yourself.'"

"Answer," yelled Alice. "Answer."

"Okay," said Dotty. "The real beneficiary of Miss Wyzansky's two years in Zinzin will be whatever lucky doctor takes care of her when she gets home. I mean, think of the contribution to medical knowledge. I've had diarrhea, dysentery, driver ant bites, toe fungus, three colds, fever from unknown causes . . . what else, Alice?"

"Leg sores," said Alice promptly, "and acute isolationism."

"What's that?" asked Ted.

"Just a minute." Alice went to the book locker and rummaged among some pamphlets on the bottom shelf. She returned with a mimeographed sheaf.

" 'Medical guide for Peace Corps volunteers in Kalya,' " she read. "I quote verbatim. Subhead Number Two: 'Isolation. It is normal for everybody to have times of depression relative to their usual mean. These depressions may be increased by isolation, culture shock and the frustrations of working and living in a foreign country. Don't throw in the towel right away. Try and keep busy. Retain your sense of humor' . . . That's underlined . . . 'If the trouble persists, talk it over with your housemate if you feel like it or contact the PC physician.' "

"Did Zerwick write that?" asked Lew.

"No, that Doc what's-is before him," said Alice.

"Talk it over with your physician," scoffed Dotty. "I mean take the money bus, twenty-eight bucks round-trip, and if you survive as far as Ft. Paul, you'll feel so good, you won't need a doctor."

"Also, Dotty," said Arch, "you've had inflammatory, erotic allergy, but bad." When Dotty looked blank, Arch ogled her. "Running for your life and virtue from Hulbert Booth and his pal Tommy."

"Oh yes, those two." She wrinkled her nose, then picked up the paper again. "That brings us to another matter I'm supposed to ponder. Quote. 'With reference to Peace Corps Goals Two and Three, they are defined as follows in the Peace Corps basic act: To help promote a better understanding of the American people on the part of the peoples served and a better understanding of other peoples on the part of the American people. Do you think your own experience has furthered either of these goals?' "

Dotty paused and seemed to be thinking seriously for a moment.

"Yes, I do," she continued. "I mean, now a lot of Kalyans know enough about Americans to want to steer clear of them, and vice versa."

"Oh, Dotty," said Arlene, "please don't be so flip. I think I'll remember Oon Gilli and his wife all my life, and I know they'll think of me often. Isn't that worth something? You always sound so cynical."

"Honey," said Alice, "wait until you've been here two years. Then you can talk."

"Arlene's right," said Cindy. "We've all made good friends in this town, maybe not as many as we should have. But . . . oh, I don't know. . . . I think it's good."

"A hell of a lot better than bombing people in Vietnam," said Ted sourly.

Round and round went the argument, more strident than usual, Lew thought, to take their minds off the news from USAID. When talk flagged, Dotty touched it off again by reading another proposed question at her final interview. What recommendation would she make for improvement of training of future Kalya groups? Learn how to drink the Kalya beer without choking, said Ted. Practice teaching to a blank wall, offered Alice. Arlene agreed with the absent Osterlord's pet theory: an intensive course in the Mola language. Cindy thought classroom specialists should consider new methods to combat the traditional rote learning of West Africa. Lew listened in detachment. He had heard the same endless debates for months. This one raged for several hours, through the pre-dinner drinks and then through the meal, jointly prepared by Alice, Arlene and Joe-Joe. They ate Zinzin fare tonight, country chop and couscous with hot pepper sauce.

Out of deference to Lew, they intentionally avoided the topic of Moses Harter and his contracts. But after dinner Ted Kramer revived it.

"You suppose one of those new schools will be a replacement for ours?" he asked. "I hope so. The thing's about to collapse."

"I'm not sure," said Lew. "The memo to Forrest didn't indicate."

"If so, I'm glad I'll be gone," said Cindy. "I couldn't bear to teach in a building Genghis made a fortune off of—even if it did have desks and screens."

"You wouldn't have to bear it long," said Alice. "Genghis believes in building for today. The hell with tomorrow."

"Kalya's champion of the economic theory of rapid obsolescence," said Ted.

"Seventy-five grand!" intoned Arch. "Man, we're in the wrong racket."

Lew left for Ft. Paul early the next morning after Jim Osterlord handed him a letter from Steve Muo for delivery to Lincoln Beach.

"Forge business," said Jim laconically. "The Forge isn't dead. It's just getting started."

But the statement seemed less realistic than hopeful, and Lew drove toward Loli and Ft. Paul more dispirited than he had ever been in Kalya. Once a money bus cut sharply in front of him, almost scraping his fender, and he cursed the driver. Red dust swirled on the laterite road, and above the high bush, hooded vultures, with their obscene purple necks, circled on motionless wings. For the first time in weeks, Lew counted his remaining days: forty-eight.

17

He first saw it when he was about ten miles north of Ft. Paul. The jeep rounded a masked curve on a slight rise and, when Lew righted the wheel on the slope's straightaway, he noticed far ahead a glow on the horizon. The time was almost midnight, and the glow had the appearance of a pink derby absurdly tucked into the fold of the night.

Lew thought at first that a festival of some sort was in progress at the capital, perhaps a forerunner of the annual Founders Day celebration a few days hence. He rubbed his eyes. He was tired. He had been delayed time and again along the road from Loli by niggling complaints. Then at Kpapata, Katherine and Barbara enlisted his aid while they dressed the wound of a Fizi boy who had slashed his ankle with a cutlass. Lew held the boy as they cleansed and bound the ugly gash, then he drove the boy to his hut in a small clearing deep in the bush. The side road was an incredible jumble of rocks, sinkholes and ruts over which the jeep lurched like a drunk. The round trip to the jungle enclave took three hours although the village probably was no more than four miles from Kpapata.

Day drained into dusk while Lew was still far from Ft. Paul. The eerie dry spell, strangely troubling to men and animals in a land accustomed to the cadence of the summer rains, had stretched to its eighth day. The road became a chain of dust clouds stirred by passing vehicles. The rains seemed a distant memory, and the earth baked without a trace of moisture. Leaves drooped, their thin veins etched with dust at the jungle's fringe. Lew kept his canteen of boiled, filtered water on the seat beside him, and drank from it even after the sun had set and the moonless night brought some relief from the smothering heat.

Now, as he sped along the macadam section of the road toward the outskirts of Ft. Paul, the pink derby expanded into a large orb from which streaks shot upward like illuminated javelins thrown into the night sky. The bowl of light had a jagged, mobile beauty, but then, as the jeep drew nearer, Lew saw that the bowl was in reality a large fire. With a start he realized that the core of the city must be burning.

When he drew abreast of the Peace Corps hostel, Lew could see a single light flickering at a window from a kerosene lamp, and he sensed that the place was deserted. His friends must have gone to the fire. Lew pressed down on the accelerator. The city's center lay about three miles ahead.

Then, about a mile from the blaze, he could see the flames and feel the heat. There was a strange, steady roar compounded of a score of lesser noises. As his ears became attuned, he could pick out separate sounds in the immense symphony of the fire—a woman's shriek, a timber falling, an explosion, the crackling of wood and the frenzied barking of a dog. When Lew turned off the highway into a street leading toward a shower of light, he found the street impassable. People, cars, bicycles, carts, dogs, chickens and goats thronged toward the blaze like a rabble army. On a hunch, Lew backed up, regained the highway and parked the jeep a block away. Then he ran at a trot toward the fire.

Lights were out on the downtown streets. A power connection must have been destroyed. But the burning center illumined the city in weird formations like those seen inside a grotto. The people became a dense, churning mass in the streets, and Lew had to fight his way forward. Children raced about his legs. Tribal women gabbled in a score of tongues. Mandingos, wrapped in tight swirls of blue, green or orange cloth, strode along like moving candy sticks, their heads bobbing above the throng.

The blaze, Lew saw, was ravaging the same tribal section of

the city where he had delivered Steve Muo one morning at the dilapidated boardinghouse. It was an area of shanties, refuse dumps, lean-to shacks, small stores and ancient wooden houses which served as tribal "hotels." The frame houses, many with Victorian gables and sagging front porches, had once been the residences of The Family. Then came the era of the concrete mixer, and The Family had moved to cement-block homes and apartments on the other side of Founders House, the monument of demarcation between the poverty and the affluence of Ft. Paul. Now the fire was sweeping through the combustible frame houses like a torch through piles of dry leaves. Lew looked at his wrist watch. It was 12:32.

The night breeze was blowing to the west and so was the fire. Lew found himself to the east, about three blocks from the perimeter of the blaze which vaulted into the sky in great lances and sheets of flame. Even at this distance, the heat could be felt on the skin, and the dark faces about Lew shone like reflectors. Some people in the swarm obviously had escaped from the burned area, for arms and legs were smudged and there was an odor of singed clothing. Lew realized that he was in the block where the Ginger Baby bar stood between the barber shop-jewelry store and the photo shop. In hopes he might see a familiar Peace Corps face, he elbowed his way to the door of the Ginger Baby. Although the power was off, the narrow night club was lighted by several kerosene lamps.

Just as Lew reached the door, he was shouldered roughly aside by a man carrying a boy in his arms. Lew caught a glimpse of the man's tapered beard and he recognized Roger, the lord of the lepers, from Dnoga. Roger's bony body was stripped to the waist and his country-cloth shirt was bound about the chest of the boy whose face was twisted in fright.

"Out of the way, Red," ordered Roger. "The kid's been hurt pretty bad."

Lew followed Roger into the building. It was choked with people. Along the mahogany bar and on the tables lay Africans, some of them naked and many of them moaning. Lew saw about a dozen Peace Corps workers, most of them women. Peace Corps teachers bustled about the room with trays which held bottles, salves and bandages. Others were bent over the victims. One teacher stood near the wall, tearing a bed sheet into strips. The air held an acrid smell of smoke and burned flesh. The Ginger Baby had been turned into a Peace Corps field hospital.

Lew saw Sam Zerwick standing at the bar. Behind him stretched rows of liquor bottles and the mirror with its painting of the Eurasian beauty domiciled in a leopard skin. Zerwick's heavy face was knotted in concentration and, through the horn-rimmed spectacles, he peered at the raw arm of a woman who was lying on the bar. He probed at the arm with forceps, apparently extracting debris. A Peace Corps girl held the woman.

"Damn it, Betty," barked Zerwick, "keep her still."

There was a confusion of babbling, shouts and grunts of pain in the room, but Zerwick's voice rose above it. Without looking up from his work, he called out: "Remember, no bandages except on hands and feet. Let's let air get to these body burns. . . . And keep forcing fluid into these people. Somebody better locate some more boiled water." Then to the African woman on the bar in a lower voice: "Easy, Pussycat. You'll make it. Don't worry. I'm almost through."

Then Lew saw Prudence. She came striding from a back booth in her purposeful manner. She was carrying a basin of water and several towels. The sleeves of her blouse were rolled to the elbow, her hair was disheveled and she wore her most intent look. Lew caught her shoulders and kissed her before she was aware of his presence, and water slopped to the floor from the basin.

"Lew!" she exclaimed. She held the basin in front of her and smiled at him, cocking her head. "Oh, I'm so glad you got here." She leaned across the basin and kissed him again on the lips.

"What happened?" he asked. "How did it start?"

"Not sure," she said. "Heard it was a stove fire in a Fizi hotel." Her smile dimmed into a frown. "I'd like you to stay here, Lew, but I guess you ought to get up to the fire. They need help more than we do. . . . The fire keeps getting worse. Can't understand it."

"On my way," he said.

The people in the street milled frantically, chattering without purpose. There was a feeling of incipient hysteria, and occasionally a woman screamed. Lew shoved forward. The crowd thinned as he neared the thundering blaze and the heat intensified with each step. In the last block, he saw a charred dog on the sidewalk, the legs still twitching. On the slanting roof of a wobbly house, two men stood precariously and shouted news of the fiery progress to people gathered below.

The fire itself appeared to cover an area of about four city blocks, starting with a row of blackened, smoking skeletons of what had been houses and sweeping to the west in a bank of flame. Just as Lew reached the burning border, flames at the other end touched a barnlike warehouse. It ignited in a single, almost instantaneous burst and, with a stuttering roar, it hurled geysers of new flame into the sky. The noise from the burning tribal quarters was deafening. Houses collapsed in pyrotechnic showers, power poles toppled and metal roofs popped with the sound of tin cans shot aloft by firecrackers. The street bordering the east side of the ravished area was bright as noonday.

Ft. Paul's three new pump trucks, as shiny red as Christmas ornaments, stood on the street. The trucks were Prime Minister Vining's pride, purchased that spring from a West German firm for $100,000 and dedicated for duty at a ceremony which bloomed with oratory. Canvas hoses from the trucks were attached to fire hydrants, and other lines, flat and inert, crisscrossed the street like tapes on a windowpane being readied for a hurricane. Not a drop of water issued from the big metal nozzles. Several Kalyans, dressed in the yellow and red uniforms of the fire department, leaned against the trucks and used their helmets to shield their faces from the heat. There was no evidence of fire-fighting.

A crowd near one of the trucks circled a man who was shouting and waving his arms. Lew pushed in among the people. Tribal men and women, their faces lighted as brightly as those of actors on a movie set, cursed, grumbled and shoved. Lew felt the blast of heat on one side of his face. The crowd was as volatile as the fire.

Then Lew saw that the man at the hub was Lincoln Beach. Fury distorted his handsome, brown face, his white, short-sleeved shirt was dirty and torn, and blood oozed from a cut on a forearm. He was flinging his arms about wildly and exhorting his audience in a chaotic melange of Mola phrases and truncated English. The orderly, disciplined man with the Ivy League manners was transformed into an impassioned haranguer. Lew caught only a few expressions in the cascade of words.

"God-damn Fam'ly. . . . No wat' fo' fi-ah. . . ."

Then a burst of Mola invective. The crowd clamored its approval.

"Dey keep wat' fo' Found' House an' palace! . . . Tribe hut all burn down. Ever't'ing chac-la. . . . God-damn Fam'ly!"

A defiant, threatening roar rose from the hundreds of people pressed about Beach. He spit out a string of Mola words and the swelling mob screamed again.

The smoking, gutted remains of a house across the street collapsed with a booming crash. An explosion of sparks arched like an umbrella, and suddenly the hair of a young girl ignited in a pyramid of flames. She ran crazed down the street, trailed by a wail of terror. A huge, bare-breasted woman caught the girl in her arms and smothered the flame against her belly. Then she too shrieked with pain. Lights and shadows danced clumsily between the pump trucks, and the mob's shouting became a chant of anguish.

"No wat' one time dis night," yelled Beach.

"Da right. Da fo' troof," came a shouted response.

"Ol' Numb' One, he vex me cruel, man," cried Beach.

This time there was no anwering roar, only a growling rumble. Few men in Kalya had ever heard such public abuse of their leader, and Lew could see by the faces around him that the people were frightened by Beach's outburst.

Beach glanced quickly about him, caught the mood, and switched back to a more generalized culprit. "Fam'ly steal wat-ah," he cried. He cursed in English, Mola and, for good measure, Fizi.

This evoked a storm of agreement. Such unpersonalized opprobrium provoked no fear. Men egged Beach on with cries of "Eh, man."

Someone pushed Lew. He fell against the bare shoulder of a man in ragged shorts. The shover was a man in gold-rimmed goggles, white crash helmet and the uniform of the security police. It was Colonel Hulbert Booth, shoulder holster slung over his white shirt. He elbowed his way rudely through the crowd, grabbed Beach's shirt in two great handfuls and rammed him against the side of a pump truck. The people fell back, permitting Lew to edge forward.

"That's enough, man!" said Booth. He thrust his face within inches of Beach's and glared at him.

"Take your dirty hands off me," said Beach. The assault seemed to have restored his Americanized English.

Booth merely tightened his grip on Beach's torn shirt. His muscles tensed and he appeared ready to thump Beach's head against the truck. Lew moved quickly to the side of the two men.

"Knock it off, Colonel," said Lew. "You hurt him, and you're liable to have a riot on your hands here."

That seemed improbable. The crowd had fallen further back, and the people were watching in amazement. Booth released Beach, shredding the shirt, and swung around to tower over Corleigh.

"You again!" Booth was raging and his thin mustache seemed to quiver. "Always around the trouble-makers, eh?"

"No, I'm trying to stop trouble."

"Peace Corps!" Booth spit the words out.

Beach muttered something, then ripped off the remainder of his shirt and threw it at Booth's feet. He grasped Lew's arm and pulled him away from the truck, then shoved slowly through the milling clusters of people until they reached the sidewalk. They stood before the open front of a tribal vendor's lean-to shanty. Beach was trembling.

"That son-of-a-bitch, Booth," he said. "Some day . . ."

"Cool it, Link," said Lew.

"That stinkin' Family." He was out of breath and he gasped out the words.

"What's the pitch?" asked Lew. "Where's the water? I know they always turn it off at ten, but . . . tonight? Why hasn't it been turned back on?"

"You ask!" He glared at the fire truck where Booth still stood. Beach's chest heaved as he tried to regain his breath. "I had to go to Kolamon," he said after a moment. "I just got back a half hour ago. It seems . . . Oh, Jesus, what idiots! The dumb, thieving, lousy idiots. . . ."

"Link!" Lew barked it as a command. Beach's eyes darted erratically and he stood rigid, his fists clenched at his sides. "Make sense, man," said Lew.

Beach breathed heavily, making a studied effort to control himself. Then he said: "Joe and Henry, the Fess twins, have charge of the water works. They take turns every night. . . . But tonight nobody could find either one. Maybe they're off drunk somewhere. Who knows? But they've got the keys. The place is locked up tight."

"If we could break in," asked Lew, "do you know which valve controls the city mains?"

"Yeah. At least I think so."

"Come on, then. Let's get the hell over to the pump station."

Beach shot a grateful look at Lew, then stood a moment biting his lip as he thought. "Okay," he said. "I'll tell the fire-truck men, so they'll be ready."

Beach threaded back through the crowd to one of the pump trucks. Lew saw him talking to a spare man in yellow and red shorts who wore a fire helmet tilted rakishly on his head. Other firemen gathered and the bony one apparently gave some instructions. Beach returned at a jog. Behind him the firelight circled half the sky like a sun bursting into dawn across a prairie. The noise was sullen, steady, intense, punctuated suddenly by rattling explosions, perhaps a stand of oil drums. Lew could feel his cheeks flush with the heat.

"Okay," said Beach. "They're going to take the pumps around to the side where the fire's running, so there will be some chance of checking it."

"My jeep's up on the highway," said Lew. "Let's go."

They ran three blocks up the street, past the Ginger Baby bar, then another block down the main road to the car. Lew started the motor and headed toward the water control station which was located about two miles away, past the swamp, on the airport road. They were both panting.

"I goofed," said Beach after a few moments. "I should have thought of doing this right away. But I got so mad, I started popping off to the crowd."

"Action before lip," said Lew.

"You're telling me."

"How come only the Fess twins have keys to the place?" asked Lew. "How about your German boss? Or you? You guys run the Utility Authority."

Beach shook his head. "Old Number One insisted. He gave the

waterworks jobs to the Fess twins—strictly patronage. I guess he wanted to make sure nobody would divert his precious water to the rest of the city. Maybe somebody at the Palace or in the embassies might miss a bath some night." He paused, then added bitterly: "It's the system, always the god-damned system. The Fess boys took a hydraulic engineering course in the States. Actually they're not bad engineers, but since they know nobody can fire them, they just play at the job. God knows where they are to-night."

The pump station, a square, concrete, fortresslike structure, stood in a scraggly field of palmetto not far off the main airport road. Lew drove the jeep up a gravel access road and parked near the main door. The building was dark. They jumped out, Lew with a flashlight grabbed from the glove compartment. There were two doors of heavy timber with a padlocked iron bar across the middle.

Beach cursed. "It's criminal to leave this place untended," he said. "Anything could go wrong. They ought to put those twins in jail for a couple of months."

He examined the padlock, pushed a shoulder against the un-yielding doors. Then he took Lew's flashlight and began walking the area between the station and a nearby shed. He found a two-by-four and rammed it against the doors. The board cracked, and a splinter pierced Beach's thumb.

"Wait," said Lew. "Let's use the winch."

They unrolled the cable from the drum on the jeep's front end, fixed the iron hook to the bar at the building's doors. Lew worked the winch lever inside the jeep. The cable tightened, the padlock snapped and the bar flew out of its sockets.

Beach shouldered through the doors and began throwing the flashlight's beam over an assortment of dials, housings and valves. Lew rewound the cable on the drum while Beach searched for the valve which would release the water into the mains of downtown Ft. Paul.

"Got it!" Beach yelled.

Lew heard a comforting, gurgling surge as water flowed into the city main. For the first time in years after 10 P.M., another open line had been added to the single one which served the small, elite area embracing the Executive Palace, Founders House and embassy row.

"That only builds to sixty pounds pressure," said Beach as he got back into the jeep. "What we need to douse this fire is a real high-pressure emergency system. Still, it's a hell of a lot better than nothing."

They drove back at top speed, the orange halo in the sky growing larger, brighter and whiter as they approached. Lew parked again on the highway and they ran toward the city's burning center. People shuffled aimlessly over the streets, sidewalks and yards, clamoring in a dozen tongues. Once Lew stumbled over a prostrate figure. Some people, exhausted, had simply stretched out in the street and gone to sleep.

When they reached the border of the fire, Beach pulled up short and loosed another string of curses. Men from the three bright red pump trucks were standing along the curb, directing nine streams of water at inky, hissing stumps of buildings. The wind was still blowing from the east, and thus the fire-fighters were merely watering a burned-out section while, several blocks away, the fire fled to the west with the roar of a hundred trains.

Beach ran to the scrawny man who headed the fire brigade and began pleading with him. The man shook his head dubiously, obviously perplexed and reluctant to move his trucks. As he watched, Lew thought he understood. The Ft. Paul fire department was making a brave show of putting out the fire. The fact that its efforts were worthless in this sector—now only a rubbled wake— made no difference. The pumps were throwing water, weren't they? Lew could see Beach arguing with the chief. At last, the thin fireman gave in. He loped about, unleashing a stream of orders. The hydrants were turned off, the hoses thrown back on the trucks in a bewildering tangle that snarled men and valves. Beach motioned Lew to his side.

"See if you can round up some Peace Corps fellows to help," he said. "Bring them to the other side. We'll take the trucks around."

Beach swung up on a truck beside the chief, and the three vehicles moved off. Boys, men and fire-fighters swarmed like ants over the trucks. Lew pushed through the densely packed street, searching for Peace Corps faces. He located a dozen men within a few minutes, most of them teachers in Ft. Paul schools or assistants in government agencies. Several, like Roger, were in town on leave from their outcountry posts.

The fire's advancing front, four blocks away, bore little resemblance to the smoking, stuttering and expiring husk on which the fire-fighters had been lavishing water. With the wind at its back, bending flames like high surf, the van of the fire raged forward, savage and bellowing. Just as the Peace Corps brigade turned the corner on the hot side, flames attacked a two-story concrete structure set amidst the raffish sprawl of shanties and frame houses. A decorative band of wood circled the cement building. A looping arm of flame fingered the band of wood, then ran swiftly around the building like a fuse. Returning to its starting point, the fiery ribbon leaped out, groped avariciously at an adjacent shack. The shanty had walls of dried thatched palm and, although the flame did not seem to touch it, the hut suddenly ignited. At once it became a squat torch and within seconds, one end of the tin roof collapsed and the whole sheet of metal sank to the ground.

The Ft. Paul firemen scuttled about in a frenzy of bodies. Small boys helped lug the heavy hoses. The chief shouted conflicting orders, which subordinates either ignored or promptly countermanded. One hose was affixed to a hydrant, then as quickly abandoned under the fierce heat. Bare-chested men in shorts spilled over the street, yelling advice and generally impeding the laying of the lines. When one hose filled with water, it sprang from the pavement like a writhing serpent and knocked two men sprawling. The tormented chief dashed about feverishly, waving his thin, wrinkled arms and bawling instructions in a high, hoarse voice.

Lincoln Beach gradually assumed strategic command of the operation. His shirtless torso glistened like icing on a cake. He took over direction of first one hose and then another. The fire-fighters sought to retreat beyond the rim of heat, but Beach bullied and cajoled to keep them at their stations. If a Kalyan backed up too far, Beach supplanted him with a Peace Corpsman and soon the Peace Corps manned five of the nine nozzles. The others, working under Corleigh, organized a bucket brigade at a sluggish creek some three hundred yards beyond the perimeter of flame. Soon a hundred African men and women joined the Peace Corps at the buckets. The snaking line passed water hand-to-hand to slosh over parchmentlike shanties which stood in the path of the flames. It was a small effort—like trying to fill a tub with squirts of a medicine dropper—but Beach insisted that any dampness on the houses and huts was better than none at all.

The pump trucks worked admirably, stepping up the pressure from the city water mains, and nine bristling streams played on the advancing conflagration. That was the trouble. The blaze continued to advance, inexorably, like a relentless, fiery monster intent on consuming the whole city before it was surfeited. It licked forward on a front about two blocks wide. Flaming runners, like scouts of a surging army, probed for the driest wood, the flimsiest wall. After several hours of suffocating work, while throats became parched and every face and hand felt the threat of scorching, Beach could only boast that the forward prongs of the fire had been contested over every foot of ground. This slowed the fire somewhat, but failed to halt its steady, remorseless, crackling progress.

Lew's work was hampered by the residents of the shanties in the path of the marching blaze. Many of them refused to leave their sagging hovels until the last minute. Men working the buckets at the operating end frequently poured as much water over people as they did over walls and roofs. Tribal children insisted on straying too near the flames, and a number of them were burned and had to be carried around the flank of the blaze to the Ginger Baby bar. Peace Corpsmen who made the trek to the Ginger Baby reported back that the place was crammed with casualties, almost as many suffering from broken and fractured bones as from burns.

The wind was not high, perhaps only four or five knots in force, but it blew without interruption, fanning the fiery ribbons ever to the west. Near the creek, the men worked in semi-darkness. Elsewhere the illumination was brilliant, the unshadowed glare of a stadium under arc lights. The human scene was chaotic. People ran, circled and shouted, stumbled over the hoses and filled the air with tribal imprecations.

Colonel Booth appeared on the sidewalk. He was ringed by a half dozen security policemen, in white shirts, black pants and black leather puttees. Booth stood with folded arms, surveying the scramble of fire-fighters and their frantic advisers. Beach noticed the colonel, but ignored him. Once Booth took a few steps forward, toward the fire line, then seemed to think better of it. He retreated, stood silently for a few minutes, then walked away, followed by his men.

Beach, making what had now become his command rounds, came to the frame house where Lew was passing up buckets to a Kalyan on the porch roof. Beach's face was strained and his shoulders slumped with weariness.

"It's after four," he said. "We've been at it here almost three hours. We'll never stop it. Nine hoses aren't enough. For this one, we need fifty—and a hell of a lot more pressure."

"Rain?" asked Lew.

They both looked at the sky. Earlier, gaps in the rolling smoke revealed clusters of stars, but for more than an hour a black overcast had curtained the sky. Whether it held rain for Ft. Paul, neither man knew.

"Maybe," said Beach. "It's our only hope. Otherwise this baby will burn clear through to Founders House."

At that instant a tiny streak flashed in the dark belly of the sky and from afar, there was a single, muffled growl of thunder. The men in the bucket line stopped as if on cue and looked above them. A Kalya woman, carrying her baby strapped to her back, kneeled in the street and folded her hands in prayer. A muttering ran through the crowd. At the hoses, all the fire-fighters looked up.

But no rain fell. The dogged, blistering work went on. The flames advanced, a trifle slower, but with majestic, scornful arrogance. They pressed forward in a wall which flashed spectacular changes of color with each new vanquished structure. The breeze blew smoke ahead of the blaze and it curled into noses and mouths. Men doubled up in coughing fits.

The hose line retreated. One pump truck became inactive, for no hydrant could be found to attach it to. The bucket line shriveled, being forced back on the creek. The flames appeared to work methodically. First they would lick at the shingled roof of a house, spread over the crest like a burning sea, then plunge downward to consume the walls. If a tin-roofed shanty stood in the path, the process was reversed. The fire ate the mud-stick or palm-thatched walls in one fiery swallow, then sprang ahead while the roof slid drunkenly to the earth.

Lew felt himself near exhaustion, as much from heat as from exertion, and he could see the same symptoms in other people. The fire had its own rhythm of destruction which produced a hypnotic effect on the workers. Once Lew found himself hoping for nightfall, when the day's heat would moderate, then realized that it was the dawn and the sun he was about to confront.

He was raising a bucket over his head when he felt a drop of water on his forearm. He thought it had spilled from the pail, but then another drop touched his forehead and another his shoulder where the shirt was ripped. Then came an unmistakable patter on a porch roof. The tempo increased swiftly, in the manner of tropical rains, and suddenly it was cascading down from the east, slanting with the breeze. Every man stopped work in his tracks and cheered. The bucket brigade fell apart. Several men threw their pails in the air.

Beach raced through the rain—it was a merciful downpour now —to the battlefront of the hose lines. He ran from nozzle to nozzle and shouted to the men on the pump trucks.

"Keep it going! Keep it going!" he shouted. "Don't stop. The rain may quit in a minute."

But it did not. Water poured from the black sky in a full-throated thunderstorm. Lightning rifled the overcast. Thunder rolled, beating from the distance like a rockslide in a canyon. At first the rain seemed to have little effect on the fire. The probing fingers of flame grew slimmer and a great hissing, like steam escaping from a vent, arose along the forward edge of fire. But within a few minutes, the crest of flame lost its upward thrust. Gradually, minute by minute, the fire pressed closer to the ground as though someone were smothering it with an immense tarpaulin. Crackling gave way to sputtering. Lew saw one bright tongue reach for a shack, then stop abruptly in mid-air like an arm chopped off at the elbow. It withdrew and died. Across the street, another flame dissolved. Everyone watched, transfixed, while water streamed unnoticed off weary backs, soaked pants and shorts and trickled into shoes. In the block where they stood, the fire stopped its march, sullenly with hisses of protest, while the smoke billowed alone to the west in black coils.

Ten minutes later Beach ordered the pump trucks to cease. Nature had brought Ft. Paul's fire under control and, almost certainly, would soon extinguish it. Hose connectors were unscrewed from the hydrants. Winches rolled the canvas hoses back to the trucks. Small boys clambered over the sides, ready for the triumphal ride back to the firehouse through the driving rain. In the east a gray line appeared, precursor to dawn, but the rain continued to pelt down with a fury that intoxicated everyone in the street: Molas, Fizis, Peace Corps volunteers, Mandingos and—Lew realized with heartened surprise—even some young members of The Family. They too had been manning the buckets and the hoses.

A young man with an owlish look, misted glasses and a pencil stuck behind his ear approached Lew. He was Oliver Downing, a member of The Family and a reporter for the *Daily Voice*. Downing, educated in England, always spoke solicitously, clucking gravely over the woes of the hapless citizens he encountered on his beat of crime and disaster. Lew had met him several times, once at the city hospital, and he found Downing's personality as pleasant and earnest as his newspaper syntax tended to be erratic.

"You have good story on the fire?" asked Downing.

"Nope, Ollie," said Lew. "Everybody did a good job, the firemen, the tribesmen and The Family. And don't forget to give Lincoln Beach and the Peace Corps a plug. . . . Well, we were all lucky it rained."

Downing nodded. "The tears of God. He weeps for all of us." He fingered the pencil at his ear. "I won't forget the Peace Corps. You were the best—most specially those at the Ginger Baby."

Lew made his way to the fire trucks. The gutters already ran deep, carrying off charred fragments, shreds of garments and other debris from the gutted tribal section. All flames were dead now. The humble residential area where the fire had stormed was now a funereal ruin, inky skeletons of buildings and blackened, branchless tree trunks. Lincoln Beach, boarding a pump truck, pulled Lew up beside him. They sat on a tangle of hose against the big-bellied tank.

They rode without speaking, their shoulders hunched in fatigue, as the trucks circled the razed section. Eight entire city blocks had been destroyed, and the wreckage simmered and stewed in the downpour which had now reached torrential proportions. When they drew opposite the Ginger Baby, Lew motioned to Beach. They both jumped off and ran for shelter in the night club.

The place was still jammed, and it reeked of medicines, smoke and human beings. Every table held a prostrate figure. Four or five people lay on the long mahogany bar. The Peace Corps teachers had been joined by several Kalya nurses from the city hospital, and two African doctors now assisted Sam Zerwick. Lew saw Prudence binding a splint on a boy's leg. The lad grinned cheerfully, but Prudence looked as spent as Lew felt. Her face was colorless, and spots of blood flecked her blouse.

Zerwick hammered the heel of his hand on the bar. "I want all you Peace Corps girls to clear out now and get some sleep," he called. "We've got a fresh crew coming in from some of the out-country towns, and we're rousing out some more hospital nurses. Now git! All of you." He peered about the room and chanced to spot Lew. He nodded curtly, then called to Prudence: "That means you too, Prudence Stauffer. I don't need any Peace Corps casualties here. . . . Red, take her home, and don't let her come back."

Prudence went without protest. She took Lew's hand, smiled wanly at Beach and left the building with them. The rain drenched her to the skin before she had walked a few steps. They bent their heads to the downpour and plodded to the jeep. All three crammed into the front seat. Water drained off their clothes to form puddles on the floor board.

Beach began to shiver. Prudence automatically reached into the glove compartment, found a rag and began rubbing his bare back with it. Beach smiled his thanks at her.

"God," he said softly after a time, "it makes me ashamed deep down. First, that insolent ten o'clock rule robs us of water. Then the Fess boys get lost with the keys. And when we finally get water, those poor dumb bastards in the fire department turn the hoses on the wrong side." He laughed bitterly. "If it weren't so lethal, it would be pure comic opera . . . and in my country."

Prudence continued to massage his back. Lew started the motor. The dawn covered Ft. Paul now, a gray sieve through which the rain poured down and hammered at the car's roof.

"Nothing we can do about it now, Link," said Lew. "I'll take you home."

They drove to Beach's apartment house, a three-story stucco, not far from the Utility Authority. Beach groped reflexively for the door handle, then turned to them. His eyes were bloodshot, he smelled of smoke and the usual smile lines about his mouth were drawn tight.

"I've had enough," he said. "It's time to act. . . . It's time. God, but it's time."

He lurched out and slammed the door behind him. They saw him walk slowly, barebacked in the rain, and disappear into the building.

At Prudence's house, they each took a hot shower and crawled into bed.

"Do you realize," she said, "that if it hadn't been for the fire, and you and Link turning on the city water, we wouldn't have had any water here for showers?"

He nodded, kissed her once, and they both fell into a numbing sleep. On the chair where he had thrown them, Lew's shirt and trousers dripped quietly for hours.

18

The stack of copies of the *Daily Voice* melted away as soon as it was placed on the lobby desk in Peace Corps headquarters. Volunteers and staff members, eager to read the story of the fire, snatched at the newspapers. They had been waiting anxiously for several hours and they had swapped graphic fragments from the long, hot night, seeking to weave a tapestry of fact from the skeins of rumor. If they could but estimate the magnitude of destruction, they felt certain of one thing—the Peace Corps had risen to its finest hour in Kalya.

Some were merely frayed. Others, their faces puffy from lack of sleep, were still exhausted. But all were buoyed by pride, and now they raced through the tabloid's account of the fire to see how the government's semi-official organ rated the Peace Corps performance. They read silently at first like scholars in some hushed library. The story occupied the entire front page and most of the interior columns.

The account was headed, "COL. BOOTH HERO OF FT. PAUL'S WORST FIRE," and it began:

By Oliver Downing, A.B., M.A.

Ft. Paul's most vicious fire in thoughts of oldest residents today claimed maybe 100 victims, the which 25 are dead and the rest feel badly of burning and lacerated bones of the body.

Col. Hulbert Booth, chief of the Prime Minister's elite security corps, bravely spurned all threats to his own person and directed successful watering of the holocaust by the city's magnificent pump trucks and fire department.

Many were saying, in the tragic light of dawn, that Col. Booth deserves the nation's most highest award, the Vining Medal of Honor first class, for his heroic efforts which vanquished the fire.

Col. Booth himself, with modesty, said: "The rain made heroes of us all."

The fire did have two victors above it: Col Booth and the rain. The affable, lion-hearted colonel kept the blaze under control and then the rain, truly the tears of God, began falling at 4:30 A.M. and at last distinguished the catastrophic blazes.

Yet, notwithstanding, the toll was fearsome. Eight blocks of Ft. Paul are burned to the soil. Twenty-five people perished and many of the smaller casualties were horrible to contemplate. Had not Prime Minister Alexander Vining purchased at great cost the new pump trucks, the whole city was fallen in flames. Thus Kalya gives tribute to his generous foresight. . . .

Lew Corleigh and Prudence Stauffer sat at her desk reading the story. Around the office they could hear protesting murmurs, a few indignant exclamations and curses. The article ran for several thousand words, even displacing the editorial page and the letters to the editor which customarily rhapsodized over lustrous deeds of the Vining administration. Downing's account included his own vivid observations, tributes to a dozen Kalyans, chiefly members of The Family, and a box score of other Ft. Paul fires since 1900. The article concluded with a list of victims, compiled with a thoroughness which indicated Downing's ability to amass vital statistics under pressure of a deadline.

Prudence put down the paper with a look of bewilderment. "It's incredible," she said.

"Not a single damn word about the Peace Corps," said Lew.

"Or about Link Beach or Sam Zerwick or the nursing at the Ginger Baby," added Prudence.

Lew turned back to page one. "And I thought Ollie Downing was a pretty decent guy," he said, staring at the lead of the story. "I can't believe it. Ollie told me himself that the Peace Corps did a great job. Especially at the Ginger Baby, he said."

"Ollie's okay," said Prudence. "Wonder if . . ."

"You wonder what?"

Prudence did not answer. She shook her head, a puzzled look on her face as she studied the newspaper.

There was little wonderment elsewhere in the office. The first scattered protests became a medley of angry shouts and profanity. Roger, normally unruffled by any incident that boded no ill for his lepers, stalked about the lobby waving a copy of the Voice and damning the writer and publisher. The women who taught in Ft. Paul schools, last night's nurses, were shrilly indignant. Outcountry Peace Corpsmen from nearby villages milled about, arguing heatedly over the identity of the person responsible for the newspaper's distorted version.

Sam Zerwick was a mountain of wrath. He had come directly to the office from treating the scorched bodies at the Ginger Baby. His face was unshaven and he held his copy of the newspaper in a trembling hand. He glared red-eyed about the lobby from behind his heavy, horn-rimmed glasses.

"That ties it!" he said to nobody in particular. "We work halfway around the clock—and who gets the credit lines? Hulbert Booth. Ladies and gentlemen, you can take this whole stinking country and stuff it. I wouldn't waste my energy."

"Amen, Sam," said one volunteer.

They gathered about the physician in mutinous mood. Carter Williams elbowed his way to Zerwick's side. His plump face was flushed and his usual fretful anxiety had given way to anger. Lew realized that not once before in the two years he had known Williams had he seen the Peace Corps chief openly belligerent.

"This one they won't get away with," said Williams. "Booth was a complete zero at that fire. It was a Peace Corps job from start to finish."

"And Lincoln Beach," said Prudence. "He got the water turned on, Carter, and he ran the fire department."

Williams nodded assent. "And Beach too. . . . I'm going to call

Ambassador Milbank." He flourished the newspaper. "This kind of reporting is an outrage."

Williams apparently sensed that this time, unless he became the funnel for Peace Corps protest, his influence with both staff and volunteer would crumble.

"So what are you going to say?" asked Zerwick. Clearly the physician's confidence in Williams' maiden role as an activist was less than total.

"I want Milbank to deliver a full, written account of the Peace Corps performance to the Voice," said Williams, "and request that it be printed in tomorrow's edition. And that story ought to name names, starting with Dr. Samuel Zerwick. If it weren't for you, Sam, they might have had one hundred dead."

"The hell with me," said Zerwick, scowling. He swept his arm about the room. "It was a Peace Corps job."

"You leave that to me," said Williams, his voice for once charged with authority.

"Did you see this?" asked Roger. He showed Williams an item tucked into a column at the bottom of the last page of the Voice.

Williams read the article aloud. Headed "Give for Freedom," it was an account of all Kalya government employees contributing a month's salary to help finance the Founders Day celebration. This mammoth festival, to be held two days hence on Sunday, annually commemorated the birth of Kalya as an independent republic.

"Voluntary!" scoffed Zerwick. "Anybody who doesn't contribute loses his government job."

"That includes teachers too," said one woman. "And the Kalya girls teaching at our school only make about forty dollars a month."

"Thirty-eight to be exact," prompted Prudence.

"Nobody contributes," said Roger. "They just get docked their pay."

The item provoked more vehement speculation about the Voice's fire story. Some felt Colonel Booth had been lionized intentionally to fan public interest in the Founders Day celebration. Some contended the two articles had no connection. This afternoon no one had any but vigorous opinions, most of them voiced with passion. The customary demarcation line between staff and volunteers fell away.

The only person who did not take part in the strident exchange was Rachael Frisson. She stood quietly with folded arms beside Lew Corleigh. Like the others, she had fatigue pouches under her eyes, for she too had worked throughout the night at the improvised Ginger Baby first-aid station.

Lew could not resist the temptation to goad her. Their hostile parting the night of her dinner party still rankled.

"I suppose you think your friend Hulbert Booth really rates all that glory crud in the Voice," he said.

"No, Red, I don't," she said. Whether it was weariness or a change of heart, Lew didn't know, but she evidenced no antagonism.

"The Peace Corps got a raw deal," she said. She smiled. "I ought to know. I was up all night too."

"So how do you figure it?" asked Lew.

"The Family's afraid," she said. "I know them and I understand. They're afraid if the Peace Corps gets too much credit for things, it might help loosen The Family's hold on the tribes. It's pretty simple, really."

"And you approve?"

Rachael patted at her luxuriant hairdo, miraculously in place despite her long hours at the Ginger Baby. "I don't approve and I don't disapprove," she said. "I understand . . . which, as I recall, is more than you'd say about me the other night."

Lew passed up the opportunity to renew the personality critique. "I think I understand what motivates The Family too," he said, "but that doesn't mean I have to like it."

She hunched a shoulder. "They've got a country to run. They do it the best way they know how. I guess the whites who run the States think they're doing their best too."

"You're sure tolerant today, Rachael," said Lew. He paused. In this pliant mood, she might be willing to talk about Zinzin. "Say, you remember you told me you had an idea and went to Bruce Kellogg with it?"

She nodded. "I don't forget a thing like that."

"Did it, by any chance," he probed, "involve a school and road contract to Moses Harter?"

"Maybe," she said. Her smile had veiled pride beneath it. "And maybe not. How many ways are there to skin a cat?"

"More than one, they say."

"And I told you I believed in compromise," she said, enjoying the fencing. "The school's reopened, isn't it? So Moses Harter makes a little money. Everybody's happy."

"Not everybody," said Lew. He paused again. "And that bright idea of building a water system for Zinzin. Who thought that one up?"

"I think Horace Magruder is a very intelligent, receptive man," she said. "He's the kind you can talk to."

"The great Frisson compromise," said Lew.

"No credits, please." She beamed at him. "Unlike the Peace Corps, I'm not insecure. I don't need applause. . . . And Red, I lied to you the other night. I not only understand you, but I like you."

She walked away toward her office, and Lew wondered whether his dislike for her cynical conception was as strong as his admiration for her ingenuity. Rachael, he mused again, was a complicated one.

The afternoon wore away amid sputtering castigations of the Vining regime. Ft. Paul schools were closed in the wake of the fire, and the volunteers had little but their own frustration to occupy their thoughts. Williams left for his conference with Ambassador Milbank. In late afternoon Roger tried to organize a platoon of Peace Corpsmen to assist the Kalya government in the monumental task of clearing away the rubble strewn over eight city blocks. The proposal drew derisive retorts. The men said that if Colonel Booth had quenched the blaze in solitary grandeur, he could clean up the debris by himself too. In the end, Roger enlisted but two people for his cleanup squad.

Lew went home early to the hostel. He felt drained, and he planned to go to bed as soon as he finished his soup and a sandwich of canned sardines. He was watching Arthur stack the still greasy dishes in the drying rack—and wondering why the houseboy's antipathy for household aids included the unopened box of detergent—when he heard a call of "bock-bock" at the back door.

A small barefoot boy with leg sores beneath his torn khaki

shorts handed Lew an envelope and promptly ran off like a frightened rabbit. The envelope bore Lew's name and the typewritten sheet inside read:

"It's time. Pick me up at the Ginger Baby tonight at 8. Urgent. L.B."

And so, thought Lew, no sleep tonight for a long time yet.

The Ginger Baby was back in business as an emporium of liquor, music and random romance when Lew parked the jeep in front at eight o'clock. The jukebox blared rock-and-roll music and a group of white-shirted Kalyans lounged by the doorway. Beach was standing at the curb. He got in beside Lew without bothering to say hello.

"Drive out the Kolamon Road," he said. "I'll tell you where to turn off."

Beach wore a business suit and tie, rather formal garb for the humid Ft. Paul night which threatened to dissolve into more rain at any moment. He put a slender dispatch case on the floor board, glanced at his watch and then sat tensely like a businessman late for an important appointment.

"What's up?" asked Lew.

"The Forge," said Beach. "We're meeting. You'll see. . . . Take a right on Banks Boulevard."

Lew remembered the letter from Muo which the feverish hours of fire-fighting had blotted from his mind. He pulled to the curb, found the letter in his wallet and handed it to Beach.

Beach read it by the light of a street lamp, then put it in his dispatch case. "Zinzin troubles," he said. "They'll have to wait now. First things first."

Banks Boulevard was a residential area of modest, cement-block homes inhabited chiefly by minor employees of the embassies and foreign commercial firms.

"Okay," directed Beach. "Now your next left."

The unlighted street had a crumbling coat of tar over the gravel roadbed. Lew knew the street well. Prudence lived at the end of the second block.

"Park here," said Beach. "We'll walk the rest of the way."

Lew pulled off the road into a vacant lot of banana trees and scrub palms. They walked rapidly down the road which was flanked by one-story concrete houses, all with rogue bars at the windows. The yards contained flowering shrubs and a few scrawny trees, but no lawns. Stone walkways led to front doors through puddles, mud and mounds of goat-nibbled range grass. Beach turned into the last walkway in the second block. The house was dark.

"Hey," said Red. "This is Prudence's place."

Beach did not reply. He led Lew around the house to the back door and rapped lightly on it three times.

Lew was somewhat prepared by now. Still, it was a shock to see Prudence Stauffer open the door. He and Beach walked into the unlighted house. For some reason, Lew felt a whisper would be more appropriate than a normal tone of voice.

"You too?" he asked Prudence. "You could have told me."

"Keep my promises if I give my word," she replied, taking his arm. "Just like you, no?"

At once several nagging questions shaped their own answers . . . Jim Osterlord and Prudence talking in code over the Peace Corps short-wave radio . . . Jim saying laconically one morning that he knew more about Prudence than Lew realized.

"You knew all the time I was helping?" asked Lew.

Prudence tightened her fingers affectionately on his arm. "Sure. I hated not telling you, but Link insisted. He didn't want you brought all the way in until he was one hundred per cent certain of you, he said."

"Oh." His surprise already had faded. Somehow it seemed thoroughly in character for Prudence with her intense commitments. "Got to be involved," she had said once. Still, he felt nettled over his own lack of perception. Why hadn't he guessed?

"I was always sure of you, Lew," she whispered. She kissed his ear, a fleeting brush, and he realized again how warm and comfortable he felt when she was near. He felt pride in her too. The stubborn little missionary turned conspirator. . . . Well, he had his own secret too: his decision to marry her.

Prudence led them into the main room, which had one goose-necked desk lamp angled down to throw a small circle of light on a center table. The venetian blinds were lowered and drawn and, as an added precaution, a bed sheet had been tacked over the blinds. A group of men, only faintly distinguishable, sat on chairs in a ring about the table. Lew counted eight of them. With

Beach, himself and Prudence, they numbered eleven persons. The room was clammy and almost unbearably hot, for Prudence spurned the window air-conditioners which Peace Corps staff members were permitted to requisition. She carries the hair-shirt idea too far, thought Lew. For himself, he always believed in snagging whatever creature comforts were available.

"This is Lew Corleigh of the Peace Corps," said Beach. "He's helping us too. Steve Muo and Jim Osterlord up in Zinzin both vouch for him. So does Miss Stauffer."

Beach translated his English into Mola. Then another man made a second translation. Lew recognized the liquid singsong of the Fizi tongue. Beach introduced each of the eight Kalyans to Lew. Five were Mola and Fizi tribal leaders. Two were government employees who spoke English; like Beach, they were men of tribal roots who had been schooled abroad on scholarships. The identity of the eighth person in the dim circle gave Lew a start. The man was a member of The Family, Oliver Downing, the *Daily Voice* reporter.

"I'm as surprised as you are," said Downing. "I had no idea you were helping us."

"But that story today?" Lew was baffled. "I don't get it."

"They made me do it," said Downing. "Link wants me to tell about it after the meeting starts."

"We'll wait a few minutes for Billy Number 15," said Beach. The sentence was repeated in Mola and Fizi.

The wait was a brief one. Billy Number 15, the most influential of Ft. Paul's colony of Mandingo traders and peddlers, glided in as silently as a dark ghost and immediately seemed to dominate the room. He was a man of impressive height, perhaps six feet five or six, and he wore a togalike sheath of purple cloth gathered tightly about his gaunt body. His feet were shod in thong sandals. Billy Number 15's skin was coal black but his somber countenance had a vaguely Arabic cast. With his narrow nose, thin lips and proud bearing, he could have been a Moslem prophet come to spread the teachings of the Koran.

The Forge, Lew realized, tapped the four elements of latent power in Kalya: the Molas, the Fizis, the Mandingos and the new, foreign-educated generation of The Family. The Molas and Fizis were by far the largest of the welter of Kalya tribes. The

Mandingos lived in a world apart, considering themselves Mandingos first, Moslems second, traders third and Kalyans a poor fourth. They had none of the apathy and slovenliness of the run of Kalya tribes, for they were the historic entrepreneurs of Africa, thrifty, industrious and as unflagging as the sales drummers who beat their way across nineteenth century America. The Mandingos' Moslem self-discipline and abstemious habits set them apart from other tribal Kalyans whose basic animistic religion under a veneer of Christianity gave them full latitude to enjoy the few worldly pleasures available in their bareboned battle for survival.

Lew noted something else about the group. Except for Billy Number 15, a man of indeterminate years, no one in the room appeared to be more than thirty years old. Kalya's secret opposition to Old Number One rested in the hands of youth.

Beach took charge of the meeting. He leaned forward, his elbows on his knees, and began to speak in a chopped English which Billy Number 15 could understand. He kept his voice low and there was a strained, urgent quality about it. When he finished a few sentences, the remarks were translated into Mola and then Fizi. The men sat silently and for the most part self-consciously in the fringe of light from the desk lamp. Chairs were unfamiliar objects to most of them, for tribal palavers were conducted by men who sat on the bare earth of palaver huts or squatted on their haunches.

This turned out to be the first meeting in a month, and Beach described the defeat of the Peace Corps and Forge member Steve Muo in Zinzin. Lew noted that in the lengthy explanation, Beach never mentioned the devil's dance which so frightened the town, and Lew surmised the omission was intentional. Tribesmen, no matter how opposed to The Family, would have difficulty believing that the town devil could be used as a tool for personal ventures. The devil's role as a transcendent supplicant of the jungle spirits stemmed from the lore of centuries and no amount of school-bred logic could persuade the average bush man that the dancer in the grotesque straw costume was not supernaturally inspired. Instead Beach bore down heavily on the potential enrichment of Moses Harter as another example of Family greed.

But Zinzin quickly gave way to the Ft. Paul fire in importance. Beach declared that the lack of city water after 10 P.M. was a symbol of everything evil in The Family's rule of Kalya. The Executive Palace, the embassies and the luxurious Founders House, primarily a showcase for the use of wealthy foreigners, had water all night, he said, while the tribal area was denied the water that might have put out the blaze in its initial stages. One of the dead was the most admired Mola in Kalya, a selfless, white-haired woman who headed the Ft. Paul orphanage where several Forge members had spent their boyhood. Beach bitterly described seeing her framed by flames at a third-story window of the rickety asylum. She had re-entered the burning building to make sure all the children had escaped, then had become trapped on the top floor. Her dress was ablaze when she finally leaped to her death on the sidewalk below. Ft. Paul's fire department had no rescue equipment.

When Beach finished speaking, Oliver Downing took over. His voice had the same hushed urgency and he squinted owlishly through his glasses.

"My article in today's *Voice* was a fabrication of immense magnitude," he said. Oliver had the same gift for richly upholstered speech as his uncle, J. Richardson Downing, the education commissioner. And strangely, when talking, Oliver managed to handle his syntax with fewer vagaries than when he confronted a typewriter as a newspaperman.

"I had been writing," he said, "a truthful recital of great exactitude for more than two hours when Colonel Booth came into the city room and demanded with the editor to witness my presentation. He saw the rightfully singing praises of the Peace Corps and of Lincoln Beach, our leader, and also the many paragraphs in which I most earnestly related the absence of water to dampen the holocaust. The colonel deplored loudly my article and ordered that it must be written over again to preserve, he said, the truth and eliminate falsehoods. I protested, but the editor said my errors were clearly obvious.

"Whereupon Hulbert Booth dictated to the editor the many points of fact he said the article must contain. Booth left in much insolence, saying he was amazed to see a Downing being deluded by the 'known revolutionary Marxist, Lincoln Beach.'

The editor then wrote over again my whole article against my most sincere wishes. He left my name on the article, stating that I was the expert on Ft. Paul calamities and the readers deserved to see my thoughts. It is a hated humiliation to see my name on lies in a journal which states that it is the daily voice of truth, justice and liberty."

Young Downing concluded with an oratorical swell in the manner of a man delivering a formal address. Several tribesmen looked blankly baffled, and Beach swiftly repeated the story in truncated English. The usual Mola and Fizi translations followed. The little Forge had as many language tribulations as the United Nations.

Each man in the circle spoke in turn. The soft cadence of the two tribal tongues had a lulling quality and, in the stifling heat of the room, Lew found himself fighting off sleep. The speeches, all delivered without interruption in the tradition of the palaver hut, consisted for the most part of a catalog of personal and tribal grievances against The Family. One man said the Kalya health department contended it had no more yellow fever vaccine, yet he saw the inoculations being given to Family children. Another deplored the recent rise of money bus fares within Ft. Paul from three cents to five cents as a harsh and unnecessary burden on tribespeople unable to afford the taxis and private vehicles used by The Family. The head of the franchised money bus fleet, he said, was growing rich and was dividing his inordinate profits with the Commissioner of Motor Vehicles. Billy Number 15, speaking with sober mien and great dignity, stated that when he sought to renew his peddler's license last week for the required two years, the Commissioner of Weights, Measures and Commercial Licenses demanded a personal payment of three hundred dollars above the legal ten-dollar fee. The commissioner, of the Booth branch of The Family, finally settled for a dash of one hundred twenty-five dollars, but renewed the license for one year only.

These Kalya censures of The Family all had a familiar, universal ring, the outcry of the citizenry against corruption in the seats of authority. With the change of a name or a title, the incidents might have taken place in Boston, Cairo, Hong Kong or Teheran. Yet Lew sensed unusual tension, an electric quality, charging the already heated room. These men were challenging the ruling power in a country where the will for such assertion, let alone the means to curb injustice, had been unknown for centuries. They were struggling to articulate smoldering desires for freedom and they did not know the lexicon of liberty. The wish was a fierce one, but the tools were rudimentary. Lew felt somewhat like a man witnessing a woman's labor pains beside a bed where no doctor or midwife was in attendance. He felt a nameless exultation. The birth of an idea had all the elemental fascination of physical delivery.

The feeling deepened when Beach swung the palaver from cause to cure. Beach himself had a wild urge for action, yet he knew The Forge was but a small and frail band to contest the deep-rooted power of The Family. His chief recommendation had the weakness of all long-range plans, a sense of remoteness. Beach urged that The Forge should launch a nation-wide effort to build a real opposition party in the parliamentary elections two years hence. As a starter, he counseled that they should attempt to recruit heavily for The Forge from some two hundred graduates who would be returning next month from universities in the United States and Europe.

He did have one specific idea for immediate action: The Forge should print two leaflets to be distributed clandestinely throughout Ft. Paul. One would brand the 10 P.M. water rule a matter of criminal negligence which cost the lives of twenty-five Kalyans. This handbill, he argued, should demand that Prime Minister Vining provide water for everybody in all city mains at all hours. Such conservation measures as were necessary should apply equally to rich and poor alike.

The other printed broadside would condemn the "voluntary" contribution of a month's salary by government employees, ostensibly to finance Founders Day festivities. Actually, said Beach, this was "squeeze" money which placed an intolerable burden on underpaid teachers and government clerks. The funds really flowed through channels of Old Number One's Democratic Justice party and wound up in the pockets of The Family and a few favored tribal chieftains.

Beach said the leaflets should be posted all over the city

in the pre-dawn hours of Sunday just before the start of Founders Day games and ceremonies.

Palaver followed in the hallowed tradition. Each man spoke gravely and lengthily with no interruption save for translation. The musical cadence of the tonal speech again had a soporific effect on Lew, but when he listened carefully to the translations, he realized that nobody was really saying anything. They were lauding Kalya and one another, condemning The Family, beseeching relief. As for practical suggestions, they were shackled by the old Kalya bond which imprisoned so many minds—a delight with form and an impatience with substance. Although Lincoln Beach listened with seemingly imperturbable courtesy, Lew could see that he was growing restive.

Only two men addressed themselves directly to Beach's proposals or any others. One clerk in the Foreign Ministry suggested that he be the one assigned to scatter the flyers along Embassy Row under the cover of night. Oliver Downing volunteered to print the throwaways on an old hand press located in the basement of the Department of Agriculture building. There were no type cases but he remembered some boxes of jumbled hand type stored with the press. The typesetting would take time and be rudimentary at best, but Downing was sure he could get it done late Saturday night.

When each had had his say, they sat mute for several minutes. Then Beach arose and announced that he would summarize the consensus of the meeting. For the future, he said, they would cautiously enlist returning students into The Forge. For the present, they would print and distribute the leaflets which he would write.

"When would it be safe for you to start working, Ollie?" he asked.

"Any time after midnight," said Downing. "The building has only one watchman. He can be taken easily from behind. He is an old man. One cloth to gag him and another to cover his eyes."

"Da build' good idea," said Billy Number 15. "No Forge man work dere."

"You're right, Billy," said Beach. "Booth will immediately think some Agriculture employee printed the handbills. That's good for our side."

Beach laid down a time schedule. He would deliver copy for the leaflets to Downing tomorrow afternoon. Then at midnight, Beach and Billy Number 15 would seize, gag and blindfold the old watchman. Downing would arrive at 12:10 A.M. to start the setting. Other Forge members would come to the back alley of the building at ten-minute intervals after the press run started and pick up leaflets. Each man was given a section of Ft. Paul in which to distribute his package of handbills. And, said Beach, everyone should circulate in the tribal areas, interpreting and stirring talk about the broadsides, fanning resentment and inciting fellow tribesmen to protest.

"I want this whole damn city riled up against The Family," said Beach. "Do anything you can to keep the pressure on. Just make sure you don't get caught by one of Booth's goons."

He said he was sorry there was no prudent way to put flyers in the Kalya National, Ft. Paul's only movie theater. There, at nine o'clock Sunday night, Prime Minister Vining would climax Founders Day festivities with his annual hour-long oration on the state of the republic. Beach said he would like to put a handbill on each of the theater's one thousand seats but the Kalya National would be guarded by security police throughout the day. Still, the leaflets fanning over the city should cause consternation in The Family. Beach said that he, for one, intended to be present for Old Number One's address Sunday night to see how Vining would handle this first open opposition to his twenty-two years of "benevolent" rule.

"Any questions?" asked Beach.

There were none. Beach's leadership was accepted as tacitly and as completely as though he were a monarch invested with the divine right of kings. They were so accustomed to follow without questioning—town chiefs, clan chiefs, paramount chiefs, national prime ministers—that even in revolt now there was no dissent. They had exchanged one form of one-man rule for another and they did it passively, with equanimity. The Forge, Lew realized, needed a hundred Beaches if it was to succeed. He felt discouraged and he became aware that the room had become brutally hot. Prudence caught his eye and shook her head sadly. At least there was some comfort in knowing that she shared his dismay.

In the silence, there was a faint rustle at the window and Lew saw the corner of the sheet move. There was a noise at the window bars.

"Rogue!" shouted Beach. They heard a thud on the ground outside.

Beach ran from the room to the back door. Lew ran after him, followed by Downing. Lew left by the front door, hoping that he and Beach might trap the snooper between them. But on the front porch Lew saw that he was too late. A man in dark trousers and dark shirt was running swiftly down the walkway. Beach came running around the corner of the house, but by the time he reached the road in front, the man had cut through the opposite yard and disappeared behind an unlighted house. Beach pulled up at the road, then shook his head and walked slowly back to the porch of Prudence's house.

"Let's have a look at that window," he said.

The three men went to the side of the house. From the outside, there was only a thin line of light around the borders of the sheeted venetian blinds. A prowler might have guessed that the light was filtering through from another inner room. The window stood about five feet above the ground and a box had been placed against the house. Beach examined the rogue bars, found no evidence of tampering at the juncture where the iron bars were imbedded in the concrete wall. He reached through the bars and felt along the bottom of the screen.

"He cut a hole in it," he said. Beach put his hand through the hole, lifted the lower slats of the blind and the sheet behind and peered into the room.

"He could see people all right," said Beach, "but the way that desk lamp was slanted down, he couldn't identify any faces. No way of telling who we were."

"But he could hear," said Downing.

"That's what bugs me," said Beach.

When they returned to the meeting room, Beach explained what they had found. "I think it was just an ordinary rogue," he said casually. "If the room had been empty, he'd have gone ahead and tried to pry off the bars. The voices made him curious."

"Maybe," said Downing. He fingered his glasses with the air of a professor weighing a problem in logic. "But what he hears, he can tell." The others in the room mirrored Oliver Downing's look of concern.

"This is no time to let it humbug us," said Beach sternly. "Let's break this thing up. We've got a lot of work to do tomorrow night."

He gave final instructions for the handbill operation, declared that neither Lew nor Prudence should take part in the distribution. The color of their skins, he said with a wry smile, hardly blended with that of the night. However, he wanted Prudence to inform Jim Osterlord of the plan in code over the short-wave radio tomorrow morning.

Then Beach ordered members to leave Prudence's house at three-minute intervals by the back door. One by one they glided away into the moonless, overcast night. Beach remained until the last.

"They didn't produce many ideas for you tonight," said Lew. "Is it that way at every meeting?"

Beach nodded. "That's the worst result of Old Number One's system. Nobody thinks. They leave it all to big daddy." He gestured with his hands. "Well, we'll get some ideas when the new batch of students comes home."

"We'd better go," said Lew. "Come on, I'll ride you home."

"No," said Beach. "You stay with Prudence. I'll make my own way. Besides, after that rogue, I'd just as soon not be seen riding around with you in a Peace Corps jeep at midnight."

"You think he was a spy, don't you?" asked Prudence.

"Could be," said Beach. "I don't see how they could have found out about us, but you know Booth's reputation—the man with the thousand eyes. . . . Well, nothing to be done about it now. I'm going home to bed. I'm beat."

When they closed and bolted the door after Beach, Prudence sank limply against Lew's chest.

"Beat myself," she said. "Three hours' sleep isn't enough."

"I'm proud of you, Prude," said Lew. "I hear you were great last night at the Ginger Baby."

"Had to be done," she said. "It wasn't so rough. We just did what Sam told us. He's a sweetheart, that man."

They sat on the sofa and soon her head was nestled against

his shoulder. Lew felt a hunger for her and he kissed her lips, a long kiss. She responded tenderly.

"Want you so," she said, "but I think I'm too tired tonight to make love. Do you mind, Lew?"

"Of course," he said. "I want you every night."

"You do?" Her look was one of frank surprise. "Won't you wear out?"

"Not until I'm eighty-three. I'm guaranteed, like a tire, for thirty thousand miles." His finger traced the ridge of her nose. "And, you see, a woman needs that because her desire grows and grows, year after year, or so Kinsey tells me."

"Sounds great," she said. "But does that go for women who use up their energy in revolutions too?"

"Not unless they give with some explanations," he said. He pushed himself upright on the sofa. "How long have you been working with The Forge? And why didn't you tell me? Some broad. Playing games with the guy she claims she loves."

Prudence looked suddenly serious. "I wanted to tell you right away," she said, "as soon as you agreed to carry messages to Zinzin, but Link said no. He said you still had doubts, and so he wasn't sure of you."

"You take me to your bed, but you keep secrets from me," he said.

"Two different things." She smiled and nuzzled his neck.

"And I thought you were the soul of honesty," he said, "the outspoken, artless missionary. But underneath, you're really a plotting conspirator. So when did you dive into this double life?"

Prudence seemed to sense that behind his gibing, Lew was irked. She looked contrite, and she spoke a trifle faster.

"It was about six months ago when that teacher in Gbinga refused to promise to contribute a month's salary for Founders Day," she said. "You remember?"

Lew did. The young Kalya girl had startled everyone with her refusal. A few days later she was convicted of a robbery charge and sent away to Kpali prison camp.

"She never stole anything," said Prudence. "I felt terrible about it because I'd gotten to know her. She was a spunky, dignified—and honest—girl. Anyway, I was at dinner one night and Lincoln Beach was there. I told him frankly I thought the way they treated that girl was abominable. I guess the more we talked, the more he began to trust me. Finally, he made some comments of his own that showed how he felt about Old Number One. A couple of days later he called on me at the office and we talked some more. One thing led to another and, pretty soon, I began helping The Forge."

She paused, pursing her lips, looking to him for approval. "I'm not sure I did right, Lew. But I just couldn't sit by and watch the way the tribal people were being treated without doing something. Maybe we shouldn't become involved in Kalya politics, but I did. It's done and that's that."

"Ditto," said Lew. "Except that after my trip to Washington, I'm convinced we should take a stand. This isn't just a Little League game over here. It's important. I just don't think the U.S. can play ball with those who exploit the people and get away with it much longer. We'll wind up being hated all over the world."

"I know," she said. "In some places, we already are."

"Senator Demarest—he's quite a guy—said something that impressed me. He said he wanted the world, when it considered America, to think of the Statue of Liberty again—and not the CIA."

Prudence smiled at him. "I'm glad we think so much alike," she said. Then the familiar, sober look took over. "And that settlement in Zinzin was nauseating, wasn't it? It made me want to throw up. . . . Just flood the place with money. The almighty dollar can fix anything, they think. Well, they're wrong. . . . For one thing, it's terrible for volunteer morale all over Kalya. Reports of the deal, or the fix, or whatever you call it, have spread like wildfire through my district. Everybody's sore at Williams and Milbank and Washington."

"You can say that again," said Lew. "At the hostel they all want to beat my ear about it."

"The Molas around Zinzin will never have a chance until Genghis is cut down to size," she said. "And if he's not, it'll hurt the Peace Corps all over the country."

"I know," said Lew, "but now he's in more solid than ever."

They sat together in silent sharing of their fatigue and their discouragement, and so they heard the patter on the roof, a soft overture of the heavy rain they knew would soon come. It did, within minutes, rattling overhead like thousands of stones bombarding the roof from a cliff above. Then came the deep, steady drone of a Kalya summer rain and, in the distance, the convulsion of thunder. Through the open windows they could hear the rain swishing in the feathery palm fronds and splattering into the puddles in the yard. This rain, they knew, was good for hours.

Prudence moved closer to Lew and linked an arm with his. "I've been thinking about Zinzin," she said, "and maybe I have an idea that would work." She had raised her voice to be heard above the storm.

"It's too late for ideas," he said. "The contracts with Genghis are all set."

"Not too late for this idea," she said.

Prudence did not amplify and Lew waited, listening to the beat of the rain. It was a cascade now.

"Well," he said after a time, "what is it?"

"Don't want to say yet. I want to get it worked out first."

He laughed. "You know something, Prude? . . . I had you all wrong. That candid look of yours is just a front. What you really love is mystery and intrigue."

"You said that before. It's not true. It's just that I care a lot about what happens."

"Well, so do I."

She turned to him, framed his face in her hands and looked deep into his eyes. "Yes, you do care, don't you, Lew? I didn't think so at first. You seemed so . . . oh, kind of flip, taking everything so easily, like nothing really mattered. Honestly, I thought you were one of the day-counters."

Well, thought Lew, he was once. And he still counted when he felt low. Just the other day, driving down from Zinzin, he had calculated the remaining time. How many days? He couldn't remember. Too much was happening. The hours and the weeks were telescoping.

"But now I know you," said Prudence. She paused, then lowered her voice. "Lew, I love you."

"We do have a pretty good combo going," he said lightly.

"You dig my spiritual qualities, and my mouth waters for your pure, snow-white body. . . . I've got a proposition to make."

She grinned as she released his face. "No, please. Tomorrow. Not tonight, honey."

"This is long-range." He tried to sound casual. "My proposition is that we get married."

Prudence's eyes lighted. "Oh, but you're late. I decided several weeks ago that we would."

"You decided! You've got a helluva lot of nerve. What made you think you'd be asked?"

"Female intuition." She looked abruptly shy, and lay her head against him. The rain hammered on the roof and spilled off the eaves like a waterfall.

"Now what?" he demanded. "The roof must be leaking."

"That's not the roof, lover," she said. "Those are tears. I'm crying."

19

Punctually at 9 P.M. Sunday the wail of sirens ruptured Ft. Paul's languorous night air and a resplendent motorcade sped along the boulevard to the Kalya National theater. If his subjects were indifferent to such rigorous measurements of time as minutes and hours, Alexander Vining definitely was not. He admired brisk schedules and he honored them.

First came a "V" of elite security police on blustering motorcycles. Colonel Hulbert Booth rode at the apex and twenty cyclists fanned out behind him. A miniature flag of Kalya, white star on alternating stripes of red and yellow, flew at the handlebars of each motorcycle. The officers' white, gold-trimmed crash helmets glinted under the street lights and their uniforms were immaculate. All wore black pants, black puttees and white shirts with the Vining family crest on the right sleeve: leopard rampant holding the scales of justice in his jaws.

Behind the cycle escort purred a dozen shining black limousines: Cadillacs, Mercedes-Benzes, Imperials, Lincolns. Snowlike patches could be seen within the cars, for white-tie-and-tails was the prescribed attire for the Prime Minister's annual Founders Day address. Each limousine flew the banner of Kalya at its radio antenna. The parade of automobiles was flanked by staggered lines of elite motorcyclists and the yellow and red Volkswagens, called "bug-a-bugs" by Kalyans, which the Ft. Paul city police used to patrol their beats. In protocol order, the first limousines held the ambassadors to Kalya, the next were filled with the commissioners of government bureaus followed by the fifteen members of the cabinet.

The last car, a black, custom-built Lincoln, with shatterproof panes and sides of hidden steel plate, flew two flags instead of one. On the right was the flag of Kalya and on the left, whipping in the muggy air, flew the Prime Minister's own banner, the white leopard with the scales of justice in a pale, sky-blue field. In the rear, closed off from the chauffeur by a glass partition, sat but one man, the Prime Minister of Kalya.

The one thousand seats of the Kalya National had been filled for hours. Perhaps another thousand people crammed the two side aisles and spilled into the garish lobby. The center aisle was kept free by a moving line of security policemen. Outside, the sidewalks were packed with people and more thousands stood on the far side of the divided boulevard.

The climax of the Founders Day celebration always drew a motley crowd, the costumes ranging from the formal dress suits and gowns of The Family to cotton dresses, faded blue suits, rough country-cloth shirts and multicolored African wrappers. Outwardly the gathering appeared much the same tonight, but through the hall coursed a kind of mass tremor of anticipation. It heightened the pitch of voices, doubled the craning of necks and seemed to ripple in the buzz of conversation.

For The Forge had done its work well. All over the city that morning the leaflets had appeared. They were fastened to doors, power poles and signboards. They could be found on the trunks of trees, spiked on tips of shrubbery and even stuck with pitch to the iron standards of the city's traffic lights. They littered the sidewalks and blew fitfully along the streets where small boys gave chase and then hurried to their parents with the prizes. Owners of parked cars that morning found the handbills stuffed into the cracks of windows. Few Ft. Paul tribal residents could read, but those who could soon found themselves at the hub of groups clamoring to have the yellow and red sheets declaimed aloud. By the standards of Europe or the United States, the broadsides might have seemed but the amateur carpings of a disgruntled minority, but in Kalya, with its strict, though unwritten censorship, the leaflets were incendiary.

The one printed on yellow paper was headlined: THE GREAT WATER CRIME. The first paragraph read: "Prime Minister Alexander Vining's government is guilty of gross criminal negligence. Its nightly ten o'clock rule of 'water for the rich only' deprived Ft. Paul of the water to combat the city's worst fire of the century. As a result, twenty-five persons were burned to death. We accuse Kalya's notorious Family tyranny of being an accessory to murder and we demand immediate opening of all city water mains at night. . . ."

The flyer printed on a poor stock of red paper was headed: END THE ROBBERY OF GOVERNMENT EMPLOYEES. It began: "The so-called 'voluntary' contribution of a month's salary by all government workers is a mockery of free institutions and supposedly free men. Anyone who declines to contribute is summarily fired or worse. The plea that the funds are needed to finance Founders Day has become a grim national joke. Actually 90 per cent of the money goes into the pockets of prominent Family members as a political subsidy. We demand that this outrageous rape of poorly paid government employees be ended once and for all. . . ."

Security and city police ranged Ft. Paul throughout the day, tearing down the flyers from trees and poles, snatching them from the hands of children and plucking them from gutters and sidewalks. By noon, the story was abroad that an elderly watchman at the Agriculture Building had been overpowered by men who used the department's equipment to print the seditious material. They all wore gloves and left no fingerprints, it was said.

Colonel Booth issued emergency orders that any person found with one of the leaflets in his possession would be arrested. But the order only whetted the city's appetite for the forbidden fruit. The sheets were passed furtively from hand to hand, and small groups gathered in tribal hotels or amid the burned-out skeletons of buildings to have "tellers" read for them what they could not read themselves. For the second time in two days, Ft. Paul was aflame—this time with an idea. So swiftly did its sparks spread that by afternoon scores of tribesmen who had never heard of

The Forge began putting the handbills back up in public places whenever they were certain no officer of the law was lurking in the vicinity. The "water crime" flyer even appeared mysteriously on a signboard outside the Kalya National theater just ten minutes before the official motorcade was due to arrive. A security policeman ripped it down and stuffed it in his pocket.

The act heightened the tension at the theater, and by the time Colonel Booth's gleaming "V" of cycles thundered into view, many patrolmen on foot were nervously pushing at knots of people to keep them from the area under the marquee.

Lew and Prudence had arrived three hours earlier and had found seats off the center aisle near the rear. Along with the audience in the old, ornate building, they could sense the mounting trepidation—who knew what Old Number One might do?— as the cavalcade drew up at the curb outside. They stood up to watch the grand entrance in the garishly lighted theater.

Down the center aisle in single file marched the ambassadors and ministers of some forty nations. They were led by the senior emissary in residence, the ambassador of Italy, a fragile, little man with a fussy stride who kept mopping his brow with a handkerchief. Lew spotted Ambassador Willard Milbank mid-way in the procession. The American wore his white tie and tails with the aplomb of a seasoned operagoer in mid-winter. He was lean and handsome, he nodded and smiled at friends and he seemed unaware of the smothering heat in the theater. The ambassadors filed solemnly into the front row of seats reserved for them. They were followed by the government commissioners and then by the cabinet, the dark faces all set in self-consciously grave molds like men attending the wedding of a daughter. The Kalya officials mounted the stage and stood by their seats, which fanned out in a semicircle from the high-backed armchair reserved for the Prime Minister.

Above this intricately carved tigerwood chair dangled a huge, illuminated glass globe of the world on which the borders of the continents were sketched in faint, black lines and Kalya itself emphasized with red and yellow bands. The globe, given to the theater by Vining himself, hung perhaps twenty feet above the stage. It was the bane of moviegoers, for as high as it hung, it still obscured the top center of the screen.

Alexander Vining's entrance was no anticlimax. As he came slowly down the aisle, the Kalya army band at the left of the stage struck up the national anthem, a majestic, swelling and interminable air that broke occasionally for a fierce stutter of snare drums. Vining was escorted by ten security officers, four in front, four in back and one on each side of him. He marched in cadence with the music, an unhurried stride of confidence and dignity.

Vining, though a man of unimpressive height, exuded a sense of power. He had heavy shoulders and his almost theatrically massive face rose in foothills to prominent cheekbones and a broad nose with high, beaked ridge. His head was bald and it shone under the theater lights like an upturned bowl of ebony. A fringe of hair, beginning above the ears and ringing the back of his head, was as white as his pleated shirt front and his formal bow tie. A few wrinkles spread from his eyes, but for the most part his face was surprisingly unlined for a man of advanced age. The Prime Minister was seventy-three, seventy-four, seventy-five or perhaps seventy-six. Nobody really knew. It was Vining's smile that attracted the eye. It was a smile of pride and assurance, but a magnanimous one, the smile of a man who has lived long in authority and who knows the virtues and the excesses of his people.

As Vining came abreast of the row where Lew and Prudence stood, Lew caught a glimpse of Lincoln Beach jammed into the standing crowd in the far aisle. To Lew's surprise, he saw that Hulbert Booth was standing near Beach. It was Booth's custom, at any public appearance of the Prime Minister, to station himself out in the crowd along with dozens of his men. Still, tonight, Lew thought it an odd coincidence that Booth, the chief guardian of the status quo, and Beach, the covert architect of the leaflet rebellion, should be standing so close to each other. Booth was scanning the audience with professional wariness and if he was aware of Beach's presence so near his elbow, he gave no indication of it.

Vining continued his measured march down the center aisle. As he passed the front row of foreign emissaries, he bowed and smiled to each side. He paused at the foot of the stage while his ten bodyguards spaced themselves across the theater. They stood with folded arms in front of the footlights and stared fixedly toward the rear of the theater. The army band concluded the national anthem, then sounded a ruffle of drums, the traditional salute to the chief of state, as Vining mounted the stage and walked to the high-backed armchair behind the rostrum. He stood there a moment to acknowledge the applause and cheers enthusiastically led by the government officials on stage. If the acclamation sounded less than tumultuous, it nevertheless could be graded as satisfactory, and Vining seemed pleased. He smiled benignly, waved a hand in thanks and seated himself. With a rustle of antici-pation, the audience settled into its seats.

The ritual for the climactic hours of Founders Day had been established long ago. First came the invocation, rendered by the Reverend Clark Philip Archer, pastor of Vining's own church, the First Methodist. A well-fed prelate with rubbery facial muscles and an eye tic, the Reverend Archer invoked divine solicitude for Kalya, Africa, the world, outer space and Alexander Vining in that as-cending order. The subsequent speeches continued the ladderlike climb toward the Vining pinnacle. The Speaker of Parliament, a Booth, introduced the Secretary of Agriculture, William Fess, who introduced the Chief of Staff of the Army, a Vining, who introduced J. Richardson Downing, the Commissioner of Educa-tion. The telescoping introductions extended for a half hour each and hued faithfully to the style of Kalya oratory: florid, lavish in encomiums, precise in diction, as rococo and as lush as the jun-gles of the country.

Since Commissioner Downing was the acknowledged master of this brand of declamation, the summit of honor was his even though this bruised the sensibilities of some Family members whose government rank stood higher than the Commissioner of Education. But Vining doted on Downing's luxuriant verbiage, and for the last five years the commissioner had been Vining's choice as the man best fitted to extol the character of the nation's leader.

Tonight Downing was in top form. The tall, kinetic commis-sioner clutched the lectern as he would an old friend and promptly unleashed a display of rhetoric as gorgeous as his white brocaded silk vest. He had superlatives for Alexander Vining's boyhood, for his youth, his apprentice years as a humble public servant and his crowning decades as the premier statesman of Africa. He saw in Vining a man whose qualities blended the best of Hannibal, Aristotle, Washington, Churchill, Schweitzer, Solomon, Lyndon B. Johnson, Michelangelo, the Apostle Paul and Horatio R. M. Banks. The last-named gentleman was the founder of the Republic of Kalya.

"And so, my beloved fellow citizens of Kalya," Downing concluded, "it accords me the highest accolade of my pedagogical career to introduce the man whose towering beneficence, prolific devotion to the cause of justice, unsullied generosity and effulgent statesmanship have transformed the ancient dream of Kalya into the most copious reality on the entire continent of Africa. He is my friend and your friend, the man who sips the cup equally with the humble and with royalty, that human miracle which the Almighty wrought in our land, the prime minister of a proud and resourceful nation, Alexander Vining!"

Downing turned with such a sweeping bow toward Vining that his forked coattails sprang into the air like battle pennants. Vining arose with the dignity of a patriarch, nodded his thanks to Downing and walked the few steps to the rostrum. A wave of cheers and applause, punctuated by a few shrill tribal yells, rolled from the audience. Vining waited patiently, his bald head glistening and his rugged face mellowed by his most benevolent smile.

Lew, who had been whispering to Prudence, automatically looked toward the side aisle to see how Lincoln Beach was reacting to this second Vining ovation of the night. As he turned his head, his eyes searching for Beach, Lew saw a confused movement in the tightly packed far aisle. From a tangle of heads, he saw Beach's right arm being raised high by Hulbert Booth. The colonel was grasping Beach's arm just below the wrist. In the flash clutter of motions, Lew could see Beach's upraised fist clenched as if he were trying to wrench free.

At that moment, a shot rang out, splitting the crowd's applause like a knife. A bullet crashed into the big glass globe, with its map of Kalya, hanging over the stage. Shards of glass showered down. Lew, turning back to the stage, saw several fragments fall on Vining and saw the Prime Minister brush quickly at his shoulder. There was a confused, frightened roar in the hall, then shouts, and fingers pointed toward the far aisle. There Lew could see Booth grappling with Lincoln Beach. A gun was waving in the air, apparently held by both men. The struggle forced their faces close together and on each was a look of fury. Beach slammed the colonel against the wall and locked his free arm about Booth's neck. But two nearby security policemen, who had bulled their way through the crowd, reached the grappling pair. One grabbed Beach about the waist while the other tore Beach's arm away, leaving Colonel Booth with the weapon. The crowd fell back and Booth brandished the pistol before Beach's face. Lincoln Beach yelled something indistinguishable and the colonel crashed an elbow into Beach's mouth.

"Assassin!" Booth's shout could be heard above the clamor in the hall.

Beach tried to shout a response, but his words were muffled by a policeman's arm thrown over his face. Beach had keeled over with the colonel's blow and he hung in the arm of the security officers with his feet trailing on the floor. The policemen dragged him up the aisle toward the theater's entrance and his efforts to cry out became only strangled, gurgling noises. One officer now had an arm crooked firmly about Beach's throat.

Prudence pulled at Lew's sleeve. "Oh my God, what'll they do to him? What happened?"

"I don't know," said Lew. "It all went so fast."

The pounding of a gavel could be heard at the rostrum. Eyes slowly turned back toward Prime Minister Vining. He stood stolidly, his face devoid of emotion as he rapped on the lectern. The crowd began to quiet down. Outside could be heard shouts and the sound of a motor being gunned. Vining continued to rap. At last there was silence.

The Prime Minister spread a wide, confident grin.

"Kalya," he said, "welcomes target practice at all hours."

A few people giggled. Then came a roll of laughter. The government officials on the stage sprang to their feet, extending their arms toward Vining and applauding him. Soon the entire audience was on its feet, giving the Prime Minister another ovation—this time for gallantry under fire.

He accepted the applause with a humble, grateful air and he let it continue for several minutes. Then he raised his arms in a pacifying gesture and the audience slowly took its seats once more.

"Free nations, large and small, have their madmen," he said soberly. He paused, then smiled. Vining, Lew thought, was a master of timing.

"I'm happy," said Vining in a lighter tone, "that Colonel Booth managed to deflect the assailant's aim. I must say that, even at this late hour in my life, I would rather lose an expensive, illuminated globe of the earth than my own head."

The crowd laughed again in admiration. The Prime Minister evidenced not a trace of nervous aftermath. He was poised, cool and as completely in control of himself as a national leader should be.

Vining launched into his prepared address with no further allusion to the shooting and no mention at all of the handbills which had thrown Ft. Paul into such turmoil. He did refer to the fire, extolling the bravery of the fire department and the Kalyans who aided it. Of the part played by the Peace Corps and of the lack of city water, he said not a word. He soon switched to the early trials and hardships of the republic, and it became apparent that he intended to build toward his customary tributes to modern Kalya and its progress under the Vining administration.

Lew could not keep his mind on the speech. Lincoln Beach riveted his thoughts. He whispered to Prudence: "There was something queer about that shot."

"Why?" she asked. "I didn't see anything until it was too late."

"I'm not sure," he said. "I'm trying to think back and reconstruct what I saw."

The tableau in his mind was that of Booth clawing at Beach's hand, trying to wrest a gun from it, and of the pistol being aimed at Prime Minister Vining, then fired. . . . But no, he told himself on second thought, that was not the way he saw it at all. When the shot was fired, there was no pistol in Beach's hand. Lew was sure of that. He re-created the scene from the moment he looked toward the side aisle. . . . Beach's right arm in the air . . . Pushed there by the colonel . . . ? An object in Colonel Booth's hand . . . The shot . . . Lew's eyes on the rostrum, for perhaps five seconds? . . . Ten? . . . And when he looked back at the far aisle, a pistol waving in the air, Link and Booth wrestling, both holding the gun . . . What did that mean?

He ran through the swift sequence of events several times, but each time he came back to the central thought: Lincoln Beach held no weapon at the moment the shot rang out. Booth, however, did have something in his free hand. Yes, that must be it . . . The security chief must have fired, intentionally high, at least twenty feet over Vining's head, then swiftly clapped the pistol into Beach's upraised right hand. In his mind, Lew swiveled his body into Colonel Booth's position, trying to separate left from right . . . Yes, it had to have been Booth's left hand which held Link's right arm below the wrist just prior to the shot. That would mean Booth would be free to shoot with his right hand. Booth was an excellent marksman. Even shooting while clutching with his left hand, he would have had no difficulty sending the bullet safely high, far above Vining and the rostrum. The shattering of the globe might have been chance, or again, Booth might have aimed at it.

Now Lew knew. There was no doubt about it. Beach had been framed in an attempted assassin's role by the chief of the elite security police. Everything fit. Booth despised Link. The colonel had fumed when Beach forced him to pay his utility bill. They had clashed the night of the fire. Booth probably suspected Link's guiding hand behind the day's avalanche of leaflets which had so bedeviled the colonel's force. And Booth had taken a position in the theater next to Lincoln Beach. True, it was Booth's custom to mingle with the crowd when Vining spoke, but why only a few feet from Link? And the reaction of Vining himself had been curious. The Prime Minister seemed too poised, too nerveless. It was almost as if he knew his life was in no danger. Had Vining seen Booth fire the high shot? Or, a more Machiavellian thought, had Vining known in advance that his security chief would stage a spurious assassination attempt? Stranger things had happened in West African politics. Could it have been a stratagem to magnify Vining's qualities of leadership on the day that his rule had been attacked in print for the first time? If so, was the involvement of Beach merely an added bit of luck? Would any stray Kalyan have fitted the dupe's role into which Booth forced Lincoln Beach?

Lew could only speculate on the intrigue, but of one thing he was absolutely certain now: Beach did not fire the shot.

"Link was framed," he whispered to Prudence.

"Sure? How do you know?"

"I'm positive," he said. "I'll tell you later."

Vining held his speech mercifully short for such an occasion, reaching his peroration of administration laurels only forty-five minutes after he began. The audience cheered again, some people from obvious relief that the oratory had ended. The march from the hall, to the strains of the national anthem, duplicated the stately arrival. Vining strode out at the end of the official party, escorted by his elite bodyguard. Motorcycles gunned hoarsely and the motorcade of limousines sped up the boulevard to the Executive Palace where foreign and domestic officialdom, this time with wives, would be feted in a rare midnight buffet supper in Vining's penthouse dwelling.

On the sidewalk amid the churning crowd, Lew and Prudence debated what to do. They had to know what had happened to Beach, but if they were to ask about him at police headquarters, they might risk being questioned themselves about their possible connection with Beach. Running quickly through members of The Forge who might make inquiry without stirring police suspicions, they settled on Oliver Downing as the only logical one. As a newspaperman Downing made routine nightly checks with both city and security police. Probably he already had the facts.

They cruised Ft. Paul's streets for several hours in Lew's jeep, hoping to spot the young reporter. The streets were thronged with Kalyans, many reeling under the burdens of palm wine which had been downed in lavish quantities throughout the day in commemoration of the founding fathers. But thousands of sober Africans were in the streets too. The triple combination of a national holiday, a shower of mutinous handbills and an assassination attempt on Old Number One proved a heady stimulant. People gathered at every corner. Motorcycle police roved the city in force. All of Ft. Paul was in ferment and nobody wanted to go home to bed. As they halted at intersections, Lew and Prudence caught snatches of the extravagant rumors which sputtered through the city like so many fuses. . . . A band of insurgents intended to storm the Executive Palace . . . Lincoln Beach had been spirited

to Kpali where his hands and feet would be cut off at dawn . . .
The unknown distributors of the leaflets were already rounded
up and in jail . . . In reprisal for the threat to his rule, Old
Number One would turn off the city's water nightly at 7 P.M.
instead of 10 . . . Actually the ringleader of the insurrectionists
was Hulbert Booth himself. The colonel was plotting to overthrow
Vining and assume power for the Booths. . . . The later the hour,
the wilder became the rumors. But young Downing could not be
found.

It was after two in the morning when Lew spotted Billy Number 15 loping along the sidewalk of a street which bulged with
refugees from the fire-razed section of the city. The tall Mandingo
was wrapped in his purple sheet. Lew maneuvered the jeep to the
curb and halted. Billy Number 15 quickly came to the vehicle
and leaned through the open window.

"Where's Beach?" asked Lew.

"Eh man. He wit' da leopard," said Billy Number 15. In Kalya
slang, "to be with the leopard" was to be in Ft. Paul city jail.
"Boot' man say Beach shoot one time Ol' Numb' One."

"Where's Ollie Downing? Do you know?"

The Mandingo peddler shook his head. "He palavah plenny dis
night." He made a motion of writing in his palm.

"Do the police know who distributed the leaflets, Billy?" asked
Prudence.

"No," he said promptly. "Boot' ver' vexed. Da Forge humbug
dat man plenny. Tell you one time . . ." At that moment a motorcycle policeman rounded the corner into their street and Billy
Number 15 quickly faded into the sidewalk crowd.

Lew turned to Prudence. "This is needle-in-the-haystack stuff.
Let's give it up for the night. We'll get the word tomorrow."

"Official cover story, you mean," said Prudence.

Although they were both too tired to think properly, they sat in
the jeep in front of Prudence's house while Lew again went
through what he had seen at the theater. They parted, convinced
of Beach's innocence, but fearful of his fate and at a loss to know
what the Vining government had done or proposed to do.

It was the next afternoon before they knew with any degree of
certainty. Copies of the *Daily Voice* arrived at Peace Corps headquarters shortly after two o'clock to be snatched up as swiftly as on

the day following the fire. Oliver Downing's familiar byline headed the story of the attempted assassination. Downing, it was obvious to Lew, sought to give as impartial an account as possible within the limits allowed by a semi-official organ of the Kalya government.

Lincoln Beach, 28, chief of the Utility Authority's billing section, is in Ft. Paul prison today, charged with almost eliminating the life of Prime Minister Alexander Vining.

Police said Beach tried to kill Kalya's chief of state by pistol bullet while Mr. Vining was ready to deliver his annual Founders Day address at Kalya National theater.

Col. Hulbert Booth, hero of the disastrous fire, again was to the rescue of the nation. He deflected the hand of the alleged seeking killer Beach just as Beach fired. The bullet destroyed the beautiful globe of the world hanging behind the Prime Minister.

Beach was dragged by security police from the scene of the crime and, at 11:46 P.M., was booked at Ft. Paul prison on the charge of trying to slay the benevolent leader of Kalya. Upon conviction, Beach would be sentenced to death by firing squad at Kpali prison camp.

Beach states that he is all innocence, but many think the facts are too grotesque for doubt. By a great stroke of fortune for the nation, Col. Booth was stood beside Beach all evening and can testify to everything.

Attorney General Archibald Fess is saying the trial will be held in three weeks, on date of July 2. He has the opinion the trial will not take many hours, if that.

The story ran on for several columns, giving fairly accurate details of the turbulent scene at the theater. Nowhere was there any mention of the handbill distribution. If the Kalya officials believed Beach was implicated in the flyer incident, they obviously thought it wiser to pretend that no such challenge to authority ever occurred than to gain an extra count against Beach. The only motive ascribed to Beach in the article was a quotation from Colonel Booth. He said Beach was a "Communist-trained saboteur and notorious Marxist revolutionary and assassin with malevolent hatred for Kalya law and order."

Lew and Prudence read Downing's story in the office of Dr. Sam

Zerwick. The physician held the paper while Lew and Prudence leaned over his shoulders.

"Some yarn," said Zerwick when they finished. "Never a dull day in this burg."

"It's a damn frame-up," said Lew. "Link never fired that shot. He didn't have a gun in his hand until Booth put it there. I know. I saw it all."

He described what he had seen. The doctor listened attentively, then lowered his horn-rimmed glasses on the bridge of his nose and peered over them at Lew.

"So you're on a spot, aren't you?" he asked.

"Me?" Lew replied. "It's Link Beach who's in real trouble."

"You too," said Zerwick. "If you tell what you know, they'll brand you a liar and an enemy of the state and kick you out of the country—maybe the rest of us with you. If you keep quiet, it'll rot your conscience for the rest of your life. I'd call that being on a spot, to put it mildly."

Lew shook his head. "Nothing's going to bother my conscience, Sam. Link is my friend. He's being railroaded. There's no question about telling what I know. The question is how."

"My hunch is Williams and Milbank won't like your decision," said Zerwick, "to say nothing of Washington."

"To hell with them!" exploded Prudence. The two men looked at her in surprise.

"My, my," said Zerwick. "Such language from our missionary."

"No time for wisecracks," said Prudence. "Lew's right. He must tell exactly what he saw—and everything he saw."

Zerwick grinned. "Well, now that that's been settled by both of you, may I say you're a couple of damfool firebrands—and if you weren't, I'd throw you out of the office."

They were silent a moment, then Lew said: "But what to do? I could offer to testify, but how do I know they'd let me? I'm not even sure they'll let Link have a defense counsel."

Zerwick scratched at his big head and pondered a bit. "Yeah, well, tell you what," he said. "I've found that anything on paper that looks official makes an impression on these people. I can yell my head off for supplies at the city hospital and nobody could care less. But if I put a formal request in writing, they pay attention—and sometimes they do something. . . . Look at those throwaways that went around the city yesterday. They scared hell out of Booth and his pals."

"So?" ask Lew.

"How about an affidavit?" suggested Zerwick. "Very very formal. Peace Corps stationery, your signature, witnessed by two, three people. I'll even use my office time-date stamp on it to make it look impressive. Then you tell Williams and Milbank you're going to present it formally to the attorney general. That'll get action."

Lew thought a moment. "Okay. Let's do it right now. I'll tell it over again and you put it in formal language. Okay?"

Zerwick swung around to his typewriter and pulled a sheet of paper from a drawer. "Shoot," he said. "Prudence, you help me with all the legal, who-struck-John lingo."

They worked for two hours, writing several drafts before they were satisfied. Then Prudence typed out a clean copy with three carbons: "Affidavit of Lewis N. Corleigh on Events at the Founders Day Celebration at Kalya National Theater." The account covered three pages. Lew initialed the first two sheets and signed his name with a flourish at the bottom of the third. Prudence and Zerwick signed on the lines marked for witnesses. Zerwick pounded the paper with the time-date stamp of his Peace Corps physician's office, then handed the document to Corleigh.

"Here you are, Red," he said. "Your exit visa."

"First stop, Williams," said Lew. He took the papers, hugged Prudence's shoulders and left the office.

Crossing the lobby, he saw Rachael Frisson by the water cooler. Today a white carnation was tucked in her imperious hairdo.

"What's all that?" she asked, looking at the batch of papers.

"Business," he said. "Actually, I'd like you to read it and sign. You know, just witness my signature. I've got two, but three looks better."

Rachael took the papers with a smile which faded as she perused them. She read the first page slowly, skipped through the other two and handed them back to Corleigh.

"No thanks," she said. She fingered the carnation and looked quizzically at Lew. "You know you have no business on earth getting into that shooting. Just when I think I understand you, Red, I don't. Always stirring up trouble, aren't you? I guess you mean to keep at it until they ship us all out of the country."

"A decent guy is being framed," he said. "That's all there is to it. It has nothing to do with the Peace Corps."

"That's what you think. You and Beach." She shook her head. "Some pair. I won't say I wish you luck, because I don't."

His reception was more cordial in Williams' office. The Peace Corps chief pumped Lew's hand with both of his and his face folded in smiles. Lew's performance at the fire had won Williams' genuine admiration and their old differences over Zinzin had been put aside. Williams was immensely proud of the entire Peace Corps these days, and he had written a confidential report to Washington, lauding both volunteers and staff for ingenuity and bravery in the great Ft. Paul fire. He had also castigated the Kalya government for its failure to give the Peace Corps public recognition.

"What a night, huh?" He clapped Lew on the back. "But how come you're not hitting the road to Zinzin? Monday's your day to go up, isn't it?"

"Yeah," said Lew, "but when you read this, I think you'll understand why I'd better stay in Ft. Paul for the next couple of weeks."

Williams took the papers with a quick, darting glance of apprehension and seated himself rather abruptly behind his desk. As he read, an expression of brooding doubt came over his face. He fished reflexively in his shirt pocket, drew out a clasp knife and began cleaning his fingernails. By the time he finished the affidavit, he had the look of a man reading the stock market quotations on the day of a bad slump.

"I know you well enough to know that you feel you have to go through with this," he said. "Still, I hope you appreciate my position. If Zinzin was a bad dream, this is a nightmare."

"I couldn't live with myself if I didn't tell what I saw," said Lew. "That may sound corny, but it's true."

"But can you be sure of what you think you saw?" Williams' penchant for avoiding a head-on collision with bad news was instinctive. "Shouldn't you think it over some more? You know how it is when there's a lot of commotion. Your own eyes can deceive you."

"I went all through that a dozen times," said Lew. "Right after the shot was fired, and again in bed last night and this morning.

That paper tells exactly what happened. Link Beach is up against a phony charge."

Williams sighed, shot a last glance at Lew as if to gauge the firmness of his resolution, then rose from his chair and went to the hall-tree. He pulled on his jacket.

"In that case," he said, "we'd better go see the ambassador right away. This one is way over my head."

There was no delay in seeing the U.S. ambassador in the air-conditioned chancery with its atmosphere of subdued efficiency and its bevy of pretty young women looking up from their electric typewriters. The ambassador's overfed secretary barely had time to give their names when Milbank was at the door with a shirt-sleeved arm extended in greeting.

"Come in, come in," he said. "Glad to see you again, Lew. How's your health, Carter? . . . Well, after last night, the Peace Corps was the last thing I expected to see today. The Kalya Army would be more like it—or Booth's security investigators. Some night."

He glanced casually at the manila envelope Lew was carrying, arranged chairs for them and settled himself behind the uncluttered desk with its neat stacks of paper.

"Sorry I couldn't do anything for you at the Voice, Carter," he said. "They're jealous of the Peace Corps or any other foreigners getting any credit for fire-fighting or rescue work. The old inferiority complex, I suppose. . . . I thought I knew these people pretty well, but I must say I wasn't prepared to see a Kalya citizen rear up and take a pot shot at Vining. You've got to hand it to the old bird. He was cool as ice afterward at the reception. Gracious host, too. You'd have thought he'd just returned from a state visit to Algeria or Morocco—instead of being shot at."

He paused, rubbed his chin reflectively. "It caused a bit of a flap outside Kalya. Apparently the Reuters man sent one of his colorful dispatches. Washington has cabled me for background."

Milbank centered his gaze on Corleigh. "What do you make of it, Lew?" he asked. "As I recall, you know this fellow Beach pretty well. No question about his antipathy for Old Number One. But trying to kill him in a crowded theater when there wasn't a chance in a thousand of getting away? Doesn't make sense. What's your hunch?"

"It's more than a hunch, Mr. Ambassador," said Lew. "I saw it all—or almost all—and Beach never had a gun in his hand when the shot was fired. He was framed. I can't prove it, but I'm sure that shot was fired by Hulbert Booth."

"Booth?" Milbank's look was one of incredulity. "Oh, come now, Lew. I know Beach is your friend, but that's a bit far out. Why, even from my seat in front, I could see the gun in Beach's hand."

"But not before the shot," said Lew. He undid the flap on the manila envelope. "Actually, sir, that's why . . ."

"That's why we're here, Willard," finished Williams. "This is going to be a rough one for you. You see, Lew has drawn up an affidavit and . . ."

His voice melted away apologetically as Lew opened the envelope and handed the stapled three-page paper to Milbank. The ambassador glanced quickly from one man to the other.

"I think you ought to read it first," said Williams.

"Mmm." Milbank already was skimming the paper. He scanned all three pages, paused to read the three names at the end, turned the paper to get a better view of Zerwick's time-date stamp. Then, snapping the papers to straighten them, he turned back to the beginning and read through slowly. Except for a tightening of his lips, his face was expressionless. His only reaction came when he finished. The gingerly way he laid down the document on the desk blotter, Lew thought, it might have been an ancient, precious parchment. Milbank's eyes questioned Lew's.

"What do you propose to do with this?" he asked.

"I intend to take it to Attorney General Fess," said Lew, "and ask to testify at the trial. If he says no, I'll insist that the affidavit be read in court. If he says no again, I . . . well . . . I'm not sure. Maybe give it to the Ft. Paul Reuters correspondent and get it over to the Associated Press man in Lagos."

"I see." Milbank creaked back in his swivel chair and folded his hands on his stomach. "Lew, I'm sure you've thought of all the consequences of this, the international repercussions."

"Yes," replied Lew, "I have. Plenty. But the fact is that they may execute an innocent man."

"And, of course," added Milbank, "you've weighed all of Bruce Kellogg's material on Beach?"

Lew nodded. "Frankly, I don't believe Kellogg's conclusions, sir. Link is no Communist. He's for Kalya. If he favors any system, it's ours, I guess. I know the guy pretty well."

"And you also know this affidavit might kill off the Peace Corps in Kalya?"

"I know it might," said Lew, "but not as dead as they can kill Beach. The penalty for attempted assassination of the Prime Minister is death. I can't . . . well . . . I've got no choice, have I?"

A flicker of a smile played on Milbank's face. "You're nimble, Lew. By making it a question, you're turning the moral issue over to me."

"That was subconscious, I guess," said Lew. "But . . . well . . . if you were in my place, do you think you'd have any alternative?"

Milbank sighed. "An ambassador always has alternatives. Too many of them." He fell silent and his eyes drifted above them to the window which framed a panorama of Ft. Paul, from the imposing bulk of Founders House to the scorched and blackened area where tribal shanties had once stood. A dark poniard of cloud plunged toward the lowering sun, and Milbank knew that soon another downpour would flood the city, and the streets and gutters would course like rivers.

"If I were a young man today, I'd join the Peace Corps," he said with seeming irrelevance. His eyes were still on the window and there was mingled envy and sorrow in his voice, which for the moment reminded Lew of Forrest Stevenson's. "Right can be so right," said Milbank, "and wrong can be so wrong. I'd almost forgotten, but for the young, there are no grays."

Not quite true, thought Lew, remembering his own qualms about Zinzin, The Forge and U.S. policy during his trip to Washington. But he sensed what must be going through Milbank's mind and he sympathized with the older man.

"Well . . ." Milbank lowered his gaze from the window and, with a perceptible effort, he turned back to Corleigh. "I suppose, Lew, you know enough psychology to realize that no witness to a scene of sudden violence can be one hundred per cent sure of just what he saw. And, if we happen to be emotionally linked to one of the people involved in the fracas, we all tend to remember it the way we really wanted it to happen."

Lew noted that Milbank had failed to answer the question of moral choice, but he realized this was no time to pursue the issue. "Of course—" he began.

Williams interrupted. "I went over that possibility with him, Willard. Lew is convinced he saw exactly what he put down on paper."

Milbank nodded. "In that case, Lew," he asked, "what do you suppose Booth's motive was in trying to fix it so your friend Beach looked like the assassin?"

"That's pretty obvious to me," replied Lew. "Booth knows that Beach opposes the Vining regime, and I guess he's got the same kind of data that Bruce Kellogg showed me. Also Booth is sore as hell about the other night, the night of the fire. The colonel found Link haranguing a crowd about the city water being turned off, and they almost started throwing punches."

"I don't blame Beach," said Milbank. "That water business is a damned piece of witless arrogance. Old Number One ought to have better sense. . . . But about the motive. How about those leaflets? Was that a caper of Beach's too? The writing in them was suspiciously literate."

"I don't know whether the handbills figured or not in Booth's put-up job," said Lew, skirting the question. "I suppose Booth would jump at conclusions and think that Link had something to do with the flyers. After all, Booth heard him raising hell, as I said, over the lack of city water the night of the fire."

Milbank leaned back in his swivel chair again and folded his arms. "I don't have to give you a blueprint of what's going to happen when you present this." He tapped the affidavit. "We went all through that on the Zinzin school. You're getting to be quite a veteran of these foreign policy snarls, Lew."

Milbank grinned briefly, then continued. "We were able to . . . er . . . handle that one, thanks to a bright idea from down the line. But Lew, this is no Zinzin. This involves the personal integrity of Vining's top bodyguard, undoubtedly the second most powerful man in Kalya. You're calling Booth a liar and accusing him of a criminal act. What's more, you're saying the Vining administration will resort to murder to get rid of minor political opposition. Those, my friend, are very serious charges. They could pretty well explode the Peace Corps right out of Kalya."

"I know," said Lew, then doggedly: "All I know is that I have to tell what I saw."

"Yes," said Milbank quietly, "I suppose you do." He sighed. "This kind of collision with a host government was inevitable from the moment Kennedy decided to set up the Peace Corps. It was bound to happen sometime, somewhere. . . . Still, I hope you won't think harshly of me if I say I wish it had happened in some other country."

"I know how you feel," said Lew. It occurred to him that he would not care to trade places with the American ambassador right now.

"I'm glad you understand," said Milbank. "In that case, Lew, let me ask a favor of you. Give me two or three days to cable Washington for instructions. Attorney General Fess says the trial won't be held for three weeks. That gives us a breathing spell."

Lew looked away from Milbank's direct gaze. There was no humiliation in the ambassador's voice, yet Lew understood how he must feel, throwing himself on the mercy of a much younger man.

"To be blunt, Lew, I want off the hook," said Milbank. It was a statement, not a plea.

"Why, sure," said Lew hurriedly. "That's okay. But regardless of what Washington says, I'm going to hand over that paper to Fess."

"I know that," said Milbank calmly. He mused a moment, then suddenly grinned and moved quickly from his chair. He came around the desk and shook Lew's hand.

"I'll get the cable off right away," he said, "and we shall see what we shall see."

Milbank turned to Williams. "By the way, Carter, I may need your help. What's the top age limit on Peace Corps volunteers?"

"None," said Williams. "I've got a sixty-seven-year-old retired schoolteacher up at Pjoole."

"Well," said Milbank, "save me a spot. I may need it."

The next three days inched by a minute at a time. Lew and Prudence tried to visit Beach at the city jail, but were denied permission. Colonel Booth arrested a Fizi tribesman on charges of distributing literature without a city license. But Lew and Prudence did not become alarmed for The Forge. The Fizi was not a member. Lew turned over his Zinzin route to a substitute, gave him a sealed letter for Jim Osterlord describing Beach's plight and the situation at the embassy. The *Daily Voice* reported that the attorney general had new, but undisclosed, evidence of a highly damaging nature against Beach.

Forge members kept up their covert agitation. Rumors convulsed the city, and fist fights broke out between tribesmen and the police. Booth threatened to impose martial law. All of Ft. Paul was restive. But for Lew, the hours dragged and he found sleep to be elusive under the hammering hostel roof. The rains were flooding down in all-night torrents now. Clothes, food and bed sheets all had the clammy feel of crawling, amphibian creatures.

Late on the afternoon of the third day, an embassy messenger arrived at Peace Corps headquarters, and a few minutes later Williams called Lew to his office and handed him a sheet of flimsy paper:

PECTO
CARTER WILLIAMS
U.S. EMBASSY
FT. PAUL
KALYA

White House concerned lest whole African policy be toppled by one incident. PCVL Lewis N. Corleigh ordered not to testify or submit affidavit. Details available in State dispatch to Milbank.

Frank Sherrod

"Sorry," said Williams.

"The hell you are," said Lew. He walked from the office and slammed the door behind him.

20

Arch Lettermore fingered the two letters as he sat on the edge of Lew Corleigh's bunk at the hostel. Occasionally he squirmed and shifted his weight. He felt uncomfortable in his light gray suit. Not only had he not worn city clothes for a year, but also, unlike most of the Peace Corps in Zinzin, he had gained weight during his year in Kalya. He listened attentively to Lew's instructions, and his sober expression seemed as unnatural for him as did the suit, tie and white shirt with cuff links. Beside the bunk stood a canvas suitcase.

"No problem, Red," he said. "When I get to Dulles in the morning, I call both of these cats, Emmett Shannon, Illinois, in the House, and Alvin Demarest, New Hampshire, in the Senate. I say I'm calling for you, and I insist on talking to them personally. If I connect with one or the other, I give the whole spiel, and then mail the two letters special delivery from the airport. If I can't get 'em on the phone, I tell their secretaries the letters are in the mail and to watch out for them."

"That's right," said Lew, "and for God's sake, don't lose the letters."

"Don't worry, man," said Arch. He placed the envelopes in the inner breast pocket of his coat. "Right next to my passport and my health card. You give ol' Archie an assignment, and it's done. I'm with it, man. Who gave you that testimonial award you didn't earn, huh?"

"Don't bring that up again."

"Listen," said Lettermore. "I'll figure out some way back in the States to fix Genghis's wagon. He'll get something else to chew on besides that USAID lettuce he's going to eat."

"I'd almost forgotten him, Archie," said Lew bleakly. "This bum rap on Link Beach has got me down. Unless we can figure a way, he's had it."

"Yeah. I know what you mean."

"I'm sorry about your dad, Archie," said Lew. "This is a helluva time to be asking you to run errands for me, but I've got to be sure Shannon and Demarest get the word."

"It's okay," said Lettermore. "It will be the first time the old man ever did anything for somebody else." The fleeting grin on his chubby brown face was sardonic. "That's life for you. Some men have to die before they do anyone a good turn." His tone grew bitter. "Not that he'd give a damn. He couldn't have cared less about what happened to a cat like Beach. Oh, well. . . ."

It was a stroke of good luck in an otherwise hapless sequence of events, thought Lew, that Lettermore had been granted emergency leave right at this time. And the fact that Arch obviously felt no grief over his father's death made it easier to ask him to make contact with Shannon and Demarest in Washington.

"No sweat," said Lettermore. "I got two hours at Dulles before I catch the plane for Raleigh."

"Trouble is, it'll be Saturday morning," said Lew, "and they probably won't be in their offices."

"Quit worrying," said Arch. "I still know how to use a telephone book. I'll raise one or the other, somehow."

Lew looked at his wrist watch. "Okay. Well, it's time to take you out to Vining. Let's go."

Although the daily deluge had ceased several hours before, pools of water lay like dingy mirrors on the poorly graded airport road, and the jeep shot spray to either side. So much rain had fallen in recent days that the conical bug-a-bug mounds had eroded and now seemed but warts on the skin of the earth. Frogs raised their hoarse lament in the swamp and the plantation's

rubber trees drooped oppressively. The moist night air clung to
the body like a diver's wet suit.

But the seeming stagnation which settled on Kalya in the
season of its big rains was an illusion, it occurred to Lew. In fact,
events had moved so swiftly that he had been only vaguely
aware of the news that Lettermore's father had died. After the
cable to Williams yesterday, Lew had sat up late with Prudence at
her house, trying to decide what to do. He had considered defying
Washington and taking the affidavit to Attorney General Archibald Fess anyway, but soon thought better of it. Without the
backing of Ambassador Milbank, he was sure Fess would ignore
the paper. They debated giving it to the Reuters news agency
stringer in Ft. Paul, a Lebanese whose allegiance to the facts was
cursory, but decided against that course too. A Reuters dispatch
doubtless would cause a stir outside Kalya, but whether enough
to exert pressure on Old Number One was uncertain. Such a move
on Lew's part might enrage Vining, provoking him to any of a
number of drastic steps, including the advancement of the date of
Beach's trial and almost sure execution. No matter what approach
they weighed, Lew and Prudence realized that they needed
official U.S. embassy support—or at least permission to testify—
to save Lincoln Beach's life. But how to generate pressure on the
embassy in the face of Washington's orders?

It was Prudence who hatched the plan. Lew, she argued, had
to get in touch with Shannon and Demarest as quickly as he
could. With their mutual interest in Kalya and their sympathy for
the Peace Corps plight in Zinzin, they might exert influence to
get Sherrod's order countermanded. But the commercial cable
and the Kalya mails abroad could not be used safely because of
covert censorship by the Kalya government. And there seemed
scant chance of persuading Milbank to let Corleigh use the embassy's daily air mail pouch to Washington as a vehicle for protesting letters to congressmen. The best procedure, Lew agreed,
was to write Shannon and Demarest at length and then take
the letters to Vining Airport and hope that some passenger for
the United States could be induced to mail the letters upon
arrival.

No, said Prudence, there was a simpler and more dependable
way. She had informed Jim Osterlord, via the short-wave that

morning, of the death of Lettermore's father. Jim had assured
her that he would have Arch packed at once and on his way to
Ft. Paul by the first money bus. The whole situation, she said,
could be explained to Arch, and the letters for Shannon and
Demarest could be entrusted to him.

Lew and Prudence worked past midnight, drafting the letters
which described the incident at the Kalya National theater and its
hectic aftermath. Then they drove to the Peace Corps office,
where Prudence typed the letters in triplicate.

Now, after bringing Lettermore to the airport, Lew watched
while the paunchy Negro, his city suit straining at the seams,
bickered with officious Kalya guardians of the various booths and
counters—outgoing customs, exit visa stamp, tickets, health card
inspection, embarking fee. The big Pan-American jet flew in for
its brief halt en route to Dakar and Washington. Lew walked
Arch to the gate.

"If you get up to Zinzin," said Arch, "stop by my place and
pinch-hit for me on the side of the Lord. Ted gets lonely if he
doesn't have somebody to argue religion with. I'll be back in a
week."

"Williams says to take as long as you have to," said Lew.

Arch grimaced. "The only guys who dig funerals are the under-
takers."

"Special delivery on the letters, Archie."

Lettermore turned out his inner breast pocket. "Stop buggin'
yourself, man. They're next to my heart. . . . So long, whitey."

Then came the long wait for some word from the United
States. If an hourglass had been measuring time, the interval
between each falling grain of sand would have seemed interminable. With no way to make direct contact with Shannon, Demarest or Lettermore, Lew could only speculate and hope. At the
hostel Saturday night, turning restlessly under his mosquito net,
he guessed that Lettermore was already home in the little North
Carolina town near Raleigh. He tried to visualize Arch speaking
to Shannon and Demarest, and mailing the letters from Dulles
Airport, but gave it up when his imagination kept picturing all
sorts of accidents that could nullify the plans.

Sunday dragged at Prudence's house. Lew suggested a game
of gin rummy to speed the hours, but Prudence sniffed that

playing cards was a waste of time. Instead she read a bulky volume on West African anthropology and Lew dawdled alternately over solitaire and a tattered Agatha Christie paperback mystery. He found it difficult to fix his mind on either the game or the story and once, while he was puttering aimlessly about the kitchen, Prudence snapped at him. They quarreled, then blamed it on the humidity and hastily kissed to make up. But neither was in a mood to share her bed, and that night after dinner they speculated on what they should do if no messages ever came from Washington. How long should they wait before they tried another tack? A week was the limit, they decided. Then, Prudence urged, Lew should go direct to Old Number One and threaten to expose the whole story, including Booth's attempt to kill Corleigh with a mamba and the Zinzin sellout. If Vining ignored the threat, Lew should resign from the Peace Corps and fly back to Washington and hold a press conference. In the capital he could attract the largest press audience. Lew agreed, although he had private doubts about the impact a lone Peace Corps volunteer could make on skeptical newspapermen. The mamba incident, especially, would sound more fanciful than plausible in such surroundings.

Monday was gloomier than Sunday, for Prudence had to make a two-day circuit of her district by jeep, and Lew had no one but Sam Zerwick in whom to confide his growing anxieties. Zerwick was sympathetic in his rough, profane way, but he was more concerned about three outcountry teachers who were suffering from some tropical disorder that defied his diagnostic talents.

Tuesday morning Lew got into another abrasive wrangle with Williams. The Peace Corps chief thought that Lew should resume his Zinzin route, now that Washington's order prevented him from helping Lincoln Beach. Why hang around Ft. Paul? Williams demanded irritably. Since he could not tell Williams about the letters to Shannon and Demarest, Lew tried to beg off with vague references to other chores requiring his presence in the capital. When Williams insisted, Lew complained that he was running a fever from unknown causes. Williams assumed his most injured look and his eyes, reflecting his skepticism, accused Lew of malingering.

The afternoon, closing out the fourth day without word of any kind from Washington, ticked by with excruciating slowness.

Lew spent several hours on his refrigerator inventory report, but became so choleric over his own assessment of volunteer morale should the boxes be removed, that he twice tore up what he had written. He paced the reception lobby, drank two Coca-Colas and tried without avail to concentrate on an old copy of *Newsweek*. Had Arch failed him after all? Or had his letter made no impression on Shannon and Demarest? He felt isolated, boxed, as shut off as Beach in his cell.

Then, just as the receptionist was locking her desk for the night, a messenger arrived from the embassy, carrying a manila folder. Lew hovered nearby as the man extracted a small envelope and handed it across the desk.

"I think it may be for me," said Lew, but the girl shook her head and went to Williams' office.

A minute later Williams came to the door and beckoned to Lew. Inside the office Williams eyed Lew without pleasure and closed the door with a bang. He handed Lew a thin, tissuelike sheet, which Lew recognized as a copy from the embassy cable room.

"I'm not very happy about this," said Williams.

PECTO
CARTER WILLIAMS
U.S. EMBASSY
FT. PAUL
KALYA
  Change of instructions per ours of 6/13/1500 Z. PCVL Lewis N. Corleigh authorized to submit affidavit and/or testify exactly what he saw in theater night of Founders Day incident.

  Sherrod

Lew grinned. He could feel the quick thrust of exhilaration within him. Who said you couldn't fight City Hall? Arch Lettermore, thank God, must have kept his pledge to raise either Shannon or Demarest. One or both of them apparently had gone to work in a hurry.

"I know how you feel," said Williams, his face as apprehensive as Lew's was elated. "I can't blame you, but for me, that cable spells trouble with a capital T."

Williams' concern with harmony in Peace Corps-Kalya relations seemed an absurd obsession at this moment. The thought strangled Lew's brief feeling of exhilaration. He stared at Williams.

"A guy's life is at stake," he said curtly.

"What are you going to do now?" asked Williams.

"Take the affidavit over to Archibald Fess."

"First," said Williams, "I think you owe the ambassador the courtesy of notifying him and consulting him. He may want to suggest some procedure. I think you ought to hold off until the first thing in the morning and see Milbank. Then you'll be free to do as you think best."

Williams' attitude implied that whatever Lew did, it would be for the worst, not best. But Lew decided swiftly that, whatever he did later, he would comply with the Peace Corps chief's request. This was no time to bypass channels, especially since embassy support might be needed if the Kalya authorities tried to suppress or discredit the testimony.

"Okay," he said. "I'll go over to the embassy in the morning."

He left Williams standing with a hand on the doorknob and a look of chagrin on his face. Williams seemed to be saying, mutely, that the ordeal was not Beach's, or Lew's, but his own.

But as Lew drove to Prudence's house to await her return from the circuit, he became swept up again in the good news from Washington. Now he could make the move that might save Link's life.

Prudence arrived only a few minutes after Lew parked the jeep in the yard. She was grimy and tired from her trip, but she became jubilant when she heard the news. In a burst of shared triumph, she kissed him again and again, made him repeat exact phrases from the cable and said she was dying to meet Senator Demarest. The senator, she said, must have been responsible. They celebrated with a candle-lit dinner and a bottle of Italian red wine that Prudence had been hoarding. They were both keyed up, looking forward to the next day with nervous hope.

Official Peace Corps mail via embassy pouch always arrived early each day at headquarters, and the next morning it included a letter for Lew. The envelope bore the imprint of the

House of Representatives and it was marked "Personal and Confidential." Lew tore it open at once. It was from Emmett Shannon.

Dear Lew:

Your friend Lettermore got me at home Sunday morning. A more eloquent plea I've never heard. The man should be a preacher of the Gospel.

I took the liberty of telling him to special delivery Demarest's copy to the senator's home instead of his office, but then I drove out to Dulles to pick up my letter from Archie personally. We had a short but useful talk before his plane left, and I think it helped me understand the gravity of the situation there in Kalya.

At any rate, I reached Al Demarest by phone Sunday afternoon. Your letter had arrived that morning and he was very perturbed by the turn of events. I went to his home Sunday night and we had a long session. We agreed 100 per cent with you that this is a kind of microcosm of our whole foreign policy dilemma, and also that this miscarriage of justice in Kalya could not be passed over in silence. We decided that we had to back you up and that Demarest, because of his position on the Foreign Relations Committee, should be the man to carry the ball.

The senator went to work bright and early Monday with calls to the Peace Corps and the White House. He got some static, so he threatened to blow the case wide open in public with a floor speech unless the instructions were changed and you were permitted to testify. Meanwhile I made a few backup calls to some friends at State, just to impress the administration that we meant business.

Skipping the details, our strategy worked better than either of us had dared hope. The White House yielded and authorized the Peace Corps to change its instructions to you. Frank Sherrod called Al and me personally to check out the wording of the cable which went to the Ft. Paul Peace Corps representative and which you undoubtedly know about by now. I had the distinct impression that Sherrod was not unhappy about the switch and that he was privately delighted he could give you the green light.

Of course, it was the mass of detail in your letter that gave us just the ammunition we needed. The attempted assassination of Vining made all the papers here, but the stories were short and carried no hint of a phony shooting. I doubt many people particularly noticed the items, and those who did probably assumed that some dissident nut had taken a pot shot at a strong man in another of those involved African affairs which aren't much understood here.

Please keep us abreast of developments if possible. We're with you and, incidentally, we admire your guts. Good luck— and just tell the truth.

In their previous meetings, Ambassador Milbank had treated Lew with courtesy and a disarming air of give-and-take between friendly equals, but this morning a new element was added. Lew thought he detected a touch of respect in Willard Milbank's attitude as he went through the routine exchange of greetings.

"Are you from New Hampshire, Lew?" he inquired.

"No, Illinois—Evanston," said Lew.

"Oh, I see," said Milbank. He eyed a sheaf of papers which he had centered on his blotter. "That explains this fellow Shannon then, I suppose. Do you know Senator Demarest as well?"

Lew nodded. "I met him one night in Washington on that trip. Well, Shannon too. I talked to both of them at the Jefferson Study Club."

"Mmm." Milbank studied Lew's face as if appraising him anew. "You're a quick learner, young man. You found your way around Washington in a hurry."

"Not really," said Lew. He waited for questions about the manner by which he had enlisted the aid of Demarest and Shannon for Lincoln Beach.

Instead the ambassador squared the papers on his desk, and settled back in his swivel chair.

"Well," said Milbank, "now that you've got the go-ahead, I suppose you want to make tracks for the attorney general's office?"

"With your permission," said Lew.

"You don't really need that now, you know. . . . Let's see, if you get in to see Fess this morning, I'll probably be called over to the Executive Palace this afternoon . . . And if the Peace Corps is still a going concern here next week, we'll be lucky." Milbank was ruminating aloud, seemingly oblivious of Corleigh. "No telling about Old Number One. Depends on his mood. He could blow the roof off, order you to pack up at once and get out . . . Or, again, he may want to palaver. The old man loves deals—any kind. They appeal to his bargaining sense. He knows that he's craftier and smarter than most of the people who want something from him. As I say, it all depends. I wonder . . ."

The ambassador's voice trailed off and, since it had been more soliloquy than conversation, Lew felt no need to say anything. Milbank arose, shook hands and escorted Lew to the door.

"A word of advice, Lew," he said. "If I were you, I'd be quite dignified and correct with Fess. He's the kind who prizes the status of his position."

"Thanks," said Lew. "I appreciate the way you're handling this. I know it means another headache for you."

"That's what I get paid for," said Milbank. "Frankly, Lew, I'm not sorry you knew how to get some action on this." He lowered his voice and looked with mock concern at the closed door. "I wouldn't want this repeated, but I hope you give Vining's outfit a few bad hours. It's about time somebody blew the whistle. Good luck."

The imposing Cathedral of Justice, with its fluted columns, mosaic tile floors and high, marble-faced halls, was physical proof of the high rung which the machinery of the law held in the Kalya scale of values. The legend carved over the entrance, "Justice and Mercy, Blood Brothers Forever," a quotation from founder Horatio Banks, admirably fitted the aspirations of the Republic. If the quotation had thus far chiefly benefited members of The Family, rather than tribesmen caught in the toils of the law, the motto still retained its validity of intent. Justice, after all, was an elusive commodity, and as for mercy, some men obviously merited more of it than others.

The trappings of the law intrigued Kalyans, Family and tribesmen alike, far more than the law itself. Thus the Cathedral housed a complex of sumptuously appointed courts, jury rooms, judges' chambers, bailiff quarters, offices of the various prosecuting attorneys and a huge, domed room where the Superior Court met. The five Superior judges were, however, cramped for space. Lew had been told that the room was jammed with rusting automatic voting machines which an enterprising American vendor once sold to Prime Minister Vining. Old Number One had tried out the machines, with their fascinating levers and automatic curtains, in three Ft. Paul test precincts at the national elections ten years ago. The results were so startling—Vining's subsidized, dummy opponent polled 32 per cent of the vote on the machines as against a national average of less than one per cent in the traditional paper-and-pencil voting booths—that Vining destroyed the returns and announced that the American firm would be compelled to make immediate repairs on the patently faulty machines. That was the last use of the electric ballot, and the machines continued to squat under their canvas hoods like wintering furniture in a summer seaside mansion. Thus limited in space, the Superior Court shortened its annual two-month term to three weeks. The abbreviated term produced no noticeable deterioration in the quality of the Court's judicial opinions, all of which were proofread at the Executive Palace for typographical and other human errors.

The attorney general's office, a hushed suite of rooms with solid red-oak furniture and crystal chandeliers, commanded the marble stairway leading to the third and top floor of the Cathedral. Lew announced himself to the receptionist, a young lady whose jaws moved constantly to accommodate a wad of gum. She disappeared through a heavy, paneled door and returned a few minutes later with the news that Attorney General Archibald Fess was laboring under a particularly burdensome schedule, but would try to spare Mr. Corleigh a few minutes sometime before nightfall.

Lew seated himself beside an end table which held a 1931 paperbound edition of the Kalya criminal laws and a two-year-old *National Geographic* featuring an article on the remnants of Kalya's ancient village iron foundries. Several Kalyans sat on chairs in the chapel-like room, their faces betraying some apprehension, if not outright distrust, about the immutability of the alliance between justice and mercy.

The minutes sidled into an hour and Lew was growing bored with the topless charms of the Kalya females displayed in the magazine. He looked up to find Oliver Downing in whispered conversation with the receptionist. Lew was not surprised, for the omnipresent journalist could turn up almost anywhere along the law's labyrinth in his pursuit of news. Downing, however, was obviously surprised to see Lew in the attorney general's waiting room.

Downing walked over to Lew's chair, his somber expression alert and questioning.

"What brings you here?" he asked in a voice too low for the receptionist to overhear.

"An affidavit," said Lew in similar key. He tapped the suit jacket which he had donned in honor of the occasion. "It's about the Vining shooting. . . . Ollie, Link was framed. I'm here to make a pitch for him."

Downing looked baffled. He motioned with his head. "Come on out in the hall where we can talk. I am tremendously curious."

Downing led him down the hall and they stood shielded behind a pillar. Lew handed Downing the typewritten account, and Downing read it while Lew kept an eye out for Kalya officials who might be passing.

"I wanted to ask your advice on this, Ollie," said Lew, "but Prudence thought it best not to get you involved. On the other hand, you saw me here, and you've got a right to know."

"It is amazing," said Downing. He adjusted his glasses and reread several paragraphs.

"Why?"

Downing dropped his voice still lower. "Because I saw it all too, from the other outside aisle, but I saw something you did not. I actually saw Booth fire the gun with his right hand and then push the pistol into Lincoln's hand."

"For God's sake. I wish . . ."

"I've been debating what to do," said Downing. He handed the papers back to Lew. "I have a great desire to rescue Lincoln, but if I come forward and talk, they will merely find some law I have broken and put me with the leopard too." He shook his head. "I don't know. I confided with Billy Number 15, and he said if I could not evolve an answer, we should call a meeting of The Forge again."

"Don't open your mouth," advised Lew. "Leave it to me, Ollie. The worst they can do to me is chuck me out of the country. Booth wouldn't dare hurt me, not right now anyway."

"But if Fess rejects your paper, as he is almost sure to do?" asked Downing.

"We could bust the case publicly," said Lew. He told of Prudence's idea for a press conference in Washington.

"I'd get out with you, somehow," said Downing with quick enthusiasm. His eyes widened behind the thick lenses. "With a Kalya national affirming a Peace Corps man's story, they'll know it is the full truth."

"Take it easy, Ollie. You're two steps ahead of me. Let's wait and see what Fess does after he hears me and then checks in with Old Number One. We've got time. What do you hear about Link?"

"He's in the section for political prisoners," said Downing. "It's not the worst. He has a toilet, and he gets fed what the warden eats. But my sources say he can see no one, and there are walls between him and other prisoners. But he has not been harmed—yet."

"Listen, Ollie," said Lew. "Let's see what happens with Fess. Then I'll be in touch. Okay?"

Downing nodded. "I can see Fess any time. I will go now and ask him, with much innocence, why an American Peace Corps man is waiting to see him."

Downing emerged from the attorney general's office a few minutes later, frowning over a last-minute note he was jotting in his pad. He nodded almost imperceptibly to Lew and left the room. Soon the receptionist beckoned to Lew and held open the thick, paneled door for him.

The room was immense, at least fifty feet long. The arched windows, with small panes of faintly colored glass, carried out the architectural theme of the Cathedral of Justice. The walls were oak paneled and the tiled, carpetless floors were designed to moderate the Kalya heat. Actually, the room did seem cool in contrast with the brutal insistence of the sun outside.

Archibald Fess looked up from a paper he was signing and smiled a noncommittal greeting. His light brown face was unlined. Lew judged him to be not more than thirty-five years old. He wore the dark blue suit favored by Kalya officials and a sedate tie of silver and black stripes. Fess's demeanor was one of pleasant neutrality and if he showed any emotion, it was in a nervous rippling of his fingers. They scampered about the desk like small children at play. Fess arose and shook hands with the Kalya snap of the index finger.

"I am honored," he said. "My last visit from the Peace Corps was in the person of your esteemed Carter Williams. He had a small problem . . . Some accusation of disreputable conduct against a volunteer by a woman of the night. She was not to be believed . . . A small-small thing. We disposed of the case forthwith. . . . A pleasure to oblige such a worthy institution as the Peace Corps. Your colleagues have bestowed enormous benefits on my country."

"It is a privilege to be granted this interview," responded Lew, recalling Milbank's advice and choosing his words with care. "I realize that your schedule is a crowded one, and I'm grateful you could spare me the time."

"For the Peace Corps, I repeat, it is a pleasure," said Fess. His smile remained fixed, but there was wariness in his eyes. The fingers of one hand trotted to the edge of the desk, performed a tiny dance there. "This is, indeed, a busy morning, but if you require it all, Mr. Corleigh, it is yours."

"I'm afraid my mission is more complicated than Mr. Williams'," said Lew. "I am here, Mr. Attorney General, on a very serious matter. Others have counseled me to hold my peace, but with me this is a matter of conscience. So, of course, I came to you."

"Without a conscience, we would all be animals," said Fess. His smile tightened a trifle.

"I was a witness to the alleged attempted assassination of the Prime Minister," said Lew. "And I have come to you with facts bearing on that unfortunate episode."

Fess's smile did not quite mask his surprise. A hand moved to his shirt front and the fingers purled about the tie. "I note with approval," he said, "that you use the word 'alleged.' That is the restrained, mature approach. The trial has not been held yet. In Kalya, every man is presumed innocent until proved guilty."

"Actually, Mr. Attorney General, from what I saw, I believe that Lincoln Beach is innocent. But in this paper I make no judgment." He drew the affidavit from his pocket and handed it to Fess. "I merely state the facts as I saw them."

"Very wise, very wise indeed." Fess took the document like a man being asked to accept a platter of scorpions. He placed the papers cautiously in the center of his desk, ran his fingers around the edges, reached for a pair of black-framed spectacles and fitted them to his nose and ears with elaborate care.

"If you'll pardon me a few minutes," he said.

He read slowly, occasionally hunching forward and drumming on the desk with his fingers. When he finished, he pushed the affidavit far out on the desk as if seeking to place its contents beyond the limits of the law. When he looked up at Lew, the fixed smile was gone. The attorney general's face was as blankly equivocal as a placid sea of early morning.

"Of course," he said judiciously, "this is not a true affidavit under the terms of Kalya law. It would have to be notarized before an attorney of this department and affixed with the national seal. A technicality, you may say, Mr. Corleigh, but what is the law but orderly process?"

"I assumed there was some legal provision I was not aware of," said Lew, "but naturally I'm prepared to comply with it at once."

"Unfortunately, there is more to it than that," said Fess gravely. "Affidavits from foreigners, under Kalya law, must be witnessed by the chief of mission of the deponent's country, in this case, your gracious ambassador Milbank. Again, a bothersome technicality, but one on which the courts here are particularly insistent."

"I see," said Lew. "Well, I can get that done this afternoon and bring it back tomorrow for the notarizing. After all, there's plenty of time before the trial."

"Ah, the trial." Fess's fingers reached toward the affidavit, then beat a slow retreat. "That too presents certain problems from your point of view. Under a Superior Court decision, an affidavit cannot be offered in court if the person who signed the document is able-bodied, competent of mind and available to testify in person."

"That's really no problem. Frankly, I'd rather testify than have the paper read. I don't mind at all opening myself up to cross-examination."

"Oh, but you see, that too would not be possible." Fess sighed as he shook his head. "Under Kalya law, a non-citizen can testify in a court of law of the Republic only in his own self-defense or in a criminal case in which a member of his immediate family is the accused.

"Now, admittedly, this presents a seeming contradiction. You could not have your affidavit accepted by the court, but neither could you testify in person. It is one of those lamentable legal contradictions which we find in all countries." Fess sighed again. "We take the fundamentals of our law from the West, where such cul-de-sacs are not unknown either, as no doubt you are aware."

Fess's voice was faintly accusatory. If there was an incongruity, he seemed to be saying, it was the fault of the West, not of Kalya.

"As a matter of fact," continued the attorney general, "this collision of procedural provisions has struck me as so patently unfair that I intend to present a test case to the Superior Court at its next session."

"And when will that be?" asked Lew. He felt like a man trying to extricate himself from quicksand.

"Not until next spring," said Fess. He was a well of regret.

Lew had a mental image of the attorney general lecturing the Court on the law's inequities while the five justices sat brooding above the cloth-covered mounds of abandoned voting machines. Lew knew that Fess's presentation would be a learned one.

"So there is no way for me to present my eyewitness account at Beach's trial?" asked Lew.

"Lamentably—and most unfairly—no," said Fess. He spoke like a physician informing a patient that the operation would be useless. His fingers beat a fatalistic tattoo on the arm of his chair. "It is especially painful for me personally to have to inform you of this, because my admiration for the Peace Corps is unbounded."

Lew recalled a boyhood afternoon at the circus and his absorption with the high-wire performer. The man, with a leonine mane of hair, had dropped into the net below the wire. His feet seemed to sink further with each step and it appeared he would be enmeshed there forever. But suddenly he grasped the edge of the net and swung himself easily to the ground. It was time to swing away from Archibald Fess's juristic web.

"I anticipated that there might be difficulties," said Lew, "so I decided on my next step. In the event I can't get my evidence before the court, I would feel forced to resign from the Peace Corps, return to the United States and present the facts at a press conference before both American and European correspondents. Also, you should know that I have at least one Kalya citizen who is prepared to accompany me and present corroborating material."

Fess could not hide his look of astonishment. He cleared his throat before he asked: "And do the American authorities—Mr. Williams and Ambassador Milbank—know of this decision?"

"Not exactly," replied Lew, "but they know I'm determined to tell the truth somehow. I have been given official permission to present this affidavit to you."

"Well, well. That indeed throws an entirely different light on the situation." Fess's face reflected the new light. His broad smile was one of relief. "In that case, we're at the international level, aren't we? We have climbed considerably above the station where you and I could make the appropriate decisions. I shall be forced to consult the Executive Palace, refer the matter upward, so to speak. After all, this has become a government-to-government matter."

"I assumed that would be the outcome of our meeting," said Lew. He could not suppress the tartness in his voice. Negotiating with the attorney general was like trying to spoon a fly from a pot of glue.

"Well!" Fess stood up and beamed at Lew. "May I take the original document—we can hardly, of course, describe it as an affidavit—to the Palace? I'm sure the Prime Minister will want to peruse it at his leisure."

"Sure," said Lew. "I've got three carbon copies."

Fess frowned. "A normal precaution, I suppose. . . . Well, Mr. Corleigh, once more, it has been a pleasure. It is this kind of meeting, the cross-fertilization resulting from discussion between men of good will of varying cultures and traditions, that makes the Peace Corps so valuable. . . . I assure you there will be no delay in your matter."

Nor was there. At eight o'clock that night, at the moment that Lew fell asleep at the hostel, Ambassador Willard Milbank was ushered by a houseboy into the air-conditioned penthouse apartment of Prime Minister Alexander Vining.

Milbank had been there a number of times for the stilted, agonizingly formal, receptions which Vining staged for the diplomatic corps and high government officials, most recently on the

night of the shooting at Kalya National. This was, however, the
first time Milbank had been summoned to a private audience in
the Prime Minister's home. His previous conferences with Vining
had all taken place in the rather spartan office on a lower floor.

Stepping from the private elevator, Milbank saw again the cool
sweep of rooms which paraded to Vining's study—the tiled lobby,
the huge living room, the dining room with its long tigerwood
table. One side was a sea of glass, for the rooms all fronted on the
parapet of the Executive Palace. From a stone wall, perhaps only
three feet high, the glass extended upward another fifteen feet to
the roof, yielding a panorama of the city below. The glass was so
clear from its daily washings that Milbank always had the queasy
sensation of standing on the edge of a cliff with a sheer canyon
below. The grandeur of the view was only slightly diminished by
Milbank's knowledge that the glass was bulletproof and that it
vastly increased the cost of air-conditioning the apartment at a time
when Kalya was so near insolvency that foreign banks were refus-
ing further credits.

For all of Vining's ferocious chauvinism, there was little of
Kalya in the decor of the apartment save for the predominating
national colors of yellow and red. The furnishings, installed by a
Parisian interior decorator, were severely modern. The armless
lounges, deep basket chairs, tiny pillows and hanging brass lighting fixtures might have as easily dressed affluent homes in Paris,
New York, Copenhagen or London. Since Kalya itself was as
yet impoverished in the arts, the paintings on the walls presented
an expensive international face—Chagall, Siqueiros, Pollock,
Klee, Le Brun and one Picasso.

Milbank knew that the apartment contained four ornately appointed bathrooms and a splendid, tiled kitchen with all the latest
electrical devices. As he walked toward the Prime Minister's
study behind the softly padding houseboy, Milbank mused again
on the change which Vining and his sumptuous penthouse sym-
bolized. Vining had been reared in a Ft. Paul that was little more
than a bush town, a filthy, festering place where The Family and
tribesmen alike drank creek water that was polluted with sewage.
Ft. Paul changed but little in the first six decades of Vining's life.
The first flush toilet and first automobiles had arrived only fifteen

years ago, the first electrical appliances even later. And now, this. . . .

The houseboy bowed low at the open door of Vining's study, ushering Milbank into the presence, then closing the door discreetly behind him. Save for the spectacular expanse of glass on one side, the room's walls were solid with books from floor to ceiling. Vining sat behind a mahogany desk on which rested a single document and an unlighted brass desk lamp fashioned into a leopard rampant with dangling scales of justice. The room was lighted indirectly from hidden ceiling fixtures, and the softly diffused glow simulated the delicate tones of early evening.

The air of quiet forbearance ended abruptly at Vining's person. He sat with his heavy shoulders hunched forward in the tailored dark blue suit coat. The massive face bore no smile of greeting, and above the beaked nose, his eyes seemed to drill into Milbank. Vining delayed perceptibly before rising, and when he did, it was with a small, stiff bow.

"I'm honored that you could come on such short notice, Mr. Ambassador," said Vining with wintry formality.

Milbank noted the title—he had always been "Willard" at these conferences—and the brief duration of Vining's handclasp. It was a mere prelude to motioning Milbank to a chair placed several yards distant from Vining's desk.

"The honor and pleasure is mine, Mr. Prime Minister," said Milbank. As he seated himself, he was aware that Vining's eyes fixed his like magnets. The black, bald head, with its fringe of white hair, could have been a wharf piling from which the tide had receded. Vining sat immobile for long moments.

Then, suddenly, he seized the document on his desk and tossed it contemptuously to the corner nearest Milbank.

"That is the so-called affidavit from your Mr. Corleigh of the Peace Corps," said Vining. His voice was low, taut, forcibly controlled. "As I recall, he also figured in that outrageous Peace Corps political meddling in Zinzin. Quite an emissary of good will is your Mr. Corleigh from Chicago—in all the ripeness and sagacity of his twenty-seven years."

Vining arose from his desk, walked to the window, looked out for a moment, then wheeled toward Milbank.

"Did you authorize that young man to take his package of lies to Archibald Fess today?" he asked. His voice quivered.

"Yes," said Milbank quietly. "Washington at first prohibited him from intervening, but yesterday the orders were countermanded. Corleigh, however, is acting entirely on his own. The embassy is not involved."

"Not involved?" It was a roar. Vining gripped the edge of the desk. "Milbank, what kind of imperialistic gall impels the U.S. government to give official sanction to this brash upstart? Who are these high-handed, insolent men in Washington who think they can interfere in the domestic affairs of a sovereign nation?"

The rhetorical questions were flung at Milbank like lances. "Do you realize precisely what your Mr. Corleigh has done in this vicious document? . . .

"He has branded Colonel Hulbert Booth a liar and a thug. . . .

"He has implied, and not very subtly, that the chief of my security police would frame an innocent man. . . .

"He has indicated that the Democratic Justice party of Kalya would send an innocent man to his death merely to rid itself of inconsequential political opposition. . . .

"He has taken the part of a known, Communist-trained saboteur, Lincoln Beach, against the lawful security forces of this country. . . .

"And not content with putting such depraved accusations on paper, he had the effrontery to tell Attorney General Fess that if his affidavit were not honored in the Kalya courts, he would resign from the Peace Corps, return home and hold a press conference. That, sir, is blackmail!"

Vining pounded a fist in his palm to emphasize the point.

"I hardly think those interpretations are justified, sir," said Milbank. "Corleigh's affidavit merely sets out factually what he saw. While I have no personal knowledge of the facts, I would like to say in his behalf . . ."

"You're not telling me, Mr. Ambassador," broke in Vining. It was a shout. "I'm telling you. And I hope you repeat every word I say verbatim to Washington. What exactly is your government up to? What is the hidden motive? Are you, for some strange reason unknown to me, trying to jettison your best friend in Africa?"

Again came the bursting rhetorical questions, hurled at Milbank in a harsh voice. Oddly, Milbank had the impression that two men were raging at him, for on the great windowpane he could see the reflection of Vining's bald head, gleaming like a dark sapphire.

"Do you want Kalya to desert you at the United Nations?" barked Vining.

"Do you want us to reject your USAID dollars? . . .

"Throw out the Peace Corps? . . .

"Expel every U.S. agency from Kalya soil? . . .

"Do you want me to eject Itambel? . . .

"Or perhaps tax my good friend Horace Magruder to the wall? I can do that, you know, with the stroke of a pen. . . .

"Do you want every U.S. concession bundled out of the country? . . .

"Is it your game to force the Republic of Kalya to turn elsewhere for the help and funds it needs to become a self-supporting nation? . . .

"Or perhaps you'd like the five hundred American missionaries ordered home—never to return?"

On came the questions, thrown at the U.S. ambassador so swiftly that they lost their individual identity. The single shafts became a barrage. Milbank marveled at Vining's ability to enunciate so clearly while in a temper tantrum, though he knew that the Prime Minister had been one of the first Kalyans to be sent abroad for schooling—University of Michigan, then Princeton for a master's degree in . . . political science, wasn't it? Vining, pausing only long enough to renew his breath, shot his questions over every facet of U.S.-Kalya relations, from the trade treaty down to such a minute token as the information clearinghouse on U.S. fellowships which was operated in Ft. Paul by the CARE representative.

The cold fury which marked the Prime Minister at the outset had long since turned hot. He pounded the desk. He paced the floor, often turning suddenly to shoot an accusing finger at Milbank. He scornfully recalled his state visit to Washington, when the pledges of eternal friendship outnumbered the twenty-one guns of his salute. He stressed his magnanimity in his talk with Milbank which resolved the Zinzin dispute. Once he strode to a bookshelf, extracted a brochure which cataloged the extent of U.S. commercial interests in Kalya and threw it into Milbank's lap.

Again, he stood directly over the ambassador, demanding to know why he did not answer, yet not pausing long enough to permit Milbank to open his mouth. Milbank, huddled in his chair, had the feeling that Vining had been blustering at him for an hour, although logic told him it could not have been more than ten minutes.

Then abruptly, like a fireworks display that has spent itself in the vault of night, the harangue ended. Vining ceased his pacing and sat down heavily in his chair. He folded his hands on the edge of the desk in an obvious effort to compose himself. His chest rose and fell, and he stared fixedly at Milbank as if he were in a trance. Milbank waited—until he became conscious that a clock was ticking so loudly it could have been a spoon beating on a dishpan.

"Mr. Prime Minister," he said, "I cannot answer for Washington directly. What I know of its reasoning was obtained from one dispatch which did little more than indicate that Lewis Corleigh had official permission to present his story. But while you were talking, I did reflect some about the nature of my own government. Do you mind if I give you some of my thinking?"

"No!" It was more of a challenge than an assent. Vining was still breathing deeply.

Slowly, in a tone he hoped had soothing qualities, Milbank began to explain the fabric of American government, the separation of powers, the roles of the legislative, judicial and executive branches, the ingrained distrust of any concentration of power that upset the historic balance.

"I know all that," said Vining impatiently. "Please don't talk down to me as if I were a child. Get to the point."

"I'm sorry," said Milbank. "I was really trying to explain aloud to myself. The background is necessary to understand the Peace Corps. The late President Kennedy established it as an independent agency in 1961. Right from the outset, there was a full understanding that the Peace Corps would never be used as a foreign policy tool. The volunteers were to be sent out to help the peoples of other lands, period. Regardless of the temptation, no other branch of government was ever to use or manipulate the Peace Corps for its own aims, whatever they might be."

Milbank hunched forward in his chair. "In the five years of

its existence, the Peace Corps has never been used for ulterior purposes. Not once. The pledge has been kept. Regardless of what Mr. Nkrumah used to say in Ghana, the Peace Corps has never spied, never been allied with other U.S. agencies, never tried to subvert a government to further American ambitions."

Vining grunted. Milbank inched forward in his chair and appealed to Vining with a gesture of open palms. "Look, Mr. Prime Minister, let me remind you of a discussion we had last winter. Remember our talk about the Dominican Republic? You denounced the intervention of American troops, and you said the U.S. government had prostituted the grand ideals it was always proclaiming. Without endorsing that view, I replied—remember? —that you must specifically exempt the Peace Corps from any such charge. Once the military tried to use the Peace Corps for a secret survey of some kind, but Sargent Shriver, then the Peace Corps director, flatly refused. The Peace Corps was trusted by both sides in the Dominican Republic, and nothing was allowed to disturb the fine relationship between the volunteers and the people they worked with. Then I said we had the same situation in Kalya, and, Mr. Prime Minister, you agreed with me."

Vining flicked his wrist dismissively. "I remember the talk and my praise for the Peace Corps here," he said, "but I fail to see the connection." He was much calmer now. His breathing had returned to normal. "I think, Willard, you're engaging in an old American practice. You call it filibustering, don't you?"

The casual use of his first name heartened Milbank. Perhaps the bomb had been defused.

"I'm not filibustering," said Milbank with a grateful smile. "I'm just building up to my central point—and that point is the character of the young man involved here—Mr. Lewis Corleigh. With all deference to your estimate of him, Mr. Prime Minister, let me try to give my own personal appraisal. I sincerely think that Lew Corleigh, this red-haired, suburban boy from Chicago, is an epitome of the best qualities in the Peace Corps. He's idealistic yet practical. He is dedicated without being a fanatic. He's involved in the lives of the poor tribal people of Kalya— the same people you've done so much to help, sir. Lew Corleigh just naturally assumes he should oppose any threat to individual liberties. Now, and here's the real point, Corleigh is convinced he saw exactly what he's outlined in that paper. He may be wrong. I think it's entirely possible that he is . . . but he is not lying. He is not involved in any machinations of policy. All he wants to do is tell the truth as he sees it."

Milbank could see that Vining was about to erupt again, so he hurried on. "Let me appeal to you as one diplomat to another, Mr. Prime Minister. My government is deeply embarrassed by Corleigh's statement here." He pointed to the corner of the desk where the affidavit still rested on the spot where Vining had tossed it. "We don't want a breach in the excellent relations between Kalya and the United States."

"Then, by God, why do you let him go ahead?" demanded Vining.

"Because," said Milbank, "we're powerless to stop him. Corleigh is one of those men who are looked up to as the all-American ideal, as a man who can't be bought off or dissuaded from doing what he thinks is right. And if he can't have his say in court, he'll have it someplace else. In brief, we're confronted with a young man of conscience—and we can't stop him."

"Very fine speech, Willard," said Vining drily. He folded his hands on his stomach and leaned back in his chair. He was the patriarch now, patient, calm, judicious. The fringe of white hair seemed again a wreath of benevolence.

"There's only one trouble with it," said Vining in his familiar deep voice which measured each phrase like a bank teller counting money. "If you're not telling a falsehood, you are coming mighty close to it." He paused for effect, peering at Milbank to gauge his reaction. "Nobody can tell me that the great United States government, with all its space rockets, atomic bombs and aircraft carriers, can't control one young man from Chicago."

"If he were a soldier under military discipline, perhaps," said Milbank. "But Corleigh is an individual member of the Peace Corps with the same right of free speech as any other citizen." Milbank paused. "Besides, he has a potential for—well, shall we say—friction back in Washington."

"You mean powerful friends in the White House?" Vining flashed the shrewd, intuitive look Milbank knew so well.

"In the Congress is more likely." Milbank tried to sound vague, but he thought of the State Department dispatch and its account

of the sudden interest of Demarest and Shannon. "Unlike the
Prime Minister of Kalya, the President of the United States is
not a free agent. He must deal with constant pressures."

"And some of those pressures come from politicians who think
I'm a ruthless old tyrant, is that it?"

"I'd put it another way," said Milbank cautiously. "They are
congenitally opposed to any semblance of one-man rule. The fact
that they do not understand the special demands and circumstances here in Kalya is immaterial to them. They are ideologists
primarily. Still, they have influence and they must be reckoned
with."

"And you think I don't have pressures too, Willard?" It was
another rhetorical question, but put without heat. The tone was
quietly philosophical. "You know my problems. On the one hand,
the Molas, the Fizis, the Mandingos. On the other, The Family.
Sometimes I wonder how I've managed. The Molas, especially,
need to be brought slowly into government."

His voice rose suddenly. "But that young firebrand Mola,
Lincoln Beach, wants to change things overnight. I've got
pretty good evidence that he's in some kind of secret underground
formed to destroy me. You've got the same data, I believe, in
your CIA files. . . . And those leaflets the other day were curiously
familiar. They read like Beach has been known to talk. . . .
And now, to top everything, he tries to assassinate me. And
you want me to let the Kalya courts entertain this flimsy, baseless
story from your young crusader, Mr. Corleigh?"

Milbank recalled Vining's cool, poised posture on the stage of
Kalya National theater after the shot shattered the huge globe
above him. Did Vining know in advance that the shot would be
fired? There was no question that Vining was a man of courage,
yet how else to explain his unruffled demeanor? . . . Or, if he
did not know in advance, did he really believe Lincoln Beach
fired the shot? Had the thought crossed his mind that perhaps
Booth did frame an innocent man? Milbank decided to probe
delicately.

"Let me presume to ask a frank question, Mr. Prime Minister,"
he said. "Did you see the shot fired the other night?"

"No," said Vining promptly, "but I saw the weapon in

Lincoln Beach's hand immediately afterward. Nobody else could have pulled the trigger."

"But suppose Corleigh is right—and Colonel Booth did fire the shot, then place the gun in Beach's hand?"

"Impossible," said Vining with a snort of derision. "Colonel Booth told me exactly what happened. He is a man of honor. Lincoln Beach tried to kill me. Hulbert deflected his hand just in time."

"The colonel, of course," said Milbank, "would have no motive in trying to stage an attempted assassination so that the blame would fall on Beach."

"None," said Vining.

Milbank wondered. Did he detect a flicker of doubt? No, the massive face was fixed in a mask of certainty.

"So you refuse to call off Mr. Corleigh?" asked Vining.

"As I explained, I can't."

"I could order him out of the country tomorrow," said Vining. He had retrieved the affidavit and was fingering it. Milbank recognized Vining's tentative tone. It signified he was in a mood to bargain.

"Then, I suppose, Corleigh would go ahead with his plan to hold a press conference in Washington."

"Mmm." Vining deliberated a moment, his expression as smoothly pensive as it had formerly been bunched in rage. "Willard, our relations have been of the best—I mean personal, as well as those between Ft. Paul and Washington."

"I know that, sir," said Milbank quickly. "There will always be bruises, but I would never want to see anything resembling a rupture."

"Then let's discuss this rationally—as friends." Vining clothed each word in the vestments of sincerity.

Milbank relaxed inwardly. His hand went to his coat pocket and he fingered a slip of paper there. On it was written the figure $23,040,000—the latest estimate of annual U.S. aid of all types in Kalya. He had been prepared to mention the precise figure. He was thankful now that would not be necessary.

"I would like nothing better," he said. "We've always resolved our differences fairly in the past."

Vining nodded. "Do you have any suggestions, Willard?"

"Yes, I do." Milbank had done his mental homework before leaving the embassy. "Corleigh's paper creates an unfortunate contradiction in testimony. Its repercussions can be needlessly embarrassing to both governments. Therefore, why not obviate that entirely. Suppose, for instance, I could persuade young Corleigh to destroy his document and never to allude to it again? And suppose, in return, you dismissed the charges against Beach?"

"Absolutely not." Vining said it without heat, but with unmistakable emphasis.

"Why not? It seems to me to be eminently reasonable."

"You forget, my friend," said Vining, "that Lincoln Beach tried to kill me."

Milbank studied the impassive face. If there had been collusion between the Prime Minister and Hulbert Booth prior to the shot, Vining was a superb actor. No, Vining was convinced of Beach's guilt. If Milbank thought he had seen a flash of doubt earlier, he had been mistaken.

"I have my own proposal," said Vining. "If your Mr. Corleigh will agree to tear up his paper—it is not an affidavit, you know—I will give my word that if Beach is convicted, I will commute the death sentence to twenty years in prison. Furthermore, he will not be harmed in any way—ever."

"Twenty years in Kpali!" said Milbank. "Mr. Prime Minister, he would never come out alive."

"I came within a few feet of not leaving the Kalya National alive," said Vining dispassionately.

There was silence. Both men gazed at each other. On the desk rested the lamp, the brass leopard holding the scales of justice in his mouth. Milbank thought the animal's expression to be less menacing than canny.

"No other suggestions, Willard?" asked Vining.

"Well . . ." Milbank hesitated. "I had hoped there could have been more . . . well, more leniency in view of the discrepancy of the evidence."

"I'm sorry," said Vining, "but attempted murder is a crime. It is not a misdemeanor . . ." He smiled wryly. ". . . even in Kalya."

"I'm in a curious position here," said Milbank. "My main

concern is to preserve the fine working relationship between two governments. But also, in a sense, I'm acting as an agent for a private citizen of the United States. And if I know Corleigh, I'm afraid he won't be willing to trade what he believes to be the truth for a twenty-year prison sentence for Beach."

"The judgment of the young is notoriously faulty," said Vining. He paused. "And however his story came out, it would be overwhelmingly contradicted. Attorney General Fess tells me he already has seven witnesses who will testify they saw Beach try to shoot me."

"Still," said Milbank, "from your viewpoint, it would plant the seeds of doubt among some tribesmen."

"I realize that," said Vining. "Frankly, I was a bit surprised at the excitement those leaflets caused in some quarters. Nothing serious, but . . ."

"But a little doubt can be poisonous," said Milbank. "As I see it, both your government and mine have something substantial to be gained if that affidavit is never made public."

"That is what I've been trying to tell you for the last half hour."

Milbank smiled. "And I've been telling you that we have no control over Lew Corleigh."

"Nonsense." But Vining smiled too. Milbank knew he was fencing.

"The Peace Corps has been good for my country," observed Vining. "It is especially popular in the Mola territory. More than one Mola leader has expressed his gratitude to me for bringing the Peace Corps to Kalya."

"And Lincoln Beach is a Mola." Milbank tried to make the observation sound casual.

Vining eyed him sharply, then smiled. There was guile in his expression now. "I'm perfectly aware of that. I alluded to it earlier."

"What about exile?" asked Milbank. He hoped it sounded as though it were a sudden idea.

"I've thought of that," said Vining. "Precisely what do you have in mind?"

"Corleigh burns the affidavit and pledges never to mention it again," said Milbank slowly. "In return, you quash the charges against Beach—in deference to his Mola boyhood perhaps—and exile him for six months."

The scales held by the brass leopard wavered slightly in a current of air from the humming wall air-conditioning machine.

"Five years," said Vining.

"One year."

"Three," said Vining.

"Two years," said Milbank. "That would carry you just beyond the next national election."

"I don't care for that implication, Willard," said Vining. "I refuse to consider anything less than three years."

"Three years then," said Milbank. "May I consider that a deal?"

Vining nodded. "Provided, of course, that Mr. Corleigh destroys the paper and all copies and agrees never to disclose the contents."

Vining arose, walked across the room and pressed the button for the houseboy. Milbank joined him at the doorway, and they shook hands.

"One further thing," said Milbank. "Does Corleigh have your permission to visit Beach at the jail and discuss this with him?"

"Of course."

"You're a reasonable man, Mr. Prime Minister." At his eye level, Milbank could see the whole expanse of Vining's glossy, bald head. He kept forgetting how much shorter Vining was.

"'Reasonable' is hardly the word," said Vining. "I am about to free a man who tried to kill me."

"Perhaps not. There is always the chance that Lew Corleigh actually saw what he believes he saw."

"That's inconceivable," said Vining.

"Well," said Milbank with a hand on the doorknob. "Now it's up to Corleigh. I can only recommend that he accept your offer. I can't force him. I have no control over him."

"That too is inconceivable." But this time Vining grinned.

Over the Prime Minister's shoulder as they said their goodnights, Milbank caught a last glimpse of the brass leopard. He too seemed to be grinning. And the scales of justice were swaying in his jaws.

21

Prime Minister Vining's word was good. There was no delay the next morning at the jail, a converted fortress dating from the days when The Family warred against the fractious tribes.

The Family had finally won control of the Ft. Paul area with the aid of a single cannon, purchased from the French, which once fired with erratic ferocity. The rusted gunpiece now crouched arthritically above the entrance of the square structure which had been built in the era before concrete. The prison was not so much a building as a huge, mud-stick quadrangle, fifteen feet thick in places, which embraced a bare, rutted courtyard. The cells were cavelike burrows which had been dug out of the wall. No windows had been cut on the street side of the jail, and thus prisoners saw light only through the courtyard doorways. Even here the light was halved, for the doors consisted of heavy wooden planking at the bottom and iron bars at the upper half.

From the prison entrance, where four Kalyans in limp army uniforms took turns trying to spell his name for the prison ledger and inspecting his Peace Corps credentials, Lew was led by a corporal to a cell at the far end of the yard. The man carried a circle of chicken wire from which dangled a thicket of mammoth keys. The corporal tried one after another, grousing to himself, until he found one that fit. He held the door open for Lew, closed it behind him, but did not lock it. He squatted on his haunches, facing Beach's cell, about twenty yards out in the yard, and began picking at the toes of his bare feet with a knife.

Lincoln Beach stood in the center of the dirt-walled room. In the half light, Lew could see that he still wore the white shirt and dark trousers in which he had been arrested. His suit coat hung on a wall peg. The only furnishings were a washstand with basin, a sheetless army cot and a small metal container with toilet seat on its upper rim.

Beach himself appeared unchanged save for a cut at the corner of his mouth. His face, with its rich brown coloring, was newly shaven, and little smile creases fanned from the brown eyes. Beach shook hands with a tight squeeze and the Kalya index-finger snap, then patted Lew on the back.

"Long time no see, man," he said. "You're my first visitor."

Lew pointed to the mouth cut. "Did they give you a working over?"

Beach shook his head. "Not in here. I got that in the theater. Booth cracked me in the mouth with his elbow." He opened his lips wide and pointed to an eyetooth. "Loosened that one. I guess I'll have to have it pulled. Otherwise I'm okay."

Beach's eyes questioned and Lew said quickly: "I know you were framed, Link. I saw what happened. So did Ollie Downing."

"Thank God you did," said Beach. "I haven't heard a word. They wouldn't let me have a lawyer. I was afraid nobody knew and that I'd be shipped to Kpali before . . ."

"We're working for you," broke in Lew. "In fact, we've got a deal out of Old Number One. But first, let's hear more about you. How they treating you? Ollie says you have a toilet."

Beach pointed to the cylindrical container. "I do," he said cheerfully. "They empty it twice a day. Very hygienic."

"And no rough stuff?"

"Nothing," said Beach. "The corporal's the only man I see and he treats me fine. Three meals a day, same as the warden. Fresh water for the basin morning and night. Of course, we don't talk much. He's a Gnebe. That's all he can speak, and I don't know the language. . . . Oh, hell. I do miss reading. I'd give a hundred bucks for a book."

"Then you owe me two hundred," said Lew. He produced two paperbacks from his hip pockets, De Tocqueville's *Democracy in America*, and Thoreau's *Walden*. "That's about all I could find in the hostel book locker. The outcountry teachers carry them off and forget to bring them back."

"What a man!" If Lew had brought papers releasing Beach from prison at once, he could not have been more grateful.

Beach placed the books on the washstand, then motioned to the cot. "Let's relax in my living room," he said, "while you give me the word."

Lew told everything germane that had happened since Beach was dragged out of the Kalya National by two security policemen. Except for a few questions, Beach made no comment. He hunched forward on the cot, his elbows on his knees, and appeared to study the earthen floor. Lew wound up giving as exact an account as he could of Milbank's conference with Vining.

"I think that's everything," he said. "Milbank's driver got me out of bed last night and took me to the embassy, so I wasn't too sharp. . . . Haven't had much shut-eye recently. . . . But I don't think Milbank held anything back from me. . . . And so, that's the deal. If we burn the affidavit and shut up about what really happened, you get off with three years in exile—assuming Old Number One doesn't come up with some new gimmick."

Beach shook his head. "He won't. He boasts he's never broken a promise, and with the American ambassador his word would be solid. . . . Strange thing, Lew. Maybe it's being cooped up here alone, but I had a wild idea that The Forge might bust me out of here some night. But then I realized I was just daydreaming. . . ."

"To be honest, Link," interrupted Lew, "The Forge doesn't amount to a damn without you. Ollie and Billy Number 15 talked some about a meeting, according to Ollie, but you can bet nothing much would have happened."

"I know." Beach continued to stare at the packed dirt of the floor. "But if somebody did get me out, so what? This isn't a big country. No place to hide, unless you want to dog it to some mountain village where you couldn't operate anyway. No, I'd just have to beat it over the border. Anyway you look at it, I guess it means exile."

"Milbank called the deal 'reasonable,'" said Lew. "Personally, I think it stinks. First they try to frame you, and when they get mousetrapped doing that, they pack you out of the country for three years. Milbank thinks there was no put-up job between Vining and Booth. He says Vining is convinced that you tried to kill him. That's hard to believe. Old Number One was one cool customer on the stage that night."

"No," said Beach, "it could be. Old Number One has a lot of guts. And I can't see Booth having the nerve to suggest an assassination frame-up to Vining. The two men just aren't that thick. . . . Nobody trusts anybody too far in Kalya, thanks to Old Number One. . . . I think Milbank is probably right."

"In that case, you have no choice but to accept, do you?"

"Well, of course," said Beach, "you could go ahead with your plan to hold a press conference in the States. But first, if I know Fess, he would parade not seven, but more like seventy, witnesses at my trial, all claiming they saw me shoot at Old Number One. So when you sounded off, you'd be the one guy against seventy. And I mean one. Ollie could never get out of the country. They wouldn't let him. Furthermore, Ollie's use to The Forge would be shot. They'd watch him like hawks from now on. And right now, we need him. He's the only Family boy we've got."

Beach gripped the edge of the cot and looked at Lew. "And, meanwhile back at the ranch, I'd be dead. What good would that do? Even if I didn't mind being shot, which—god-damn it—I do. Without me, the only men capable of running The Forge are Ollie or Billy Number 15, maybe Steve Muo. They're all good men, but frankly, the wheels don't go around too fast up here." He tapped his head, then paused a moment. "Kalya's no country for martyrs, and I'm not martyr material anyway."

"Alive you're worth ten dead ones," said Lew.

"Maybe, maybe not," said Beach. "I've got another problem too, Lew. It's Cindy. I can't get that girl out of my mind. It's worse here. I think of her constantly."

"I know what you mean. Cindy's special."

Beach stood up. "Well, then, that's it, isn't it? We accept the offer?"

Lew nodded. "I'll go along with anything you say."

"Okay," said Beach. "Get word to Old Number One that he's got a deal. When does he spring me out of here?"

"He told Milbank 'next week.' I'll try to nail it down to a specific day, say Monday."

"All right. And if you get in another trip to Zinzin, how about talking Cindy into coming back to Ft. Paul with you?"

"She'd better," said Lew, "or I'll kidnap her."

They parted with another handshake, but this time Beach continued to hold the grip.

"I won't forget what you did for me, Red," he said. "You could just as easily have ducked the whole thing. I'm not sure any of my Kalya friends would have come through for me like that."

Would they? Lew wondered. Ollie had offered to substantiate Lew's story, but would Ollie have gone it alone? Perhaps it would be impossible for a Kalyan to understand that Lew himself had never once considered the possibility of remaining silent. But Kalya lived too close to the bone to nourish such concepts as loyalty, conscience, honor. Two peoples, two ways of life, shaped by the centuries and by history.

"I was just lucky," said Lew. "I happened to be looking at you when Beach grabbed your arm. All I did was report what I saw. I wasn't risking much—except maybe being shipped home."

"You saved my life," said Beach. "I wouldn't have had a chance at the trial."

"Any time," said Lew. They both grinned.

Beach called to the guard, who was still squatting in the sun, absorbed in his toenail excavations. The corporal locked the door behind Lew and escorted him back to the entrance office, where the four army officers crowded around Lew while he signed the "out" column of the moldy ledger.

Lew drove to the Peace Corps office, was admitted at once to Williams' office and told him of Beach's decision. Lew knew he could save time by reporting directly to Ambassador Milbank, but he also sensed that Williams had begun to chafe over his own indifferent role in the negotiations. Williams did, indeed, seem grateful that Lew checked in with him first, thus sweeping the Peace Corps chief back into the tides of diplomacy. Williams made a few notes, then hurried off to inform the ambassador.

Within two hours, Williams returned with the news: Everything was settled. Lew was to burn the affidavit and all carbon copies in the presence of Ambassador Milbank. Beach would be released Monday morning and given time to collect his belongings before the evening plane to Lagos. The exile in Nigeria would last exactly three years to the day. The *Daily Voice* would carry a brief story, stating that the Prime Minister, out of his deep compassion for the Molas, Beach's boyhood tribe, had requested the attorney general to call off the trial and had ordered authorities to grant Lincoln Beach an exit visa.

The burning of the papers that evening became a festive, if somewhat comic, ceremony. It was performed over the kitchen gas stove in Milbank's home in the embassy compound. Lew, Milbank, Williams and Attorney General Archibald Fess attended the rites. Lew held the original over a flaming burner, kept it there until the paper almost burned to his fingers, then doused it under the kitchen tap. He crushed the wet embers and threw them into a pink, plastic trash basket. Fess followed suit with one carbon, then the other two men ceremoniously burned the remaining copies. There was one casualty. Williams scorched the tip of one finger, and Ambassador Milbank personally fetched salve and Band-Aid.

Then Milbank poured Scotch-on-the-rocks for all hands, and they drank a toast to Prime Minister Vining, followed by one to the President of the United States and yet a third one to undying Kalya-United States amity. The drinks ate into the attorney general's magisterial façade like a benign acid, and by the third round he became definitely chummy. He even accepted Lew's offer to drive him home in the Peace Corps jeep. Williams and Milbank saw them off at the portico of the embassy residence.

"You're in violation," chided Williams in parting. "You're carrying a Kalya national in a Peace Corps vehicle. I may have to dock you a month's pay."

"Make it my contribution to Founders Day," called Lew. They all laughed.

Lew drove off, slightly tipsy, chattering with Fess about the success of the Kalya soccer team which had just bested Sierre Leone, 3 to 1, for the West African championship. Lew felt lightheaded and he told himself that compromise wasn't such a pernicious practice after all.

The next morning a cable, addressed to Lew, came to Peace Corps headquarters via the embassy. It was from Washington and it was signed by Frank Sherrod:

The President wishes to thank you personally. When you terminate next month, come by for a talk. Until then, good luck.

Williams was in an expansive mood when Lew showed him the cable. That dreaded impasse—a contest of wills—had been averted. Reasonable men had reasoned together in the admirable pattern fashioned by Lyndon Baines Johnson, and they had reached a reasonable solution. In a word, Williams was off the hook, and relief flooded his plump face like a sunrise.

"You're a diplomat now, Lew," he said, beaming. "I always said that once those rough edges were polished off, you'd make ideal Peace Corps staff material." He pointed to the cable. "Matter of fact, Sherrod may have that in mind. He says to drop by for a talk when you terminate. What else? Eh?"

"I hadn't thought of that," said Lew. He pondered a moment. He knew he'd welcome a chance for a three-year assignment, the normal tour for a staffer. Latin America, maybe? But what about Prudence? What were the rules on husband and wife?

"Well, we'll see," he said.

"But first," said Williams, "back to Zinzin. You've been off the route long enough. I know you'll want to see Beach when he gets out Monday, but you can be up and back by then."

"On my way."

Lew whistled as he loaded the jeep. It was good to be going back again. He wondered what new crises were shaking the Franklin-Wyzansky menage, whether Ted Kramer's disposition was as sour as ever, about the state of Cindy's night class and Jim's water system. Had the first coils of cynicism ensnared Arlene yet? He crammed in the last of the kerosene drums and textbooks, the medical supplies and the weird assortment of sundries—toothpaste, hair nets, cold cream, beer, nail polish, books, radio batteries, a package of roofing nails, a basketball and, for Roger, a how-to brochure on pottery. Roger wanted to set up a ceramics workshop among his lepers. Lew had just slammed up the tailgate when he heard a shout.

"Hey, Redhead! Wait for me."

It was Arch Lettermore, fresh off the morning jet from the States. His suit coat was thrown over his single piece of luggage, his shirt was unbuttoned to the navel and he was sweating copiously.

"Haven't you got this lousy country air-conditioned yet?" he demanded. "I'm hardly gone a week, and you jack up the temperature ten degrees. . . . Give me time to check in with Williams, Red, and I'll cadge a ride up with you."

The ordinarily long drive to Loli passed swiftly. Arch, in a buoyant mood, might have just returned from a weekend party rather than a funeral. He regaled Lew with descriptions of the lugubriously greedy mortician, the friend of his father's who had stayed drunk for two days and the minister who could find only one favorable quality in the deceased to praise. That, said Arch, was "patience," a virtue which the pastor repeatedly sandwiched between verses of the Twenty-third Psalm. Arch showed Lew the present he had brought for Kramer, a Gideon Bible that he had filched from a hotel room in Raleigh.

"Times are changing," said Arch. "The desk clerk let me register without me even trying to pretend I was an Indian. . . . Wait'll you hear that ol' atheist Kramer holler when I give him the Bible. The only okay thing about it, he'll say, is the fact that I stole it."

They grew serious only when Lew outlined the deal that would send Lincoln Beach into exile. He pledged Arch to secrecy on the contents of the letters to Demarest and Shannon. Lew had made his own exceptions to the agreement binding him to silence on the shooting episode: Prudence, Sam Zerwick, Jim Osterlord, Arch and members of The Forge. All of them, he felt, had to know.

Arch's vow to remain quiet was buttressed by the raising of his right hand and an improvised oath on which "whereas's" hung like heavy fruit.

Lettermore's irrepressible humor became a portent for the journey. Peace Corps households along the route were remarkably free of caviling. In Kpapata, Lew found both Katherine and Barbara in school, where they were supposed to be, and neither one had a complaint. Even more rare, they had been in good health since Lew's last visit. Bart, stroking his silky chin whiskers, grumbled over some minor distress, but Lew felt he was merely playing out a role. Actually Bart seemed to be content for once, and he even looked cheerful when he announced the remaining days for Group V—thirty-three. Lew realized with a start that he himself had lost count. One month more to go in Kalya. The thought settled about him, a wreath of nostalgia.

They spent a lively night at Forrest Stevenson's home at Loli, which they reached after dark in the midst of a pounding rain that once almost mired the jeep. Geronimo, after his first frenzy of barking, snuffled happily at their trousers. Stevenson served them mint juleps, and Grace Stevenson apparently had signed her own truce with Africa at last. She quaked only once, when a streak of lightning drove into the hillside like a spear and illuminated the whole parkland knoll. But she quickly laughed, for the brilliant flood of light revealed the ancient Mola watchman cowering against the dabema tree. His quiver of arrows was slung over his back, but his bow was nowhere to be seen.

Stevenson listened to Lew's story of Beach's imprisonment and approaching exile with polite, but insistent, skepticism. Lew, of course, could not disclose his own part in the compact.

"Something peculiar about that story," said Stevenson. "I can't believe Old Number One is softening up, even in his old age. If Beach took a shot at him, Old Number One won't rest until he's got Beach six feet under."

"The story's kicking around Ft. Paul that Beach was framed," said Lew. "Maybe Old Number One is afraid some VIP—an American or what have you—will blow the whistle on him. Anyway, they say Beach only has to stay with the leopard until Monday. Then off to Nigeria."

"If they don't find some way to bump him off on the way to the airport," said Stevenson. He shook his head. "It doesn't make sense. Wait for Wawa. It'll turn up, sooner or later."

Stevenson still relished Moses Harter's victory in Zinzin. It appealed to his sense of congruity as much as it still grated in Lew's mind. The settlement with Genghis Khan had a distinctly Kalyan flavor. Had Genghis emerged the loser, Stevenson would

have had to question the validity of his own perceptions etched
by thirty-five years in Africa.

"It's really rich," he said, his thin, blue-veined hand cupping
a third mint julep. "Genghis is merry as a troll. His mouth is
watering over all that money he's going to eat. He's been down
here twice in his red Mustang to see how the school plans are
coming along. He's even trying to pressure me into buying some
of his land for the high school. But there, I put my foot down.
Maybe I have to let him fatten on those contracts, but I don't
have to put up with a land swindle too. Oh, that man is a corker,
believe me. His cupidity is so open, it's positively luminous. He
kind of radiates all the time now. Makes you feel good just to
be around him. For a guy who claims his life was blighted because he never managed to get into a college, he's sure making
education pay off now."

"Forrest," said Lew, "you're one of those characters who secretly admire con men."

"Secretly, hell," retorted Stevenson. "I admit it. The freebooters
and the musclemen live an uninhibited life. No anxieties, no
doubts, no self-delusions about improving the lot of mankind like
you Peace Corps toilers. Just a straight, single-minded drive to
loot. It's great for mental health. I'll bet you never heard of a
successful bandit who consulted a psychiatrist."

"Oh, Forrest, for heaven's sake," protested Grace Stevenson, "are
we going to have to listen to that harebrained philosophizing of
yours tonight? Why can't we talk about something interesting for
a change?"

"You mean the gossip in Ft. Paul, dear." When Stevenson became a little drunk, the gentle tone he used with his wife took on
vestments of velvet. "The search for meaning is the age-old quest
of the male. The ladies, God bless 'em, have never bothered
much. In the female vocabulary, philosophy is a dreary word. . . .
Oh, well." He sighed and centered his gaze on his tall, frosted
glass.

"At least when *we* run off at the mouth, what comes out is
worth hearing," retorted his wife.

But the threat of another domestic squabble passed, and the
talk did turn in the direction Grace Stevenson favored—the gossip in Ft. Paul, Loli and Zinzin. The men, too, were equally at

home with the chitchat despite Stevenson's disavowals. The talk ran until midnight, enlivened by Arch's recital of events at North Carolina's most flamboyant funeral of the year. Lew went to bed in a state of serenity. The Stevenson household had not changed a bit.

The next evening had all the flavor of a long-postponed homecoming. It was raining savagely when Lew and Arch arrived in Zinzin, and their fresh clothes became soaked on the short dash from Arlene's shower hut to her house. At his own mud-stick dwelling, Arch made a formal presentation of the Gideon Bible to his roommate, and Kramer responded predictably with a morose recital of the mishaps that had plagued him during Arch's absence. The rats were invading again, his feet hurt and Houhab, the Lebanese storekeeper, was bugging him for payment of his old liquor bill.

Later the Peace Corps turned out in force to greet Corleigh and Lettermore at the home of Dotty and Alice. Lew felt the tug of familiarity at once. The living room had slipped back to its old state of sloth and neglect. The record albums were scattered over the floor again, dust coated the Scrabble board and soiled batting bulged from the decrepit sofa. Joe-Joe obviously had not washed his Sweet Briar sweatshirt in days. Alice and Dotty were blissfully untidy. The lenses of Alice's glasses were smeared with thumbprints and Dotty's hair hung uncombed in lank strands. The air in the house had the moist, stagnant feel of a cave.

Jim Osterlord caught Lew's elbow the minute he came in the door and pulled him to one side. Jim's hair had begun to look shaggy again after the ceremonial haircut, a cigar jutted from his mouth and his olive face wore a professionally conspiratorial look.

"Prudence briefed me on the short-wave," he said. "But all they know here is that Beach went to the leopard for taking a shot at Old Number One, and now he's going to be released. Nobody knows about the affidavit. You'd better play it cool."

"I figured that," said Lew. "We'll talk later."

Jim nodded and faded into a recess of the room. He loved the undercover bit, thought Lew. Jim would make a great secret agent.

Questions tumbled at Lew from all sides. Did he think Beach had really fired at Old Number One? If so, why was he being released? What was the real word from Ft. Paul? Had anybody yet given the Peace Corps any credit for its work the night of the fire? Lew fielded the inquiries as adroitly as he could, but found himself resenting the fact that he couldn't disclose his own role in the shooting episode. He was, after all, rather proud that he had maneuvered the U.S. government into changing its policy of inaction, and now he realized that his small triumph must forever remain unsung in public. Arthur Schlesinger, Jr., and Theodore Sorensen could lift the curtain of history, but not PCVL Lewis N. Corleigh. It didn't seem fair. . . . The Peace Corps representative scorching a finger at an embassy gas stove during an official paper-burning would make a wonderful "inside" anecdote. . . . Oh, well, perhaps memoirs in twenty years. But who, then, would care?

"But I still don't see why Old Number One has been so easy on Beach, I mean if Beach really tried to assassinate him," said Dotty. She gestured with her cigarette, and ashes dripped over her paint-daubed Levi's.

"Psychology of the leader's charisma," said Ted sourly. "It polishes his image as the great black father, fearless, compassionate, a man who can't be harmed by mere mortals."

"Oh, can that egghead jargon," said Alice. "Old Number One is a vindictive, cruel old man. Look at the schoolteacher at Gbinga who wouldn't kick in for Founders Day. They framed her on a robbery charge and sent her to Kpali. Her hands may have been cut off by now, for all we know."

"Right, cellmate," said Dotty. "I mean, it's out of character."

"A man can mellow with age," said Arch. "I know just getting back here, looking at your tired, young faces, makes me feel ten years older. But I've learned to be tolerant. Some day I may even get to tolerate white people."

Cindy Fuller grinned. The rose ribbon in her hair matched her disposition. She had been in a state of subdued euphoria ever since Jim brought word from the short-wave that morning that Beach would be released from prison.

"Let's you and I go outside, Archie," she said, "and see if they talk about us. We'll listen at the window."

The Peace Corps chatter soon turned to the news in Zinzin, and Lew noted that the bubbling air of speculation quickly dissipated. School met daily and Cindy's night-class attendance had climbed back to an average of twelve persons. But Moses Harter's public air of smug triumph cast a pall over the Peace Corps contingent. He strutted like a rooster lording it over his hens, complained Dotty. Arlene said Genghis now greeted her effusively each time they met. The guy was oily, ingratiating and repellent, said Kramer.

"The worst of it is Oon Gilli," said Cindy. "Ever since Morfu was killed in bush camp, he hasn't set foot in night class. Who knows, maybe he blames it on me."

"No, I think he blames the whole Peace Corps," said Arlene. "He never speaks to me any more or Jim either—and Oon was Jim's best worker."

From his seat in the corner of the room, Jim Osterlord shook his head slightly at Lew through a haze of cigar smoke.

"Cripes, Red," said Dotty, "I mean, nothing has changed in this sinkhole—except for the worse." She glanced involuntarily at the Canada Dry wall calendar with its date boxes hatched by red crayon.

"I still can't bear to think of Oon and that 'small-small' night in our class," said Cindy.

"Well, at least Genghis won't make an extra killing out of land," said Lew. He recounted his conversation about it with Forrest Stevenson.

"You kidding?" hooted Alice from her perch on the tattered sofa. Her short legs dangled just off the floor. "How naive can these USAID people be? Genghis owns all the land where they're going to build one elementary school—only he holds it in the name of that runt who's supposed to be the town devil."

"Wawa!" shouted Dotty with the gusto of one whose suspicions of knavery have been confirmed.

"Wawa!" echoed Alice and Ted.

"Where's a drink in this place?" asked Ted. His tone was sepulchral.

"Make mine double," said Dotty.

Alice brought a round of rums, whereupon Ted launched into a theme which had long been his pet, but which he had suppressed recently under the weight of adverse public opinion.

"It goes back to what I always said," he declaimed. "The Molas won't pay much attention to us up here because they think we're a bunch of idiots, living in the same cruddy, mud-stick houses they do. They figure all Americans are rich, but they see us putting on the poor mouth, eating country chop, wearing old clothes and getting diarrhea the same as Kalyans. If we're so smart, why don't we wear good blue suits like Forrest Stevenson? Who's going to pay any attention to people who don't have the savvy to ride in a red Mustang like Genghis? What the hell do they know about the Peace Corps hardship image they promote out of Washington? . . . Christ, this do-it-yourself poverty is for the birds."

"Bravo," said Alice. "Remember Sally in Group IV, and how she carried her baby on her back Mola-style? The Kalyans all thought she was making fun of them. . . . And now, to make it worse, Washington wants to take the kerosene refridges away from us. Oh, Holy Mother, I'm glad I'm getting out of this joint next month."

But Cindy, Arlene and Arch took prompt issue, and the dispute headed toward the name-calling stage while the rain drummed on the metal roof and a spanking sound from the bathroom announced that the unrepaired leak was in business again. Jim Osterlord sat mute in his corner, wrapped in cigar smoke. Joe-Joe moved about, his bare feet slapping the floor like ping-pong paddles. The bone-searching dampness in the room made them shiver despite the heat. Nothing had changed, thought Lew. The thought comforted him. Zinzin wore the trappings of home, and any marked shift of mood would have jarred. He sat contentedly while the others wrangled.

After a dinner of canned pea soup and noodles with over-spiced meat sauce, Lew packed five Peace Corps friends into the jeep and drove them home. At Cindy's house, he walked her to the door under his poncho while Osterlord waited in the car. They stood for a moment in the shelter of her living room.

"Link wants you to drive down with me tomorrow," said Lew. "He'll only have a few hours after he gets out Monday, and he wants to see you before they put him on the plane for Lagos."

Her brown eyes widened, but her smile was a brief one. "I don't see how I can," she said. "I've only got one more month, and exams are coming up . . . but . . . Oh, I'm dying to see Link again."

"Get Arlene to sub for you," said Lew. "Her classes are in the afternoon at the mission. She could take yours in the morning."

Cindy looked torn. "I wonder if I should? I'm always cracking the whip, telling them not to miss school."

"Have you skipped a day yet when school was open?"

"No, but . . . Oh, Red . . . what about the night school?"

"Make Ted do it," he said. "It'll do him good to get off his duff for a change."

"I suppose . . ." Suddenly her lips tightened and she wore the firm look of decision he had seen the day she confronted Moses Harter. "All right, I will. Just give me time in the morning to contact Arlene and Ted."

"I'll pick you up at nine-thirty sharp," said Lew. "Bring your perfume."

At Osterlord's house, Jim shed his taciturnity as promptly as he did his raincoat. The houseboy was asleep. Jim lit the kerosene lamp and seated himself backward on a wooden chair, his arms folded over the top.

"Don't believe that stuff about Oon Gilli," he said. "Steve recruited him for The Forge and Oon's going to be a damn good member. He's convinced now that his kid was murdered in bush school to scare him off working on the road."

Jim's eyes shone in the light of the lamp. "And listen, Red. Oon's not the only one. Steve has got two more damn smart Molas working with The Forge now. Give us a year, and we'll have half the men in town. Why, what with the waterworks, and building a real political party up here against Old Number One, this joint is going to be jumping. I wouldn't go home when my tour's up if they paid me."

"What's new on the water system?" asked Lew. Jim's fever was contagious. The dour mood of Dotty and Alice's house seemed years away. Jim's Zinzin had the tension of theater on opening night.

"It's going ahead," said Jim. "Steve and I have been up to Itambel twice already. The training course will start as soon as we can finish the rough plans, maybe in a couple of weeks. . . . And listen, pal, Steve's getting cagey. The guys he takes up there for training will all be members of The Forge. That way, we mix politics with pipe lines."

"I don't know about The Forge," said Lew. He described the meeting at Prudence's house, the lack of ideas and inventiveness, and he told of Beach's fears that The Forge would waste away during his exile.

"The hell it will," said Osterlord. "Not up here. Listen, something happened to Steve when he heard Link went to the leopard. Steve figured that was the end of Beach, and that he'd better be ready to take over. Honest, he's a new man—aggressive, on the muscle, quick with the decisions. The Forge is on the way. Steve's already come up with ideas about recruiting college boys this summer. And I'll be helping for two years more, if Williams lets me extend. . . . You tell Link to quit worrying. Steve and I are going to make this a go-go outfit."

Jim's eyes were aglow and he shifted fitfully in his chair as he talked. The combination of the waterworks and the clandestine nature of The Forge fired his imagination.

"Harvard was never like this?" said Lew.

"You said it, brother." Osterlord waved a derisive hand in the direction of the Franklin-Wyzansky house. "They don't know the score. They mope around, teach a little school, nag at each other and get all lathered up over the kind of crap Ted is always putting out. . . . This is a great town. It's on the move."

"I guess it's that deal with Genghis that bugs them," said Lew. "I take it that never bothered you." Lew could not resist needling his fervent friend. "Not as long as you can build the waterworks— Osterlord's private Aswan Dam."

"So they've been grafting around here for a thousand years," said Jim, "long before they thought up some new gimmicks in the slave trade. So what? Wait'll The Forge gets operating. We'll ride Genghis Khan out of here on the ass end of a money bus."

"One water system sure changes your tune," observed Lew.

"Balls! You still haven't learned the way it works around here, Red. One thing at a time. But we've got to get some muscle first."

They talked for another hour, and when he went to bed, Osterlord was whistling "Hello, Dolly." Lew was almost asleep when he realized that Jim had said not one approving word about Lew's affidavit or his role in forcing the switch of signals from Washington that would free Lincoln Beach. James Osterlord, master builder, was afloat in his own dreams of empire. And somehow, Lew did not mind.

Except for two brief downpours in late afternoon, the rains held off during the return drive to Ft. Paul. Cindy, elated by the prospect of seeing Beach, became positively garrulous, chattering about her girlhood in Atlanta, her painful bouts with segregation, her love for the Peace Corps and her new teaching plans for the adult night class. The hours passed quickly and the jeep slogged past the dripping walls of jungle and the sinking bug-a-bug mounds with only one mishap. A rear tire blew. Lew stood in muck up to his ankles to put on the spare while Cindy stationed herself at the other side of the blind curve to warn off any gladiatorial money bus drivers who might be approaching. Their shoes and socks were wet and muddy when they climbed back into the jeep, but they harmonized for an hour on old songs and reached Loli in good spirits. The Stevensons were in Ft. Paul for the night, so Cindy and Lew stayed with Susan, Cindy in the spare bed and Lew on a cot in the kitchen. They arrived on schedule at the Ft. Paul hostel at dusk of the second day.

Lew showered and changed clothes, then drove to Prudence's house.

The sound of the jeep, grinding through the mud in low gear, brought Prudence to the front door to welcome him. She stood with folded arms in the doorway, and he could see that her hair was combed in a soft arc over her forehead the way he liked it. Her trim, hard legs, showing several bush scars against the tan, were bare beneath her green cotton dress. He realized again how slight and vulnerable she was, standing alone, framed in the deep orange haze of a Kalya sunset.

She kissed him with the hunger that continued to surprise him. Then she pushed him away and studied him with that questioning look of hers. The appraisal, as if she were seeking reassurance for her love, brought a freshness to every reunion, but as usual, along with a feeling of tenderness, Lew was amused. She was such a serious one at times.

"I'm so glad you're back," she said. It seemed to be a punctuation mark for her scrutiny. She had weighed him—and the feelings he evoked—once more and found the gift abundant.

She let him lift her from the floor, but then she struggled to be let down again.

"I'm in a terrible box, Lew," she said. "Waiting to tell you,

I realized how much I need you. If you hadn't come back tonight, wouldn't have slept at all. Guess I'm scared."

"You know Doc Zerwick's sleep prescription for keyed-up Peace Corps women executives," said Lew. "You take one man, stir moderately, mix with two rums, place in a large bed and . . ."

"Not now, please." She broke into his teasing. "This is serious. Here, look."

She stepped to the coffee table and handed Lew a sheet of paper. Its appearance had become familiar in recent weeks. It was a tissue copy of an embassy cable. He read:

PECTO
CARTER WILLIAMS
U.S. EMBASSY
FT. PAUL
KALYA

Staffer Prudence Stauffer relieved of duty Ft. Paul. Recalled Washington via first available air transportation for reassignment.

Frank Sherrod

"But . . ." He was stunned. "What's it all about?"

"Being kicked out of Kalya by demand of Old Number One," she said. "I'm on tomorrow night's plane. If there had been any space, Williams would have shipped me out tonight."

"But why?" Suddenly all their personal plans were scattering like clouds before a gale. Reassignment? By the time he got back to the States a month hence, she might be in Chile, Afghanistan, Guinea, God knew where.

"Wait'll I make us some tea," she said, "then I'll tell you."

Tea! He watched her hips as they swung toward the kitchen. Prudence cataloged beverages in terms of mood and event. Alcohol was reserved, sparingly, for moments of rejoicing. Coffee was for heavy thinking. Tea meant a crisis of mind or spirit.

She returned, set the cups and saucers carefully on the coffee table, then sat silently while she wiggled the tea bags in darkening water.

"Thanks a lot," he said.

She looked up, startled. "Why, what's the matter?"

"Damn it," he said. "You tell me you're being yanked home. Who knows when we'll see each other again? And then you give me tea. Why not offer me something real exciting, like hot milk, for God's sake?"

"Oh . . . Guess I didn't think, honey. I'm so upset." She looked at him questioningly, suddenly anxious. "Would rum be all right?"

"A rum would be fine—straight."

When she returned from the kitchen, she had two glasses of rum, one almost full, the other a modest two fingers high. Her smile was almost timid when she took a sip of the smaller portion. "Guess I'm more chicken than chick sometimes."

"No. You're just too much rooster sometimes."

"Oh . . ." There was a dawning in her puzzlement. "Do you think I try to boss you, Lew?"

"Now and then."

Her lips trembled. "Are you going to be mean, Lew? . . . I couldn't stand it. I feel so low—and kind of lonely."

He crossed quickly to her and kissed her. "No fights," he said. "Come on now. Down the rum and then drink some tea, and tell me."

She did both, but did not look up after sipping the tea. "Well," she said, "it all blew up in the last twenty-four hours. Carter called me in yesterday noon. He said he had a very disagreeable matter to take up with me. Milbank had just relayed an urgent inquiry from the Palace. The government, said Carter, had information that my house had been used as a meeting place for plotters who were trying to overthrow constitutional government. What did I have to say about it?"

She paused, then raised her eyes, looking at him for understanding. "Naturally, it shook me. I thought at once of that rogue, of course. He must have been an informer. . . . So, I knew it would be useless to try to deny that a meeting took place, even if I were a good liar, which I'm not. . . . So I thought fast and said that never at any time did I take part in any meeting that threatened free, constitutional government. Guess I stressed the 'free' and the 'constitutional.' Williams looked at me kind of funny—funny peculiar, I mean—and said, well, what about a meeting at my house? I said I would not answer that question, that I considered my home a place where what anybody said or did, including Kalyans, was a private matter. Would I tell him who was there at this particular session the Palace seemed to be referring to? I asked what night? He said it was just two nights before the yellow and red handbills were strewn all over town. I said I could not name names."

"At which point," said Lew, "Carter put on his injured, why-do-you-of-all-people-have-to-do-this-to-me look—and you relented and told him."

"Did not," she said. "He looked hurt enough, but instead of pressing me, he just kind of deflated like a punctured tire. Then he said too much was happening too fast, and that some members of the Peace Corps were getting way, way over their heads into Kalya politics that they didn't understand. He couldn't see why we didn't just teach school, do our jobs and let the Kalyans run their own country."

"He wouldn't," said Lew caustically. "Carter thinks you can be on all sides at once. It's a way of life with him."

"He never gets outcountry to see the people," said Prudence. "We do. . . . Anyway, he said he'd have to report back to Milbank at once, but I might as well start packing because Old Number One was raging mad—he remembered my name as a witness on your affidavit—and there was no hope of compromise this time. That's all I know, except that this afternoon when the cable came, Carter said Old Number One wouldn't settle for less. Either I left voluntarily, or Vining would order my deportation and have Booth's men personally escort me to the plane.

"Then Williams added, in that hurt way of his, that he could hardly blame Old Number One. The gathering at my place, said Carter, was held only two nights before the handbill distribution, and Old Number One could put two and two together as well as Williams and Milbank could."

Prudence took a sip of tea and smiled, a bit self-consciously, when Lew lifted his glass of rum for another swallow.

"What about the rest of us?" Lew asked. "Do they have the names?"

She shook her head. "I don't think so, or else there'd be some big blowup, arresting Billy Number 15, Ollie and some others, ordering you out too and maybe breaking the deal Old Number One made on Link. No, my guess is that it was the rogue, that he got caught breaking into some other house, and then tried to talk his way free by reporting on the doings at my place. Only, I don't think he could identify anybody. He probably just spotted two white faces and a lot of dark ones, and figured there was a plot of some kind."

They talked and speculated until after midnight, through the dinner of cold-cuts and during the hours that they spent sorting rugs, carvings, appliances and knickknacks into a series of piles. Prudence intended to parcel out her Kalya acquisitions among her Peace Corps friends and, with her instinct for instant order, she insisted that the division be made tonight. Tomorrow, she said, she would be too busy with other things.

The housebreaking seemed more definitive than Prudence's words, and soon Lew felt the old mood of dejection—the one that often enveloped him in the jungle twilight along the Zinzin road —lowering about him again. The luster had faded from the deal that freed Lincoln Beach. Lew had been swept up in the maneuvers, had been lured by the sense of being an insider, of pulling strings in international politics.

But what had happened really? The Peace Corps had been routed all along the line. Beach got off with his life, but he was being shipped out of the country, far from the tribes for which he battled. Beach lost. Hulbert Booth won. . . . Prudence, the best of the Peace Corps staff, shipped home. . . . In Zinzin, Moses Harter was about to become a rich man—at the expense of the Molas and the U.S. Treasury. . . . And Jim Osterlord, spiritually bribed by a waterworks. . . . The old system, the arrogant rule of The Family, marched on with hardly a break in its phalanx. . . . And Lew himself? What had he succeeded in doing after two years? He was still a truck driver, and Kalya hadn't changed a whit since the day he made his first haul up the long, red road.

It was past midnight, and he and Prudence lay in bed after their lovemaking. They lay in silence for a time, their bodies limp and surfeited. He could feel the soft down on her arm as it rested across his chest, and he could hear the measured, muffled breathing. But he could not shake his mood of depression.

"Maybe Williams is right, Prude," he said. "Maybe we did get in over our heads. With all our moralizing about right and wrong, about the tribes and The Family, what do we really know about Kalya? Everything seems to be going down the drain. I guess we're just amateur do-gooders, after all."

"It's partly Williams' fault to begin with," she said. "If we'd had a rep who knew the score, who understood Kalya politics and wasn't afraid to use a little Peace Corps pressure now and then, things might have been different. But he wouldn't. So we did."

"As it is," said Lew moodily, "we've had it—from Ft. Paul to Zinzin."

"Don't be so sure about Zinzin," she said. She sat abruptly upright, holding the sheet over her bosom. She grinned down at him.

"Lew," she said, "you've really stuck your neck out—in Washington after you were threatened with a mamba, and then again with the affidavit. I'm so proud of you. I'd like to do something too."

"About Zinzin?" he asked. "But what could you do?"

"I'm not going to tell you." She flicked a finger at the tip of his nose. "I'm entitled to one secret."

"You're worse than Jim Osterlord," he said. "Code talk on the short-wave, holding subversive meetings in your house behind drawn blinds—and now secrets."

"You're just envious," she said. "Envy already. Some lover, you are."

"Some missionary, you are," he grunted. "We'll be lucky if they don't throw you out of the country before tomorrow night."

There was a loud knock at the door, then another.

"Just a minute," called Prudence. Then to Lew: "Who could that be? It must be almost one o'clock."

They both dressed hurriedly.

"I'm coming," called Prudence. She went to the front door while Lew seated himself on the divan, turned on the floor lamp and grabbed a book from the end table. It was Graham Greene's *The Comedians*. He opened the book in the middle and pretended to be engrossed.

"Oh, Carter," said Prudence at the door. "Come in, please."

"No," said Williams. "I'm looking for Lew Corleigh. Is he here? I couldn't find him at the hostel."

"Sure," called Lew. He went to the door.

"Could I see you a minute out in my car?" asked Williams. "It's urgent."

The two men sat in the dark on the front seat of Williams' staff jeep. The Peace Corps chief rubbed a hand nervously along his jaw.

"Lew," he asked, "were you at the meeting here—the one that's prompted Prudence to be sent home?"

Lew hesitated. There was no time to think. "I'll have to take the Fifth on that."

"In that case, you're in serious trouble." Williams' face was a shadowed moon and he spoke with the bored irritation of a judge sentencing a chronic drunk to another thirty-day stretch. "Colonel Booth now has a signed statement from the rogue who saw the meeting here. The rogue identified Lincoln Beach as one of the participants. Furthermore, he says he saw a white man whom he could identify on sight. Booth and the Prime Minister are convinced that the white man is you."

"Me?" Lew thought fast. "I'll bet the rogue was tortured," he said. "Under Booth's caressing—and those two 'leopard men' assistants of his—the fellow would say anything Booth wants."

"That's possible," said Williams fretfully, "but hardly relevant. The main point is that Old Number One is storming again. He called Milbank over to the Palace a few hours ago and read him the riot act. He says the Beach deal is off. Beach must stand trial —and the trial has been advanced to next Wednesday morning."

"But we burned the affidavit—after he gave his word." Lew tried to sound incensed, but he felt as though he were sinking.

"Vining says he'll keep his word on that. He won't deny you the right to testify," said Williams. "But after you tell your story on the stand, at least seven eyewitnesses will contradict you. Then the rogue will be put on to discredit your testimony by showing that you and Beach were fellow plotters who attended a secret meeting just before the handbills were circulated."

"In other words, they've got me boxed." Lew's feeling of helplessness was compounded by Williams' attitude. The Peace Corps chief seemed professionally pleased to enumerate Lew's burdens —like a doctor ticking off the symptoms of cancer.

"The ambassador is concerned for your safety," said Williams. "He can send you home tomorrow night on the same plane with

Prudence. Otherwise, after Beach's trial, you could be indicted and tried for perjury. Where that might end, nobody knows."

"Is he ordering me home?"

"No. Milbank knows better than to try to order you." The words were steeped in the resignation of a man who deals with habitual offenders. "I don't think he's even interested in advising you. You're still operating under the last cable from Washington. You're a free agent."

Williams rubbed his chin again without looking at Lew, and Lew assumed that Milbank's true feelings had been distorted in the transmittal of the message. Williams, patently, was fed up with Lew Corleigh, mischief-maker, plotter, prospective felon.

"I can't go home," said Lew. "Tell the ambassador I'll have to testify."

Williams put his hand on the ignition key. "Of course, I knew you'd put your own grandiose sense of honor before the welfare of the Peace Corps. We'd never survive here if you were convicted of perjury."

"For Christ's sake, Carter," Lew exploded. "Do you think I lied in that affidavit?"

"I think your memory was influenced by your alliance with Lincoln Beach." Williams' fingers played with the ignition key. He was anxious to be gone. "I really don't know what you saw. I hope you do."

"Thank you." Lew slammed the door as he got out.

Williams drove off without looking back. Lew watched until the taillights became two tiny embers in the sultry night.

Prudence had made two cups of tea and this time Lew drank his without protest. Prudence toyed with her cup while she listened. Her face was bare of make-up. Love so often left its communicants shorn of the most commonplace of shields.

"Maybe you should go back with me," she said. "It's different now. You don't have a chance in a million of saving Link's life."

"Prude, I couldn't. You know that."

"Guess I do." Her mouth tightened. "But I'm afraid for you, Lew . . . and it may be months before I'll see you again."

"I know." He checked himself. The idea had come like the sudden visit of a zestful friend. "Prude, let's get married now—tomorrow—before you leave."

"I . . . I'd love it. . . . But how? . . ." She glanced at her wrist watch. "There are only, let's see, twenty-one hours until the plane goes. . . . I don't . . . Oh, we'd never make it."

"Sure, we would. Let Sam Zerwick handle it. He can get around any red tape on papers or the license. Cindy could be the maid of honor. Sam can be the best man. He can get a preacher somewhere. Is it a deal?"

"But what would I wear?"

Lew laughed. "Now we're getting somewhere. Wear that pink dress you bought for the party. It's a natural. No sweat. . . . We can get married right here in your place, then beat it to the airport. They can toss rice all the way."

"I like that. Getting married at the scene of the crime." Color flooded her cheeks. She was ebullient now. "What about the service? I'm Unitarian. You're Presbyterian. Oh, I think the Episcopal one is chic. Very stately. Who'll give me away?"

"Maybe we could smuggle in Billy Number 15—or Ollie. . . . What time? How about six P.M.?"

"Too late," she said. "We've got to have a honeymoon here, in late afternoon. . . . But, oh dear, don't we need a reception?"

"It's a deal, then?"

She nodded, suddenly serious. "It is a deal, Lew—our last one in Kalya."

They both rose to their feet at the same time, and Prudence's knee knocked her tea, cup and saucer, to the floor. They kissed above the scatter of fractured china.

Five minutes later they were in the jeep, headed for Sam Zerwick's house to arouse him and trumpet the tidings. Prudence feverishly made a list of all the things Sam had to do. The time and place were settled. They would be married at 3 P.M. in Prudence's house.

22

At 9:32 A.M. an explosion shook the amiable torpor of downtown Ft. Paul. Pedestrians shuffling along the streets broke into runs and headed in the direction of the short, powerful blast. Private cars, motorcycles, bicycles, taxis and even two money buses raced toward the Mandingo enclave.

By 10:30 A.M. Ft. Paul had resumed its lethargic pace, clucking over another grisly incident in the always hazardous life of the capital. The Elite Dry Cleaning and Photographic Supply Shop, owned and operated by Billy Number 4, had been demolished and, deplorably, Billy Number 4, his wife and one of his three children had been killed. The other two children, weeping, were being comforted in the nearby home of their uncle. Colonel Hulbert Booth and the Ft. Paul police had both investigated and, provisional to a full-dress inquiry, had issued a tentative finding: Billy Number 4 had been experimenting with a new dry-cleaning solvent. The volatile vapors had exploded inexplicably, killing Billy Number 4 instantly. His wife and child, blown against the adjoining wall of the Ginger Baby bar, died a few minutes later. The damage was confined to the one building, but it was a total loss and all equipment wrecked without hope of salvage. The rubble lay inert, like a historic ruin, and, on the sidewalk, someone found a child's sandal.

Lew heard the noise from the hostel, a remote but emphatic sound as if a cannon had been fired from a distant hillside. He was too busy with his wedding chores to pay much attention, and it was noon before Arthur, the houseboy, returned from town with a hashed version of the tragedy. Lew thought it symbolic, and consistent with everything that had happened in recent days, that three Kalyans should be blown apart on his wedding day.

But if there were an omen in the coincidence, Lew could not worry over it. There was too much to do. Sam Zerwick had agreed, or rather decreed, that he would give the bride away. After all, he said, he was fifteen years older than the bride, and in Kalya, that would make him of an age to be her father. Cindy, bunking at the hostel dormitory, was delighted to be the maid of honor. Cindy fully expected Lincoln Beach to be released that day from prison, and Lew did not have the heart to tell her—yet. He hedged, saying Beach's release had been delayed until evening. He privately vowed he would tell her immediately after the ceremony—or rather, he hoped that Prudence would do it. Cindy had brought her pink sheath from Zinzin, and again Cindy and Prudence would be wearing identical dresses.

Lew had roused Ollie Downing from bed shortly after dawn and prevailed upon him to be the best man. They both knew it would be risky, but it intrigued them that a Forge member should take part in a wedding uniting two of its helpers. In any event, they felt Ollie's part could be kept a secret, for there were to be no invited guests—only Prudence, Lew, Cindy, Zerwick, Ollie and the minister.

Zerwick pledged himself to find the minister and at 11 A.M. he drove by the hostel to report success. He had enlisted the chaplain of the U.S. Army engineer unit which was drafting plans for a new Ft. Paul reservoir—upon completion of which Ft. Paul would have water all night. The chaplain would use the Episcopal service, said Zerwick, and fortunately he was able to send Lew and Prudence copies of the ritual.

Lew glanced at the typewritten extracts from the prayer book and read:

Minister: Bless, Oh Lord, this ring, that he who gives it and she who wears it may abide in thy peace and continue in thy favor unto their life's end through Jesus Christ our Lord. Amen.

Lew looked up at Zerwick. "The ring! I forgot all about the ring."

So he drove into Ft. Paul, and at a Lebanese jewelry store he found a simple gold band which was priced at $13. The amount tapped a latent vein of superstitution in Lew, and after bargaining he got it for $11.50.

But honoring the taboo against the groom seeing the bride before the ceremony on the day of the wedding proved frustrating. There were so many things he wanted to ask Prudence about. Did she want flowers? How about music? Were they to be married in doleful silence? Had she cabled her parents? Should he cable his? Did they have to tell Carter Williams? There had been seven marriages of Group V volunteers that spring. Had any, or all, obtained Peace Corps permission? Was such permission necessary?

Zerwick, shuttling between Prudence's house and the hostel, resolved most of the questions himself. He appeared at the hostel the last time at 1:45 P.M. with the license. Under Kalya law, applicants had to wait three days before issuance of the national license, but Zerwick had bribed the clerk with a ten-dollar bill. Names were immaterial. The license brought by Zerwick authorized the union of "John and Mary Doe or whichsoever names shall hereafter be substituted for the above."

Zerwick gave Lew his final briefing at the hostel. Lew and Oliver Downing should drive to Prudence's house in the jeep, Downing keeping out of sight. At the house, where they should arrive promptly at 2:55, they should wait at the side door where they would be screened on three sides by the tool shed, the house and a trellis of bougainvillaea. The chaplain would beckon them into the house a few seconds before the 3 P.M. ceremony. He was a beefy man with a whiskey nose, added Zerwick. Remember, Ollie must keep the ring until the chaplain indicated the moment when Ollie should give it to Lew, who in turn hands it to the chaplain, who later hands it back to Lew. Got it?

There would be no music, said Zerwick. Prudence would wear a short white veil, and she would carry a bouquet—pink camellias. Zerwick had picked them in his own yard. There were three bottles of Algerian champagne—Zerwick's gift—for the tiny reception. They would all clear out of the house within an hour after the ceremony.

"Good luck," said Zerwick. "You're a brave man. Personally, the word 'husband' gives me the shakes."

"Married men live longer," said Lew. "You can find the statistics in the World Almanac."

"I know," said Zerwick. He peered over his spectacles. "Every minute seems like an hour. . . . See you at three."

Lew showered at the hostel and dressed with exaggerated deliberation, and it occurred to him as he donned his one city suit that this was the last hour he would spend as a single man. The thought unnerved him and he wished that he were a smoker. He needed support, if only an acrid loop of smoke of the kind that Jim Osterlord wrapped protectively about himself. Lew buttoned his shirt collar, straightened his tie, disliked the shape of what he saw in the mirror, and reknotted the tie.

At last, at 2:30 P.M., the appointed hour for Oliver Downing to arrive in a taxi, Lew went to the front door and waited just inside. The hostel and its environs slumbered in the full heat of day. Even the Fizi squatters were dormant, dozing under the sheltering eaves of their thatched roofs. Lew could feel beads of moisture on his chest, and he hoped his white shirt would remain reasonably fresh for the rites. He tried to be calm, but he found himself rubbing his palms together, an uncharacteristic gesture. He sent Arthur out to the road to watch for the taxi. The houseboy leaned against a post, expertly scratching a leg sore with the big toe of the other foot. Heat shimmered on the road's pavement like glassy dancers. The minutes passed. Lew glanced repeatedly at his watch . . . 2:35 . . . 2:40 . . . then 2:45. Oliver Downing was only slightly more punctual than his fellow Kalyans, but this morning he had promised Lew faithfully that he would not be late.

At 2:48—it was a good ten minutes to Prudence's house—Lew decided that he could wait no longer. He went to the back of the hostel, where the jeep was parked. He climbed in, carefully adjusted the crease of his trousers and started the motor.

At that moment a taxi careened off the road and slid to a halt behind the hostel in a shower of muddy water from a puddle.

To his consternation, Lew saw Billy Number 15, wrapped in his purple toga, get out of the taxi behind Oliver Downing. Even more upsetting, Ollie was not dressed for a wedding. He wore an open-necked sports shirt and held no suit coat. The taxi departed, leaving the two men.

"What the hell, Ollie," said Lew. He got out of the jeep and nodded, a trifle curtly, to Billy Number 15. "We're late already—and you're no best man in that getup."

Downing peered through his glasses as though he had not heard. "I've got something to show you—at this very instant. It is most important."

"Important! Good God, man. I'm late to my wedding. Where the devil have you been?"

"You will learn," said Downing. "You must come inside to the hostel. A private room where we cannot be seen or heard."

Lew could see Prudence waiting in her home and Zerwick glowering at his wrist watch. He appealed to Billy Number 15: "What's this guy talking about, Billy? I'm supposed to be getting married right now."

"Eh, man," said Billy. He stood tall in the sun, casting a shadow as straight as a pole. "Ever't'ing chac-la. Da Forge need you one time."

Lew tried to tug Downing toward the jeep, but Downing pulled away.

"Beach is in great danger," said Downing. "But you can, perhaps, rescue him. We must show you something inside the hostel."

"I'll do anything you say an hour from now," said Lew, "but right now I'm getting married." He looked again at his watch. "Hell, man. It's two fifty-one. I can barely make it."

Downing shook his head. "There is no time for that." The sun glinting on the glasses obscured his eyes. "Prudence would approve. She would do what she could to save Lincoln Beach. The wedding can take place later."

Billy Number 15 moved closer. Lew found himself hemmed

between the jeep and the two Kalyans. He had the distinct impression that if he tried to get into the jeep, they would physically block him.

"Please take us to a secure room in the hostel," said Downing with commanding insistence. "Then you can decide what you must do."

"All right," he said, "but let's make it fast."

While Arthur watched with languid curiosity from the shade of the dabema tree, Lew led the two men into the hostel. He took them to the cluttered bunk room he shared with three other volunteer leaders, all of whom were absent now on outcountry trips.

Downing closed the door.

"Is there a key?" he asked.

Lew shook his head. Downing closed the two casement windows and latched them. He stationed Billy Number 15 with his back to the door. Then Downing stood near Lew's mosquito-netted bunk, where he could not be seen through the windows. He beckoned Lew to his side.

Downing reached into a side pocket of his pants and withdrew a yellow cardboard holder about six inches long. It was a packet open at one end and, printed in red ink, Lew could read the legend: "Dill's Pipe Cleaners." Inside the holder was something wrapped in tissue paper. Downing placed the packet on a table and began to unwind the paper.

"I did not want scratches on these," he said.

Lew watched with as much fascination as he would have if he were about to be shown the Hope diamond. Inside the last of the wrappings were two stiff, narrow strips of photographic paper. Each tiny strip, less than an inch wide, appeared to contain three pictures in sequence. Downing handed one strip to Lew.

"Be careful," he said. "Hold it by the edges only."

Lew held up the pictures to get better light from the window. He recognized them as contact prints. He could see two heads that appeared vaguely familiar.

"Here." Downing handed him a magnifying glass.

Lew held the glass to the strip, then he gasped.

He was looking at three photographs of Hulbert Booth and Lincoln Beach. The first showed Beach's right arm being held up by Booth's left. Booth's right hand held a pistol at shoulder level. The arm was extended. Around the two men were a tangle of faces, blurred, and lower in the picture, three rows of heads of seated persons. The picture was clear, taken from perhaps not more than twenty feet away. Lew recalled that the lighting was brilliant that night inside the Kalya National—a security precaution.

The second picture was identical except that Booth held the pistol pointed slightly upward. The third showed only the pistol with a white smudge at the muzzle. Could it be smoke? Obviously the camera had been jerked off its focal target, for all that could be seen was the pistol, the smudge and a black hand holding the weapon.

"But where did you . . ." Lew began.

"Notice this," broke in Downing. He pointed to the first two pictures. "This row of heads is somewhat lower than this one, and this one still lower. The seats in the Kalya National slope toward the stage. Now look at the pistol. Booth is pointing the gun at the stage."

While Booth's face was shown only in profile, there was no mistaking him . . . the thin mustache . . . the security uniform with epaulet . . . the dark goggles. Beach's face showed completely, for it was turned in bewilderment, the eyes centered on the gun in Booth's right hand.

"It's fantastic," said Lew. "It must have been taken just as Booth was about to press the trigger. Then the third one looks as if the gun is going off. In God's name, Ollie, where did you get it?"

Downing took the strip and turned it over. On the back, stamped in pale blue ink, was a legend on the middle frame which extended into the other frames on both sides. Lew read:

Developing service. Billy Number 4's Elite Dry Cleaning and Photographic Supply Shop. 8 to 6 daily. 143 Founders Street, Ft. Paul, Kalya.

"What's the other picture?" asked Lew.

"It is another print from the same negative," said Downing. "It is altogether a blessing, for the negative was destroyed with everything else this morning in the dynamiting of the shop. There are only two prints in the world."

"Dynamiting?"

Downing nodded. "Colonel Booth increased his murders by three today."

"Eh, man," said Billy Number 15 from the door. He was pressed against it like an exotic barber pole of purple and black. "Boot' kill t'ree Mandingo dis day."

"Give me the word, Ollie," said Lew. He could see Prudence, waiting in her pink dress, a bouquet of pink camellias clutched to her breast, but the thought was crowded quickly off the screen of his mind by the faces of Booth and Beach in the narrow contact prints.

Downing rewrapped one strip in tissue paper, tucked it inside the pipe-cleaner holder, and handed the holder to Lew. Then he rewrapped the other one and slid it carefully into his pants pocket.

"You will want the packet," said Downing, looking owlishly at Lew, "after you have heard the story. I will make it short, because we confront a problem in time." He sat on the edge of Lew's bunk and spoke in a low voice.

"Billy Number 4 was devoted to the art of photography. On the shooting night, he was in the audience with a small Minox camera. It could hardly be seen in his hand. When the commotion between Booth and Beach started, close by Billy Number 4, he snapped three pictures rapidly. But then the gun went off and he became frightened, hiding the little camera under his robe. That night he developed the roll and found these pictures. But he knew that Lincoln Beach had been taken to the leopard, so he told no one out of fear. He was even more feared the next day when my story in the Voice said that Beach would be tried for seeking the assassination of the Prime Minister."

Downing glanced at the pipe-cleaner holder in Lew's hands as if to make sure it was still there. "Billy Number 15 is—was—a very close comrade of Number 4. They had talked some of politics, especially the day after the handbills were sown. Last night Billy Number 15 went to Number 4's house over the photo shop. He was hoping he might encourage his friend discreetly toward The Forge. At last, in great secrecy, Number 4 showed the

pictures to our Billy. They were very clear because Number 4 used
his flashlight magnifier which, woefully, perished in the explosion.
There were only two prints, he said, that he had made. Billy
Number 15 asked if anyone else knew of the pictures. Yes, said
Number 4, he had told another Mandingo named Tule in much
confidence that afternoon."

"Tule bad man," said Billy Number 15. "We t'ink he spy for
Boot'."

"We think Tule is a paid informer," explained Downing. "Unfortunately, Billy Number 4, while a good man, was of the trusting kind—too trusting of his friend Tule. Billy Number 15 asked
to borrow the pictures and Number 4 agreed with no problem.
Early this morning, Billy Number 15 looked for me, but could not
find me. Then came the explosion of the dry cleaning and photo
shop. One of Booth's men is my cousin, and he confided to me
that dynamite had been used to destroy the place. He did not
know why except that Billy Number 4 was an enemy of the state.
Obvious, as you can see, that Tule, the Mandingo, told of the
pictures. . . ."

"I suppose Booth has the negative," said Lew, cutting in. "He
must have searched the place."

"I cannot be sure, of course," said Downing. "Maybe he did
find the negative, and perhaps the shop was blown in retaliation.
Or maybe not. Either way, it makes no difference to us. We have
two prints."

"Of course," said Lew, "these pictures have to be shown to Old
Number One somehow. It's a terrific break, especially since Vining
is apparently convinced that it was Beach who shot at him. . . .
But, Jesus, why can't I get married, and then work on this tonight?"

Downing shook his head. "No time," he said. "For you have not
heard all. Billy Number 15 finally found me just an hour ago.
He also hears this: Since the rogue identified Lincoln Beach as
being at the meeting at Prudence's house, and Vining has moved
up the trial, Colonel Booth is much eager for a big intelligence
coup. It is believed, upon a very good source, that Booth will go
to Beach's cell late tonight and torture him until he confesses
that he attended the meeting and also planned the distribution of
the leaflets. And, most naturally, Booth hopes to get the other

names from Lincoln—especially yours, because Booth is sure you were there. At the trial, he wishes to make you out a plotter against the state."

Downing paused and moistened his lips with his tongue. "The leopard men are alerted for tonight. That I have from a perfect source."

The "leopard men" were Hulbert Booth's reputed torture experts, two stout men who played cards all day at security headquarters. The one with occasional gold teeth was said to be the more proficient of the two, but both were heralded as remarkably imaginative in their art, and their professional efficiency was equaled by the pleasure they took in it. The leopard men, it was said, prided themselves that no judge had even seen a mark on a defendant entrusted to their care. They never bruised the face.

"I see," said Lew. He thought a moment. "I'll take the pictures in this holder to Ambassador Milbank. When he sees them, I hope he'll show them to Old Number One. If he won't, well . . . You'll keep the other one, Ollie?"

"Yes. Insurance."

"But first I've got to beat it by Prudence's house and get the wedding fixed for later," said Lew. He looked at his watch again. "It's three-twenty now. Maybe we could be married just before she has to leave for the airport."

"I think that must be left to me," said Downing. "Explanations of a late groom consume much time. . . . And a waiting bride gets angry. . . . You should go direct to the embassy. . . . Do not worry. I will tell Prudence in the smallest detail so she will understand."

Lew thought of Prudence, a white veil at her forehead, and then he saw the gold teeth of the fatter of the two leopard men— like frosted light bulbs strung in a cave—and he saw Lincoln Beach sitting alone on his cot, perhaps reading—what was it again?—De Tocqueville and Thoreau?

"All right," he said. He put the packet in his trouser pocket where he could feel it next to his thigh.

"And this," said Downing. He handed Lew the magnifying glass and Lew put it in a pocket of his suit coat.

"Let's go," said Lew.

Billy Number 15 stepped toward Lew. Again he seemed a mobile barber pole of purple and black.

"Boot' kill t'ree Mandingo," said Billy. "Old Numb' One betta' do somet'ing dat man or . . ." He rushed into a volley of chopped English that Lew could not understand. The outburst lasted for almost a minute, then subsided.

Lew looked helplessly at Downing.

"Billy says that Booth murdered his best friend and two of his family," said Downing. "If Old Number One does not invoke severe penalty upon Colonel Booth, Billy will find his own way to revenge."

Except for a slight nod, Billy Number 15 stood as fixed as a statue. Lew could feel that the Mandingo meant what he said.

"Come on," said Lew. "I'll drop you fellows off downtown where you can get a cab."

But there was a long delay outside Ambassador Milbank's office. Milbank was in conference with the Italian and Belgian ambassadors. Something weighty, involving Itambel, Lew supposed. He tried to read the copy of *Life* on the waiting-room table, but could not concentrate. After a few minutes, he wrote a note, "Urgent I see you at once, Lew Corleigh," and sent it in by the obese secretary. Her waddle irritated Lew almost as much as her reluctance. She returned with an unconcerned smile and a note scribbled under Lew's on the same paper: "Patience, unlike virtue, is rewarded many times over. W.M."

It was half an hour before the envoys came out. More time slipped by while Milbank introduced them to a Peace Corps volunteer. It was 4:10 P.M. by the time Milbank led Lew into his office and closed the door.

"It seems to me that your business is always urgent," he said. His voice fenced his customary cordiality.

"I think you'll understand." Lew removed the tissue paper from the pipe-cleaner holder, unwrapped the paper and handed the contact strip to Milbank. "Please hold it by the edges, sir. . . . And you'll need this."

The ambassador took the strip and the magnifying glass, frowned, then applied the lens to the pictures like a jeweler inspecting a gem. He swept the glass from left to right.

"Who took these?" he asked, not looking up from the glass.

"Look on the back."

Milbank turned the strip over and read the stamped legend. Then he placed the strip on his desk blotter beside the glass.

"Isn't that the place that blew up this morning?"

Lew nodded. "The negative may be gone along with three people. I have it from a reliable source that Booth dynamited the shop after hearing about the picture and what it showed." Without mentioning Downing or Billy Number 15, he told Milbank the circumstances, including the report that Beach would be "questioned" that night by Booth and his two leopard men.

"I see," said Milbank, "and I suppose you want to . . ."

"I think it's vital that Prime Minister Vining be shown those pictures as soon as possible," broke in Lew.

"I hardly think my duties include the protection of a Kalya national from the ministrations of the security police," said Milbank pensively. He paused. "On the other hand, I do have an obligation to you—a fairly constant one, it seems—and these pictures show that you were telling the truth."

"When I said 'urgent,' I didn't just mean Beach," said Lew. "You see, I was supposed to be married to Prudence Stauffer at three P.M. Then I . . . er . . . came into possession of that contact strip. She's still waiting. And her plane leaves at ten."

"Prudence Stauffer? . . . Well, the plot does thicken, doesn't it? The Prime Minister suspects that you were at that meeting in her home too. What about it, Lew?"

"I'd rather not answer that, sir."

"All the privileges that your embassy can accord you, but no co-operation. Is that it?" Milbank shifted in his chair. Lew wondered whether there was anger beneath the ambassador's obvious annoyance.

"Your attitude will make things sticky," added Milbank. He shrugged. "I'm not sure I understand your generation at all." He held up the picture again. "Is this the only print?"

"No. There is another one in a safe place."

"You're a meticulous man for details, Lew," said Milbank. "But if I may say so, I think some of your associations with Kalyans have been considerably less than prudent. If it is one of the aims of the Peace Corps to help overthrow governments, somebody

failed to inform me of it. In fact, I was at some pains to tell
Vining just the opposite the other night."

Lew said nothing. He was still standing and he felt a sudden
stiffness in his neck from the tension. He moved his head in an
effort to loosen his collar.

Milbank handed the pictures back. Lew, welcoming the chance
to occupy his hands, quickly rewrapped the strip in tissue and put
it again in the cardboard holder, then slid the yellow packet into
his pants pocket.

Milbank stood up. "Frankly," he said, "I think the Peace Corps
—at least some of you—have been playing with fire in this country.
Secret dabbling in the domestic politics of any foreign nation is
a dangerous game—especially African nations right at this time."

He gazed fixedly at Lew. "On the other hand, I found Old
Number One's righteous endorsement of that bully boy, Hulbert
Booth, just a bit overripe the other night. I would love to see Mr.
Vining's face when he sees those pictures."

Milbank motioned toward the door. "So let's go over to the
Palace."

Lew's tension snapped like an abruptly cut wire, and his legs
felt unsteady as he followed Milbank at a brisk pace past the nest
of secretaries and their softly clicking electric typewriters. Milbank's personal secretary was feeding herself from an open box of
chocolates.

The embassy driver sped them to the Palace in a green Chevrolet
sedan with diplomatic plates. They halted briefly at the security
building and were waved on by one of Booth's goggled motorcycle patrolmen. They drove up the curving roadway, bordered
by its roses, jasmine and tulips, and past the two flagpoles, one
flying the ensign of Kalya and the other Vining's personal leopard
rampant. The great lawn, wearing its automatic sprinklers like a
woman in curlers, swept in solid green to the Executive Palace,
that baroque pile of marble which the Peace Corps had dubbed
"hangover Hilton."

They halted under the imposing portico, where six more security police stood at what passed for attention. Lew looked again
at his watch. It was 4:50. By the time they reached the fifth floor
reception room of the Prime Minister's business office and were
smiled upon by a slender, fawn-colored receptionist, Milbank had

shown his embassy card repeatedly at various guard stations. Now
it was 4:58 P.M.

The receptionist, chic in a tan, belted dress, was not surprised
at their sudden appearance and her finely plucked eyebrows lifted
not at all. In a nation without telephones, diplomacy moved on
an endless chain of comings and goings. Milbank stated his request for an audience.

"I'm so sorry, Mr. Ambassador," said the girl. Her eyes danced
with regret. "The Prime Minister is occupied outside the Palace
on state business. He will return at six."

Lew realized that the phrase "outside the Palace" was probably
a discreet embroidery of the facts. Once a week in the late afternoon, in a continuing test of his renowned virility, the old man
bedded a woman in the penthouse five floors above. It was of a
piece with his own luck today, thought Lew, that Vining should
choose this one day out of seven.

"Ah, yes," said Milbank. His face reflected his sympathy for
Vining's burden of statecraft. "May we wait?"

"Of course," trilled the girl. "I'm sure the Prime Minister will
be available at six. He is always punctual."

Milbank and Corleigh seated themselves in the uncomfortable,
straight-backed tigerwood chairs, and the girl offered them their
choice of *Paris Match*, *Look*, the *Daily Voice* and the 1966 Kalya
yearbook. Lew chose the yearbook and found that Kalya, a parliamentary democracy, had 102 miles of paved streets, 744 miles of
graded, dirt highways, 26 tribal languages, abundant natural resources, the same prime minister for 22 years and elaborate plans
for national telephone, power and postal systems by 1970.

But the facts dripped on his brain like drops from a leaky faucet
heard from a bed at midnight. He absorbed each new one as
he would the blow of a sledge hammer. Were the pink camellias
in Prudence's bouquet wilting? Who was helping her pack? Had
she cried? Who would take her to the airport? The $11.50 ring
was in his coat pocket, but against his thigh he could feel the
rectangular shape of the cardboard packet.

He tried not to look at his watch, but when he did, the hands
read 5:30. He moved his chair closer to Milbank's.

"Do you think your driver could take a note to Prudence

Stauffer?" he asked. "I ought to tell her something. I was supposed to be married two and a half hours ago."

"Sure," said Milbank, "but we'd better send for him. With your credentials, I'm not sure you could get back up here." He addressed the receptionist. "Would it be possible to send a messenger for my driver? We'd like to send him on an errand."

"Most certainly." Her smile was the flutter of a dove. Her high heels bore her rhythmically to the door, where she beckoned to a guard and told him to fetch the American chauffeur.

"Vining ought to have some means of communication in this building," whispered Milbank. "Short-wave or something. But he prefers it this way. Until the nation gets its telephone system, he'll do without too. Frightful bother sometimes."

Lew borrowed a sheet of the Palace stationery, crested with the inevitable leopard teething on the scales of justice, and wrote his note: "Dearest Prude: You know the score by now. It may be a couple of hours yet. Could you possibly get the chaplain to go to the airport and marry us there? Hope you understand. I love you. Lew."

More time passed before the driver appeared and took the enveloped note along with Lew's directions to Prudence's house. Lew's watch read 5:50.

At two minutes past six, a Kalya messenger of the Palace entered the room, whispered with the receptionist and left. Five minutes later, he was back. More whispers.

"The Prime Minister," said the girl, "decided to go directly to the penthouse. I told him you have been waiting. If you wish, he will be pleased to receive you now in his study."

Lew had heard descriptions of the Vining penthouse, but he was unprepared for the cascade of light pouring through the high wall of glass. The sun was beginning its final descent, and the glass glittered with the false brilliance of the day's last hour. It would be dark before eight o'clock. The houseboy padded ahead of them, past the severe furniture and the modern paintings which lined the walls of the sweep of rooms.

The Prime Minister stood erect behind his desk, a sturdy, black oak of a man. His bald head glinted in the pouring sunlight and before him rested the brass leopard desk lamp with its scales of justice in subtle motion. Vining squinted at the window, then motioned to his houseboy to draw the curtains. Vining switched on the leopard lamp as the houseboy withdrew.

Milbank made the introduction, and Vining shook hands with Lew with the Kalya snap of the index finger. His rugged face seemed at peace. Lew hoped, for his own sake, that the lovemaking had renewed Vining's confidence in the durability of his manhood.

"So this is the young man that has cost us so much time and palaver," said Vining. He seemed genuinely curious. "Could it be that red hair? It flames like a torch."

Lew felt better. Whatever had happened in the bedroom, Vining was not displeased with himself. There was a lassitude in the Prime Minister's movements as he seated himself and gestured at two waiting chairs for his guests.

"What is it this time, Willard?" he asked. "If you've been waiting more than an hour, it must be important."

"It is," said Milbank. "Corleigh has something to show you that he thinks bears on our recent talks."

"Frankly, I don't think there is any more to be done or said," said Vining. There was a querulous note in his voice, but no manifestation of anger. His recent violent sessions with Milbank could have belonged to other men and other eras. He folded his hands on the vest of his dark blue suit.

"Lincoln Beach will be tried Wednesday," he said, "and your Miss Stauffer is leaving tonight. A witness will testify Wednesday that Beach attended a meeting at Miss Stauffer's house two nights before some very scurrilous literature was dumped on this city. I would not be at all surprised if the witness also placed Mr. Corleigh at that same meeting."

He looked sharply at Lew, who tensed. Lew had no idea how to evade the inevitable question. But, strangely, Vining did not ask it. Instead, he shrugged.

"I would imagine the judge would look askance at the testimony of a young American who attended a patently seditious meeting," he said. "I say 'seditious' not from any certain facts in my possession, but from my long experience with men and politics. . . . So, Willard, just what is there left to discuss?"

"I'm not quite sure," said Milbank. "Mr. Corleigh wishes to show you some pictures."

Lew sensed that he should make this a dramatic production. He removed the cardboard holder slowly from his pocket, placed it on the edge of Vining's desk and then, very deliberately, unwrapped the tissue paper. Vining's eyes followed every movement, and the only sounds in the room were the purr of the air-conditioner and the soft crinkle of paper.

Vining took the strip of pictures from Lew's hand, glanced at it, then moved forward and held it under the lamp. Lew fished the magnifying glass from his coat pocket.

"Perhaps this would help, Mr. Prime Minister," said Lew. He offered the glass.

Vining grunted, took the handled lens and held it and the contact strip under the glow of the lamp. He held the strip in several positions, then turned it over and read the lettering on the back. When, at last, he laid the pictures and the magnifying glass down on the desk, his expression was inscrutable.

"That was the shop that blew up this morning," he said.

"Yes, sir," said Lew. "The negative is thought to have been destroyed, but this print and one other had been given to a friend earlier by Billy Number 4. They were brought to me this afternoon."

"Curious that they should be brought to you," said Vining.

"It's known in Ft. Paul that Lincoln Beach and I are friends."

"You're more than friends," snapped Vining.

"I brought Corleigh here," put in Milbank hurriedly, "only because these pictures throw an entirely new light on his story. No one can doubt now that he is telling the truth about what happened at the Kalya National."

"You mean," said Vining coldly, "that I have been lied to by Colonel Booth?"

"I didn't—" began Milbank.

"Don't try to quibble, Willard." Vining's voice shot up a notch in pitch. "You come in here with three pictures which say: 'Alexander Vining, your security chief is a villain who frames an innocent man and then lies to you about it. You are an old fool, Vining, who has been betrayed by a trusted subordinate.' Isn't that what these pictures say, Mr. Ambassador?"

"I can't say what the prints mean to you," said Milbank quietly. "I brought them here to show that a Peace Corps volunteer, an

American citizen for whom I'm in part responsible, acted in good faith."

"That's another one of your half-truths," said Vining hotly. He pointed to the pictures. "Why are they so small?"

"The prints are the same size as the negative," said Lew. "From a very small camera called a Minox. Of course, contact prints like these can be blown up to any size."

"Oh."

Vining's face was a dark mask, and Lew could only guess at the extent of his anger. But was he incensed at Milbank? Angry at Booth? Or at himself? Perhaps all three?

The Prime Minister sat perfectly still for several minutes. His eyes shifted from Milbank to Corleigh, but seemed to bore through them to a point beyond. A shaft of the lowering sun slipped through the curtains and fell on his head. The fringe of white hair might have been a ring of snow on a dark peak. The tiny brass scales in the leopard's jaw swayed with a hypnotic motion.

"I want you gentlemen to wait in the living room," said Vining finally. "I'm going to send for Colonel Booth. I wish to speak to him privately. Later, we can continue our talk."

He arose and took the pictures in his hand.

"May I keep these here, Mr. Corleigh?" he asked. "I assure you I'll return them to you after the colonel leaves."

"Of course," said Lew. He decided to chance saying that had been eating like acid at his mind. "There's a rumor in town, sir, that Colonel Booth intends to question Lincoln Beach tonight at the city jail—along with two of his . . . well . . . assistants in such things."

"Such things?" Vining darted a glance at Lew. "If you're implying what I think you are, Mr. Corleigh, third-degree methods are not permitted in Kalya."

He strode to the door and held it open. "Until later, gentlemen." Then he rang a hand bell at the doorway and the houseboy came at a trot.

Milbank and Corleigh went to a settee in the living room to begin their wait. The houseboy passed them, walking rapidly.

"I think that last remark was a great mistake on your part," said Milbank. "It might spoil everything for you."

"I had to let him know—somehow—that time was running out," said Lew. He looked at his watch. Time was, indeed, running. It was 6:31.

And yet another half hour passed before they heard the front door open and saw Colonel Hulbert Booth stalk through the sweep of rooms to the study. He was in full uniform, but he had removed his goggles and was carrying them in his hand. The sun, pressing into the horizon now, flooded the room with a medley of orange and red, and Booth appeared to be striding confidently through his own warped rainbow. The colonel did not see them.

A few minutes later the phoneless penthouse became the scene of a quick series of movements. First, the bell summoned the houseboy to the study door. The man left the apartment and returned five minutes later with Major Felix Booth, the assistant security chief. The dapper little brother of the colonel went to the study, but emerged almost at once. As he walked swiftly through the living room, he saw the two Americans on the settee in a corner. Major Booth stopped short. His look was one of startled comprehension. Then he bowed briefly and hurried out the front door.

The suite was in the shadowing gauze of twilight when Colonel Hulbert Booth left the study. He walked slowly, with his eyes on the floor, but a last shaft of light caused him to blink and he looked up involuntarily toward the wall of glass. It was then that he saw Milbank and Corleigh.

He stopped. He glanced briefly at Milbank, then stared at Lew. The colonel swung his goggles in a slow circle.

"I might have known," he said.

He looked fixedly at Lew for perhaps as much as thirty seconds. The thin mustache appeared oddly dainty on the rugged face. Then Booth shrugged, a shake of his epaulets, and strode on.

The front door closed behind the colonel. Lew looked again at his watch. It was 7:45. Prudence would be leaving for the airport.

Vining himself stepped from his study and called to them: "All right, gentlemen!"

The living room was almost in shadow now, but as they passed one of the paintings, two bright yellow circles seemed to leap from the frame. Both men noticed it.

"The Siqueiros, I think," said Milbank.

Save for the glow from the brass lamp, the study was almost dark now and it was difficult for Lew to see the Prime Minister's face clearly. They all resumed their seats.

Vining handed the picture strip to Lew.

"As I promised," he said.

"I have made several decisions, gentlemen," he said after a pause. His voice was brisk, vigorous. "While I'm under no obligation to inform you of them, I think it would clear the air all around if I did so."

The brass scales were motionless now, and the leopard stared at Lew over his open jaw.

"I decided," said Vining, "to revert to our original agreement despite the recent evidence implicating Miss Stauffer of the Peace Corps staff. I summoned Major Felix Booth here some time ago— I'm sure you saw him—and told him to release Lincoln Beach immediately from incarceration and to escort him to the airport where he can make his originally scheduled flight to Lagos tonight. Beach will have time to pick up his clothes. The rest of his belongings will be sent to him."

Vining was speaking rapidly. "In our arrangement, Willard, Beach was to be exiled for three years. That will stand as first stated. . . . Colonel Booth has been temporarily relieved of duty and will leave Thursday for France where, fortunately, he had been invited to attend a three-month course in intelligence and counterespionage operations. I think, in view of what I have learned tonight, that Colonel Booth cannot help but profit by a three-month course in security methods. One may understand zeal to protect the state, but one cannot condone certain excesses. . . . His brother, Felix, has been placed in command of the special Executive Palace police during the colonel's absence."

The Prime Minister paused again. "I think that is all, except for two things. Officials of my administration who lie to me will always be punished. Likewise, I will not tolerate any foreign organization interfering in the politics of Kalya. You might keep that in mind, Mr. Corleigh, and perhaps pass it on to Carter Williams for such instructions as he may care to issue to the Peace Corps."

Vining rose from his chair. The two Americans followed suit automatically.

"I have but one request, Mr. Corleigh," said Vining. "When both Beach and the colonel are at their new stations—let us say a week from tomorrow—I would appreciate it if you would make an appointment with my secretary and deliver those two photographic prints to me personally."

Lew stiffened. His mind splintered in several directions. He had not anticipated this.

"They are, of course, your pictures," continued Vining. His tone was low, casually conversational. "However, if you do not see fit to give them to me, I shall be forced to speak to Mr. Williams about the whole future role of the Peace Corps here. There are a number of facets of it that trouble me."

Lew glanced involuntarily at Milbank, but the ambassador's head was averted. It was Lew's decision.

"I will bring in the pictures a week from tomorrow," said Lew.

"Good," said Vining. He smiled for the first time that night. "Then I think everything is in order. Good night, gentlemen."

The houseboy had lighted several hanging lamps in the suite, and as Lew passed one, he looked once more at his watch. It was 8:02. The drive to the airport took at least forty minutes, and he still had to go by the embassy to pick up the jeep.

"I'll tell the driver to step on it," said Milbank.

The two men exchanged grins. Then Milbank put his hands to his forehead and flicked off imaginary drops of moisture with a loud snap of his fingers.

23

Lew wheeled the jeep into the airport parking lot, searching for a space near the terminal. There were none. He drove slowly between two lanes of parked cars, cursing his luck. He had never seen the lot so crowded. Finally a gap appeared like a missing tooth, and he eased the jeep into the opening. He was near the far limit of the lot.

He switched off the lights and slid out of the front seat, not bothering to lock the car. A man stepped forward in the dark from the fender of an adjacent car. It was Oliver Downing.

"I've been waiting," he said. "I knew you'd have to park out here. . . . Quick, what happened?"

"Link's free," said Lew. "He ought to be at the ticket counter now. He's on the nine-thirty for Lagos. . . . Ollie, I've got to beat it." He squinted at the luminous dial of his wrist watch. "It's nine already. Prudence leaves at ten."

He turned to go, but Downing caught his arm.

"One second," said Downing. "What about Colonel Booth? I've got to tell Billy Number 15. He's waiting in town for me."

"Old Number One is shipping him to France for some kind of intelligence school," said Lew. "He's relieved of duty—for three months."

"Three months!"

"That's all. And I've got to turn both prints over to Old Number One. . . . Best I could do. There wasn't time to bargain. . . . I'll see you later about it."

"Three months," repeated Downing. "Billy will never take that. His best friend, and wife and child, blown up. When I tell him three months . . ."

"I can't help it, Ollie."

"When is Booth leaving?" asked Downing.

"Thursday, I think Old Number One said. Yes, Thursday. . . . Sorry, Ollie, but I've got to go."

Lew turned away, walked to the rear bumper of the jeep and then broke into a run. The terminal was a good quarter of a mile away.

The familiar air of bedlam at the big building, with its pulsing yellow lights, was compounded tonight. In addition to the confusion attending the sandwiched arrival and departure of a half dozen international planes, there were the precautions made necessary by the exit of two persons for political reasons. Security police were everywhere, their gold-trimmed white crash helmets bobbing about like balloons.

Lew saw Major Felix Booth, grinning proudly, at the entrance. He stood with a bantam's command stance and seemed to be giving orders to several patrolmen at once. The crowd was thick and contentious. Apparently every coming or going passenger was to be feted by at least ten Kalyans. There was even one tribal woman, a baby on her back, apparently at the terminal on some obscure errand unconnected with expensive air travel. Members of The Family, most of them dressed in funereal blues and blacks, shouted directions at bag-laden porters, and Europeans struggled for position in the counter lines.

Lew shoved his way forward, searching frantically for Prudence. Someone stepped on his shoe, mashing the toes. A straw hamper banged against his knee. A portly German cursed when Lew pushed him aside. Children weaved through the thicket of legs. The crowd swelled in bodies and tumult near the line of official booths.

Then he saw her. She was standing at the emigration counter, where exit visas were stamped, and beside her were Lincoln

Beach and Cynthia Fuller. Prudence wore a light blue traveling suit, her face was pale and, for the first time, she looked distracted, almost panicky. She was holding a little bouquet of drooping pink camellias.

"Prude!" he yelled.

She looked wildly about. He raised an arm and shouted again. This time she saw him.

"Lew!"

They elbowed toward each other and met beside two over-wrought Kalyans who were wrestling with several bulging suit-cases. Prudence buried her head against Lew's chest, and some-one's arm knocked her blue beret askew. She wept.

"Oh, Lew. I thought you'd never make it."

He kissed her. There was a taste of salty dampness from the tears. She kissed him in turn, repeatedly, then thrust the bouquet into his hands and began fumbling in her purse.

"Help me, Lew. Can't find my handkerchief. Have you got one? . . . The chaplain waited until ten minutes ago, then he had to leave. . . . What are we going to do? . . . I've never been this way before. Can't think straight."

She began to cry again, but this time she soon smiled with relief and squeezed his hand so tightly that he winced. He took out his pocket handkerchief and dabbed at her eyes and cheeks. His other hand held the flowers, crushed and forlorn now.

"No," she said. "Okay now. Let me do it."

She took the handkerchief and dried her tears. Then she drew a mirror from her purse and traced on fresh lipstick. The little mirror reflected her disapproval.

"Terrible," she said. "Oh, come on. I've still got to get the exit stamp."

He took her arm as they pushed forward to the counter.

"I've got it all figured, Prude," he said hurriedly. "I'll be back in the States in just four weeks. We'll be married the next day at your mother's place."

"Here." He stopped her, took the ring from his pocket and pressed it into her hand. "You keep it for us."

"No, I can't," she said. "It's bad luck. Oh, please don't, Lew. I'll start bawling again."

But he closed her fingers about the ring. She looked at it a moment, then kissed him with a smile. She slipped the ring into a small zippered compartment in her purse.

"All right," she said. "Lew, what happened? We don't know a thing. Link showed up suddenly here a few minutes ago in the tow of Felix Booth. Cindy was with me, and she almost had a heart attack. We know about the pictures, but Link knows absolutely nothing else—except that he's on the plane for Lagos."

"Let's get that stamp first," said Lew. "Then I'll tell you."

They were back at the counter now. Lincoln Beach's arm rested on the counter. He was wrangling with the official over his papers. Cindy stood to one side.

"Pardon me," said a voice behind Lew.

It was Major Felix Booth, ploughing his way to the counter like a small tugboat in a bustling harbor. He spilled a torrent of chopped English at the emigration officer. The grinning major made it clear, with excessive civility toward Beach, that nothing was to obstruct the imminent departure of the esteemed billing chief of the Utility Authority. At that, the passport was stamped and Beach had cleared the last link in the chain of officialdom.

"Hey, Red," he said as he turned from the counter. "See you at the gate."

Now the emigration officer, a man with long, pointed sideburns and an inquisitorial air, balked at Prudence's papers. He pointed out that her airline ticket read "Prudence Stauffer," while the slip of paper permitting her exit, procured that morning in Ft. Paul, proclaimed her to be a Mrs. Lewis N. Corleigh. Which was she, if either? Prudence tried to explain. She was to have been married, so that morning she gave her married name. The ticket was purchased before she knew she would be married. But, really, she wasn't.

"Doesn't make sense, I know," she said. Her lips trembled and she clutched Lew's arm.

Again Major Booth intervened. He did so with a bow and his most ingratiating smile.

"Stamp the exit visa, officer," the little major ordered. "She is Miss Stauffer and she is leaving the country at the invitation of the government."

The man with the pointed sideburns appeared mystified, but he stamped the passport as ordered. Prudence stuffed it into her purse along with her ticket. Major Booth bowed again with a truly admirable flash of teeth.

At last Lew and Prudence joined Beach and Cindy at Gate 2. It was 9:25. The Air France plane for Nigeria, inbound from New York, was late. They huddled together while Lew told, as rapidly as possible, of his conference with the Prime Minister.

"I'd sure like to see those pictures," said Beach.

"I've got one strip here," said Lew, "but you can't see much without a magnifying glass. We couldn't risk it." He turned to Cindy. "I hope you won't mention the pictures to anyone, Cindy. I've given my word to turn both prints over to Old Number One after both Link and the colonel are outside the country."

"Don't worry," said Cindy. "Anything, just so Link is safe."

"That's Vining for you," said Beach bitterly. "Booth kills Billy Number 4 and two of his family—and as a punishment he gets sent to a school in France."

"You're free," said Lew. "That was what mattered. I was in no position to bargain. There wasn't time. As I say, the two leopard men were going to call on you tonight with Booth."

"Bastards," said Beach.

They explored other facets of the palace meeting, then they stood self-consciously, sorting their own fragmented thoughts and trying to ease four sudden stabs of loneliness with small talk. Two security guards stood at a respectful distance, out of earshot.

"Three years is a long time," said Beach. "But at least, they say the humidity isn't so bad in Lagos."

It was oppressive at Vining Airport at this moment. One half of the sky was starlit, but an overcast brooded to the east and its fringe seemed to be moving threateningly toward the airport. The air lay heavy on the skin like a full, warm sponge.

"What are you going to do when you terminate next month, Cindy?" asked Prudence.

The question was aimless, put to consume time, not demanding a specific answer. Cindy was standing with an arm linked in Beach's.

"I'm going to Lagos," she said. It was an announcement.

"Oh," said Prudence. "You mean . . ."

Cindy nodded. "If he'll have me proper. If not, he can figure out how to keep me."

Beach grinned at Lew. "We don't marry 'em, Red. We keep them waiting. It's cheaper."

"When was all this decided?" asked Lew.

"About ten minutes ago," said Cindy, "while you and Prudence were making public spectacles of yourselves."

They heard a whine in the black cloud above them. Two bright spears appeared above the field's far runway with its parallel rows of yellow landing lights. The Air France jet from the United States was letting down a few minutes behind schedule.

On impulse, Cindy took the rose ribbon from her hair and handed it to Beach. He fingered it a moment, then tucked it into a side pocket of his tan suit. He bent his head and kissed her. Lew and Prudence moved several steps away along the steel mesh fence. They both looked away, but the two security guards exchanged prurient grins.

The big jet moved into position beside the gate like some great, whistling fish. The shriek of the engines died away, and a line of shadows snaked toward the gate.

"Prudence! . . . Lew!"

A tailored suit, long, elegantly sheathed legs, a wave of black hair, dark glasses merging with the night. It was Maureen Sutherland, first hugging Prudence and then offering a cheek for Lew's kiss. He pecked at it, feeling as foolish as he did the afternoon in the lobby of the Peace Corps building in Washington.

"You two have kicked up such a, you know, rhubarb, they sent me over for a look-see," said Maureen. The words came out in little gusts through her full, gathered lips. "Poor Carter. I'll bet he's in a swivet."

They introduced her to Cindy and Beach, and Maureen swept the pair verbally to her heart with phrases that simultaneously flattered them and revealed the depth of her own inside knowledge.

"The capitalistic revolutionary," she said to Beach. "Our new breed." She turned to Cindy, her sheaf of hair billowing, then falling into place like a sculptured curve. "And Cindy Fuller of the adult night class! Cindy, you're the talk of the staff in Washington. Along with Roger, you're, you know, our prize exhibit in Kalya. . . . And this, I suppose, is a twin ceremony. Two exiles, one for Nigeria and one for the United States?"

True, thought Lew, but only barely. If it had not been for the photographs, only Prudence would be leaving tonight.

"The cable said reassignment for me," said Prudence.

"I know, love." Maureen adjusted her smoked glasses, little comrades of the night. "We're not going to lose you if I can help it. Not Prudence Stauffer."

"It may be Prudence Corleigh soon," said Prudence. "We tried to get married today, but . . . well . . ."

"No!" It was a shriek. Maureen hugged Prudence all over again, then turned to Lew. "What smashing news! When did you break down, Lew? I never thought you'd give up all those, you know, predatory bachelor nights. And to get a heavenly female like Prudence!"

Lew became conscious of the pink camellias he still held. He handed the bouquet, torn and wilted, to Prudence, and Maureen beamed knowingly on the transfer.

Maureen motioned them closer and lowered her voice. "I've got a simply t'riffic wedding present," she continued. "I'm supposed to let Carter announce it, but I can't resist, you know, telling you people. Washington has decided to let Kalya volunteers keep the kerosene refrigerators. Isn't that tremendous? Of course, it's a gamble, what with that old dinosaur, Phil Taggard, rooting around for something to hang us with. But I argued that the, you know, morale of the volunteers comes first. Right, Prude?"

Prudence, uneasy under the gush of news, did not answer. And suddenly, the irony of the situation—Washington countering a political exile and a deportation with a battalion of shiny, kerosene-fed coolers—struck Lew. It was preposterous, an absurd non sequitur. He started to laugh, tried to cut it off, but found that he could not. Prudence and Cindy smiled at first, then they began to giggle. Lew gripped the top of the mesh fence to steady himself.

"What's so funny?" Maureen looked hurt and baffled.

"I'm sorry, Maureen," began Lew, but another fit of laughter smothered his apology.

"I don't get it, baby," complained Maureen.

"Well . . ." Lew checked himself. No, if Maureen needed an

explanation, she would not understand what she heard. The black mamba . . . Genghis Khan . . . a framed assassination . . . The Forge . . . a fire raging with no city water to extinguish it . . . a Kalya revolt simmering just below the surface . . . some of the Peace Corps committed on the side of the tribes. And then those kerosene refrigerators!

"I apologize, Maureen," said Lew at last, rubbing at his eyes. "Maybe it's just that they're such unreliable boxes. I'm forever turning them upside down to get them to work. Over here, kerosene refrigerators are a laughing matter, I guess. That's all."

"Oh, I see," said Maureen. She patently did not.

"Air France Flight Four-Oh-Two for Lagos!" The amplifier had a gritty, impersonal tone. "Boarding now through Gate Two."

Lincoln Beach pulled Lew to one side. "On your next trip to Zinzin," he said, "tell Steve Muo I'll be in touch somehow."

"I forgot to tell you, what with everything else going on," said Lew, "that Osterlord thinks Steve will be a real leader now. Since you went to the leopard, he's become more aggressive. Jim thinks The Forge will grow."

"Good," said Beach. "Tell Steve I'm counting on him and Ollie Downing to keep things moving. . . . The students next month. They've got to enlist some of them. . . . And Red, thanks again for the affidavit and then putting the pressure on with those pictures. It kept me alive. I'll never forget."

He gripped Lew's hand, then put his arm around Cindy's waist and walked her to the gate. They kissed briefly. Beach swung into a file of passengers. He walked swiftly, carrying a small flight bag, and he mounted the ramp and disappeared into the plane without looking back.

"If you'll wait until Prude's plane leaves," said Lew to Cindy, "I'll give you and Maureen a lift into town."

Cindy shook her head. "No, we'll leave you two alone. We'll get a taxi."

" 'By for now, Prudence," said Maureen. "I'll see you soonest in Washington. . . . And Red, baby, save me an hour tomorrow. I want the real, you know, lowdown on Zinzin."

Prudence and Lew watched while Beach's plane sped down the runway, nosed up into the night and became a fading, lighted toy in the distance.

"I wonder if he'll ever come back," said Prudence. She leaned over the steel fence, the camellias drooping from her hand. "And what will The Forge become without him?"

"I don't know," said Lew. "Osterlord thinks Steve Muo has the stuff to take over. . . . All I know for sure is that Beach is quite a guy. If he lives, and comes back, he might remake this country some day."

"He is one of the best human beings I ever knew," said Prudence. She turned and took his hand. "Lew, I think I should ask for reassignment in some country where we can both serve on the staff. If they say no, then when we're married, I'll resign and go as your wife wherever they send you."

"Suppose I don't get a staff job," he said. "After all, Sherrod just said to come by for a talk. That's not a commitment. . . . And now there's this last flare-up with the pictures. . . . Maybe we ought to think of something outside the Peace Corps."

"Hate to leave the Peace Corps," she said.

"The trouble is," said Lew, "we're both marked. Whatever country they sent us to—or sent me to—somebody on the staff would get the idea we were coming to cook up a revolution."

"If the Peace Corps does its job right," she said, "there's bound to be revolution—or anyway, pretty fast evolution."

"That's what Link says. I guess he's right. Maybe Congressman Phil Taggard realizes it too, and that's what really gets under his hide."

"Lew, if we can't get another Peace Corps job, let's try for something else abroad." She was absorbed in plans now. "Maybe CARE or some kind of foundation. There are scads of them."

"I'm with you," he said. "Somehow, with everything I've seen and learned here recently, I just couldn't be satisfied with grad school—or the damn fuel oil business either. Maybe I'm spoiled, but I want to be out . . . well . . . trying to help."

"Me too." She nestled against him. "And Lew, let's have a real church wedding, please? With my folks and yours, organ music, lots of flowers, the works."

"Done," he said. "A girl who gets left at the altar deserves the real thing the next time. We'll make it big and schmaltzy."

"Thanks."

They stood silently, wrapped in their separate thoughts of life and of each other, until new lights, winking out of the overcast, signaled the approach of Prudence's plane.

Waiting passengers began to bunch toward the gate in the irrational manner of all departing travelers, each seemingly fearful that if he were not first aboard, he would be left behind. In the jostling, Lew heard his name spoken in a familiar, precise enunciation which gave each syllable its own identity.

He turned to see a yellowing face, a scar on one cheek and mouth lines which ran downward like empty creek beds. It was Moses Harter of Zinzin, dressed in a suit which resembled those worn by J. Richardson Downing, Harter's superior in the Kalya educational hierarchy. The gray suit of synthetic fibers shone and crackled as though electrically charged. The creases of Harter's suit were sharp as knife blades and his tie flashed the yellow and red national colors. He carried a thin dispatch case of new leather.

"A pleasure to see you, Mr. Harter," said Lew without warmth. "Seeing someone off? Or vacation in Dakar?"

"Neither," said Harter. The sinking mouth lines gathered into a smile that seemed to propound a riddle. "I'm going to the United States."

"Oh." Lew eyed him blankly for a moment, then remembered Prudence. He drew her toward him and made the introduction.

"Prudence Stauffer . . . of the Peace Corps staff," said Lew. "She's going to the United States tonight too."

"Delighted to have such company. Perhaps we can be seatmates?" said Harter, hissing the sibilants. He smiled broadly. "There is so much I need to learn quickly. I've never been to the United States."

"How long will you be gone?" asked Lew.

"Two years!" Harter said it proudly and his smile lighted into a beam of triumph.

"I don't understand."

"Fellowship," said Harter. He fingered his tie in a sprucing gesture as if to congratulate himself. "One of your fine foundations has seen fit to grant me a fellowship for two years' study in political science. It has been my dominating interest, you know."

"How perfectly marvelous!" said Prudence. Her voice had an unnatural silky purr, and Lew glanced sharply at her.

"I deem myself most fortunate," said Harter with an effort at humility. He whistled the s's. "I only hope I can repay my benefactors with a solid accumulation of knowledge that can be put to some use here in Kalya."

"What school?" Lew was still stunned.

"Oberlin," said Harter. "I selected it after much consideration, primarily because its heritage of independent scholarship seemed to best fit our needs here in Kalya. Above all, we need new ideas, new visions, new vistas." His precise diction invested each word with a halo of dedication.

"I'm so happy for you—and for Kalya," said Prudence. Her smile was almost feline, and Lew looked at her in disbelief.

"But what about the USAID contracts?" asked Lew.

Harter waved an arm in the vague direction of Zinzin. "Oh, Mr. Stevenson is searching for another contractor. I hesitated to disappoint him at a time when he requires, above all, an experienced builder, but this was too great an opportunity to pass up. . . . Forrest is a sympathetic man. He agreed with my decision. He knows his burden is increased now, but I'm confident he will find someone to replace me."

"Well, good luck," said Lew slackly. In his bafflement, he did not know what else to say.

"Thank you," said Harter. "My graduate school term does not begin until September, but I wanted to see the country first . . . New York skyscrapers, the Rockies, Los Angeles. . . . Well, I'll leave you to say your good-bys. Perhaps if we cannot sit together, Miss Stauffer, we can have a drink on the plane at least."

"I wouldn't miss it for the world," said Prudence. Her voice had a lilt.

Harter elbowed his way forward toward the gate, his dispatch case bumping the legs of fellow travelers. Harter was one man who certainly did not intend to be left off the plane.

"God, you sounded ecstatic over having a drink with that bandit," said Lew. "And earlier, you were purring like a kitten. What's got into you?"

"To quote Confucius," she said, " 'he who studies in Ohio cannot eat money in Zinzin.'" Then she put her head against Lew's shoulder and began to laugh.

"You!" He pushed her away and held her by both wrists. "The secret?"

She nodded, and the little, intense frown came in the wake of the laughter. "I started working on it right after he got the USAID contracts," she said. "It seemed so natural. After all, we all knew Genghis was itching to go to the States and get some kind of degree to tack after his name. So, I had a long talk with the CARE man in Ft. Paul who also makes recommendations to a batch of foundations. And . . . well . . . I must say the timing was superb, wasn't it?"

"But, my God," countered Lew, "Genghis in graduate school? Why, his education stopped at the sixth grade."

"Know it," she said. She grinned. "Mine didn't."

"And how about college credits? He hasn't got any."

"Busy hands at Commissioner Downing's office can turn out very impressive certificates," she said. "Richardson Downing couldn't do enough for the favorite love-son of Old Number One."

"What a broad," said Lew. "First you plot with The Forge and then you turn around and hand a big present to one of the leading thugs in Kalya. Why, that fellowship must be worth eight or ten thousand dollars."

"Learned from Rachael Frisson and Horace Magruder," she said. "If they can play the game with U.S. dollars, so can I. What is it again? Reasonable people can always reach a reasonable compromise?"

"I'll be damned," said Lew. "Be sure to tell Shannon and Demarest about it when you get to Washington. It'll break them up."

"Good-by, Red—but only for a month."

Her Pan-American flight was being called and the crowd surged forward. Lew and Prudence kissed while the pressure of other passengers jammed her purse into his ribs and the bouquet was crushed once more.

He watched while she joined the line winding toward the waiting jet with its blinking wing lights and its long shark's snout. The plane faced toward the black cloud which now squeezed the few remaining stars into a handful of sky. Prudence, as if to reassure herself, walked with her purposeful, emphatic stride, her shoulders squared. Although she could not see Lew, she turned at

the top step of the ramp, held the mangled camellias to her lips
and blew a kiss into the sultry night.

Lew walked slowly back to the jeep, his hands jammed in his
pockets and his mind turning from Prudence to Genghis Khan
to Lincoln Beach. The compromises which once repelled him had
enmeshed them all. They were trapped in a skein of accommodation, their lives caught in a web of promises, bargains, trades.
Reasonable men had reasoned together. And a veil had dropped,
delicately, softly, over the huddled form of Oon Gilli's wife as
she sat with her son's clothes and a piece of iron ore at the stoop
of her mud hut. It was difficult to visualize her now, nor could he
quite recall the shape and texture of the Washington skyline—
that night he sat on the hotel roof and vowed to battle for the
tribes lest the world be lost in a thousand Zinzins. Lew walked
unseeing past a knot of Booth's security men. He felt the sadness
of lost resolves.

Had they betrayed the plain people of Zinzin, or had the Peace
Corps—Jim, Cindy, himself, Prudence—fought the best they
knew how? What was it that seemed to freeze such men of good
will as Sherrod and Maggiore into postures of inaction, their
hearts willing but their feet unable to move? Did the ideal he
glimpsed that night in the words of Senator Demarest still glow, or
was it sputtering out? What had become of the American beacon
in this tangled chain of "reasoning"? Was this what in Washington went under the grand, billowing banner of "foreign policy"?
Lew did not know. There was so little he could be sure of these
days.

He stood for a moment at the end of the muddy parking area,
looking at the boxlike outline of his jeep. Dirty, rugged, stubborn, 100,000 miles under its angular hood. It was the mobile
monument to his two years in Kalya. But were they years of
victory or defeat, accomplishment or frustration? He kicked a front
tire, affectionately, as he would pat the withers of a horse or
ruffle the nape of an old, family dog. Then he thought of his staff
sergeant in Germany, the spare, knobby Kentucky hill man. Nothing counts in combat, he had said, but you and your outfit. All else
is the enemy.

So they had lived and they had survived. In Zinzin, Jim Osterlord bristled with his building plans, for the water system and for

The Forge. . . . Let's see, how many more days to go . . . twenty-eight, twenty-seven, twenty-six? . . . Four more trips to Zinzin. Perhaps tomorrow he should load some empty oil drums for Jim. If Osterlord resumed work on his road now, with Genghis gone, he might need the drums for culverts. . . . And new textbooks for Arlene . . . and chalk. Cindy needed chalk for her adult night class. . . . Another batch of termination forms for Alice Franklin. She had lost hers somewhere. . . . What else? Oh yes, Bart was out of kerosene, and Dotty Wyzansky had vowed he'd never get another meal in her house if he didn't bring up a jar of cold cream. Lew began to hum as he walked around the jeep's front bumper, with its balky drum of towing cable, toward the driver's door.

He became aware of a group of people clustered about a car a few yards away. They were laughing and chattering over some incident at the air terminal. They were Americans—Lew caught snatches of a southern accent—and one man was having trouble with his key in the car lock.

"Once more," said one man. "Wawa!"

"Not always!" Lew shouted at them. They turned, their faces showing dim surprise in the night.

He waved to them, got in the jeep and started the motor. The Americans were still staring at him as he drove off.

The black cloud had swallowed the whole sky as he drove toward Ft. Paul, past the swamp with its indignant bullfrogs, past the stately rubber trees, all at parade rest in the still, heavy night, and past the cowering bug-a-bug mounds. Along the road walked a tribal woman, swinging gracefully at the hips, yet plodding at the heels to balance her headload of wooden sticks. Further on walked a withered tribesman, sheathed cutlass dangling from his waist.

A lone jungle sentinel, a dabema tree, towered its umbrella of foliage high above its white trunk, so like a pillar of soiled concrete. The fringe of the headlight beam flushed a long-tailed coucal with its splash of white breast. The bird lumbered from its branch and flew across the road, trailing its "coo-coo-coo" call, a lonely pennant of song.

His thoughts drifted to Prudence as he drove into Ft. Paul and headed for the street which led to the road for the hostel. He could see Prudence sitting in the plane, the splash of freckles between her eyebrows, the head tilted as she listened to Moses Harter's whistling sibilants . . . or standing in the nave of a church, holding, curiously, a bouquet of pink camellias, fresh and dewy . . . or kissing him while broken china lay at their feet. . . .

The jeep's headlights picked up a dark, moving mass directly ahead. Lew's foot went instinctively to the brake. He slowed the car and brought it to a halt. The street was blocked by a large crowd which spilled between a row of cement-block houses on one side of the street and a high hedge on the other. By the tumble of carmine bougainvillaea over the hedge, Lew recognized the yard of the Japanese embassy. Three other cars were parked in mid-street, one of them a red and yellow Volkswagen of the city police. Another, painted white and topped by a flashing red light, was Ft. Paul's lone ambulance. A number of motorcycles stood against the curbs, their motors idling. At least a dozen white crash helmets of the security force bobbed about amid the forest of dark figures. Chaotic milling marked any Ft. Paul street crowd, but this one seemed seized by an undertow of near hysteria. People shouted, shoved one another or jumped up and down like pogo sticks to get a better view. The sullen night air, certain to burst into rain at any moment, failed to muffle the clamor.

Lew caught the arm of a white-shirted young Kalyan who had just leaped into the air and swiveled his head in a quick arc.

"What is it?" asked Lew. "What happened?"

"Eh, man. Big fella cut bad one time." The young man made a slashing motion with his arm, as though wielding a bush cutlass, then plunged into the wall of bodies in the general direction of the ambulance.

The white crash helmets appeared to converge into two lines leading from the entrance of the Japanese embassy to the ambulance. The crowd surged toward the staggered bowls of white. Lew hurried to the hedges where the ranks of people appeared to be thinner. He elbowed his way forward and managed to reach the side of a policeman who stood with arms thrown wide.

Two security officers were bulling forward with lowered heads, trying to keep a narrow corridor cleared through the throng. Behind them came two other elite patrolmen carrying a stretcher. On it lay a man with policemen's coats thrown over his legs and torso. As Lew looked, a weird, red band passed over the stretcher from the ambulance's flashing light, but the victim's face was unrecognizable. Lew could only see that it was a dark one. The cortege forged ahead and the crowd swept in behind it like water through a broken dam.

Lew was left in the wake, one of only three or four stragglers at the entrance of the embassy driveway.

"Lo, the wayward groom—finally," said a familiar rough voice.

It was Sam Zerwick. He had suddenly emerged from the gloom of the embassy yard and he stood on the edge of the gravel driveway, wiping his spectacles with a tail of his blue sports shirt.

"Prudence get off all right?" he asked.

Lew nodded. "Yes . . . I . . . but what the hell happened here, Sam?"

Zerwick replaced his glasses. "A very neat slicing. Both hands cut off at the wrists. Cutlass job." He looked at his own hands in the dark. "Nice and juicy too."

"But who was it?"

"Your friend, Colonel Hulbert Booth," said Zerwick. "As I get it, he was about to call on his lady friend. He left his cycle down the block with a couple of his men. Then, in the embassy yard, he was ambushed from behind the hedge. Quick work. He must have lain there five or ten minutes before somebody heard his moans."

"Who did it?" asked Lew.

"Haven't got the foggiest. Nobody knows."

"Is Booth dead?"

Zerwick shook his head. "Nope. Big loss of blood, but I think he'll make it." Zerwick clapped Lew on the shoulder. "Got to go. They want me at the hospital."

He walked quickly toward a car parked in the middle of the street, and now Lew saw that it was the staff jeep of the Peace Corps physician.

Lew walked back to his own jeep. The ambulance was pulling away, throwing out its flashes of light like bloody spears. Motorcycles gunned and white helmets formed two protective lines on the flanks of the ambulance. The crowd broke apart. People began running down the street.

Lew started the jeep's motor and switched on the headlights. At that moment the rain came. The roof rattled, the noise of a thousand stones. Before he could roll up the driver's window, Lew's left arm became soaked. Water sluiced over the windshield, at first in rivulets, but quickly in a wide sheet. Lew turned on the wipers.

In one sweep of the blades, he saw a tall, straight form standing beside the hedge. Lew had the swift impression of a barber pole, bizarrely striped in purple and black. He moved closer to the windshield, sighting along the beam of the headlights. But on the next sweep of the blades, the figure was gone.

He stared for a moment at the hedge. The small leaves bent downward under the force of the rain. Closer to the car, the gutter was already filling with swirling water. A chorus of hammers beat upon the jeep's roof. Lew sighed. Tomorrow's road to Zinzin would be a long, red, muddy trench.